Dark Secrets

Dark Secrets

Eileen Stafford

PIATKUS

Chapter One

Lily walked slowly into the chapel on her brother's arm. She closed her eyes for one brief moment and supposed herself in white instead of black, imagined that she heard the wedding march instead of the sombre strains of Handel's 'Largo'. This should have been her wedding day instead of her mother's funeral.

She was comforted by her brother's presence. William, her twin, was a source of constant strength. She glanced up at him and realized that if it really had been her own beautiful day, he would still have been beside her, for their father had been killed on the Somme two years ago, or was it three? It seemed so long now, and the events of the last few weeks had almost blotted out that earlier loss.

Arthur, whom she had loved so much, would have been standing there at the front of the chapel waiting for her. If she closed her eyes she could almost see him turning to smile at her, that gentle loving smile that she had last seen at the railway station when she waved him goodbye after his leave. The Armistice had been as good as signed when he had died in one of the last useless skirmishes of the war. She could feel his ring on her finger beneath the long black gloves. Then, as if that was not enough, her lovely mother had fallen victim to the influenza epidemic that had raged through Bristol just as everyone thought the worst was over.

She held herself tall and proud as she walked, determined that she would not cry, not here anyway in front of all these people. Her grip tightened on William's arm and eventually she slid into the seat indicated, stood at the right times and sang the familiar words of her mother's favourite hymns automatically without comprehending any of them.

Then it was over, and after the interment there was the gathering at home where family and friends must be regaled and refreshed with the sandwiches and cakes she had prepared beforehand. Lily wondered who had thought up this grisly ritual as she smiled first at one and then another, nodded at their compliments about her mother, and pressed them to cups of tea and food she could ill afford.

'Is the landlord going to let you stay in this house?' The bossy voice of Aunt Agnes cut through the clatter. She had set her cup and saucer down on the window sill and was staring at Lily critically. Now and then she looked pointedly at her empty plate, clearly expecting to be offered more food.

'I hope so, Aunt,' Lily replied, hoping that the other visitors were too busy with their own conversations to listen to this one. 'William reckons that his wages at Evans's will pay the rent, and my job at the bookshop might just about feed us. We'll manage somehow.'

Agnes sniffed disparagingly. 'That won't be easy with four of you.'

Lily knew that this was perfectly true but she was not going to admit it, not here anyway. The words worried her though, destroying the composure she had been trying to maintain for the past week. She glanced across at twelve-year-old George. He had an enormous appetite. In fact she could see him busily demolishing the last of the fishpaste sandwiches and wished that William would remind him to hand round the other plate instead of devouring its contents himself. Ivy, at eleven the youngest of the family, was sitting on a low stool in the corner looking doleful in her black dress. She was doing nothing to help, but not eating either.

'You'll have your work cut out to look after those two,' Agnes persisted. 'They both need a firm hand if you ask me.'

But no one is asking you, Aunt Agnes, Lily wanted to shout. Instead she said, 'I'll manage. Don't worry about us.'

'Can't help worrying. If you were all a bit younger I suppose I'd have had to move in and look after you.'

Lily shuddered at the thought and hoped her aunt wasn't aware of the horror she felt at such an idea. 'That won't be necessary. William and I are eighteen. Thank you though, Aunt.'

Agnes nodded and looked at the plate of cakes that lay just out of her reach. 'Your mother was clever with her needle. Pity you don't take after her. Books are all right but they never earned anyone any money! Folks don't need books but they always want something to put on their backs.'

Lily checked the angry retort that rushed to her lips. 'I've learned to type, Aunt Agnes,' she said. 'If we can't manage I shall have to find a job as a lady clerk. The wages are quite good.'

'Not natural,' Agnes said. 'Girls weren't meant to be in offices. You'd do better looking for a husband with a bit of money.'

Lily stared at her aunt in amazement. Agnes had never married and she had always made it clear that she held men in very low esteem. Possibly there had been a fiancé killed in the Boer War though. When Lily's romantic fantasies ran in that direction she was inclined to feel a little more sympathetic. Perhaps she had something in common with her father's angular and pernickety sister after all!

'I'll never marry now that Arthur's dead,' she said firmly, and suddenly feeling sorry for her aunt she fetched one of the plates of little fancies that she had baked and offered them to her.

Agnes took one and bit into it thoughtfully. 'Not marry indeed,' she said when she had finished the first mouthful. 'Stuff and nonsense. That was the mistake I made. You're not bad-looking, and by the taste of these ...' she licked some of the sticky icing sugar from her fingers ' ... you're quite a reasonable cook too. I think I might know someone who'd do.' She looked Lily up and down as though she were in a cattle market. 'Yes, come to think of it, it would be a good match.'

Lily was horrified. 'Please don't say such things, Aunt,' she said. 'I've told you, I couldn't possibly think of anyone else.'

3

'That's as may be,' Agnes declared. 'We shall see. I shall talk to your brother about it.'

'William? What on earth do you mean? He has no say in what I do with my life.'

'He's the eldest son and so the head of the house,' Agnes stated decisively.

'I thought you didn't believe in such things, in men being the bosses and all that? You always said that you'd have liked to be a suffragette.'

Agnes grinned at her. 'Maybe, but you're only a slip of a girl, and now that you've no parents you need someone else's protection. William will do nicely.'

'But William is my twin. Half an hour older, Ma always said. How can that make him wiser?'

Agnes shrugged her shoulders. 'It doesn't, but he's a man and folk look up to a man more than to a woman. Not that I agree, mind you, but sometimes it's sensible to go along with things, and that's a bit of advice you'd do well to remember, my girl.'

Much later in the evening, when the clearing up was done and the house looked almost normal again, Lily damped down the fire and went through into the back room. This was where the family always gathered, where they usually ate, where George and Ivy did their homework after school, and where the range was always hot and comforting. The front room, or parlour as it was sometimes grandly called, was only used for special occasions such as today.

Ivy had reluctantly helped with washing up the vast array of crockery, much of it borrowed from neighbours, and then had gone silently to bed. George was sitting at the table where the light was brightest and was reading a lurid comic. Such things had not been allowed when their parents were alive but Lily doubted that she had enough authority to ban them now.

William was, for once, sitting in the sturdy arm chair, his feet toasting on the fender. Usually he put on a thick outdoor coat, gloves with the tips of the fingers cut off, a hat and scarf, and then would go up to his small unheated bedroom and study for the accountancy exams which he was so anxious to pass. He often worked until midnight at least.

'I can't face going up there tonight,' he said. 'Come and sit down, Lil. We ought to talk.'

Lily settled herself in the smaller chair on the other side of the range. 'Did you hear Aunt Agnes going on?' she said.

'I heard bits of it. She asked if we were going to be able to keep the house.' He paused and bent down to open the front doors of the stove so that they should feel more of the heat. 'Actually she may have a point.'

Alarm shot through Lily. This was the only home she had ever known. It meant security and shelter. However hard she had to work, they had to keep this house. Her mother had made her promise that she would look after the two younger ones, keep the family together, see that William continued with his studies. They were death-bed pledges and Lily knew that she must keep them at all costs.

'What do you mean, William?'

'There's the rent to find, and even if we can do that, we don't know if the landlord will transfer the tenancy. It was in Father's name. The landlord let it go to Mother, but now she's dead too he might not be so happy to let us have it.'

'But he can't turn us out!' Lily took up the poker and jabbed angrily at the coals so that they flamed and flickered before dying again to a smouldering glow. 'I made our Ma a promise just before she died.'

'What promise?'

'That I'd do everything in my power to keep the family together here and to see you through your exams. Your studies were almost all she cared about. She wanted above everything to see you a proper qualified accountant.'

'You shouldn't say that. She loved us all equally. Anyway it's up to me now. If I have to get a job that pays more, I will.'

'No, you won't. I'd never forgive myself if I let Ma down. You got to get those exams passed first.'

'And what about you then?'

Lily shrugged her shoulders. 'Me? What I want has nothing to do with anything. When you're all launched, then's the time for me to think about myself, and that'll take a few years yet.'

'We'll see,' William said. 'I won't have you leaving your job in your precious bookshop. I know how much you like it.'

George looked across at them. Lily hadn't thought that he was listening.

'I could deliver papers or some'at. Keep chickens in the garden and sell the eggs?' he suggested helpfully.

'Thanks, George,' she said. 'We'll see. If only Father had bought the house years ago we shouldn't be in this mess. Ma told me that it was offered to him once.' She sighed at the thought. 'Wouldn't it be wonderful if it belonged to us? It would be like a castle, our fortress against the world.'

William shook his head. 'Now you're being fanciful,' he said. 'It doesn't do to have improbable ideas and dreams.'

'Oh yes it does,' she objected. 'If you never have dreams, you never achieve anything.'

'Rubbish,' William said, but there was fond amusement in his voice. 'It's all those books you spend your time with. You've become a bit of a romantic. Castle and fortress indeed! What would we want a fortress for?'

In spite of the sombre day they had spent, Lily laughed a little. 'To keep us all safe,' she said. 'And now I'm going to bed. Don't forget to lock up, William.'

'I'll do that,' George said, closing his disreputable magazine. 'Time I shouldered some of the jobs.'

Lily looked at him fondly. He was so unlike his elder brother, always hating school work, always wanting to be out in the streets up to some mischief or other. Perhaps Aunt Agnes was right. He certainly wasn't easy to manage.

Ivy was fast asleep when Lily crept into the bedroom. She put her candle down on the dressing table for there were no gas lights upstairs. She took off the soft grey blouse that she had worn all day, handling it with reverence for it was one her mother had made for her. It had a high neckline and many tucks running down the bodice, every one handstitched. The style was not the height of fashion now but Lily loved this garment. She remembered the care her mother had put into its making and the pleasure she had felt when she had taken it from its layers of tissue paper on her seventeenth birthday. It was the most beautiful thing she possessed. She folded the blouse carefully and put it away. It would be a long time before she wore it again. She wanted to keep it for ever in memory of her mother.

Just a week later their landlord's agent paid his expected visit. William was upstairs in his bedroom studying as always, Ivy and George were supposed to be doing homework and Lily was standing at the ironing board trying to get her brother's shirts as wrinkle free as her mother always could, when she heard the knock.

He was a short dumpy man with thinning fair hair and a face covered with freckles. He took off his hat and held it tightly in his hands as though frightened that it might become contaminated if he put it down anywhere.

'Come in,' Lily said reluctantly. She showed him into the icy cold parlour and left him standing there while she went to the bottom of the stairs and called up to her brother. 'Will, come down. It's about the house.' She was glad that she was wearing her best serge dress and that she'd pinned her hair up afresh after she got home from work. At least her appearance gave her a measure of confidence. She tried not to anticipate trouble or to show that she'd been dreading this interview. She knew that as long as her mother was alive they had been safe, for it wouldn't have looked good for a war widow to be turned out of her home. But in the landlord's eyes, they were now merely a bunch of children. She guessed he wouldn't feel any responsibility towards them.

When William appeared their visitor came straight to the point. He ignored Lily altogether, directing his remarks only to her brother.

'Well, Sir,' he started. 'I was never one to beat about the bush as the saying goes, and my boss what owns this property thinks that now's the time when it should be sold.'

'I see, and how much would you be wanting for it?' William said.

This remark obviously took the little man by surprise. He shook his head. 'As to that I couldn't say, Sir. I wasn't sent

7

to offer it to you so to speak. The boss just said that he wants you out by the end of January next if that suits?'

A flicker of annoyance crossed William's face. 'And what if it doesn't suit?'

'All the same if it do or if it don't in a manner of speaking. Out you got to be by January 31st 1919. That's what I was instructed to say.'

'Even if we are able to pay the rent?'

'Even if you can pay the rent it won't make any difference. The tenancy can't be transferred. Sorry, but that's final.'

'And where are we expected to go?' Lily exploded.

The answer was pat and ready as if rehearsed. 'Well now, for a start there's the orphanage just at the end of the road. Your father having been in a position there, teacher and governor so I'm told, they'd certainly take the young ones. Proper orphans they are and no mistake. And as for you, Miss, they'd give you a position in the kitchens and Mr William here could follow in his father's footsteps. My boss has enquired and they said they'd be pleased to have the young Mr Penrose as a teacher, live in of course, all found.' He nodded in William's direction and looked pleased that he had a solution to offer.

Lily however was boiling with rage. Who were these strangers, the landlord and his foolish little minion, who presumed to order their lives? 'Never!' she said. 'It's a good place no doubt, but not for us, not for George and Ivy, and I'm certainly not going to spend my life skivvying in a kitchen.

The little man shrugged his shoulders. 'That's up to your brother to decide,' he said firmly. 'But you've just got the rest of December and then January, like I said. Come the end of the month you've got to be out. Don't forget.' He twisted his hat in his hands, and shuffled to the door.

William followed him while Lily stayed where she was, her hands gripped tightly together, knuckles showing white and eyes blazing with anger.

'What an odious creature,' she said when her brother returned.

William sat down wearily on one of the cold unwelcoming chairs. 'What are we to do?'

8

'Find another house of course.'

'That won't be easy. Haven't you noticed that there are loads of men home from the Front now? They get priority.'

Lily sighed. 'Of course I'd noticed. What are we going to tell George and Ivy?'

'The truth.' William got to his feet again and they went through to the other room.

'You got to find somewhere,' George said when the dismal news was relayed. 'I ain't never going to live in that orphanage.'

Ivy was more positive. She looked at the calendar that hung on the wall beside the hearth. 'About six weeks left, Lil. That's a long time. Something's sure to come up.'

That night Lily prayed desperately that something would.

Agnes Penrose was a tall angular woman with no time at all for men. Her maternal grandmother had left her enough money to bring in a small regular income and so she was independent, a cause of great personal satisfaction. The fact that she had no need either to earn a living or to seek a husband had moulded her life, and she had lived alone doing just as she wanted ever since her twenty-first birthday. She sometimes reluctantly hinted at an admirer killed in the Boer War for this gave her a little air of mystery, but it had never been more than a hint, and now, whenever she thought about it, which was seldom, she mixed fact with fantasy and wasn't quite sure which was which.

She was not rich, of course, but if she was careful she knew that she would never need to seek financial help from anyone as long as she lived. She often thought with disapproval, even now long after his useless death in one of those useless battles, of her brother Edward who, having received a similar sum of money, had squandered the lot on that wife of his and his four children.

It was the fate of these nephews and nieces that had been causing her some concern. William she approved of. He was doing well, had always been clever and would cause no problems. She had strong misgivings however about the other three. Lily, William's twin, eighteen now, she

9

considered to be a self-opinionated young woman, though pretty as a picture of course, with all that unruly curly hair and those big brown eyes. Then there was George. Whenever Agnes thought of her youngest nephew both apprehension and horror filled her prim heart. He was uncouth, unruly, badly spoken, and would surely come to no good. Ivy, the youngest, had always had temper tantrums if she couldn't have her own way. Thoroughly spoilt, that one!

On the whole Agnes was quite horrified at the prospect of giving any of them a home. She had a tiny house that was as prim and exact as her own person. There was never a pin out of place, never a cup or dish left unwashed, and over everything was an air of peace and quiet. No, she couldn't begin to contemplate what dire consequences would follow if she had to house any of her brother's family. It was this fear that had caused her to be rather too critical at the funeral. She felt guilty about it now.

There was however one thought that kept returning to her, a wildly extravagant idea that might rid her of two problems at once. Her next-door neighbour had always been a thorn in her flesh. Harry Coney the coal merchant had his yard at the end of the road and lived in the house next to hers. He had lived alone since his son had been killed at Ypres and she was aware of the threatening masculine presence of him just through the wall. She could even hear him snoring sometimes when the night was quiet, and occasionally he would call out, presumably in his sleep, for she could never make out the words even though she crept to the wall and held a glass tumbler against it, the bottom pressed to her good ear.

He seemed to be a jovial sort of man and sometimes asked himself into her house, usually to borrow something. His jaunty clothes and bright beady eyes challenged her uncomfortably. Mr Coney needed a wife, that was obvious, and he had money. He was one of the few who'd done well during these last four years of war, and he'd told her that since his son's death he was looking for a good woman. There had been an unpleasant gleam in his eyes and she'd thought in a moment of extreme alarm that he was propositioning her, but he'd gone on to say that he'd like a new young family.

She'd breathed a sigh of relief. At forty-eight that put her firmly out of the running.

Young, he'd said, and the idea of Lily began to grow in her mind. She was certainly young, might soon be homeless and penniless, and there weren't many marriageable men around now, what with all those lying dead in France and Belgium. Well, it was a thought! Take Lily, take George and Ivy too, and he'd have the ready-made family he craved. Meanwhile she, Agnes Penrose, could sink again into the peace of her blissful spinsterhood, nothing to think about but herself!

She wouldn't want them next-door of course, couldn't have unimaginable things going on noisily in the bedroom next to hers! The house was too small anyway. Well, he could buy the house up in Bishopston, the place that she'd always told her brother to buy and not rent. A splendid idea! Eventually she had it all worked out, and because she was Agnes Penrose and had never allowed herself to be thwarted in any way, she had no doubt whatsoever that everything would come to pass just as she wished and planned.

The following day she asked her neighbour in for tea and cakes and he accepted the invitation with both surprise and alacrity. By the time he left he was quite convinced that the whole plan had been his own. He assured Agnes that of course he knew the family. He'd been delivering coal to them for years. Yes, the girl was presentable, a cut above most of the other women he had considered. And yes, he knew that her father had been a teacher and her brother was training to be an accountant. That would be a bonus! He'd never want for someone to sort out the coal yard accounts when the tax man chased him! And the girl could type, could she? Quite a family firm they'd make of it!

Harry Coney was confident of his own powers, his ability to charm, and more than that, he had a nice fat bank balance. He could get the little Penrose family out of their troubles, buy their house so they'd not have to leave, take young George into the business, and as for that pouting Ivy, he'd soon lick her into shape, had always wanted a daughter in fact! He grinned to himself. Two for the price of one. Not a bad bargain. He'd not let any grass grow under his feet, never one to do that

11

was Harry Coney. He'd certainly give the idea his full attention.

Agnes Penrose went to bed that night well pleased with herself, but when she heard her neighbour shouting out in his sleep through the wall, she felt a shiver of apprehension and wondered what on earth it would be like to be married to Harry Coney! But she firmly suppressed her doubts. It was in the hands of the Good Lord anyway. She was just helping His plans along a bit.

A few days later the door bell clanged imperiously. It was seven o'clock, and William looked up from the big ledger in which he was writing. Who could be calling on them at this hour? There were usually no visitors at this time in the evening. The last person to call had been the unwelcome landlord's agent. He put his pen down, wiping the nib carefully, and then ran down the stairs and opened the door, getting there before Lily who was in the scullery washing up. The man outside was well dressed, tall and smart, and William looked at him enquiringly.

His visitor took off his hat and bowed slightly. 'You must pardon my calling unannounced,' he said, 'but I'm a neighbour of Mrs Agnes Penrose. Your aunt, I believe.'

William was immediately suspicious. What could the old woman be up to now? 'Yes, we have an aunt of that name.'

'She told me about the sad death of your mother. I want to offer my condolences. My name is Harold Coney.'

Then William placed him. The clean face and smart clothes had been a perfect disguise. 'Mr Coney,' he said. 'Yes, of course I know you. Coney and Son, Coal Merchants. You've been bringing us sacks of coal for as long as I can remember.'

The man nodded. 'You're right, but it's not *and Son* any more, I'm sorry to say. My son James was killed at Ypres.'

William immediately repented of his initial antagonism. 'Would you like to come in?' he offered. 'My sister is often very downcast lately. She likes someone to talk to.'

Lily was as surprised as her brother, but she mellowed eventually and they passed a reasonably pleasant hour. It was only after he had left that she began to wonder why he had come. She had liked him on the whole. He was presentable, clean, obviously doing well, and he was polite and attentive especially to her and to Ivy. She had made him a cup of tea and they had gossiped about the war and the neighbourhood. He'd told them that his wife had died giving birth to his only son whom he'd brought up alone. 'Never looked at another woman in twenty years,' he'd said proudly. 'Too busy building up the business in hard times. No time for women.'

'Decent chap,' twelve-year-old George announced later over his bedtime drink of Ovaltine. 'Why'd 'e come?'

'I expect he's just lonely,' Lily said. 'With his son killed, I suppose he wanted to talk to someone who was in the same boat.'

'Got any bread pudding, Lil?' George asked, obviously more concerned about his stomach than their recent guest.

'There's a bit left, I think,' she said, fetching the tin for him. 'I'm glad you like Mr Coney. He works hard at the coal.'

'It's a good job, better'n all this learning I got to do at school.' George chose the biggest slice of the spiced and weighty pudding and started to munch. 'I'd like to work at some'at like that. You be nice to him, Lil, and he might give me a job. Is 'ee coming visiting again?'

'I don't suppose so,' she replied. 'There's no reason why he should.'

'I'll bet he does,' George said, his mouth full of stodge.

Lily looked at her younger brother, watched the bread pudding disappear rapidly, and wondered why she too had an uncomfortable presentiment that they hadn't seen the last of Harry Coney. In her bones she felt that he was to play some part in their lives, although exactly what she couldn't imagine.

Lying in her narrow bed later on she couldn't get him out of her mind. She'd seen him often, clad in his scruffy coal-covered clothes, a sack round his shoulders as he delivered coal to all the houses in the road. She'd never

13

thought of him as anything other than the coalman. Now he had an identity. He owned the business, two carts, two horses, and had another man working for him. What could he want with her family?

Then she thought of Aunt Agnes and was immediately suspicious. What had Aunt Agnes to do with it, for goodness sake? A few tears slid from under her closed lids. If only her mother were alive she wouldn't feel so vulnerable and alone, and if Arthur hadn't been gunned down in that last fruitless battle just before the peace was signed, well, she'd have no worries in the world.

When sleep came to her at last it was full of dreams, not of her Arthur but of Harry Coney. He looked at her with great staring eyes out of a coal-black face, and she woke up bathed in perspiration in spite of the December cold of the unheated bedroom.

Chapter Two

Harry Coney sat in his lonely little back room after that first impulsive visit to the bereaved family and had to admit that he was quite taken with the Penrose girl. In fact, to his amazement he lusted after her. Although he boasted that he'd not looked at another woman since his first wife had died all those years ago, it wasn't strictly true of course. A vigorous man like himself couldn't live like a monk! But until now there'd been no one he'd ever thought of marrying. His son had come first.

He drew deeply on his pipe, leaned back in his vast arm chair, put his feet on the mantelpiece and came to the conclusion, after half an hour of careful contemplation, that Lily Penrose might suit his purposes very well. She was young enough to be biddable, looked a good breeder and he wanted children, and it'd be jolly pleasant to have a wench who'd never been with a man before. He grinned to himself lasciviously as he thought about teaching her a few things! Yes, he'd definitely call again. Not too soon, though. Let them stew a bit, worry about what to do. And there was the house. He'd have to make enquiries about that, buy it over their heads. Not a bad place, Sefton Road.

He wondered what they'd made of his first visit. He'd been careful not to give himself away, merely offering condolences in their loss. After all, he'd known the family for a long time. Nice woman the mother had been, always ready with sugar lumps for his horse, and often a cup of tea for himself. Daughters were supposed to grow like their mothers, so Lily Penrose should turn out all right. He went to bed that night his mind quite made up.

Meanwhile Lily and William were agonizing over what to do about their plight. Thoughts of their visitor of a few days before had faded from their minds.

'I've made enquiries,' William said as they sat round the table one evening. 'No luck with another house. In fact, there aren't any to be had for love or money.'

Ivy stirred her dish of stew angrily so that some of it slopped over the side on to the table cloth. 'I'm not going to that orphanage,' she said. 'Even living with Aunt Agnes would be better than that.'

'Cor lummey,' said George, 'I ain't going to neither of they places!'

'If you don't both mind your manners you'll have no choice in the matter, either of you. For goodness' sake, George, talk properly.' Although fond of her young brother, Lily was heartily ashamed of him too.

'Why? I want to talk like me friends.'

She sighed. 'Then you'll get nowhere in life, believe me. You'll be judged by how you speak, especially when you go for a job. How do you think I keep my position in the bookshop? I'd be out on my ear straight away if they heard me speak like that.'

'I ain't going to work in a bookshop.'

'Stupid boy,' Ivy said, joining in the air of disapproval. 'You'll just be a navvy then, or a coalman like Mr black-face Coney what came courting our Lil.'

The words stung Lily almost into silence. She felt the colour rise quickly to her face.

William sprang to her defence. 'Mr Coney did no such thing, Ivy, and I'll ask you please not to make ridiculous statements like that again. He came to offer his condolences, that was all. And look at the mess you've made with that stew. Don't you know that your sister has to wash and iron that cloth?'

Ivy was slightly crushed by her brother's rebuke. 'Sorry,' she muttered. 'I'll wash en myself after supper.'

After supper of course she did no such thing and George took himself off to see some of his friends.

16

'Make sure and be in by nine,' William called after him.

'Ten,' he shouted back as he slammed the front door.

The twins looked at each other in despair. 'What on earth are we to do?' Lily said. 'They need a firm hand, that's obvious. Ma walloped both of them often, big though they are, but they wouldn't take that from you or me.'

William got up wearily and helped clear away the dirty dishes on to the wooden draining board beside the sink in the scullery. 'I can't do anything with George,' he said. 'I'm ashamed to admit it, but although he's my brother I've nothing in common with him at all, more's the pity.'

It was true of course, Lily mused. Her two brothers couldn't be more unlike. William with his tall fine-featured good looks might have come from a different family altogether. George had no respect for book learning. Brawn was all that mattered to him.

'He'd have to change his ways if he went to the orphanage,' she said.

William shook his head. 'It would never work. He'd run away.'

'It's going to be hard enough bringing them up,' Lily said wearily, 'but without a house and without enough money it'll be almost impossible. I can't see any way forward.'

As the days passed all hope of a satisfactory solution to their problems faded. Lily tossed on her bed each night and the only possibility open to them was what the landlord's agent had suggested: the orphanage. They had already received offers of help from this establishment for their father had been much respected there. He had been a member of both staff and management. Lily could work in the kitchens, the Principal said, and help out now and then with the little ones, William could teach arithmetic, and George and Ivy would be received as inmates, uniform, rules and all. If William and Lily were willing to surpervise at weekends and evenings as well they could live in.

'On the face of it, it seems a good idea,' Lily said to Ivy one day in the scullery when they were preparing the evening meal together.

'I'd rather die,' Ivy said dramatically. 'Those children

all look alike, all speak alike, think alike too, I shouldn't wonder.'

'Then what can we do?'

'You could marry someone rich,' Ivy said. 'Someone who'd carry us all off to some nice house and we wouldn't have nothing to worry about ever again.'

'And where am I to find such a paragon?'

'What's a paragon? Don't use such long words, Lil.'

'It means wonderful person. Where is such a one to be found then?'

'Harry Coney.' Ivy grinned at her sister. 'He ain't quite what you said, but he got money.'

Lily took her hands out of the hot soda water and stared down at the red chapped skin. 'I'm not going to marry Harry Coney,' she said. 'He hasn't been to see us again, hasn't asked me, and he's too old, so forget about it. I really don't know where you got such a stupid idea from. Money's not everything anyway.'

'Oh yes it is,' said Ivy. 'Money's absolutely everything!'

Christmas Day was disastrous. There were only tiny home-made presents, a small piece of ham, and the fruit and vegetables that were being sold cheaply late on Christmas Eve. Lily had gone down to Grosvenor Road in St Pauls to do the shopping as prices were lower there than in the slightly more prosperous district just up the Ashley Hill where they lived.

On Boxing Day, when their spirits were at their lowest ebb, Harry Coney made his second unannounced visit. Ivy stood at the front door and looked him up and down with her candid grey eyes. Yes, he was old, but fairly presentable. 'Mr Coney,' she said. 'Nice to see you again.'

'Is your sister in?' He took off his trilby and appeared to be relaxed and confident.

Ivy turned and called mischievously into the empty passageway, 'Lil, are you in?'

A flustered Lily appeared. She blushed when she saw who their caller was. 'Of course I'm in,' she said crossly to her sister. 'Come in, Mr Coney. My brother will be down in a minute.'

The house was narrow and had three rooms and a scullery all in a line, the parlour at the front, cold and with a faint smell of mildew, the dining room in which they never dined and which also was cold and for most of the time unused, and the back room, a comfortable little den with its constantly burning coal-fired range, two big red plush arm chairs, a large oak table covered with a red chenille cloth, and in the corner, a china cabinet. This was the hub of the house. The scullery, down two steps and with a stone sink, led from it.

Harry Coney was familiar with houses like this, for most of those in Sefton Road were built in long terraces with no back or side entrances. Apart from this drawback they were fairly spacious and pleasant, with small front gardens and bigger ones at the rear, but when he delivered coal he had to carry the sacks right through the passage, through the back room, and out into the yard or scullery in order to dump the contents in the coalhouse. When the householder could afford a ton it meant twenty sacks to deliver, twenty dirty dusty journeys right though the house. If their husbands were affluent enough, housewives preferred a ton at a time, for the business of laying newspapers over the carpets or linoleum, covering the chairs against the coal dust and then washing everything afterwards was a laborious chore, almost as bad as having the chimney sweep in. The fewer times that it had to happen the better.

At the back of this road stood the great ugly Orphan Homes so there was no chance of improving things with the making of a back entrance. It was the one thing Harry didn't approve of. But on the whole the house was sturdy and strong. He looked around it with a proprietorial air as he followed Lily through. He'd already enquired about buying it, but wasn't going to say anything of this to the family yet. He'd bide his time, wait until they were feeling really desperate.

He'd brought presents: a bunch of grapes, oranges, a large fruit cake, a catapult for George, pen for William, ribbons for Ivy and a tortoishell comb for Lily. He placed the bag on the table. 'Forgive me,' he said in a suitably humble voice which he assumed for the occasion, 'but I've no family.

Christmas isn't what it was. Thought you'd like these.'

William and Lily were immediately suspicious, but Ivy fell upon the things with glee, her few doubts about their donor quite forgotten. George handled the catapult with reverence.

'No aiming at cats or birds,' Lily told him. 'Else it gets taken away from you.' Privately she thought it a most unsuitable present.

'I'll set you up a place for target practice in the garden if your brother agrees,' Harry said hurriedly, guessing that his gift had been a little misplaced. 'When you're good, you can try for the rats.'

It was the middle of the afternoon when he arrived and Lily found herself wondering how long he would stay and whether they should invite him to share their evening meal. They had finished the last of yesterday's meat at mid-day and there was little in the larder for supper. She'd planned nothing more exciting than bread and jam and a piece of cake, not the rich fruit variety that their visitor had brought but a simple one she'd baked herself from the cheapest of ingredients.

'If we'd known you were coming we would have lit a fire in the front room,' she said apologetically. 'It's a bit cramped in here.'

He laughed. 'Perhaps I should have brought a sack of coal,' he said. 'Never thought of that for a Christmas present. I've always got plenty myself.'

Ivy stared at him without laughing at his little joke. 'When we last went to see Aunt Agnes we passed your yard,' she said. 'You got mountains of the stuff.'

'So I have, so I have. A coalman without coal wouldn't be much use, would he?' he replied, winking at George who was also staring at him.

Ivy ignored both the remark and the wink. 'I'm going to try my new ribbons,' she said, flouncing to the door.

'Have you thanked Mr Coney for them?' Lily reproved.

'Thank you,' she said ungraciously and was gone in a second, closing the door with a bang behind her.

Harry Coney followed her with his eyes. Lily, watching him, didn't quite like the expression on his face. Was it amusement she saw there or something more disquieting? Well, yes, she knew perfectly well that the child often needed a good hiding, but she wasn't going to have her sister either criticized or laughed at by anyone outside the family. She felt immediately protective. 'She's had a lot of grief for so young a child,' she said. 'First our father, and then the final blow, so unexpected and so quick.'

He inclined his head slightly, the trace of amusement quickly banished. 'Your dear mother. Yes, of course. Very sad and so needless. One wonders how the Good Lord can do such things.'

Lily stared at him. Pious expressions sat ill upon him but she'd often asked herself the same question. 'Shall we all have a cup of tea?' she said quickly in order to change the subject. With a man like this it was more comfortable to keep to ordinary mundane things.

To Lily's satisfaction the problem of the next meal didn't arise. After sharing some of the splendid Christmas cake he'd brought and the cup of tea that she offered, Harry Coney took himself off. She saw him to the door with a certain amount of relief, but just as he was about to leave he turned and looked at her closely.

'Would you care to come to the Metropole with me next week?' he enquired. 'There are a couple of good films on and I'd be honoured to take you.'

She blushed furiously. Was Ivy perhaps right about him coming courting? Surely not. He was old enough to be her father. 'What films?' she said quickly.

'A Mary Pickford, and the latest Charlie Chaplin. Thought you'd like both of those.'

'Yes — yes I would.' Lily had only been to the Metropole down in Ashley Road once before, taken by her father as a special treat.

'Wednesday then. I'll call for you at seven o'clock.'

She stood at the front door quite mesmerized, unable to refuse.

Three long strides and he was at the little iron gate. He clicked it behind him, smiled, waved, and then was gone, made quickly invisible by the high privet hedge that guarded their tiny front garden.

She turned and walked solemnly back through the passage. What had she done? Whatever had possessed her? Go to the pictures with Harry Coney! She must be mad.

Her pleasure in her job was almost overshadowed during the next few days. She loved working with books, enjoyed the day to day contact with the customers who came into the big shop, but all the time, at the back of her mind, was a niggle of worry about the evening out with Harry Coney. Eventually she talked it over with Joan, her fellow salesgirl.

'Lucky you,' Joan said with a laugh. 'Back from the Front is he then?'

'Too old. Lost his son at Ypres.'

'Then he won't have any trench problems. No shell-shock or anything. Make the most of him, my girl. Men like that are hard to come by just now. In fact, finding any man at all is pretty difficult with so many killed.'

The causal words reassured Lily and when Harry came for her the following Wednesday evening she was feeling more confident than she'd been for a long time. She had spent some hours the previous evening taking up the hem of one of her dresses at least two inches and adapting the neckline. The high frills had gone and it was now cut lower, showing her throat. She had searched for a necklace that was right for this new look, for she felt scrawny without the flattering high collars that she was used to.

Just as she was about to leave Ivy stared at her with a wicked glint in her eyes. 'Just look at you, our Lil,' she whispered. 'You look like a trollop.' And then more kindly, 'Pretty though. Have a good time.'

In spite of Lily's earlier fears everything went very well. Harry Coney was easy to be with. They laughed at the antics of the little man with his moustache and stick, and then Lily became dreamy-eyed and romantic as she watched Mary Pickford in all her glamour and filmy clothes. Harry had brought a small box of chocolate creams which they shared during the film, and in the interval he bought her a large tub of ice-cream, strawberry-flavoured and delicious, and she felt that she had never experienced such an evening of luxury in her life. He was meticulously correct, not touching her except for a moment when there was an especially romantic little episode on the screen. As the hero held the heroine in his arms, Harry grasped Lily's hand and squeezed her fingers gently, overwhelming them in his big calloused grip, and then released her. It was over in a second and she surprised herself by not being at all embarrassed. Indeed, in the dark, in the highly charged atmosphere of the warm cosy cinema, it was quite pleasant. The feel of him sitting close to her was agreeable too. Her body tingled disturbingly. She wondered if Mary Pickford up there on the big screen felt like that?

He escorted her to her gate, watched while she let herself safely into the house, then turned and strode down the road to the bus stop. He too was pleased with the evening. Nice girl, easy to mould to his ways, he decided. Yes, she'd do. He'd made the right decision. After New Year he'd call again.

The bus took him down to Old Market Street and he walked jauntily to a certain house where he knew he could get further comfort. Keeping himself in check tonight had been a strain. Had to go careful with Lily Penrose though. No good rushing things. Wait till they were properly wed before he tried anything. No point in frightening the life out of her. There were a couple of other wenches who'd be only too willing to give him all he needed at any time, and a good measure of brandy into the bargain. Came at a price of course, but well worth it. If he played his cards right he'd be able to go on with this little bit of pleasure after he was wed too he thought. A man needed more than a weedy bit of a girl.

He gave his customary knock on the door and was pulled inside by a welcoming pair of warm and friendly arms.

William was still working at his books when Lily got home. 'Well, how did it go?' he enquired, his face full of concern.

'All right, I suppose. He was kind, bought me chocolates and ice-cream, and the films were good.' She took off her hat and coat and put them carefully on the hall-stand.

'I don't mean those things.' He frowned.

She laughed at him. 'That's all there was. He just wanted an evening out, I suppose.'

'That's as may be. Anyway, there's a sandwich I kept for you, and the kettle's on. Come and sit down and tell me about it.'

Lily looked at her twin brother with affection. They had always been very close, and she knew that now their parents were dead he felt a responsibility for her. She couldn't tell him about the quick hand clasp, the unfamiliar feel of a man sitting close to her though. It would be too embarrassing.

She settled herself in the big arm chair in front of the fire, and took the plate that Will offered. He was looking at her searchingly, wanting her to add something more.

'I don't know what to make of Mr Coney,' she said, between bites of Marmite sandwich. 'He's so much older than me, but it didn't seem to matter.'

Suddenly the door opened and Ivy put her head round. 'Did he kiss you, our Lil?' She grinned impishly. 'Bet he knows how, being an old man. Plenty of practice.'

Lily was immediately flustered. Her sister suffered from none of William's inhibitions. 'No, he didn't, and it's no business of yours anyway,' she said crossly. 'And he's not an old man. Forty-two if you must know. He told me.'

'Gosh, that's ancient!' Ivy turned and ran up the stairs again. Lily could hear her singing loudly, '"Daisy Daisy give me your answer do, I'm half crazy all for the love of you."' To Lily's surprise William laughed. 'Well, it is a bit old, Sis, you must admit. Forty-two. About Ma's age.'

'You all seem to be assuming that I'm going to marry the man. He just wanted to take me to the pictures, as I've already said. His age has nothing to do with it.'

William was at once serious again. 'Well, be careful,' he said. 'If he wants to continue the friendship he'll have to ask my permission, and I'll find out what his intentions are.'

Lily sighed. Of course this was normal and she supposed that now she had no father William would be her guardian. It was rather degrading though. She thought of the women who had fought for votes just a few years ago. Had they possessed fathers and brothers who controlled their lives? The vote was won now anyway, thanks mainly to the war,

24

but not for all women. Only those of thirty and over were considered sensible enough for the privilege. She still had a long way to go, but perhaps that was the age at which a woman could call her life her own. She would look forward to it! And until then she'd just have to put up with William making decisions about things. Fortunately he was one of the best. He'd not lord it over her, and degrading or not, she'd make the most of his protection. At least she had an ally who would always be on her side whatever life might hurl at her.

She finished her sandwich and her hot milk and smiled at her brother. 'I'm going up to bed now,' she said. 'Thanks for your concern, and for the supper. Don't worry though. I'm sure our Mr Harry Coney was just lonely. Christmas and all that. He misses his son. We probably won't see him again except when we order more coal.' Privately she thought, *And that'll be never. Only a month now and we must be out. Dear God, whatever are we going to do? Will it really be the orphanage for George and Lily?*

She filled a stone hot water bottle and put one of her father's old woollen socks around it and then climbed the stairs. Her dreams that night however were not of Harry Coney with coal-grimed face as he had appeared to her before. This time he was clean and dapper, smart grey spats on his feet, a straw boater, grey flannels and sports coat, a white shirt and flashy tie. And he was holding her in his arms just as the hero had held Mary Pickford in the film she had seen. In her dreams she responded, and then she awoke covered in confusion and embarrassment and was heartily glad that it had been just a dream.

During the next few days Lily tried to recall Arthur's features, tried to remember the feel of him, how it had been when he'd kissed her goodbye on that last leave. She endeavoured unsuccessfully to compare him with Harry Coney but his features were dim to her now. It seemed that his memory was destined to perish as he himself had done in the mud of France. Sometimes she cried into her pillow at night thinking again about what might have been.

In the daytime however she was intensely practical and

when Harry asked her out again she accepted. This time it was a Saturday and they walked on the Downs. He took her to the Avon Gorge with its great suspension bridge and she was glad to hold his arm when they walked across. It was so far down. The horses and carts and the sprinkling of motor cars on the Portway below looked like little toys.

'I mean to have a motor one day,' he told her as they stopped and leaned over to stare at the muddy water and the road far below. 'But a van comes first. I'm going into general hauling, moving furniture and goods. There's a good future in that.'

She glanced up at him. It was nice to be with someone who appeared to have no money worries, who was confident and assured, and for an older man he was quite handsome, masterful too. Yes, she decided. She could do worse than settle for someone like this. Young men were few and far between now as her friend had remarked. 'That sounds grand,' she said. Then as she considered his words she added anxiously, 'But will you keep the horses? I've heard that a lot of them end up as ... as dog meat. It's horrible, and some go across to France. They actually eat horses there!'

She shuddered at the thought and he laughed at her. 'My two would be a bit tough, wouldn't they?' he teased. 'But, yes, we'll keep them to do the coal rounds for a good few years yet, so you needn't worry.'

They walked right to the other side of the bridge and then back again. Then they found a little tea house in Clifton and she marvelled at the food she was offered: pastries such as she had never tasted before, great thick custard slices that she had no idea how to eat.

'Put it on its side,' Harry said. 'Then you can slice it without the custard and cream oozing out.'

They laughed together, and when they could eat no more went out again into the January cold. The sun had just disappeared from view and the sky was a blaze of red and gold.

'It's so beautiful,' Lily said. 'I don't often see the sunset. I'm usually in the shop.'

They had wandered along a lonely bit of path beneath the trees. There was no one about. Suddenly he stopped and stood facing her. He took both her hands in his.

'Marry me, Lily, and you'll be able to see the sunset every day of your life. No more work.'

She gasped and looked up at him. It was so quick. She hadn't expected a proposal as soon as this.

'I don't know.' She thought of William.

'Just say yes and I'll do the right thing, ask your brother's permission as soon as we get home.'

She drew in her breath. Had he read her thoughts? 'But I need time.'

He dropped her hands then and pulled her to a seat by the side of the path. 'I thought that time was just what you hadn't got?'

'What do you mean?'

'The house, your brother and sister ... everything.'

'How do you know all about that?'

'I'm not blind and deaf, little girl,' he said. 'I've made an offer for your house. It's been advertised, you know.'

She hadn't known. She sprang up in sudden anger, colour flaring to her face. 'How dare you do that? Are you blackmailing me? Are you going to put us out of our house then? I knew I should never trust you, Mr Coney.'

He just sat there calmly looking at her and shook his head. 'Think about it before you judge me so harshly,' he said. 'I knew it was for sale. I've always wanted a place in Bishopston. I can wait for you to find somewhere else to live if that's what you want. You can rent it from me in the meantime. You won't need to move. No, I'm not blackmailing you.'

Emotions were chasing each other rapidly one after the other. What did he mean? Was he genuine? What was there in it for him? She guessed that he was no do-gooder.

'Why?'

'Why what?'

'Why are you doing all this, saying all this, asking me to marry you, then telling me you're buying my house?'

'Sit down again.' He patted the seat beside him. 'I'll tell you why.'

27

Grudgingly she sat down, leaving a large space between them. 'Tell me then, and be quick. I'm cold. I want to go home.'

'I've come to love you, Lily Penrose.'

The quiet remark took her breath away and for one short moment disarmed her completely. Even Arthur had not said those precious words. But she squared her shoulders, tried not to believe him. 'You haven't known me long enough.'

'Quite long enough,' he said. 'And I've watched you since you were small, remember.'

'Why buy the house then?' She was still suspicious.

He sighed. 'I thought of it almost as a wedding present for you if you should accept my offer.'

'What do you mean?'

'It would be in my name, of course, but yours in everything but law.'

'The children? You wouldn't want them surely?'

He grinned. 'I could manage George and Ivy if you allowed me a free hand and didn't interfere. They need some discipline. William would want to find somewhere else to live, I've no doubt.'

He had it all worked out. She suddenly felt helpless as though all will to plan and map out her family's future had been taken out of her hands. And then abruptly the feeling changed to one of relief. The terrible burdens that she had faced since her mother's death wouldn't be hers any more. She'd have no money worries, George would have a man to control him, they'd have a roof over their heads, her very own roof if Harry Coney was to be believed, William could go on with his studies. Her promises to her mother would be fulfilled.

He must have sensed her capitulation for he jumped up and stood in front of her. He took her hands in his, pulled her to her feet and into his arms.

'Then it's settled? You will?'

She couldn't speak. She just nodded her head in affirmation.

Then he kissed her, his lips hard on hers, and she allowed him to do so for a moment, permitted herself to respond a little. But eventually she pulled away. She couldn't look into his eyes for she was full of confusion. It was all so quick, but what else was there to do? 'If William agrees, I'll marry you,' she said.

Chapter Three

On a rare sparkling day in February Lily Penrose walked beside her brother to her wedding service. While her spirits lifted as she heard the strains of the music that was being thumped out on the old piano, another part of her mind told her that she was one of the Bible's sacrificial lambs.

William looked down at her and pressed her arm to his side. She knew that he'd been far from happy about this marriage, making her take time to consider, but she had assured him over and over again that it was what she wanted. 'Security, William,' she had said. 'No more worries about money or a roof over our heads, discipline for George, a good man to look after me. He's giving me the house as a wedding present. What more could I want?'

Love, youth, trust, William had thought in reply, but he had said none of those things aloud. He had tried very hard to believe the best of Harry Coney and eventually he had given his reluctant approval, told his sister that she went to her marriage with his blessing. That at least was true for he hoped and prayed desperately for her happiness. But he couldn't completely quell his doubts. It was the man himself who worried him. There was something not quite right about Harry Coney. The trouble was that he couldn't actually put his finger on anything definite.

As for Lily, with each measured step that took her closer to her bridegroom, she felt less and less composed. She was trading her freedom for security. But what had her mother said one day long ago? The words came back to her now. She wished that she'd remembered them earlier although whether they would have made any difference to her decision she couldn't say. 'To be independent, a woman needs money of her own,' Elsie Penrose had pronounced. 'She needs to have it and keep it. That's why I sew and why I put a little by every week. It's my hidden store, for a rainy day.'

She had given this small hoard to Lily just before she died and it was hidden beneath a special floorboard in the back room. The thought of the little leather purse gave her a quick surge of confidence, enough in fact to carry her those last steps to her bridegroom's side.

He turned and smiled at her, and although there was no answering smile in her heart yet her lips smiled, and she couldn't help thinking how handsome and assured he looked. Yes, she would banish her doubts and give herself to all the excitement of this most special of days.

Ivy, just behind her, had mixed thoughts too. Just one more week of freedom for me, she reflected, while they're away on their honeymoon, and then it'll be bossy old coal-face who'll be telling me what to do. But there were some compensations. She'd found a way of getting round him. Pay him a few compliments, flash her eyes at him, and he usually looked at her differently, stopped treating her as a naughty little sister. In fact there was a look on his face that challenged her in a frightening way. She thought of it now as she took her sister's bouquet. A small grin played across her face for a moment as she wondered what it was that happened on a wedding night. There were some lurid tales told in the playground at school, but really no one had much idea. Whatever it was it sounded pretty disgusting. Most of it she couldn't believe. But she'd find out soon enough now. Lily might enlighten her perhaps, or she could even listen through the wall when they came home next week.

'Will you take this man ... love, honour and obey him ...'

Obey. Every woman said this on her wedding day but Lily didn't want to make that promise. Yes, she'd have obeyed Arthur, but Harry Coney? Well, it was too late now. Her voice was almost inaudible, but the words had to be spoken, the commitment made.

The wedding breakfast had been prepared by Lily herself

31

with some help from the neighbours, and it was set out in the Sunday School Hall. She cut her cake, ate and drank little, smiled at everyone as they told her what a lovely bride she made, and returned her new husband's smile when required to do so.

Her wedding dress had been made by a friend from a length of white satin that had been going cheap in the winter sales. It wasn't all that Lily wished, not quite a dream-gown, but she was thrilled to have it. War-time brides had mostly gone to their weddings in ordinary suits or coats. At least she had been saved from that. The dress was cut in the latest style, still ankle-length but straighter than usual, consequently saving material and enhancing her slim figure.

She had fixed her hair in a loose bun at the nape of her neck and had pinned her mother's veil over her unruly curls. When it was time to change into her going-away suit there were tears in her eyes as she carefully folded the delicate lace and placed it back in its tissue paper. She almost felt her mother's presence for a moment and longed for her kiss, her approval, and most of all her advice.

But there was no time for sentiment. They were going for a week's honeymoon, an unexpected pleasure. Lily had never been on holiday in her life. Weston-super-Mare was the only seaside town she had ever visited.

Teignmouth was grey and cold by the time the train from Temple Meads chugged into the little station, but Lily was entranced by the sight of the sea. The railway line went right alongside the beach and for a moment she forgot her fears about tonight as she looked at the dancing waves, the ships out in the bay and the seagulls majestically riding the wind.

But her apprehension returned when she sat facing her new husband across a table in the little restaurant where he had booked their evening meal. She toyed with her food, her usual hearty appetite completely deserting her. She tried to make conversation, but with little success, and eventually he paid the bill, guided her outside, tucked her arm into his and walked the short distance to the boarding house where their suitcases awaited them in the threatening bedroom.

Unknown to Lily, of course, Harry Coney had deliberately spent the previous night with his favourite trollop, as he always called her, and now could afford to be easy and careful with his new bride. Or at least that was what he hoped. She'd have to get used to his lusty ways later, but he'd break her in gently. It was quite a novel experience for him, a young girl, ignorant about everything, never had a man before.

'You go and unpack,' he told her. 'I'll have a cigarette down here. I'll be up later.' He'd give her half an hour. That should be enough time, he told himself. By then she might be ready for him.

He puffed impatiently, watching the clock, determined to be exact. Then he stubbed out his third cigarette, looked at his reflection in the mirror above the fireplace and was moderately pleased with what he saw. There was very little grey in his hair, his stiff white collar was still immaculate. He considered himself a good catch for any woman.

Brimming with self-confidence, he strode up the stairs. It was quite dark outside now but the gas wall-lights cast a gentle glow around the room. She was already in bed and holding tightly on to the sheet as though it was a piece of armour that she needed to save her life. She was his very own possession now he thought, gloating. It gave him a feeling of great power. He laughed at her and pulled the sheet away.

'Don't be modest,' he said. 'You're beautiful. Don't hide yourself from me.'

He had always been careful with his few good clothes and even tonight he was in no rush. He stared down at her, at the frilled nightgown but then turned away, took off his jacket and placed it on a hanger. He fumbled with his collar stud, removed his shirt and trousers and placed them in the big wardrobe beside her dress and coat.

Lily watched him as a frightened rabbit watches a stoat. All she knew was that she must lie still on the bed, allow him to remove her lovely nightdress, look at her, handle her, and do whatever he liked to her. She was almost completely ignorant as to what that might be.

She'd helped to bath George when he was small so she

33

knew something of little boys, but when suddenly Harry emerged from the shadows, turned towards her, and she saw that he was completely naked, she took one look at him and closed her eyes in horror. What had happened? Why was he like that? George had never been ...

He took a step towards the bed, launched himself into it and removed her hands from the neck of her gown. 'Take it off,' he ordered.

Obey, obey, obey. The word raced through her mind and she gritted her teeth, kept her eyes tightly closed and did as she was bid, faithfully keeping the promise so unwillingly made earlier in the day.

His hands were all over her in places where no one, not even her mother, had been allowed to touch. She tried to push him off but he persisted, stroked her legs, and that at least was a little more pleasant. Then suddenly he was on top of her, pressing into her, right in. She screamed as he relentlessly thrust on and on, disregarding her fists thumping desperately on his back.

All his good resolutions about being gentle disappeared. By God she was beautiful. This was good. This conquest of a reluctant young girl was the best thing he'd had yet. And he was doing nothing wrong. She was his wife. He could carry on like this every night, and more often than that if he wanted.

Eventually he rolled from her and she felt the warm blood on her thighs, the pain subsiding a little.

She lay tense and still, not daring to move until she heard his heavy breathing and then the deep guttural snoring that surely announced that he slept. Then she crept fearfully from the bed, washed herself in the basin of cold water on the marble stand, put her nightdress on again, extinguished the lights, and unwillingly slid in beside him once more, but lay precariously right on the edge of the bed so that no part of her body should touch him. If he awoke, would it all start over again? Had there been a comfortable chair in the room she would have slept in that, but there was only a small cane one in front of the dressing table.

So this was it! This was what she had heard about in garbled sentences whispered furtively at women's gatherings

34

sometimes. Why did women want marriage so much then? Lucky Aunt Agnes! And her mother and father? Oh no, surely it hadn't been like this for them? Tears slid from her eyes but eventually, because she was young and healthy and quite worn out, she slept.

He awoke her in the morning and yes, to her horror, forced himself on her again. Wasn't once a night enough? In the daylight it was more disgusting and degrading, but not so painful perhaps, and there was no blood this time. But to have to look at him in the full light of day, have him look at her, was too awful. She much preferred him clothed!

In contrast to the horrors of the night, the luxury of the small boarding house was a pleasant surprise to Lily. She had seen little of it the night before. At breakfast she tried to regain some composure, to eat the bacon and eggs that were set before her, and to her amazement she found that she was hungry. Later they walked on the promenade, then along the sea-wall and on to the beach right down to the sea's edge. Lunch was in a small but expensive-looking restaurant and Harry seemed not to worry about the cost. During the afternoon he bought her a new handbag, a necklace, and later an ice-cream. He even made her laugh sometimes. If only marriage was just this, she thought. Without the other it would be perfect.

The second night was not quite so bad, the third more acceptable, and by the time the week came to an end, although she still found the whole performance revolting, she was becoming used to it. Resigned might be the best word, she decided. If this was what she had to put up with in order to keep a roof over their heads, to keep William at his books, and to keep them all fed and clothed, well, so be it. It was only an hour or so out of each twenty-four after all, sometimes less. She had done all that was required of her, kept her promise to her mother. She felt a glow of satisfaction. And when a baby came, as she knew one might, surely then he'd leave her alone for a bit.

William moved out of the house the day they came home. He had arranged to have a room and his food in the orphanage in exchange for weekend supervision of the boys. He would still keep his day-time job with the accountancy firm and he could study undisturbed in the evenings. It seemed a satisfactory solution on the whole, and Lily was pleased that he would not be too far away and that her promise to her mother was being fulfilled. His exams wouldn't be jeopardised.

Ivy was difficult on that first night home and Lily wondered how she would manage the child. She would be twelve next March, a tiresome age.

'Don't worry about her,' Harry instructed. 'She's my responsibility now.'

Lily didn't quite know what he meant by this. She wasn't sure that she liked the idea either. Their mother had entrusted the care of the younger two to her.

She felt sure that George would be all right. Before her marriage he had seemed to get on very well with Harry, had gone out on one or two of the coal rounds in fact, and had proclaimed that he wanted to leave school and do this regularly. 'Not until you're fourteen,' Lily had insisted, but she'd seen a wink pass between the two of them. 'We'll see about that,' Harry had said.

The first days and weeks passed in relative calm. Lily enjoyed her new role as housewife. The house became her pride and joy, and she cleaned and polished until every corner of it gleamed. Harry allowed her money for new curtains and she brought out her mother's treadle sewing machine and determined that, although she had never been much use with it before, she would try to do better. Cooking too intrigued her. Now that there was more money for better ingredients, and she had more time, she experimented, cooked a hearty meal and a pudding for the four of them each evening, and often invited William to share it as a change from his meagre orphanage fare.

Her love of reading, which had increased during her years in the bookshop, was the only thing that displeased Harry. She wasn't aware of this for some time and it was not until the long June evenings that matters came to a head. She had bought a copy of *David Copperfield* from the second-hand department of the shop in which she used to work and after supper one evening she pulled her chair close to the window for the light and started to read. It was a rare snatched moment of leisure.

When Harry came back from his visit to the pub he took one look at her and his face reddened with displeasure.

'What do you think you're doing?' he shouted.

'Just reading. The gas lights aren't bright enough to read much in winter, but now with the light nights I thought I might catch up on a few books. All the work's done. I had some time to spare.'

'Not for that rubbish you haven't!' He strode up to her and snatched the book from her hands. 'I don't want a clever wife. Reading's not for women, not for the likes of you!'

'But you can't stop me.' She sprang up, tried to take the book from him. 'I've always read.'

'Then you won't from now on, do you understand? No more books.'

Lily looked at him with complete incomprehension. Had he gone suddenly mad? Then to her dismay he opened the door of the range and pushed the book on to the glowing coals.

'You can't do that!' she screamed at him. She tried to open the door with clumsy hands for he had shut it firmly. But the flames were curling hungrily round the open pages, roaring up the chimney. She felt sudden hatred, an emotion she had never experienced before, and with it an anger that frightened her. She bunched her fists and struck him repeatedly on the chest. 'How can you do such a terrible thing?' she shouted. 'It's wicked to burn books.'

'Not for me it isn't. Have you got any more?' He grabbed her fists and held them in an iron grip. 'Have you got any more I say?'

She thought of the few volumes that were in the cupboard beside the bed. He had never looked there and she had not, until this moment thought it necessary to hide them. It was where they had always been.

She shook her head. 'No more,' she lied.

He released her and pushed her down into the armchair. 'I never want to see you with your head stuck in a book again, is that clear? I don't want books in this house.'

'But why?' Was this a drunken rage? she wondered. Or was she dreaming it all? Her face was pale and her heart thumped with amazement and shock.

Ivy came in at that moment. She'd obviously heard most of the conversation. 'I've got books,' she said jauntily. 'School ones mostly.'

'Then keep them to yourself,' he told her, and turned and stamped out of the room.

''Tis because he can't read,' Ivy said calmly. 'He don't want a wife cleverer than he is. Men don't like that.'

Lily stared at her young sister. 'What do you mean, can't read? Of course he can read. He has a business. Everyone can read nowadays.'

'No they can't,' Ivy contradicted. 'Quite a few in my class can't read. Some's good at arithmetic instead. I expect Harry was like that. He knows about money and things, but he can't read books.'

'How come you're so sure?'

Ivy was quiet for a moment. At last she said, 'He asked me to read something to him. A bit from a newspaper what William left here. I asked him why he couldn't read it for himself and he said he hadn't got his glasses. But he haven't got glasses, never had any. I've watched en since then, and I know 'tis true. We'd best keep it secret though. He'd hate us to know.'

Lily marvelled at her sister's shrewdness, and her anger with her husband subsided a little. If he truly couldn't read, no wonder he hated to see her doing so. She was horrified though. How terrible not to be able to read, and it was something that they could never share. She was condemned to a life of pretence and subterfuge. How could she possibly be married to a man who couldn't read? Why had she not discovered this truly amazing lack before? Would it have made any difference?

The following day when he was out on his rounds she took her remaining books and handled each volume lovingly: *Tess of the d'Urbervilles*, her favourite, a complete Shakespeare which she had never read but which she had meant to study one day, poems by Francis Thompson, a small leather-covered Tennyson and a much-read copy of Wuthering Heights. There were a few lesser volumes too, romantic novels she had enjoyed before she started working in the bookshop. She leafed through the pages of one book after another and thought wistfully how wonderful it would be if she could read some of them to Harry at night when they were alone. But she realized with a great surge of despair that she had nothing in common with her husband, there was nothing to share except the uncomfortable heavings and gropings in bed each night, the meals she cooked for him, and the very occasional walk on the Downs of a Saturday.

She carried the books downstairs, then carefully pulled back the carpet in the front room. This was a better place than the one where her money was hidden. No one ever came in here. She retrieved the little bag of sovereigns that her mother had given her, forty of them, a veritable fortune, her guarantee of security if she should ever need it.

She took a large flat-bladed screw-driver from the tool box in the cupboard under the stairs and prised up a board that she knew was loose. Beneath it was a space that you could even get down into if necessary. She wrapped her books in several thicknesses of cloth and brown paper and placed them in a space between the brick foundations below. She put the little leather bag of sovereigns beside them, and finally replaced everything as it had been, the fireside rug over the carpet, a chair on top of that. She put the screw-driver safely away and then returned and stared down at the place where her secret treasure lay hidden. No one should ever know of it. It was her guarantee. Guarantee of what she was not quite sure, but her mother had said that a woman should have her own money, and Lily felt that never had a truer word been spoken. This was hers. Harry Coney should never get his hands upon it or upon her precious books.

Although she knew that she would never become really resigned to this travesty of a marriage, she longed for a child. That deep hungering was all that kept her faintly willing to put up with her husband's endless lust. Yet in spite of all Harry's energetic efforts, the tell-tale signs never came. Lily's flow was as regular as clockwork and consequently there was no relief from his constant demands. Every night, whether he was sober or drunk and at whatever time he came home, he expected her to be ready for him. Sometimes it would be twice or three times for he would often wake her up and demand her body all over again. She frequently wondered how much longer she could put up with his treatment of her. She had found out about his visits to the house in Old Market Street too and when he was very late and she guessed that he had come straight from there she was completely sickened. Yet she managed to keep this knowledge to herself. It was a secret wound. She couldn't bring herself to confront him, and she certainly could never tell William.

She constantly searched for things to occupy her mind but with books forbidden and no interesting conversation in the evenings she found that the monotony of her life became gradually more and more unbearable. It almost threatened her sanity until one day she decided to use a little of her housekeeping money to go into town.

The bus took her to the Tramway Centre and as she stepped from it she was filled with excitement and a little thrill of pleasurable guilt. What would Harry say if he could see her now, out enjoying herself, when he thought her safely in the scullery slaving over the washing, or preparing meat and vegetables for his evening meal?

Yet she used to do this journey every day. How much she had taken her freedom for granted then! She walked up Park Street, pausing frequently to look at the shops, the latest fashions displayed in the windows, the bolts of cloth ready for making into dresses and coats. The university stood on the crest of the hill, its great tower dominating everything else, and just before it, on the other side of the road, was the bookshop, her bookshop, the place where she had spent so many happy hours before her marriage. She stopped and stared at the window display thinking of the times when she herself had been arranging the books there, proudly handling the new volumes, delighting in their bright covers and in the pages full of the knowledge and scholarship that she craved.

'Well, hello, stranger!'

Joan Harris, the girl who had worked with her, had just come out of the shop. 'How's married life then?' she asked jauntily. 'I'm going up Brandon Hill to have my sandwiches. Think I could spare you one. Like to join me, tell me all your news?'

Lily paused for a moment, and then beamed at her, felt suddenly young and free again. 'Yes, I'd love to.'

They climbed the green leafy hill behind Park Street and found a seat overlooking the City. Lily breathed deeply and stared at the vista below. 'I'd forgotten how lovely it is up here,' she said. 'Bristol is beautiful, isn't it? You don't realize it from down there.'

Joan opened her lunch bag and took out a sandwich, passed it over to Lily. 'Suppose it is. But we didn't come up here to talk about the view. Tell me all about yourself. It's a long time.'

Lily was hungry. She'd brought two apples but she looked at the bread and fishpaste with pleasure. 'Sure you can spare it?'

'Of course.' Joan took a bite of her sandwich and turned to look critically at her friend. 'You seem a bit peaky, look as if you could do with more than one. Are you ...?'

'No, nothing like that. Odd, isn't it? I thought all women started babies as soon as they were married.'

'Most do, more's the pity. Then one a year after that. Count your lucky stars, my girl.'

Lily was surprised by this comment. She knew that Joan was getting on for thirty and quite on the shelf. Her fiancé had been killed in the first year of the war and men were in short supply now. It wasn't likely that she'd ever be married. She thought for a moment how awful it was to be an old maid, and then she remembered that during the first weeks of her marriage she had almost envied people like Joan and Aunt Agnes, free and independent, no man to share their bed, no one to answer to. It took a lot of determination to rid your mind of the feeling that marriage was the whole purpose of a woman's life. But was it? Now in 1919 were things beginning to change?

'I suppose you might be right,' she said. 'But I'd like a baby one day. Harry wants lots.'

'Let him have them,' Joan said grimly. 'Men get the pleasure, women get the trouble. The Good Lord wasn't very fair, was He, when He doled things out?'

Lily laughed. 'I've never thought of it like that.'

'Then it's time you did. Like to come to our meeting on Friday evening?'

'What meeting?'

'The Women's Union. We fight for women's rights.'

'I thought that had all finished now we've got the vote?'

'This is different. We campaign for all sorts of things. The right of women to work after marriage, to use birth control, to have more authority in their lives. We want to get women into Parliament too. What's the use of stopping at merely getting the vote?'

Lily finished her sandwich and took out her two apples. She passed one over to Joan. 'Sounds marvellous, but pretty impossible.' She thought with horror of what Harry would say if he could hear this amazing conversation. Then suddenly she made up her mind. She wouldn't be the submissive little wife any longer. It was time she asserted herself. 'All right, I'll come,' she said. 'Where is it?'

'The room over the Butler's Cafe in Corn Street. Half-past seven. Will you really come? Will your hubby be agreeable?'

Lily scrunched the apple noisily and wanted to laugh and cry both at the same time. Her emancipation was at hand! 'Agreeable! That's a joke if ever there was one. He'll hit the roof!'

'Can he stop you?'

'He might have locked me in the bedroom if we had a lock, but we haven't.' Her state of nervous anticipation made her want to giggle like a schoolgirl.

'Good. Stand up to him.'

All day Friday Lily was in a state of tension. She did her work automatically without thinking about it, and she prepared Harry's favourite meal, steak and kidney pie, with potatoes and plenty of rich gravy. When they had finished she carried the dishes through to the scullery, told Ivy to get a move on and help her with them, and then went up to the bedroom. She decided not to put on her good coat. It might anger Harry to see her dressed up. Instead she took the old-fashioned one that trailed almost to her ankles, chose the simplest hat, and when she was ready presented herself at the door of the back room where Harry was sitting with his pipe. Ivy was at the now cleared dining table, her school books spread out before her. George was nowhere to be seen.

Harry looked up at her in amazement. 'Where you off to then?' he demanded.

'I'm going out.' She tried to make her voice sound confident and firm.

'Where?' he repeated.

There was nothing for it. She felt obliged to tell him the truth. 'To a Women's Meeting, with a friend.'

He got up slowly from the deep armchair. 'Take your coat and hat off, woman. You'll do no such thing. I'll not have you gallivanting, filling your head with rubbish. You've enough to do looking after me.'

'I'm sorry,' she said, backing away from the door. 'You have no right to stop me. My mind's made up. I'm going.' She heard Ivy gasp and realized that she could have been far more tactful.

He strode towards her, put his hand on her arm, took her by the shoulders, shook her. Then she was aware of Ivy springing up from the table so fast that the chair she had been sitting on crashed to the floor.

'Don't go, Lil. I don't want you to go and leave me.'

For a moment Lily was distracted. What was the matter with the child? Why should she not be left? She'd never been unwilling to be alone before.

The remark obviously distracted Harry too and she saw a sudden and totally unexpected grin spread across his face.

'Go then,' he said releasing her, pushing her away from him as he did so. 'Go to your meeting, and face the consequences when you come home.'

She rushed along the narrow passage, nervously pulled at the front door, felt in her pocket to make sure that she had the key and then slammed it behind her. What did he mean, face the consequences? Would he go to the pub and come back drunk, beat her perhaps? He had never done that, never hit her, and as she walked down the road to the bus stop she felt a moment's guilt. Perhaps she had not been thankful enough for that, not valued him enough. There were plenty of women beaten by drunken husbands every Friday night. Was she wrong to go and desert him? A great rush of guilt swept through her so that she almost turned round and went back, begged his forgiveness. But she only paused for a moment, then resolutely marched on to the end of the road, past the Orphan Homes where her brother would no doubt be in his room, eyes glued to his books.

The motor bus was coming. She ran the last few yards to the stop, climbed aboard and paid her fare, and as she sank into a vacant seat she squared her shoulders and told herself fiercely that she was doing the right thing. Women must stand up for themselves. She was taking the first brave steps!

She would always remember what Harry Coney meant by taking the consequences, remember it for the rest of her life. She put her key into the lock at exactly half-past nine, was surprised that there was no light in the back room, then she heard it − the noise that shot through her like a piercing knife wound, her sister's voice raised in protest, frightened terrified protest. Lily tore up the stairs to the source of the sound, flung open Ivy's bedroom door and there he was, spread-eagled over the child on the narrow bed.

He turned as the door opened, laughed, slid off the bed and faced her. 'Now you,' he said. 'Always ready for two or three. Get those clothes off, hussy, and I'll show you what your gallivanting can lead to.'

She looked with disgust and horror at his gaping trousers, which, in spite of his words, he was automatically endeavouring to do up as he spoke. Behind him her sister lay sobbing on the bed, bloomers round her feet, skirt at her waist.

In one stunned glance Lily took in the entire situation. 'You brute, you filthy disgusting brute!' she screamed.

There was a marble statue of a grotesque foreign god on the chest of drawers, one that Ivy, for some strange reason of her own, had bought for twopence in the pawn shop a few weeks before. It had been banished up here to her bedroom where it sat evilly amongst an assortment of books, pieces of cheap jewellery and an old battered teddy-bear. Without thinking Lily picked the idol up and flung it at her husband with all her strength. It hit him squarely between the eyes and she saw the look of amazement, as he fell. His head struck the raised edge of the fender that guarded the tiny never-used fireplace. He had fallen with a sickening thud and then everything was silent, and Lily could only hear the beating of her heart filling the room with fear.

Ivy got slowly from the bed, adjusted her skirt and looked down at the inert form on the floor. 'There's blood,' she whispered. 'You've killed en. Lil, you've gone and killed en.' She picked up her bloomers and put them on slowly, not taking her eyes from him for a second. 'I'm glad,' she murmured, turning away at last. 'I'm glad he's dead, but you shouldn't have gone out and left me, Lil.' Then she burst into tears, fled to her sister's arms and sobbed without control while Lily held her tight and stroked her hair.

Inwardly Lily was quite calm, cold and contained as if the terrible thing she had done had taken all feeling from her. She too had hardly taken her eyes from the silent figure, watching him even as she held Ivy in her arms, waiting for some movement. If he were not dead she would be terrified of his anger, but if he was . . .

Her mind was sharp as a knife. She was a murderess, she would hang like Tess had hanged, the wronged Tess of the d'Urbervilles, the girl she'd read about so often and never thought to emulate.

When Ivy's sobs ceased a little, Lily disentangled her clinging arms. 'We must go away,' she said. 'Now.'

Chapter Four

Lily left her husband's body just where it had fallen. The disgust and contempt she felt left no room for pity. She had no regrets for what she had done, for he had brought her to this. She was surprised at the strange coldness in her heart. There was no panic, just an apathetic nothingness as if she was moving in a dream world.

She went into the front bedroom, looked with distaste at the double bed, the scene of her nightly humiliation, and calmly opened the wardrobe and took out a dress, her best hat, and a spare pair of shoes. Then she went to the chest of drawers and removed a nightgown, underclothes, and a blouse. She bundled all the things up in her arms and went downstairs.

Ivy was watching every move for Lily was behaving as if she was in a trance. She herself was still shaking, horrified, unable to think clearly. She followed her sister down, saw her take the big shopping bag from the cupboard and cram the clothes into it. Then she watched in panic as she went into the scullery and took a large knife from the rack on the wall. Terrified Ivy shrank back into the shadows, but her sister walked past her into the front room, pulled back the carpet, used the knife to lever up a floorboard and then removed a small package.

'What are you doing?' Ivy managed at last. She had crept along the passage and was watching from the doorway, mesmerized and trembling. 'Please, Lil, tell me what you're doing. Don't go away and leave me with him.' She emphasized the last word, desperation in her voice.

46

Lily appeared to come out of her daze, and was immediately ashamed. Why was she not comforting her little sister? Ivy had suffered the most terrible shock and trauma and here she was, thinking first of saving her own skin. She replaced the floorboard over the still hidden books, flattened the carpet back as quickly as she could and put the smaller package in her pocket.

Ivy was holding on to the door for support. 'I'm coming. I'm coming with you.' She was almost screaming the words now. 'You can't leave me. They might think I killed him. They'd hang me, Lil.'

Lily wrapped her arms around her little sister. 'Hush, love. It's me who's the guilty one. It's me they'll come looking for. I shall have to go away and hide. If you come too they'll find both of us. Alone I might be able to disappear. But I promise I won't leave you here.'

As she held the trembling body close to her, she wondered grimly whether Ivy had actually been raped. Lily couldn't be sure. Perhaps she had just returned in time. Part of her mind wanted to believe that her husband could never do anything so hideous, so unspeakable. Yet of course he could. She thought of her own treatment at his hands.

Could she possibly persuade Ivy to tell her? 'Did he ... can you tell me what he did to you?' she began falteringly.

'Don't make me say, Lil. It's too bad and nasty.'

Lily held her tighter and knew that now was not the time to probe. But she wouldn't be here to find out later, to help Ivy come to terms with what had happened. She knew that she would be consumed with guilt for ever if she left Ivy at this vital time, but if she stayed ... the thought was too horrible to consider, and she wouldn't be any use at all shut away in a prison cell. 'We'll go to William,' she murmured, desperate now. 'He'll know what to do.'

Ivy wiped her eyes. 'I'm afraid to go upstairs. My things are up there.'

'No, they're not. Your coat is on the hall-stand, and your dress and night things are waiting to be ironed, so they're down here in the basket. I'll get them.'

She was suddenly all practical common-sense again. She

47

found another bag, fetched Ivy's crumpled clothes, bundled her into her coat, squashed a hat on her head and then, at last, and without a backward glance, she propelled the child to the front door, down the little path, and along the road to the orphanage gate. She knew exactly where William's room was. Hopefully no one would see them for there was an outside stairway leading to it. They reached it unobserved and Lily knocked on the door, praying that he would be in.

When he opened it, he took one look at the white distraught faces of both his sisters and ushered them quickly inside. As he heard the whole shocking story he bunched his fists in frustrated rage, and desperately wished that he had been the one to discover Harry Coney at his filthy business. At least he would have had the pleasure of punishing the bastard. As a brother he felt that he'd failed. He wished that he'd killed him himself with his own bare hands, strangled the life out of him slowly and painfully!

'I've killed him, Will,' Lily finished. 'They'll hang me.' She sank on his bed, her whole body crumpling with the horror of it.

William stared at her in disbelief at first as this further terror burst upon him. But yes, of course, she was right. His blood ran cold at the thought of his sister facing all the brutal force of the law, for he knew that there was little sympathy in the courts for a wife who had killed her husband, whatever the grounds. He doubted that even the provocation of a little sister raped would persuade them to be merciful.

He had guessed for a long time that Lily was very unhappy in her marriage, but that Ivy too should have been misused was beyond thought. Dear God in Heaven, how could a man behave like that?

He took a grip on himself. Thinking this way would get nowhere. What was to be done? He looked at the two of them sitting together on his bed. Lily was wiping her eyes, trying to be brave, and they were both waiting for him to produce a solution that would make everything right.

'You must go, Lily,' he said decisively. 'Now, straight away. Go to London. You can disappear there without any

48

trouble, then wait and see what happens, how the land lies. And try not to worry about Ivy. I shall look after her. I'll take her to Aunt Agnes tonight and then fetch the doctor to that devil. Perhaps he isn't dead after all. Have you any money?'

Lily closed her eyes with relief. So her brother felt the same way as she did, that to run away was the only option open to her. Whether Harry Coney was dead or alive she must get away, but she was sure he was dead. Perhaps it was the idol with which she'd hit him, some heathen magic that had come to her aid!

'Yes, I have money,' she said, pulling the leather purse from her pocket. The little hoard of sovereigns could mean the saving of her life. 'I've quite a lot as a matter of fact. I shall be all right for some time, until I get a job.' She removed four of the precious coins and passed over to her brother. 'Use them for any expenses,' she said. 'For Ivy if she needs anything. They were our mother's present to me before she died. She said that girls needed money more than boys!'

William laughed a little grimly. 'Prophetic words! Are you sure you can spare these?'

'Of course. The money is really for Ivy and me. Mother just wanted me to be in charge.' She turned to her sister. 'I don't want to leave you, love,' she said. She put her hands over Ivy's trembling fingers. 'If you want me to stay, I will.'

'No.' Ivy's voice was adamant. 'I'll be all right. You go, Lil, and then I won't feel so bad about it.'

Lily could hear the despair behind the brave words and her whole heart went out to her little sister. She put her arms around her for the last time and held her close.

'You mustn't feel bad. Nothing was your fault.'

But Ivy knew that the frightening thing Lily had done had been for her, and blamed herself for being the dirty disgusting cause of it all. She tried to control the shaking that threatened to take over her whole body. The least she could do was to be quiet and good, to do what her brother and sister told her. Lily mustn't ever be found or she'd go to prison! 'Go, Lil. Please go,' she whispered. 'William will look after me like he said.' She disentangled herself from the false security of Lily's arms and tried to push her away.

Reluctantly Lily got up and retrieved her bag from the corner where she had thrown it. Her heart was breaking at the thought of leaving the two people she loved most in all the world.

'How are we going to keep in touch?' William asked.

'We aren't!' Lily gritted her teeth, and knew that she was about to embark on the hardest course of action that she had ever taken in her life. If she wished to survive, then somehow the terror and despair she felt would have to change swiftly to toughness and determination. She felt anything but tough and determined!

'If no one knows where I am, not even you, the safer I shall be,' she said. 'I shall only have myself to think about. In London no one will find me, ever.' Her lips set in a firm line. Was this really Lily Penrose, Lily Coney, speaking? Was she truly saying these awful things?

Her emotions were torn in two. To walk away, to walk out of that door and know that she might never see them again, was so terrible that she wondered if there was any power on earth which could make her do it. Then suddenly she thought of the last pages of her favourite novel, *Tess of the d'Urbervilles*, remembered how she had shuddered as she read of the men coming for poor wronged Tess, the gallows that waited, and the black flag that flew from the prison tower. This would be her story too if she stayed.

William glanced at the clock, his face tense and worried. 'There won't be trains as late as this.'

'But I told you, I have money, Will.' She put the still heavy purse away in her inner pocket. 'I shall stay in a lodging house or cheap hotel near the station tonight. Don't worry about me. Just look after Ivy.' The thought of a hotel had come to her out of nowhere, and at least it would satisfy her brother that she would be safe for this first terrible night anyway.

She kissed them both quickly. 'Forgive me,' she whispered. To Ivy she said, 'Even now, lovey, I'll stay if you want me to.'

'No.' Ivy almost screamed the word. 'I don't want you

dead. But come back one day, Lil.'

They were the last plaintive words she heard as she strode with leaden heart to the door, down the outside stairway and out of the gates.

She had to grip the handrail of the bus firmly as she stepped on to it and the conductor looked at her, concerned.

'You all right, darlin'?' he asked.

'Fine,' she managed. 'The Tramway Centre, please.'

She wanted to run away into the dark sleazy streets around the station, run and run until weariness overtook her and she could sleep unseen in some alley like a hunted animal, but that was just the way to attract the attention of the police, or to be molested by someone even worse than ... she could see Harry's dead face threatening her, laughing at her round every corner!

No, she would survive. She forced her common-sense to prevail once more, put her hand thankfully on the bulge of sovereigns, and in the yellow flickering lamplight looked at the little boarding houses just before the station incline.

No questions were asked when she booked into one of them. She went straight up to her room and stared around. She had never felt so frightened and alone in her life. There was no lock on the door so she jammed a chair beneath the handle, then took out her purse and put it beneath the pillow. She removed her clothes, layer by layer, and finally pulled the hairpins out of her thick bun and put them in two piles on the small dressing table. Then she brushed out her curls in long sweeping strokes, and marvelled that she could still do such an ordinary mundane thing!

But sleep eluded her. It was not her husband's face that haunted her now, but an indistinct figure, a policeman, then more than one, a whole battalion of them bearing down upon her, handcuffs and batons displayed threateningly. Until tonight she had considered the police to be friendly figures, keeping law and order, and always on her side. Now they were enemies waiting to put a noose around her neck. Her stomach somersaulted uncomfortably again and again as she recalled in horrific detail all the terrible unimaginable events of the evening. She suffered an agony of remorse too over leaving Ivy just at the time when she needed love and understanding.

Just before dawn she fell into a fitful frightened sleep, and when the street noises below her window awoke her, she was filled with fresh despair. She felt that she had been in bed for a hundred years. She got up as soon as she heard someone else in the house moving about.

She washed and dressed quickly and wished that it was possible to leave without breakfast, but this would cause comment, so she sat down in the small dining room and looked with dismay at the plate of bacon and eggs that was placed in front of her.

'Going on holiday?' the woman said, and although the question was automatic, probably asked of all the guests, Lily was startled.

'Just to visit my aunt,' she replied, and realized that this was the start of a whole string of lies that she would be obliged to tell over the next weeks and months if she was to keep her identity hidden.

She had no intention of going to London. The idea had come to her in the night. She would set a false trail. If the police thought she was in the capital they would spend all their efforts looking for her there.

Unwillingly she went to the ticket office and booked a single third-class to Paddington. Then she went into the ladies' waiting room and changed her older hat for her best one. She speared it fiercely into her thick coil of hair with her hatpin, and hoped that she looked different enough for the clerk at the other window not to notice that she had already bought one ticket. Assuming as posh a voice as she could muster, she asked for a return to Torquay. Although she was wasting some of her precious money she judged that the little subterfuge was worth it if it put her pursuers off the trail. She tried to appear as calm and confident as possible for she knew that only by keeping her wits about her would she survive.

It was the end of July and Torquay would be busy with the first of the season's holidaymakers. Lily hoped that it would be easy to find work in one of the hotels, no questions asked. With the influx of trippers, all glad to get away and forget the horrors of the war, surely it would be possible to disappear?

But what name should she give? She sat in the train as it took her away from Bristol, away from Ivy who needed her, William her twin from whom she had never been parted for long. George who didn't need her but whom she loved in spite of all his faults, away from everything she had ever known. She felt quite unreal, as though this was all happening to someone else, another life that she was looking at from the outside.

Her mind roved back over the five months of her marriage, then the time before that, the happiest years perhaps, when she had worked in the bookshop. She thought of her parents, and finally of Arthur. She wondered if he knew what had happened to her, if the dead had any knowledge of the loved ones they had left behind. How different her life would have been if only he had not been killed in those ridiculous trenches! Her eyes filled with tears, and eventually, because she was so exhausted, she slept, a short sweet sleep in which she was in Arthur's arms, and the whole world was beautiful.

That bliss lasted until the train pulled noisily into Exter and she was jolted rudely back into a world that was anything but beautiful. In her dream she had borne Arthur's name. Suddenly she wondered what her name should be now, the name that would be hers for the next weeks and months, years perhaps. It came to her in a flash: Lilian Smith, a neutral sort of name, and just enough like her own not to sound too strange. She had never become used to Lily Coney. She shuddered at the thought of it. Coney, Coney, Coney ... the words repeated themselves over and over with the rhythm of the train as it gained speed on the final leg of the journey. She couldn't rid her mind of the hated name until she deliberately and angrily substituted Lilian Smith, Lilian Smith, Lilian Smith, her passport to a new and independent life.

But even as she mouthed the unfamiliar words she knew that the shadow of the gallows would haunt her as long as she lived – presuming that she did live of course! If she was found she would be tried and she would be hanged. She shrank back into her seat and closed her eyes as panic and dismay filled her once again. Please please, dear God, let no one discover who I am, she prayed desperately. Never let me be Lily Coney ever ever again!

Left behind to deal with his little sister's grief, William felt completely out of his depth. For the first time he was ashamed of his ignorance, for he had never had a woman. There was a girl whom he liked at Chapel and whom he saw from time to time, usually in the company of others, but his upbringing had strictly forbidden anything other than a chaste kiss before marriage, and even this was only permitted when a couple were engaged. The orphanage where his father had worked all his life and under whose roof he himself now lived upheld these values to the extent that they refused to take any child who was not the lawful orphan of properly married parents. William remembered challenging his father once about this harsh rule, but he had been firmly silenced. To take an illegitmate child, he was told, was to encourage sin.

And now, dear God, he had to deal with the possible violation of his little sister. He longed for more wisdom than his sheltered eighteen years had given him.

'Can you tell me what happened?' he asked gently after Lily had left.

'I didn't want her to go out to that meeting and leave me,' Ivy sniffed. 'I was frightened.'

'Why was that? Why were you frightened?'

'Because he was ...' More sobs, more terror.

William found a handkerchief and passed it to her. He wanted to put his arm around her, but was scared to do so. He'd always been wary of physical contact and after the events of the last hour was even more so.

'He came upstairs and into my room. He looked at me, and looked, and laughed.'

Her head was bent, the handkerchief screwed up and held close to her eyes and he had to strain to hear the mumbled words. Had Lily come in time, he wondered, in time to prevent the thing that he couldn't even articulate?

54

He realized that he had no words to describe what happened between men and women. In his family and in the circle in which he moved it was unmentionable, never discussed or talked about.

'Tell me about it,' he said and the words sounded, to his own ears, banal, unsympathetic. He longed to possess some of his mother's tenderness and compassion, and tried to think what she would have said, how she would have dealt with this crisis.

'He took off his trousers,' Ivy said, 'and there was this awful ... awful thing sticking out.'

William felt colour racing to his face and neck.

'He came and squashed me on the bed and pulled up my frock and touched where it's rude ... he hurt me! I don't like him.'

She blew her nose and William waited, unwilling to hear more yet knowing that he must discover the truth. Was Ivy old enough to have a child? He was further ashamed that he knew so little about such things.

'Then Lily came and hit him with my idol.' Ivy looked up at last. 'He's been rude before,' she said. 'I hated him, and I'm glad he's dead. Perhaps it was the idol that did it.'

Then perhaps she hadn't been raped after all? Raped! William shuddered. But it seemed from what Ivy was saying that Lily had returned in the nick of time. He wondered just how much Ivy knew about the facts of life. Perhaps she didn't understand what might have followed.

Her next words however shocked him considerably and disabused him of this idea.

'He wanted to do the same to me as he does to our Lil every night,' Ivy said, her tears diminishing now. 'He would have too if she hadn't 'a come just then.'

William hid his further embarrassment. 'But he didn't. You're sure of that?'

''Course I'm sure. I told you, he would 'a, but she killed him first.'

With the story over, Ivy's terrors about the future returned. 'What we going to do?' she whispered.

'Go to Aunt Agnes.'

'I'd rather stay with you.'

William sighed. 'You can't. You aren't even supposed to be here. No girls are ever allowed in this part of the building. It's the boys' house. I'll be thrown out if they find you, even though you are my sister, and then where shall we be?'

Ivy knew that he was speaking the truth. She knew too that if she didn't do as her brother said she'd have to enter the orphanage as an inmate, and that was too awful to think about. She still felt guilty too. Although Lily had said that nothing was her fault, she was sure that it was. She knew that she was dreadful; full of sin the Chapel elders would say.

She had sometimes smiled artfully at her brother-in-law, usually to get her own way over some rule he had instituted. She'd been able to get round him frequently, make him laugh at times. Was that what he'd meant by saying that she was a hussy, always flashing her eyes at him? Was that why he did what he did? And now perhaps God was punishing her for all her sins and was sending her to Aunt Agnes or even worse, here to the orphanage, so that she would have to learn to be good, and have her trespasses washed away and forgiven like the Bible said.

She thought of the orphanage girls with their dull grey uniforms, the long silent lines as they walked along Sefton Road every day for exercise, and the rigid regime of rules that she knew all about because her father had been a teacher there.

'Isn't there anywhere else?' she said, testing God as well as her brother, and knowing quite well that there wasn't.

'Only Aunt Agnes,' William replied wearily, 'and we'd better get going because I've to find the doctor and tell him there's been an accident.'

'That's no good,' Ivy said, shivering. 'He's quite dead. A doctor's no good, and if you fetch one he'll tell the police and they'll come and Lily'll be taken away and hanged.'

'Don't say that. Don't even think it.'

William's voice was angry now and Ivy flinched.

'Put on your hat and we'll go.'

She said nothing more. So God wasn't going to work a miracle? She'd known that He wasn't all along, of course. She picked up the bag that Lily had packed for her and preceded her brother out of the door and down the steps.

Agnes greeted them with some dismay. She was in her nightgown, a heavy shawl hurriedly thrown around her shoulders and her head bristling with curling rags. 'What on earth . . . ?' she gasped.

'Let us in quickly, Aunt. There's been an accident.'

Her nephew's surprising appearance at this hour, combined with the sound of his very shaken voice, made her open the door wider and she ushered them into the small living room at the back of the house. The remnants of a fire were still burning in the range and the room was hot and close.

'It's Mr Coney,' William said briefly. 'I've to get the doctor. Can you look after Ivy for a night or two?'

It was the last thing Agnes wanted to do, but she looked at the frightened child, took her bag from her and then her coat.

'Sit there,' she commanded, indicating an arm chair. 'What's happened then, and where's Lily?'

'Lily's disappeared,' William told her. He knew that he'd have to give her a credible explanation or she'd be worrying Ivy's life out to tell the truth and that was the last thing he wanted. 'There was an argument between them,' he continued. 'Harry fell and hurt his head. I've to fetch the doctor. Lily said she had to get away. That's all I know.'

Agnes felt a momentary stab of guilt. She'd been feeling this unaccustomed emotion with increasing frequency lately as she'd watched her niece becoming progressively more pale and unhappy. She must do her best to make amends, do all she could to help. Something to drink! That was the panacea, the cure for most ills.

'I'll get some hot milk for the two of you,' she said. 'You look as though you could do with it.' She asked no questions, merely went out into her immaculate little scullery and brought in a pan of milk which she put on the stove to heat. She fetched three large cups, and when the milk was hot and poured out, stirred generous helpings of sugar into each cup, and a tot of brandy into hers. She judged that William at only eighteen was still too young for the delights of the bottle. In fact his Chapel upbringing probably forbade it.

'Here,' she said as she handed the brimming cups to each

57

of them. 'Get this down. You'll feel better, and then you can tell me exactly what happened.'

Ivy gulped the scalding liquid and felt a little warmth flow into her shivering body, but it couldn't take away her remorse for being so bad. And her sister would be hanged because of it. It was too much to bear. She put the cup down in the grate, covered her face with her hands and started to sob again.

William was full of compassion for her, rage with Harry Coney, and desperate anxiety for Lily. Everything depended on him now. What he did and said might affect the lives of his sisters for ever. He finished his milk as quickly as he could. 'Trust me, Sis,' he said. He picked up her cup and put it with his own on the table. 'Everything'll come right. You'll see.'

She looked at him with a tear-stained face. 'How can you stop them finding her, taking her to prison? Oh, Will!'

Agnes caught the last few words and spun round to face them. 'Prison! Prison did I hear you say? What's happened? You're keeping something from me!' Her voice was rasping and harsh. Even brandy couldn't alleviate this further horror.

It was no good. William realized now that he'd have to tell it all. He took a deep breath and began.

After the story was told Agnes sat quite still and silent. She had never before been concerned with anything so vile. Of course, she mused, no one could live in a street like hers without being aware of some of the horrific sins of the flesh, as she called them, but they had never touched her before. Events like this had always happened to other families, never hers.

She looked from Ivy to William and thought about her one-time neighbour, the noises through the wall, the shouting in his sleep, his roving eyes – and she shuddered. She was filled with revulsion and disgust. So his filthy lust hadn't ended with his lawful wife, and not even with the prostitutes, for she had known that he visited one or two of these despicable creatures frequently. In spite of all that he had to take this child and defile her too.

She was not given to demonstrations of affection, but went

stiffly to her still sobbing niece and put her arm awkwardly round her shoulders.

'I'll look after her,' she said to William. 'You go and do what you think best. And we'll say nothing to anyone.' She paused for a moment. 'I know I've not been the best of relatives to you four children, but blood's thicker than water and we'll stick together. Never fear.'

Surprised, William was constrained to give her a quick peck on the cheek as he prepared to go. 'Thanks, Aunt,' he mumbled. 'I thought you'd come up trumps in the end.'

After he had let himself out she put her hand to the place where he had kissed her. She couldn't remember having been kissed since she was a girl, and not often then!

'Come on then, lovey,' she said to Ivy. 'I'll make you a nice little bed up in the spare room. Everything'll work out all right in the end. You'll see.'

Satisfied that for the time being anyway he had done the best for Ivy, and that Lily was safely away, William now had to turn his thoughts to his brother-in-law. As he left his aunt's house to walk home he was filled with loathing. He couldn't remember hating anyone before, but there was certainly hatred in his heart now, but how could one hate the dead?

He fought a battle with himself. If he fetched a doctor tonight the police would probably be called straight away and that could be disastrous for Lily. Supposing he left it until the morning when she'd be on the London train? But then there was George who'd be returning home some time, to find what? A corpse? Or might Harry Coney be alive and in need of help? The more he thought about it the more certain he became that he must go to the house before he did anything else.

It was in fact George who found Harry Coney first. He had been out with some friends and came in whistling cheerfully. He was surprised to find the front door ajar. He usually had to knock.

'I'm back,' he yelled. 'Come on, Sis. Any food going?' He threw his jacket on the hall-stand and bounced through to the back room. No one there and the room was cold, even in the summer night. 'Where's everyone?' he shouted. He looked briefly out into the scullery. That was empty too. Then he realized that the house was silent, no sound at all. Mystified he went back into the hall and sprang up the stairs two at a time. Ivy must surely be in. In the summer she sometimes went to bed early to read. Books always put Harry in a bad mood.

Her bedroom door was open and he went through and then stopped, fear ripping through him as he saw the motionless form on the floor, blood congealed in a small pool beneath the head. 'Blimey,' he said. He went over and felt the hands that were splayed on either side, not icy cold thank goodness, and then put his ear to Harry's chest and perceived movement. He was breathing, not dead, breathing steadily!

George had seen boxers knocked out, had watched some of the methods used to bring them round. Concussion they called it. Could put them out for hours. He tried to ease Harry away from the fender that had obviously caused the trouble. He snatched a pillow from Ivy's bed and put it beneath his head, and then slowly he saw the eyelids flutter open and Harry stared at him. 'What's up?' he murmured. 'Where am I?'

George was infinitely relieved. He couldn't bear dead things, always left someone else to pick up dead birds or throw a dead cat into the dust bin.

'Must have fallen and got knocked out,' George said. 'Nasty crack on your head. How long you been there?'

'How the devil should I know?' Harry was beginning to come to, his memory returning. He tried to sit up and then sank back again, groaning and holding his head. He remembered Ivy, the thrill he'd felt trying to take her against her will and her being so small. He'd never done it with a child before. But he hadn't managed it, had he? That cursed wife of his had come back too soon. Well, there was always another time! No one must know about it though. He'd have to find her, tell the silly little bitch to keep her mouth shut or it'd happen again. Well, it would anyway, but no need to frighten her beforehand. It was her fault after all, flashing those eyes at him all the time.

'You need a doctor,' George told him. 'I'll get old Jones. He was good to Ma.'

Harry glared at him. 'No doctor. Just get me to bed, son.'

Then he grinned, and George, seeing the expression, wondered what the old devil had been up to. Of course, Friday night. He'd been drinking. There was one of Ivy's books on the floor and that foul-looking idol. He picked both up and returned them to their rightful place.

Harry seemed to have sunk into unconsciousness again, but George wasn't scared now. Better get the old bugger into his own room, and into his bed if possible. No wonder Ivy had run away somewhere. She wouldn't want to stay while this repulsive lump was sprawled out on her floor. He tried to get his arms round him, but failed, so he took hold of his legs and slid him over the lino out on to the landing and into the front bedroom.

George decided that it must have been the book that had sparked Harry's drunken rage. Books always got him into a state. He'd probably seen Ivy reading and had taken the book off her, fallen over in his drunken stupor and hit the fender. But where the dickens was Lily? She ought to be here looking after things. And why was that hideous idol on the floor too? He shivered superstitiously. He'd always hated the thing, was sure it had, what did they call it? the evil eye! He couldn't think for the life of him why his sister liked it so much.

The rough handling, helped by a dousing of cold water on his face, brought Harry round again and George soon had him on the double bed with a spare blanket thrown over him. More than that he refused to do. 'Where's our Lil?' George asked a trifle petulantly. 'What happened? I suppose you got mad at Ivy reading again?'

Harry groaned and felt the two lumps on his head, one at the front where something had hit him and the other at the back, still sticky with blood. He tried to concentrate on what George was saying. A book? Ivy reading a bloody book? Was that why he'd fallen down? His mind cleared once more and memory returned again. He chuckled obscenely. 'Yes,' he said. 'Must have drunk too much, got angry. Keep off the drink, boy.'

George looked at him with distaste. They got on fairly well for most of the time, but this fetish about books was stupid, and he couldn't help despising Harry when he was drunk. 'Where are my sisters?' he repeated.

'Gone off to your holy brother, I should think,' Harry said with sudden inspiration. 'Yes, that's where they'll be.' He groaned again. 'For Pete's sake, get me a drink, and take my bloody shoes off.'

George did the latter unwillingly. 'You'll get water, nothing more,' he said.

'Water's what I want, and a cup a' tea 'ud go gown a treat.'

'Shall I fetch the doctor then?'

Harry tried to sit up in bed and collapsed again, groaning. 'No bloody doctor!' he yelled as George hurried down the stairs.

William was considerably shocked to find his brother-in-law revived and fully conscious. He was filled with relief for Lily because this meant no police, no fear of ... he couldn't bring himself to dwell on the consequences if she really had killed this despicable object on the bed, yet the brute had deserved to die for what he'd done to Ivy and, over the past weeks, to Lily too.

Lily! William suddenly realized that he must find her quickly.

He took one more disgusted look at Harry Coney lying there in state, and, horror of horrors, actually grinning at him, then strode out of the room and downstairs. 'You all right, George?' he asked his brother.

'Yes. He won't have the doc. Stupid old bugger!' George remarked casually. 'He'll be as right as rain in the morning. You'd best get Lil back.'

'That's just what I'm going to do.' William didn't wait to add any more. No explanations appeared to be necessary. George seemed quite satisfied with whatever story he'd been told or guessed.

William ran most of the way to the orphanage, pushed open the big gates impatiently and fetched his bicycle from the shed just inside. Then he cycled furiously through the quiet streets to the station. It was a long way and when he got there he realized how fruitless his search would be. Lodgings, she'd said, just for the night. She planned to get the early train. He stared up at the windows of some of the places where she might be, but the front doors were locked, everything in darkness, and only the dim light of a gas lamp here and there on the pavement. It was past midnight. Wearily he pedalled all the way back. He'd be there again in the morning for the first trains.

On a Saturday morning in the holiday season there was much rushing about. William bought a platform ticket and stayed for hours, watching every train bound for Paddington, but of Lily there was no sign.

Chapter Five

Torquay Railway Station was full of trippers down from Exeter or Bristol for a day by the sea. Lily glanced at her reflection in the refreshment room window and hoped that she looked like one of them.

There were couples surrounded by suitcases and excited children. Lily looked at them enviously. And further up the platform, where the first-class carriages had stopped, she saw wealthier holidaymakers. Some were imperiously demanding porters and taxis. She slowed her pace for a moment and wondered what it was like to be carefree and rich. If she managed to get a job in a hotel these were the kind of people she would have to serve. She looked away and walked resolutely towards the exit, towards her new life.

Once outside the station she put her bag down and breathed deeply of the fresh sea air. Torquay was quite new to her and the smell of it brought immediate memories of her honeymoon in Teignmouth. How naive she had been then, how hopeful!

She looked nervously at the first hotel she saw, the Grand Hotel. No, it was far *too* grand to start with. It had an imposing frontage, sparkling windows, and an air of intimidating prosperity. There was a bustle about it that awed her: taxis drawing up, chauffeurs opening doors and porters staggering with vast amounts of luggage. She clutched her own shabby bag and walked on until she came to a row of boarding houses that were not quite so pretentious, some a little down-at-heel, some with a friendly look about them. There were certainly plenty, but how to choose?

By the end of the morning she had knocked on countless tradesmen's entances and encountered a vast assortment of housekeepers, but no one was in need of chamber maids, or anyone to wash dishes, or any other kind of help. She bought herself a sandwich and a cup of tea and then wearily continued her search. She tried prosperous streets, narrower ones behind the sea front, and others further away from the sea. Prospective employers of all varieties stared at her critically, weighed her up and obviously found her wanting. She met very few friendly faces, and was repeatedly refused. No, they had all the staff they needed, thank you. Sometimes there was not even a thank you, merely a door slammed abruptly in her face.

Her last hope was the Imperial Hotel which stood, opulent and imposing, on the hill that led away from the harbour. She trudged towards it, her despair deepening and her bag becoming heavier with every step. As she turned into the spacious drive she saw a large motor car at the front entrance, a girl about her own age just getting out, and a bevy of attendants of various sorts fluttering around her. Lily straightened her hat with her one free hand and felt downcast and shabby. She stared at the girl's beautiful clothes, and her own seemed old-fashioned and run-down. For a moment the girl looked at her and then turned away to her handsome companion. They went laughing hand-in-hand up the steps to the gleaming front doors which were flung open for them by a uniformed attendant. Lily, tears in her eyes, turned away and walked round to the back of the great building.

The door was open and she knocked timidly, not daring to enter. The man who eventually came looked her up and down disparagingly but with a trace of amusement and she wondered if she had a dirty mark on her face or if there was something else amiss.

'No. There's no vacancies, darlin',' he said. 'Come back next week and we might have a place for a skivvy. Sometimes the girls just leaves with no notice.' He winked at her. 'No knowing why they departs so sudden. Yes, you'd do capital, but I daren't sign on more'n my allowed number. See you again then, shall we?'

Lily shook her head. 'I don't think so,' she murmured. 'I need somewhere now.'

'Good luck then. Sorry we can't oblige.' He winked again and she hurried away shivering, totally despondent. She walked down the hill in the direction of the harbour and just once looked over the cliff edge wondering what it would be like to throw yourself down on to the jagged rocks below. At least it would be quick, better than prison and the gallows! Perhaps it was even better than pretending to be someone else for the rest of your life.

The full horror of her situation swept over her like a rushing tide from which there was no escape. She'd never be able to be Lily Penrose again, never see Bristol, Ivy, William, George . . . Dear God, what had she got herself into? Perhaps she should go back to Bristol now and face her punishment? But visions of the fictional heroine swept into her mind again. The last pages of that book haunted her: Tess walking away with the men who had come to take her, the rope, the black flag. She put her hand to her own small neck and almost fainted with panic and fear. She wished she had never read Hardy's masterpiece. Perhaps there wouldn't be such lurid pictures in her head if she had not encountered those powerful lines.

Then the mists gradually cleared and she found herself on the quayside again and knew that there was no going back. She had chosen her path and must keep to it.

There was a bench at the water's edge and she sank thankfully down upon it and stared at the boats rocking gently on the little waves below, at the gulls serenely riding the balmy evening breezes, and wondered what on earth she was to do next.

Behind her on the other side of the road there was a row of houses and little shops, all facing the sea, their fronts looking across the Old Harbour and towards the headland on the far side of the bay. She had walked past them almost unheeding before but now she turned and studied them. One had an attractive bow window full of books. It couldn't possibly be of any practical help to her of course but there was no harm in looking. She was at the end of all her resources. Nothing mattered now. It had been a long time since she had been in a bookshop or in fact read a book. She thought of Harry's ban on reading and shuddered. But he was dead and she could read freely again.

Dully and without hope she got to her feet, crossed the road, and looked more closely. She read the sign painted above the door: Harbourside Books. For a moment she allowed her despair to subside a little as she feasted her eyes on the volumes arranged behind the thick panes of sparkling glass. Whoever looked after the shop kept everything in immaculate condition. No help was needed here obviously, yet she couldn't bring herself to move. The books in the window were not at all like those she had sold in Bristol. They were mostly old leather-covered volumes so it must be an antiquarian bookshop. For a moment she allowed her imagination to run riot. How wonderful it would be to own a dream place like this, to have no worries, to be free and secure!

But her common-sense and her need for a bolt-hole and a meal eventually overcame her fantasies. As Aunt Agnes had said, books seldom earned anyone a living. She turned away reluctantly, and with her increasing hunger and exhaustion, hopelessness returned in full measure.

Then suddenly she was aware of the strong smell of frying onions! It was wrong somehow, out of context here in this lovely place, but she was hungry and the smell was intoxicating. It reminded her of the old scullery at home long ago. Ma had frequently fried the juicy white onions that her father grew in the back garden behind the house and stored in heavy strings hanging from the pantry ceiling. A great pang of homesickness swept over her, not a homesickness for the house in Sefton Road as it was when she shared it with Harry Coney, but for the same house as it had been before her marriage, the house of her childhood and growing up, a place of security and love.

For what seemed to be the hundredth time that day she tried to pull herself together, and looking around for the source of the amazing smell soon realized that it came from the sleazy little café next-door to the bookshop. She walked the few steps towards it and stared into quite a different window. The glass was dirty, dead flies were massed on the old wooden window frame while their living fellows buzzed noisily back and forth or flapped despairing wings from the sticky fly-paper that hung menacingly above plates of sad-looking cakes. But there, right in the centre of the window, was a grubby postcard fastened to the glass. 'Capable woman wanted' it said. 'Cooking, cleaning, general help, live in'.

She read it two or three times in disbelief, and then, trembling, pushed the door open and walked through.

The café was even worse inside. The tables were covered with stained oil-cloth, the cakes displayed on the counter were uncovered like those in the window, and the smell of onions, appetizing enough in the fresh air outside, was overpowering in here.

'Yes, Miss? What would you like?'

What would I like? Lily thought. Oh, what would I like? To be out of here, back in Bristol, free from worry, free from guilt, free from the terrible memory of Harry Coney on top of my little sister, free from the sight of him sprawled out on the floor, blood trickling from the wound on his head, and most of all, to be free from the horrifying fear of a rope round my neck, condemned to die because of that sudden moment of outrage and shock.

She stood for a second, gasping for breath because of her thoughts and the stifling foetid smell of the shop.

The man behind the counter wiped his geasy hands on his even greasier apron. 'Cup of tea?' he queried. 'You all right, Miss?'

The voice was kind, the first friendly words she'd heard all day, and Lily felt tears threatening the last shreds of her composure. She sat down on the nearest chair and nodded.

The man was all concern. 'I'll make you a nice sandwich, shall I, Miss?' he offered. 'That'll strengthen you. The Missis got a bit of cold beef in the safe outside. Like some of that would you, and some onions? Always keep onions on the go. Trippers like 'em.'

Lily shook her head weakly. 'Just a cup of tea,' she managed. In spite of her hunger she felt quite nauseous now at the thought of beef and onions here amidst the squalor.

He appeared a few minutes later with a tray and she noticed that it had a clean embroidered cloth on it in startling contrast to the grubby one on the table. He put the tray down in front of her. 'I brought you a piece of the wife's cake,' he said. 'We don't keep that in the shop. She makes it special.'

Lily wondered why she was honoured with the special cake and the clean cloth, but said nothing as hunger overcame her qualms. It was good and when she had finished it and downed three cups of tea she began to feel better.

'Actually,' she said, when he came to clear away, 'I didn't just come to eat. I need a job.'

He stared at her in amazement. 'What, you, Miss? Work here? You'm above this sort of thing.'

She wanted to laugh hysterically at that. Was a murderer above any sort of thing, however distasteful? She tried to smile at him, and then she shook her head. 'I'm not above working hard,' she said, 'and I need somewhere to live and to earn a little money. What would you want me to do?'

'Take over really.' His voice was hesitant. 'That's what the Missis and me are looking for. Someone a bit older than you to take over. We're getting on, no children what wants to work here, and it's all too much.' He looked around at the other tables, at the fly-blown glass in the window, at the filthy floor. 'But this ain't no place for a young lady like you, pardon my saying it.'

'I'm tough, and I can work hard, just as hard as someone older,' Lily argued. 'Would you consider me?'

He stroked his bristly chin. 'Well, we'm pretty anxious to have someone. The state of everything puts most folks off. You'd best come and talk to the wife.'

Gladys Bailey was as slim and neat as her husband was rotund and untidy. Her appearance immediately resolved the mystery of the immaculate tray-cloth.

When Lily's surprising request was relayed to her she looked slightly suspicious. 'I can't think why a young lady like you should want to take this place on,' she said. 'Not run away from home because you're expecting, have you?'

Lily was taken aback by the half-truth, but no, she was certainly not expecting. 'No,' she replied quickly. 'Nothing like that.'

69

'Well, if you're honest and all's above board and you don't mind hard work, you might fit.' She sighed and looked around apologetically. 'I used to keep everything spick and span, but I can't do much now because of my rheumatics, and to tell you the truth, my dear, I'm proper ashamed of the state 'tis all fallen into.'

'I'll soon have it put to rights if you'll let me,' Lily said. She knew that she'd have to forget the words 'above board' for very little about her present circumstances could be described as that, and they certainly wouldn't want her if they knew the truth. Her heart lurched.

'Can I see the room I'd have?' she asked timidly. She was tired, so tired, and wanted to look no further. In spite of the dirt there was something that felt right about this place, and she had taken a liking to the old couple, even felt a little sorry for them. She was desperate too for a refuge, somewhere of her own, a bed, a chair and a table. That was all. A place to be, to hide, to cry unseen!

'Take her up, Reg,' the woman directed. 'It's not much, but it's big and bright. A nice room.'

Lily followed him out into the hall and up a flight of stairs, and then up another to the second floor. He gasped for breath as he reached the top.

'We hardly ever come up here,' he told her apologetically. 'We'm too old for all these stairs.'

As he flung open the door however she gasped with delight. The room was large, as his wife had said, being the attic and obviously taking up most of the top storey. And unlike the rest of the house it was clean, with scrubbed boards, and only dust and cobwebs to show that it had not been lived in for a long time. It had sloping ceilings at both ends, the single bed she craved, a table and chair, a large cupboard, a dressing table with bowl and jug, and most wonderful of all a window with a view, a little window cut into the eaves, a window with a seat where she could sit and think and try to reshape her life. It was a view such as she had never expected to have in her wildest dreams. Instead of the ugly grey orphanage buildings that she had seen across the wall from her bedroom window all her life, there was the harbour, two harbours in fact, the old one and the new.

And there was the glory of the open sea beyond, boats, a blue sky full of little scudding clouds, and most important of all a great sense of peace. Perhaps in this wonderful little refuge she would find some tranquillity at last.

'Yes, it's lovely,' she said. 'If you'll have me I'd definitely like to work for you.'

'We'll try each other out,' he insisted, 'for a week, and then see how we go. You'll get the room, and your food of course which you'd have to cook for yourself and for us, and ...' He hesitated. 'Seven shillings a week on top?' he questioned. 'Would that suit?'

Would that suit? It was absolute riches, seven shillings and this room. Could she have dreamed of more? She glanced at the sky through the little window. Was God really up there as she'd been brought up to believe, and was he looking after her? She'd secretly doubted Him lately, but perhaps He was around after all. Aloud, and more practically she said, 'And what, in addition to the cooking for the three of us and looking after the café, do you want me to do for that?'

'Would you take over completely like I said?' He sounded hopeful. 'The Missis and me are beside ourselves with the worry of it all. Like she said, her rheumatics are terrible sometimes and she can't manage no more. We live downstairs behind the shop, just in the one room. She can't climb the stairs at all now. I'll show you what to do, the buying and everything. Give you a free hand if you'd like that.'

She nodded, and smiled at him reassuringly. It wouldn't do to sound too enthusiastic at first though. 'Yes, I feel sure I could manage,' she said, and already, in her mind, was ordering soda and soap, washing and scrubbing, putting clean cloths and flowers on the tables. And onions? Well, she'd see about that. She could even smell them up here. Onions all the time might be just too much. Perhaps she could turn the little café into a tea-shop!

'We could do cream teas,' she said. 'I'm good at scones and fancy cakes. Would your wife approve of that?'

'Anything you like, Miss just so long as we gets a bit from it each week, and there's enough to pay your wages and the rent and a few shillings left over p'raps for a few improvements.

71

We like it here, see, lived here all our lives and don't want to move out. That's why we been looking for someone to take over, someone what'll let us stay and see our days out here. It was getting so rundown that the landlord told us if we couldn't do better he'd turn us out.'

It was obviously a long speech for him and he blew his nose loudly with the emotion of it all. 'Let's hope you likes it and we likes you and you'll stay.'

'Oh, yes,' she said, unable to hide her enthusiasm any longer. 'Let's hope that very much.'

Standing there in that lovely room, and with that view just behind her, she wanted to throw her arms around the little man's vast girth in gratitude.

He held out his hand to her. 'Then we'm most pleased to have you, Miss. Mr and Mrs Reginald Bailey we are.'

She took his hand and shook it warmly. 'And I'm ...' She hesitated for one moment. 'I'm Lilian Smith,' she said. 'Miss Lilian Smith.'

'Would you mind if I worked today, even though it's Sunday?' Lily asked her new employers the following morning. 'With the shop closed I could get a lot done and be ready to open tomorrow as usual.' She couldn't bear the thought of long hours stretching ahead of her in which there was nothing to do but brood about the past and about Harry and her possible fate. She wanted to get the place clean and wholesome anyway. The sooner the better.

Gladys Bailey looked a little scandalized. ''Tis the Lord's day and I don't hold with disobeying the commandment,' she announced. 'But as long as you don't make a regular habit of it, then I suppose, as you'm just starting, the Good Lord 'll make an exception.'

There was a definite twinkle in Reginald Bailey's eyes. 'I'm thinking o' that verse in the Good Book where it says them what don't work don't eat, so I say get on with it, Miss Smith. Just so long as you don't expect me and the Missis to do anything?'

'Nothing at all,' Lily assured them. In fact she hoped that they wouldn't interfere. She wanted a free hand. At least the dead flies had to be cleared away and that awful grisly fly-paper which hung luridly above the counter must be put in the bin. The floor and tables must be scrubbed and the window cleaned. The rest would have to wait because she needed to buy things. She was trying desperately to replace the hopelessness and horrors of yesterday with ideas and enthusiasm for the future, uncertain though it might be. She knew that hard physical work would help dispel a little of the grey blanket of despair that threatened to overwhelm her much of the time. The fear would probably be there for ever but it could perhaps be pushed into the background, at least during the day.

She had slept blissfully on that first night in her new room, pleased with the clean sheets and blankets produced by Mrs Bailey and even a towel too, although there was only cold water in the jug and no hot offered.

Seagulls had wakened her early in the morning and she rejoiced in the sound, and in the security, false though it might be, of this secret place. No one knew where she was. Life of a sort was starting all over again. The room had a friendly feel and in it was limbo, safety. She had been thinking over her new identity. It would become part of her, the lies eventually seeming to be the truth.

Her greatest sadness was for the loss of her brothers and sister, but she was confident that William would manage. He would look after the younger two, see that they were all right. By marrying Harry Coney she had done her part, kept her promise to her mother. That it had all gone so wrong wasn't her fault. She kept telling herself these things as if, by the affirmation of them, they were bound to be true.

The gulls screaming outside reminded her of the occasional day out at Weston when she was little, days of sand and sea and magic. In her memories those hours had always been warm and sunny and full of happiness.

Downstairs Reginald Bailey was waiting with the questions that she had guessed must come. 'You going to tell us a bit about yourself?' he enquired. 'Us ought to know why you'm here without much luggage and all that. Missis thinks it a bit strange.' His voice was apologetic. He sounded as though he had been nagged into asking these questions.

Now for the play acting! Lily was glad that she had worked it all out and that she had remembered, on the train, to take off her wedding ring. It was safely tucked away in the innermost pocket of her handbag. She had wondered if she could sell it. It seemed a pity to drop it down a drain. Gold was gold after all. The ring meant nothing to her now, was rather a symbol of her slavery, her shame and fear. There was still a faint mark on her finger where it had been, but she had covered it with her mother's engagement ring and this fitted her story.

She baulked a little now that she actually had to voice the lies she had so carefully prepared, but she reminded herself that henceforth her whole life here in Torquay was a pretence.

'My fiancé was killed at the end of the war,' she said. That at least was true, and true of a few million others, so wouldn't give away any clues by which she could be traced. 'My father too. I haven't any brothers and sisters.' She crossed her fingers superstitiously behind her back as she said this. Please God, please William, George, Ivy, forgive me for that! 'There aren't any jobs for women now in ... in Gloucester,' she continued, 'so I decided to try my luck by the seaside. I heard that there was seasonal work down here. I just packed what I could carry and got on a train!'

'You'll have to get some things,' Gladys Bailey said, looking her up and down. She had stared disapprovingly at the hold-all that Lily had carried upstairs last night.

'I didn't have much,' Lily told her, 'and I left a few clothes with a poor family I know. I couldn't carry any more than this. I wasn't sure how long I'd have to tramp about looking for somewhere.'

'The market-place is good for cheap material and ready-mades. You could go there come Wednesday and get yourself a dress or two.'

'I'll do that then,' Lily replied. 'I sold my father's watch and chain. Sad to do it, but needs must. I've enough to buy at least one frock and some aprons.'

She had found a loose board in the attic room similar to the hiding place at home, and her precious hoard of sovereigns was safely stowed away there for a rainy day.

When she went shopping she'd only buy the minimum. Anything more would cause comment and enquiry and she certainly didn't want to arouse any suspicions. She had just enough in her purse now for a few necessities.

After his fruitless search at Temple Meads on Saturday morning, William returned dejectedly to Sefton Road. He knew that he would have to face Harry Coney now, come to some sort of agreement with the man in spite of the fact that he never wanted to see him again.

He was better, still in bed and enjoying the ministrations of George, who had been bribed to carry up some breakfast and then a sandwich at lunchtime.

William went upstairs and looked scathingly at the man who had ruined his sister's life, trying to subdue the hatred and loathing in his heart.

Harry seemed unaware of his disapproval. He grinned evilly. 'Well, where is she then?'

'Left you,' William said briefly. 'And after last night, who can blame her?'

'Don't know what you're talking about. Got a bit drunk, that's all. That silly kid's to blame, always ogling me.' He had lowered his voice and William wondered why.

'Got another version of the story for you though,' he whispered mysteriously, 'and it'll be best for everyone if it's the one to be put about. George don't know all the facts, and I want 'im kept in ignorance.'

'I bet you do,' William said, clenching his fists. 'You swine.'

Harry laughed again. 'Think of your precious little kid sister. Want to keep her pure, don't you?'

William said nothing to this. There was nothing that he could safely allow himself to say.

'George had the story all worked out when I came round,' Harry went on. 'Just threw it at me ready made like. He jumped to the conclusion that I'd seen her reading, grabbed the book, slipped and fell. That's about it. Nice harmless little tale. Never could abide to see women read. No good for 'em, always makes me see red.'

'And that's what you want me to believe?'

75

'No such luck. But you can make sure everyone else believes it, that stuck up aunt of yours for a start, the neighbours and such like. The kid'll be happy to agree to it. She won't want no one knowing what happened, will she? It don't put her in a very good light.'

William was dumbfounded and stood there full of outrage, but his initial disgust for the fabrication of lies gradually gave way to reluctant agreement. The story would leave Lily quite guiltless and Ivy free from taint. That it also left Harry Coney moderately free of blame infuriated him beyond measure.

'Where's Lily gone then? You'd better get her back!' Harry's voice was louder now, imperious, as if he felt no remorse whatever.

Suddenly it was the last thing in the world William wanted to do. Tell her that she was free from guilt, yes, but fetch her home to this brute? He shuddered. No, definitely not.

By the end of the weekend the convenient story of Ivy's reading a book in her room, Harry finding her and raging because he was drunk then falling on to the fender, had been firmly established. Ivy, settled now with Aunt Agnes, had willingly accepted the story and promised silence. She felt defiled and loathsome in herself because of what had happened and wanted no one to know the truth. The fact that Harry Coney had apparently risen from the dead had very much distressed her at first for it meant that, still alive, he might repeat his revolting attentions. But of course it meant too that Lily was innocent and therefore quite safe and could come home. That was the most important thing of all.

Although she knew much of what had really happened Agnes was easily persuaded to accept the new version. She didn't want to dwell on the truth anyway. It gave her too many nightmares!

Harry Coney recovered in a few days, resumed his life as though little had happened, visited one or other of his accommodating women friends down in Old Market as frequently as he wished, and concluded eventually that he could manage just as well without his cold under-sexed wife. He told William that he'd support anything he wished to do to find her, but secretly he cared very little either way. If she wanted to run off and leave him for now, well, let her go. He was confident that she'd return to him one day, and then he'd show her who was boss! He sometimes rubbed his hands together at the thought, but he was in no hurry. The longer she was away the more she'd miss him!

George absolutely refused all offers to live with Aunt Agnes, and was even more determined in his rejection of the orphanage. 'Too many rules and regulations,' he said to William. 'Harry says I can stay here and that suits me fine. He's not a bad bloke and we get on all right.'

William was extremely doubtful about this arrangement. 'Our father wouldn't have liked it,' he objected.

'That don't matter much now,' George said with devastating candour. 'Dad's dead and gone and so he can't say nothing, can he?'

'Promise you'll do your homework and not get into any bad ways then?' William said capitulating helplessly.

George laughed. 'Schoolwork ain't for me, Will. I'm not like you, never was. Harry says I can go into the coal business soon. I works for him Saturdays and some evenings. And he pays me a bit too.' He patted his bulging pocket. 'I'll be richer'n you one day, just see if I'm not.'

Reluctantly William had to agree that this was perfectly possible. 'All right then,' he said. 'Give it a try, living here I mean, and don't think of leaving school yet. And if things go wrong we'll find something else.'

'They won't.' George sounded perfectly confident. 'When you going to get our Lil back?' he said. 'We needs a woman about the place to cook and that.'

William felt his anger rising. 'Is that all you want her back for?'

George grinned again. Nothing seemed to worry him lately. 'Dunno,' he said. 'Harry's got one or two floozies. Perhaps she'm better where she is come to think.'

William stared at him in horror. 'You mean he's got another woman already?'

'More'n one,' George said. 'It keeps him in a good mood.'

Thinking about it afterwards William decided that

although he must find Lily as soon as possible in order to tell her that Harry was alive and that she was quite innocent of any crime, he'd never let her be forced back to that devil of a husband. He couldn't bear to think of her alone and frightened in London though. He blamed himself for so stupidly letting her go without a way of contacting her. Whatever had possessed him? He determined that he'd devote every spare minute, every last penny he possessed, to finding her.

In Torquay Augustus Ash wondered what was happening in the little café next-door to his bookshop. The place had always been an eyesore with its dirty windows, fly-blown cakes, and nauseating smell of onions that penetrated his immaculate shop every time the door was opened. But for two days he'd not been afflicted by this aroma, the window was clean, the flies gone, and the cakes were covered with muslin frames. There was even a new blind to keep the sun off the window. Every time he passed he stopped for a moment to look in and to marvel at the changes.

By Wednesday afternoon he could contain his curiosity no longer. Tentatively he opened the door and looked around. Pleased by what he saw he sat down at a small table near the window. To his amazement the cloth was spotlessly clean.

Lily looked at her new customer. He wasn't the usual type. Mostly they were families wanting a fancy cake each and a cup of tea, nice ordinary people, trippers down for a day out by the sea. This one was different: tall, distinguished-looking, young, and so fair that his golden hair appeared at first to blend into his high intelligent brow. When she went to take his order he turned such brilliant blue eyes upon her and smiled so dazzlingly that to her amazement her heart thumped a resounding tattoo. She had thought that no man would have the power to affect her like that ever again.

'A pot of tea, please,' he said. 'For one. And could I have a scone and jam? They look delicious.'

'They are,' she said, quite overcome. 'All home-made.'

'By whom?'

'Myself of course.'

'In that case I'll have two.'

After she had served him a family came in noisily and seated themselves at the next table. She was busy with their order for a time but the strange young man seemed to be in no hurry. He ordered cakes and another pot of tea and when the boisterous holidaymakers had gone he was still there drinking his third or fourth cup.

He smiled at her again as she started to clear away. 'You're new here,' he said. It was a statement rather than a question. Obviously he wasn't just a tripper.

'I started on Sunday,' Lily told him. 'Mr and Mrs Bailey were looking for someone to take over. I have the room at the top overlooking the sea. It's lovely.' The words rushed out and she wondered why she was telling him all this. It was safer to say nothing about herself. She must be anonymous, completely unidentifiable. Her stomach turned one of its sickening somersaults.

He nodded. 'I'm glad for you, and for the Baileys too. They've been looking for someone for a long time. It looks as though their search is ended!'

Lily was curious about him. How did he know so much? 'You live near?' she asked.

'Next-door. I own the bookshop. My father bought it as a present for my mother, a little hobby to keep her occupied. He always had his nose in a book, and so did she.'

Lily was immediately interested and a little envious of the unknown woman who had a bookshop for 'a little hobby'.

'What happened to her ... your mother?'

'She died last year, of a broken heart, I think. People aren't supposed to die of such things but she and my father were very close, and after his death in France she just gave up wanting to live. She fell victim to the influenza epidemic and had no resistance to fight it.'

Lily was about to say 'My mother died of that too', but stopped herself just in time. How close she had come to revealing yet another bit of her old life. She said instead, 'My fiancé was killed right at the end of the war.' This was the one piece of safe information that she could give to anyone.

'I'm sorry.'

The shop was quiet, no one else had come in. Lily wondered at the way she was talking to this man. She should be in the scullery washing the dishes. But he wasn't just any old customer after all. He was special, the next-door neighbour, and more than that, the owner of the shop she had not dared yet enter, the place of dreams, the beautiful little bookshop that she had looked at enviously every time she walked past its tiny old-fashioned window.

Although she had peered into it frequently, looking at the array of books that was changed nearly every day, she had not seen the owner until now. And miraculously, it seemed to her, he had walked right into her café of his own accord. She wanted to blurt out that she had spent the happiest days of her life working amongst books, wanted to describe the big shop at the top of Park Street, the university students who bought their books there, the precious volumes she was allowed to sort and catalogue, the second-hand department with some antiquarian books like those in his shop, and her own little hoard of volumes hidden away beneath the floor boards in the front room at Sefton Road. She shuddered suddenly at the thought of Sefton Road and of what she had left there sprawled on Ivy's floor!

She put out a hand to steady herself and he looked up at her, surprise on his handsome face.

'I say, are you all right? You look pale suddenly.'

'Yes, I'm fine.' She quickly gathered herself together. She must try to stop this frightening dizziness that overcame her whenever she thought of Harry Coney and the noose that awaited her. How could she conquer it, how would she survive if she couldn't achieve some measure of peace? She supplied the answer from her common-sense: think of something else, keep occupied every minute of the day.

'Did your mother enjoy the shop?' she asked as she stacked sticky plates and cups from the neighbouring table. 'I mean, I should think owning a bookshop was quite . . . ' She stopped, realizing that she was talking too much again, but he looked enquiringly at her.

'Quite what?'

She shrugged her shoulders, picked up the heavy tray, 'Interesting,' she said lamely. She wanted to say 'wonderful, marvellous, the best thing imaginable', but concentrated instead on the pile of dirty crockery balanced precariously.

'Yes, she liked it, but after the war she lost interest in it and passed it on to me. I've been here on and off ever since – not quite the career I had imagined. In fact it's only a hobby really, but it suits me in many ways. Do you like books?'

Careful, careful, Lily Penrose, she told herself fiercely. 'Yes. I've read a few.' She hoped her answer was non-committal.

The clanging bell on the shop door rang and she jumped, nearly dropping the loaded tray. 'I mustn't stay gossiping any longer,' she said, 'or my employers will give me my cards. I'm on a week's trial.'

He stood up and looked around appreciatively. 'No fear of that. I should think you're the best piece of luck that's come their way for a long time. Goodbye then.' He smiled. 'I shall see you again no doubt.'

In the back kitchen she prepared the order for the next customers, carried it through and looked at the place where he had been sitting. She knew that she must be careful about what she said to him. He had been so easy to talk to and she was lonely and because of that, vulnerable, but friends were dangerous. She must definitely not make any friends!

She spent two frustrating hours that evening cutting out and putting together the new frock that she had set herself to make from material bought in the market. There had been no ready-made dresses that she liked. Gladys Bailey loaned her sewing machine and watched critically as Lily tried to remember the things her mother had tried to teach her long ago. But it was no good, she hated sewing.

At ten o'clock she thankfully packed it all away and climbed the stairs to her precious refuge at the top of the house. There was still a little light in the evening sky, a deep red glow from the setting sun that was reflected in the still water of the bay. Small boats were motionless and even the sea-gulls seemed more peaceful than usual.

Lily stared out of the window and tried to fill her heart with a similar tranquillity. But later as she brushed out her long curling hair, giving it the customary one hundred strokes

81

that her mother had always insisted upon, she thought about the bookshop, its fascinating owner, and about her own lack of books here. She yearned for the ones she had left behind, and resolved that she would save a little of her money each week and try to buy something to read, but she would have to find a cheaper bookshop. No good looking next-door. There were other reasons too why she must not look there ...

She glared at her reflection in the small cracked mirror over the wash-stand. There were rings beneath her eyes, deep dark rings, and she smoothed at them with her fingers. At eighteen she should not have those awful tell-tale signs of worry and distress. She resolved that when the wretched new frock was finished she would go for a long walk every evening. Hadn't her mother always said that fresh air was a magic formula for all ills? Elsie Penrose had been full of such notions, always producing some panacea that would cure any malady she came across. But Lily doubted whether even her mother could have found anything to take away the dread that was part of every moment of her life.

In spite of the beauty outside, the twinkling lights reflected in the water now that the sky was almost dark, hopelessness overcame her again and once more she crept into bed, pulled the comforting blankets up to her chin and tried to sleep.

Chapter Six

William went to London at the end of July in a desperate bid to find his sister. Apart from the yearly trip to Weston-super-Mare he had never left Bristol before and the experience was daunting and full of pitfalls. He had contacted the Salvation Army in Bristol and they had told him where to go, whom to ask. He had Lily's photograph with him, the only one he possessed. It had been taken for Arthur when he went to France and Lily stared from it innocently in sepia tints. William's heart bled for her. He longed to tell her that there was no death sentence hanging over her, that she was free to come home or to stay if that was what she preferred, and that she was completely innocent of any crime. He couldn't begin to imagine what she must be suffering.

In the capital he stared around in awe and amazement at the signs of both wealth and poverty, opulence and squalor. He toured various women's hostels, showing Lily's photograph to each suspicious warden, and mostly getting raucous and bawdy remarks for his trouble. But of his sister there was no trace.

On Saturday night he found lodgings in the YMCA, slept little and continued his search through the Sunday streets the next day before dispiritedly catching the last train home from Paddington. He sat gloomily in the carriage staring at the advertisements for various Devonshire holiday resorts. Torquay was the central picture. He had never been there and his mind hardly registered the details, the painted sea, the bathers in the frothy waves. Torquay, Exmouth, Teignmouth, they were completely foreign to

83

him. He doubted if he would ever have the money to visit any of them. All he could think of was his continuing search for Lily. He would never rest until he found her even if it took all his savings and every moment of his spare time and energy. He would leave no stone unturned, no avenue unexplored. Perhaps he should put an advertisement in a London newspaper? His heart sank at the immensity of the task he had set himself but nevertheless he was determined to go to London again as soon as possible. If he was careful he might be able to go in two weeks time.

It didn't occur to him at all that he might be looking in quite the wrong place.

On that same Sunday Lily went to church with her employers, knowing that this was expected of her. It was the acceptable thing to do. She wore the prettiest of her two hats, which she had trimmed with ribbon to match her dress. She was determined that she would make herself look as bright as possible to hide the turmoil in her heart.

Being 'chapel' she was unused to the Prayer Book and watched Gladys Bailey surreptitiously so that she should always have her book open at the right page. If she gave herself away this might be another clue that could lead to discovery.

In spite of the unfamiliarity of the words she enjoyed the service and listened with rapt attention to the sermon for it was lively and interesting and the Vicar was young. Afterwards she walked slowly down the aisle and decided that the morning hadn't been the disaster she had imagined it might be. At the gate Gladys Bailey stopped suddenly, nearly tripping her up.

'Good morning, Doctor,' she said, addressing a tall personable young man who had followed them out. 'Them pills aren't as good as the last ones. My rheumatics be worse'n ever.'

Lily turned to look at the recipient of this displeasure and immediately liked what she saw.

The young man smiled. 'I'm sorry about that, Mrs Bailey,' he said agreeably. 'I'll be coming to see you at the end of

84

the week. Persevere until then and we'll see about another change if things are no better.'

'Best go back to the old ones, I'm thinking,' she grumbled.

Her husband took her arm firmly. 'Don't bother the doctor now,' he whispered. 'You got to persevere like he said.' He succeeded in guiding her across the road.

'We'll discuss it when I call.' The young man smiled and touched his hat to her, and as they passed he smiled at Lily too.

'He seems nice,' she remarked. He had an interesting voice, she thought privately, with some sort of unfamiliar lilt to it, definitely upper class.

'He's a good doctor,' Reginald Bailey said. 'He'm new and I don't think he'm going down too well with local folks though. They'd prefer someone a bit older, more used to our ways.'

Gladys sniffed, though whether it was in agreement or derision Lily couldn't say. 'He'm all right, but too young for the likes of me,' she said. 'And from up Scotland too. I'd a liked a good Devon man what knows these parts.'

Scotland! So that was the source of the melodious and captivating voice.

'He's called Doctor MacMullen,' Gladys further volunteered. 'His family live in a place with great wild mountains, a long way up the map, past Birmingham.' She was obviously highly suspicious of such outlandish surroundings.

Lily remembered pictures she had seen in a shop window in Bristol, paintings of lakes and mountains, a ruined castle with a name that she couldn't pronounce, and a noble-looking stag with wide threatening antlers. She had always thought that Scotland looked wonderful, a magical place quite out of her experience, and it had a fearsome quality too. She wondered what Doctor MacMullen was doing in Torquay and what he thought of the gentle rolling hills of Devon and the blue tranquil sea.

'Perhaps the winter will suit him better then,' she said. 'I believe Scotland's cold. What's it like here in the winter, Mrs Bailey?'

'Mild most times, but us gets some powerful storms now and then and the sea's fierce. You wait and see, maid.'

Lily banished the young doctor from her thoughts and wanted to laugh grimly at the word 'maid'. Since she came to Devon she'd heard it used frequently of single girls and supposed she must get used to it! Her employers had been very correct until now and she had been 'Miss Smith' whenever they spoke to her, but perhaps it was to be 'maid' from now on. She must consider it a compliment! Maybe it might help to assuage memories of the last horrible months since her wedding day, but anyone less worthy of the word 'maid' would be difficult to find, she thought cynically.

During the following weeks Lily had little time to brood. August was one of the busiest months, and as Torquay filled with holidaymakers so did the café. She worked far into the night baking scones and pastries for the next day, keeping records of what she had spent and how much came in, cleaning everything fanatically, and washing the accumulation of dishes that she had not been able to do during the day. From nine o'clock in the morning until she firmly closed the door at nine in the evening, she was busy with an almost ceaseless stream of customers.

In spite of her wish to keep the café merely as a tea-shop she found eventually that she had to produce something savoury, for people came in at lunchtime and in the evening asking for more than she had time or ability to make. She eventually discovered a small bakery which could supply pasties and sausage rolls ready made, and good fresh bread too. She negotiated prices for these things, made a steady profit, and by the end of August there was a modest sum set aside for several improvements which she hoped the Baileys would approve.

'You'm doing well, maid,' Reginald Bailey told her. 'We'm real pleased with everything.'

Lily blushed with pleasure. She was little used to praise. Her father had been a strict disciplinarian, always expecting the best from all his children but seldom congratulating them when they reached his high standards. Harry too had never praised her for anything in spite of her efforts in house and kitchen.

She knew that she had done well in the little shop. The steady stream of customers and the growing amount of money in the bank informed her of that. But it was nice to be told, to feel appreciated. She needed every bit of encouragement and cheer that might come her way for although she could manage to keep her fears at bay when she was busy and surrounded by noise and bustle, the worries returned as soon as she was alone. When the shop was shut and she had finished the next day's preparations, she would climb the two flights of stairs to her precious refuge at the top of the house, and then the terrors would reappear in stomach churning profusion.

She marvelled sometimes because she had seen nothing in any newspapers about a Bristol man murdered and the search for his guilty wife. She was aware that during the day she was beginning to feel a false sense of security and reminded herself that she must not let her cover slip, must never forget that she must be a person with no identity other than the one she had assumed. Nothing must ever be revealed that could lead to her true name being discovered, her alibis exposed.

'You'm just like a daughter,' Reginald Bailey said one Saturday at the beginning of September, 'and we both feel, the Missis and me, that we could trust you to look after things for a few days while we go away and visit our son and his wife what lives away. Doctor's changed the pills again and the new ones be doing the trick, so we think we could manage the journey. Reckon you'd be all right?'

Lily looked at them fondly. ''Course I will,' she said.

They had been leaving her to run things much as she pleased lately, doing less and less to help, and she liked it that way. They had not argued with any of the improvements that she suggested. There was already a new sink with a large wooden draining board in the scullery, some big cupboards and a handsome plate rack on the wall. The tables were resplendent with sparkling white tablecloths, three sets in fact, so that there were always freshly laundered ones available. Bright curtains hung at the windows, and all the cutlery had been polished to a brilliance that had caused Gladys Bailey to rub her eyes in disbelief when she first saw it set out the day after Lily had laboured upon it.

'I shall miss you while you're away,' Lily said, 'but I'll be fine.'

She had come to like both of them, was glad of their company and of their caustic comments on some of the more amusing or unusual customers. They gave her a sense of security too. In spite of her confident words, she wondered a little fearfully how she would like being here all on her own even for a short time, but said nothing of this, waving them off cheerfully the following Saturday morning.

The day was fairly busy, but she had found, to her surprise, that there were often fewer customers on Saturdays. 'Changeover day,' Mrs Bailey had told her. Things were beginning to quieten down a little anyway. Lily sometimes wondered if there would be enough work to keep her occupied and the three of them fed when winter came and all the visitors left.

It was almost time to close. Only one elderly couple remained in the café finishing their supper of pasties and cakes when the door bell clanged and Augustus Ashe came in, put his hat on the hat-stand and sat down. Lily had discovered his name but not a lot more about him.

She had not seen him since that first meeting. There was often another young man looking after the shop next-door. She had noticed him occasionally arranging the books in the window. 'Name of Mr Dyer,' Gladys Bailey had said. 'Lives in the back and keeps an eye on things when Mr Ashe is away. An old army friend, I heard tell, and he've got shell-shock, poor soul.' Then she had added thoughtfully, 'Mr Ashe employs him out of the kindness of his heart I do believe. He's a nice man but rich, above our class.'

It was all rather a mystery to Lily. She had been tempted once or twice to go into the shop and look around, perhaps buy something, but she hadn't yet dared, and the beautiful old books that were displayed in the window were far beyond her pocket anyway. She'd found a cheaper alternative in the town.

He smiled at her as she came to take his order. She remembered that smile and the brilliance of his blue eyes.

'I'm not too late then?' He took out his watch and glanced at it briefly before tucking it back into his waistcoat. 'Almost nine. Are you sure it won't be any trouble?'

She blushed. 'Of course not. What would you like?'

'Have you any of those delicious scones left or have they all been gobbled up?'

'There are just two,' she said, remembering the ones she had kept back for herself.

'Then I should very much like two, and a pot of tea.'

In the kitchen, as she prepared his tray, she wondered what it was about him that made him appear special, different. He disconcerted her. She had to admit that she was attracted to him and this annoyed her considerably.

She served him with as much indifference as she could command, yet when he had finished and paid his bill he seemed reluctant to leave. 'My name is Augustus Ashe,' he told her unnecessarily. 'May I know yours?'

'Lilian Smith,' she said without hesitation. The lie caused her no trouble now. She had become quite used to her new identity and the name tripped off her tongue with ease.

'I've been away,' he volunteered. 'I have a house in Dorset that I need to visit occasionally.'

She stood by the till and stared at him. Dorset! It reminded her of something. Of course. It was the setting for the novel she had enjoyed so much before she was married, but which now caused her such dismay and apprehension. The author had been a Dorset man and his Tess had lived there. She counted out the change and handed it to him but he shook his head.

He was staring at her. 'Are you all right?'

She pulled herself together. 'Yes, of course I am. I was just thinking of Dorset, of *Tess of the d'Urbervilles*. I enjoyed the book at first but its ending always upsets me.'

He looked at her with more interest. 'So you read?'

She was indignant. 'Of course I read. I read a lot as a matter of fact.'

He inclined his head slightly. 'I'm sorry if I implied that you did not.'

'You think that I'm illiterate because I cook and work in a café, I suppose?'

'Not at all. You must come and look at my books some time. Maybe there's something that you would like?'

'I couldn't afford those beautiful leatherbound ones that I've seen in your window.'

'Then one day you shall choose whichever you like and I shall present you with it in exchange for your delightful scones.'

Was he laughing at her? She wasn't sure how to take this sudden out-of-place friendliness. She went to the hat-stand, took his trilby and held it out to him formally. 'That would be very kind,' she said.

'Meanwhile I wonder if you would allow me to show you one of our famous beauty spots?'

She was more confused than ever. Did he know that the Baileys were away? Was he trying to take advantage of her?

'I don't think that would be quite proper, Mr Ashe,' she said. 'We hardly know each other.'

'Tomorrow the weather is going to be lovely. I should like to walk to Cockington and would love to have your company.' He completely ignored her objections.

'Cockington?' She went to the door and opened it, indicating that he should go.

'A village not far from here. It's very beautiful. You shouldn't miss it.' He glanced round the room. 'You've worked wonders here. I should think that you need some recreation, Miss Smith, and I should be honoured if you would allow me to take you there tomorrow afternoon.'

He was looking at her with those eyes again, and feeling the embarrassing colour rushing to her face as though she were an untried schoolgirl, she turned away. He was so formal, so proper. She had never met anyone who addressed her like this and she had to admit that she was tempted. It was certainly a long time since she had enjoyed herself, had any pleasure, felt young and carefree. Would a couple of short hours matter that much?

'Thank you, Mr Ashe. Yes, I think I should like to go,' she said a trifle uncertainly. Then she looked directly into his eyes and added with sudden inspiration, 'Customers often ask me for ideas, places they should visit. It would be nice if I could recommend somewhere.'

'Then I shall enjoy showing you the beauty spots, Miss

Smith. Tomorrow is Sunday so an ideal time to begin. Two o'clock?'

He bowed slightly and then was gone. She locked the door behind him, cleared his table and carried the things into the kitchen. Dear God, what had she done? A married woman, no, not that now, rather a murderess, a widow who had killed her husband, and she was behaving like a stupid girl with no cares in the world.

In bed that night she tried to make excuses for her frivolous behaviour. Of course she needed fresh air and a change, needed to know about places as she had told him. But then she thought about home as she usually did when work was over for the day, when the sky darkened and lights from the many little boats out in the bay were reflected beguilingly on the water. Augustus Ashe with his handsome features and gentlemanly ways faded from her mind and in his place there was Ivy with tear-stained face, William worried and tense, and worst of all, the clearly remembered sight of Harry Coney on the floor at her feet.

Although she had at first told herself that her promise to her mother had been fulfilled, lately she was beginning to change her mind. 'I've failed completely,' she said to herself, and on this night she said it aloud because the Baileys were away and there was no one to hear. 'The family is split up, and all because of me. Ivy will be miserable with Aunt Agnes, William is having to live in the orphanage, and George? Well, I have no idea where George is.'

Sleep was a very long time in coming to her in the quiet house on that Saturday night. She tossed restlessly for hours. Was there no way of getting in touch with William? she wondered. She knew that in spite of the risks, she would have to communicate soon. Lilian Smith would have to give way to Lily Coney one day if she was to retain her sanity.

The next morning she awoke early in spite of her poor night's sleep, and when she pulled the curtains aside her spirits soared with the rising sun. Tiny dancing waves gently rocked the boats below the harbour wall and only a few small fluffy clouds interrupted the otherwise unbroken blue of the sky.

She stood for a long time at the window, just looking, savouring the tranquillity. It gave her peace and a feeling of serenity that was completely at odds with the turmoil she had felt last night. Nothing in her life had changed, but this morning she was just a little more hopeful, more confident of survival. Her moods see-sawed like this all the time, and for now she set her problems aside and determined that she would enjoy today. Mr Ashe was going to take her to Cockington this afternoon! Whatever his motives for asking her, and she had to admit that she was a little suspicious of them, she would still enjoy every moment.

She washed slowly, a luxury she could not often allow herself for weekday mornings were always a rush. Then she dressed with equal care, choosing her best frock, another she had laboriously fashioned for herself recently. It was made of pale blue voile with pearl buttons right down the front. She had found these on a second-hand stall and had carried them home triumphantly. The dress had a boat-shaped neckline with velvet trim, and the skirt finished just a few inches above her ankles. She had been very pleased with her efforts, and Gladys Bailey, who had helped her, was delighted too. 'You looks very beautiful, maid,' she'd said. Lily had been considerably cheered.

Now she ran downstairs and into the shop where there was a long mirror. She stood in front of it, twirled round so that the skirt spun out from the fashionable dropped waistline, and for a few moments, felt light-hearted again. She put her hands over her slim hips and marvelled that in spite of all Harry Coney's cruel violations each night she had not become pregnant. Perhaps God was sometimes on the side of women after all!

After breakfast she put on her hat and gloves, placed her collection into the little handbag that she had made to match the dress, and stepped outside into the fresh morning air to walk to church. The Baileys shouldn't think that she only went because of them.

Augustus Ashe was there too. She could see the back of his head two rows in front. And the young doctor had arrived just after her. He strode purposefully up the aisle and seated himself on the opposite side towards the front.

She glanced at him and was glad that the new pills he had prescribed for her employer were working better than the last. Mrs Bailey approved of him fully now in spite of his dubious background. Lily had seen him briefly two or three times when he had visited. On each occasion they had exchanged a few words and she had been impressed by his attitude towards her. There was no condescension in spite of her lowly position. If, heaven forbid, she should ever be ill, it was Doctor MacMullen she would want to see leaning over her bed. Lily was surprised at these slightly unchaste thoughts, especially as they came to her so wickedly in the House of God, and she banished them quickly from her mind.

The Prayer Book was becoming familiar to her now, less confusing. She switched her attention from the doctor, sang the hymns with enthusiasm, glanced now and then at the handsome upright back of Augustus Ashe just in front of her, knelt at the right times, and listened to the sermon with interest.

Afterwards it seemed quite natural that Mr Ashe should ask if he could accompany her home. They walked side by side along the quiet streets and she found that talking to him was easy. Even with William there had never been this simple and spontaneous flowing of thoughts and ideas.

When they reached the café he raised his hat to her and smiled. 'This afternoon then,' he said. 'I look forward very much to our little outing. I shall call at two. Make sure that you wear comfortable shoes. It's over a mile.'

She laughed at that as she let herself into the café, and she appreciated it too. She guessed that not many men would be considerate enough to think of comfortable shoes.

Later, as they strolled through the Royal Terrace Gardens and then walked along the Torbay road above the beach, Lily found that there was the same easy feeling as before. She had no need to search for something to talk about and not once did she feel inferior or ill at ease.

When they left the coast and turned inland he drew her attention to the many wild flowers in the hedgerows. 'Scabious,' he said. 'That's the wild variety. My mother used to grow the bigger cultivated ones at home and she

93

would make huge flower arrangements of them. She loved their delicate blue. It was her favourite colour.'

Lily detected a sadness in him sometimes as they talked. She noticed that it was apparent when he mentioned his home and particularly his mother. 'What are those?' she asked, pointing to some red flowers beside the road and diverting his attention from the scabious which she privately thought rather small and insignificant.

'Ragwort and scarlet pimpernel,' he told her. 'There are masses of them at Ashcote. I used to pick them when I was small. I was never allowed to pick the cultivated flowers.'

'Ashcote?'

'My house in Dorset.'

She had not heard its name before. 'Is it very big?' she asked him. 'Ashcote sounds rather grand.'

He laughed. 'It's quite big.' He paused for a few moments and then changed the subject abruptly. 'Look over there,' he ordered, and pointed in the direction of a flock of noisy chirruping birds sitting in a line on the ridge of a barn roof. 'They're getting ready to leave for warmer places. They always gather here. I hate to see them go. Seems as though they're telling us summer is almost over.'

For the first time Lily was ashamed of her ignorance. She had never really taken any notice of birds apart from the noisy sparrows and the occasional robin redbreast in the garden at home. Swallows, she thought. So that was what they were called. She stared at them. 'Where do they go?' she asked hoping the question wasn't too stupid.

'Warmer countries. Africa sometimes,' he said.

She gasped in surprise. 'Africa? As far as that?'

He smiled at her. 'They're amazing birds. You've never been interested in the countryside then?'

She shaded her eyes and looked at them with more attention, then shook her head. 'Living in a town all my life there wasn't much opportunity.'

'But Gloucester isn't big, is it? The Cotswold hills are lovely. Did you never walk there?'

Now the shame came in full measure. Why, oh why, did she have to lie to this man? She had nearly slipped up. If she continued this pleasant easy friendship she knew that

94

she would certainly give something away before long.

'No, I never did,' she said. 'I was always too busy.'

He looked at her for a moment and was obviously aware of her sudden disquiet for he changed the subject quickly once more.

'You've met our new young doctor, I believe?' he said.

'Yes. He comes to see Mrs Bailey occasionally. She fully approves of him now in spite of his Scottish origins. He's changed her pills and her aches and pains are apparently much better.'

Augustus laughed. 'I'm not surprised. He's full of all the latest ideas. I order a great number of medical books for him. Nice chap. I think you could say that we are friends. I shall introduce you to him one day. He keeps an eye on me, tells me that I must look after my health.'

Lily looked at him in surprise. 'I didn't think you were ill?'

'Just an occasional cough, a hangover from the war. I allow Duncan to fuss over me now and then.'

The remark, tossed out carefully, could be a façade, but for what? Lily knew that thousands of young men were suffering various unspecified complaints as a result of their years in those frightful trenches. Well, they were the lucky ones, she thought. At least they were home and alive. She glanced again at Augustus. He looked well enough.

Her thoughts returned to the doctor. Duncan ... Duncan MacMullen. She had not known his Christian name until now. Yes it suited him, rugged and sort of craggy, quite the opposite to the romantic and elegant impression that the name Augustus Ashe conveyed. And that name suited its owner just as aptly. Funny how names sometimes seemed to be absolutely right, as though fate or parents or breeding ordained the whole course of one's being. She shivered and thought of Harry Coney!

The rest of the afternoon passed uneventfully. Cockington with its quaint thatched cottages was more beautiful than she had imagined any place could be. Augustus bought her a small painting of the old Forge, and insisted on carrying it, handing it to her when they stood once more at the café door.

'I shall put it on the wall of my room,' she told him. 'And I'll always treasure it as a memory of this afternoon.'

'You sound as though it was the last?' There was a measure of banter in his voice.

She smiled at him sadly. 'I think it should be.'

He shook his head. 'I positively won't allow it,' he said. Then he raised his hat to her, turned and strode off to his own doorway.

Lily was so tired that she fell asleep quickly that night, but not before she had made up her mind sadly that she should not encourage this friendship with Augustus Ashe. There was no room in her life for any further entanglements. She had finished with men for ever.

Ivy reluctantly settled into her new home and, at the end of August, her new school. The first days were hard, but gradually she became used to her aunt's strict ways, her scrupulous cleanliness, even the frugal meals. The horror of that terrible night came back to haunt her frequently, and sometimes she would have nightmares. She was still sure that it was all her fault. Then she would cry out and fight off the constricting blankets that Aunt Agnes insisted on tucking so tightly under the matress on each side of the bed although it was still the middle of summer.

Her aunt usually came into her room and sat with her for a while when she had these night terrors. Often they shared a midnight cup of tea or Ovaltine, and sometimes for a treat a biscuit or two. During these times Ivy felt the beginnings of affection for the gaunt woman with her hair in curling rags and her body shrouded in a winceyette nightdress and vast shawl.

They hadn't talked much of Lily. For some reason that Ivy couldn't define, there was a reticence between them whenever her sister was mentioned. It seemed that Aunt Agnes felt herself to blame somehow, though for the life of her Ivy couldn't think why that could be. One night when the dream had been particularly frightening she cuddled up to her aunt, sipped the comforting drink, and sighed. 'If only we could get Lily back,' she said. 'She thinks that she killed ...' She couldn't bring herself to say his name. 'She

96

thinks that she's a murderess, but she's not, Aunt Agnes. We just got to tell her that, and I want her.'

A few moments passed before Agnes could bring herself to reply. 'Perhaps she don't want to come home. Perhaps she's happy away from him.'

Ivy considered this. She hadn't really thought the matter through fully. The only important thing was to tell Lily that she had done nothing wrong, that the police weren't lurking round every corner in wait for her. Her vivid imagination conjured up all the terrible things that she'd be thinking about if she were in her sister's shoes.

'She wouldn't have to go back there to him, though, would she? She could come here and live with us.'

Agnes shivered a little. She'd thought of this possibility and rejected it. 'I don't think that would do at all,' she said. 'She's married to Mr Coney and back to him she'd have to go, so when all's said and done I think she's better off where she is, wherever it might be.'

Ivy pulled herself out of the comforting arms and sat up straighter in the bed. 'But she must be told.' She stressed the last word. 'She must be told that she's not guilty.'

'Yes, I suppose she must. William is trying every way he knows to find her.'

'Perhaps I could help. What do you think I could do?'

'Go back to sleep,' Agnes said. 'There's nothing at all that you can do.

Chapter Seven

Lily knew that if she was to have any peace of mind she must find out how Ivy and the rest of the family were faring. She thought of them constantly, worried about each of them, and continued to blame herself for everything that had happened. Whatever the risks, she would have to contact William. How to do this without giving away her whereabouts caused her much concern and eventually she decided that an unsigned anonymous message was the only possible way.

Another three or four days passed before she could bring herself to do anything about it, but then she took a piece of paper, a nondescript leaf out of a notebook, consulted her calender, and forced herself to write:

The waiting room, Exeter St David's
Sunday 21st September, 3 o'clock

Although her fingers were shaking and the pen wouldn't do quite as she required of it she knew that William would recognise her handwriting immediately. She folded the paper, put it in an envelope, sealed it, stuck the stamp firmly in place and then held it gingerly as if it had achieved some grim life of its own.

The envelope was blank, staring up at her, white and unsullied, needing an address, but where should it be sent? The orphanage was out of the question. As far as she knew William never received any personal letters. The staff there would know that she was missing and that she was wanted by the police. Her blood ran hot and cold at the thought of it. When they saw the envelope and the postmark they would know immediately where she was.

The other possibility was Aunt Agnes, but that had dangers too. Ivy would probably guess the origin of the letter even if the address was printed in capitals, and an indiscreet word at school could easily put the law on Lily's track.

More than once she almost tore the envelope through, but eventually she settled upon Aunt Agnes. All things considered this was probably the safest of the two options. She'd have to trust Ivy to be sensible and to keep her mouth shut. She decided that the envelope should be written in her normal handwriting for that would cause no speculation. Both Ivy and William would recognise it at once and hopefully would be careful.

She wrote 'PRIVATE' very large on the top left-hand corner and with still trembling fingers followed it with her brother's name, 'William H. Penrose, Esq., Care of Miss Agnes Penrose', then the Eastville address, and finally Bristol. She looked for a long time at that word. Torquay was lovely but Bristol was home. Would she ever be able to go there freely again? There was a great well of longing in her heart as she thought about its familiar streets and saw for a moment some of the faces of the people she knew.

The posting of the letter was another small and private penance, and as it fell with hardly a sound to the depths of the old Victorian pillar box she knew that for good or ill, for life or death, she had made her choice. There was no going back, no possibility of second thoughts now. She stood quite still and stared with unseeing eyes, at the red paint and the ornate VR embossed on the front of the box, and felt that her fate was sealed inside that cylindrical tomb. Yet she knew also that to live any longer with no knowledge of her precious family was quite impossible.

The envelope was delivered the following day and Agnes, picking it up from the mat, stared at it with curiosity and totally failed to recognise the writing. Why on earth was William having his post sent here? Perhaps he had a sweetheart at last. The orphanage wouldn't approve of such goings on, and grudgingly she supposed that he did well to keep it secret.

She put the letter in her pocket and pondered how to get it over to her nephew. Ashley Hill was too far away for her to walk nowadays although she'd have thought nothing of it when she was younger, and the bus fare was not to be overlooked either. The more she thought about it the more she decided that she must tell William sternly, when she saw him, that he had to find some other route for his letters. She couldn't be postman as well as replacement mother to Ivy. It was too much to ask.

Harry Coney's yard was still at the end of Agnes's road. He'd sold the house next-door just after his marriage but he'd not been able to find another coal yard with sufficient stabling and sheds near to his new home. Every day he came early to the yard in a small motor car of which he was very proud. Then he and his workman would load the two carts, fasten the horses in the shafts, and the lumbering contraptions would go off to deliver their loads.

Nearly every morning Agnes watched the old horses bravely pulling their heavy burdens and wished that they could go to retirement in some pleasant green leafy place rather than to the knacker's yard which would be their inevitable end when those awful motor lorries took the place of the old carts. Animals were Agnes's weakness. She sometimes lost sleep just thinking of the cruelty that she frequently saw. Not that Harry Coney was cruel. There were a lot of things wrong with him but she had to admit that he was all right to his beasts.

By the way he worshipped his motor car though she guessed that he'd be changing to dirty noisy engines as soon as he could afford to do so. He already had one van but that was kept clean and sparkling for furniture removals. She was careful to say nothing to Ivy about her fears for Flo and Janey for the child was just as fond of animals as she was herself. In fact, it was one thing that they had in common.

Judging by the loads the horses were pulling each day, trade must be good in spite of the warm weather. Folks were storing up coal for the winter of course. Agnes was glad that she had a ton in the outhouse because it meant that she'd had no need to speak to Harry Coney ever since

100

Ivy came to stay. She had not wanted anything to do with him after what he'd done.

On this particular morning however as she looked out of her window she was aware of the troublesome letter in her pocket, and had a sudden idea. If, in spite of her revulsion, she could bring herself to ask a favour of that awful man, perhaps he would take the letter home to young George, who could take it to William. It was a sensible solution after all and would save her a tiresome journey.

She turned the notion over in her mind all the morning while she did her various bits of housework, and then made her decision. She'd wait until he brought the carts back in the afternoon and then force herself to go down and beard him in his den. She wasn't looking forward to it, but she couldn't see that any harm would be done. William would get his letter tonight. She'd not tell Ivy of course.

Harry Coney looked at the envelope and grinned at Agnes. So she was overcoming her hoity-toity ways at last, deigning to speak to him, and all because she wanted a favour. 'Yes, I'll take it for you,' he said. 'No trouble. George can run round with it after tea. Who's it from?'

Agnes shook her head. 'No idea. Perhaps he's found a sweetheart, someone the orphanage wouldn't aprove. Don't go gabbling about it now, Mr Coney. Make sure and tell George to pass it over without anyone seeing. They're a prissy lot at that orphanage.'

Harry had taken off the day-time clothes he kept for delivering coal and was dressed in tweed plus-fours and a reasonably smart jacket. There was a tap in the yard, and now that he'd bought the motor car he always washed and changed before going home. Mustn't get the spanking new leather seats covered with coal-dust. He put the letter in his pocket. 'Any news of that wife of mine?' he enquired. 'Silly little bitch, running off like that! She don't know when she's well off. The business is doing well.'

Agnes flinched. She hated bad language. He'd no right to call her niece a bitch. She frowned at him. 'If you'd treated her right, she'd not have gone.'

He shrugged his shoulders. 'When she first scarpered I

didn't much care, but I've decided I want her back. Silly of me no doubt, but there it is.'

He strode over to his gleaming little black Ford and turned the handle at the front so that it suddenly chugged into life. 'Come on, woman,' he ordered. 'I want to lock up.'

Agnes looked around her. The horses were comfortably stabled, the yard neat and tidy. She walked through the big wooden gates, and looked up at the notice painted on the wall outside.

H. CONEY. COAL MERCHANT AND GENERAL HAULIER.

There was a gap after the word CONEY, for the words AND SON had been painted out. For one fleeting second Agnes felt a glimmer of sympathy for the man. She could remember his boy who'd been killed in the war, nice lad, not at all like his father. Of course Harry Coney wanted Lily back, needed more sons, wanted to paint those words up there again.

But a shiver of revulsion quickly replaced the sympathy and very firmly she repeated her reproof, 'If you'd treated her right, she'd still be here.' Her words were harsh and condemning, but then she remembered that he was doing her a favour. She tried a grim little smile. 'Thanks for delivering the letter anyway. Saves me a journey.'

When Harry arrived home George was sitting at the table reluctantly doing his homework. The two of them had an easy friendship and Harry was sometimes glad of the boy's company. In fact he intended taking him into the business one day when he left school. He made no irksome rules and George had responded by becoming more responsible, less cheeky. They had found a woman to come in for an hour every day to do a bit of cleaning and washing for them, and on the whole life proceeded fairly calmly.

'Your dear holy brother seems to be up to something. Unbelievable though it is, it looks as though he been and got himself a woman at last.' Harry grinned evilly. He flung the letter onto the table. 'He's having secret mail sent to your aunt. She's asked me to play postman.'

George had been agonising over a page of composition.

102

He was no good at English, much preferring sums, and he was more than glad of the diversion. At first mildly amused he glanced at the envelope, but then suddenly, as he saw the handwriting, he picked it up, staring at it as if hypnotized.

''Tain't no fancy woman,' he said. 'It's from our Lil. It's her writing.' He jumped up and waved it beneath Harry's nose. 'Didn't you recognise it? It's from Lil, I tell you.'

Harry snatched it from him, cursing his shameful secret, his inability to read. Not stopping to think, he ripped open the envelope, held up the paper with its message that, apart from the numbers, he couldn't decipher.

'You shouldn't 'a done that,' George said, ashamed of his big mouth. Why, for goodness' sake, hadn't he stopped to think for a moment before blurting out who it was from? 'It's not addressed to you. It's for William.'

'William be blowed!' Harry said. 'She's my wife and I've a perfect right to open her letters.'

George glanced guiltily at the words and read them aloud: '*The waiting room, Exeter St David's, Sunday 21st September, 3 o'clock.*'

'Well, now.' A grin of satisfaction spread over Harry's face. 'I'll just go down and give her the surprise of her life, and bring her back. Need someone to clean the motor car now and then!' He glared at George, his amusement suddenly changing to flinty determination. 'And don't you dare say a word to no one, see. If you go and blab to your brother, you can just get out of here for ever and go and live in that silly bloody orphanage with all its rules and regulations.'

'It's not right,' George said uneasily. 'If she'd wanted to see you she'd have written to you instead.' He forgot for a moment that Lily believed Harry to be dead. He was very much regretting his further brainlessness in reading the contents aloud so readily. He could have made something up perhaps, or given the wrong time or place. Harry could decipher dates and numbers though. That was necessary to keep his business going. George comforted himself a little with that. He'd have found out anyway.

But if only he'd said nothing from the beginning, gone along with the idea that William had a sweetheart somewhere, then he could have delivered the letter as his sister intended. George knew how desperate William was to find Lily. He'd spent a fortune on trips to London looking for her, and each time he'd come home more and more fed up and despairing. And now she was making the first move, wanting to get in touch at last, and he, George, had given her away, spoilt everything. He'd never felt so wretched, so ashamed of himself, in his life.

'She wants to see William,' he insisted. 'We've got to tell him.' He picked up the envelope and studied it again carefully. 'It says PRIVATE so she meant it just for him.' Then bravely he repeated, 'You done wrong, Harry.'

'I done plenty of wrong and I don't care a damn, me lad. It's me your stupid sister is going to see, not her bloody saintly brother, and if you interfere you'll find out that I mean what I say, every word of it. Out you go, lock, stock and barrel. No more high jinks for you once you're in that holy prison of a place over yonder.' He indicated their back garden with its eight-foot stone wall behind which were some of the orphanage buildings. 'You'll have no job with me, no nothing. That'll be it.'

George had an immediate mental picture of the stark cold rooms where his father had taught. He knew that the children were well looked after, nicely dressed, taught their manners, and always left with a job to go to, girls into service, boys apprenticed to some manual occupation. So why did he shiver with apprehension every time it had been mentioned as a possible home? Because it was the end of his freedom, of course, and here with Harry Coney there was almost complete freedom, more than he'd had with his parents in fact, and he enjoyed it. Harry made him feel grown up. They were almost pals now. If only he could bury the misgivings he sometimes felt about his brother-in-law and also his feelings of loyalty to his sister, he could really like Harry Coney.

He made up his mind suddenly and closed the exercise book over which he'd been labouring. 'All right then,' he said reluctantly. 'I won't say nothing, but don't think I go along with what you're doing.'

'No need for your approval,' Harry said. 'Glad you've

seen the light though. Got to look after number one in this life, Georgie boy. You see me all right and I'll see you the same. Let's shake on it, make a pact?' He held out his hand.

George looked at the big coal-engrained fingers, the dirty nails with distaste. What had he done? Betrayed his sisters, both of them! But he'd made his decision and he couldn't go back on it. Perhaps Harry was right, you had to look after yourself first because there seemed little chance of anyone else doing it. But he couldn't take that hand and shake it for the life of him. He turned away and began to pack his school books into his shabby old satchel. 'We got some cold meat in the larder,' he said, 'and there's some potatoes ready on the stove.'

'Right ho,' Harry said cheerfully. He withdrew his hand. 'It's a pact whether or not we shake on it.' He was not at all put out, more amused by George's disapproval. He folded Lily's piece of paper and replaced it in its envelope and tucked it into his pocket. He wouldn't need the contents read to him a second time. His memory was as keen as a butcher's knife. Next Sunday at three o'clock, St David's station, Exeter. He'd be there.

He rubbed his hands together in gleeful anticipation and turned to George. 'Come on then, son. Let's have that meat and tatties. I'm starving.' As long as the lad kept his mouth shut he bore him no ill will. He supposed it was natural that after such a pious upbringing he'd want to do what he called the right thing. Harry laughed to himself again. He was constantly amused at other people's odd ways. Always do what was best for yourself, that was his motto, and so far he'd found it worked! He opened the drawer beneath the table-top and took out a white cloth and spread it over the green baize one. 'We won't have to do this ourselves when I get the dratted wife back,' he said. 'The sooner the better.'

George shivered, and decided, as he stumped up the stairs to put his books away, that he'd given himself up to Satan. He was well on the wide road that led straight to destruction just like the Bible said, while his brother, whom he was about to deceive, was plodding along the narrow way that led to life. Oh, well, perhaps there was time to repent and change course later when he was old. With that slightly comforting thought firmly in place he dumped his things on the bed, likewise tried to dump his troublesome conscience, and ran down again to Harry Coney and a substantial supper.

After posting her note to William, Lily was in an agony of suspense. Would it reach him safely? Would he respond? If so would he be able to come to her without anyone knowing?

If all went according to plan she hoped that at least her mind would be set at rest over Ivy. Concern for her little sister was a persistent heartache. And what was George doing? Was the house sold? The questions she needed to ask William went round and round in her head constantly. Even while she was serving customers, cooking, cleaning, or busy with the accounts, the thought of the coming Sunday afternoon would send her stomach into violent somersaults which she was quite unable to control. Once or twice she had looked into the mirror at her reflection and said silently to the pale face she saw there, *You will be Lily Penrose again just for a brief hour instead of this strange Lilian Smith.*

There had been no more walks with Augustus Ashe. He came into the café frequently, but she was usually busy with other customers and they hadn't talked much. On Thursday however he came later, when the shop was empty. He sat down and ordered tea and scones as usual. Her home-made scones had almost become a little bond between them, a cause for amusement because he always ordered them whatever the time of day.

'You look pale,' he said as she put the tray down on his table. 'Working too hard, I suppose. It's time they took on someone else to give you a hand.'

Alarm bells rang in Lily's head. She didn't want any close association with another woman or young girl, someone who might ask questions and one day stumble on the truth. 'No,' she said quickly. 'I can manage.'

There was concern in his blue eyes as he studied her. 'Perhaps I should ask Duncan to have a look at you.'

She blushed. The young doctor had visited Gladys Bailey

again recently and he too had remarked on Lily's pale face and tired eyes. She had laughed and told him that she was perfectly fit. 'Oh, no,' she said again, too quickly. 'I'm fine, really.'

'Be careful then.' Augustus still sounded doubtful. 'Get some fresh air whenever you can.'

She smiled. 'You sound like my mother. She was always bothered about our health.'

'Then she must have been an admirable woman. Who else did she bother about? I thought you said you had no brothers and sisters?'

Lily took a deep breath. *There I go again*, she thought, *carelessly saying things that must be kept safely hidden away*.

'My father and myself,' she hedged.

She hated telling untruths to this man whom she had instantly liked, and for whom, although she dared not admit it, she felt more than mere liking. Their friendship must not progress any further, she reminded herself. It was too fraught with dangers. And anyway, he was as far above her as the gulls soaring overhead were above the little house mice with whom she was constantly waging war in the larder. She knew that he was gentry while she was miles down the ladder, but more than those things, she was false, a non-person, a wanted criminal.

But he was still looking at her, and she blushed as she set out his cutlery. Then she lifted her eyes for a moment from the table and looked straight at him. There was a flush on his face that seemed out of place on a man. She noticed that the colour was high up on his cheekbones. Into her memory flashed a picture of a girl she had known once who had looked like that, always the pale face and the vivid splashes of colour. It was a long time ago, but she remembered her mother telling the family that she was ill and was to be sent away to a special place where she could be cured with lots of good food and fresh air. Surely Mr Ashe couldn't be ailing in any way? He had told her that he had a cough now and then, but so did most people.

When she had set the plate of scones on the table, the tea pot with sugar and two sorts of cream, thick and thin, to his right hand, she looked at him again and frowned. 'Why do you think fresh air is so important?'

She watched him spread the thick Devonshire clotted cream carefully on each scone before he replied. Then he reached for the jam, held the dish in his hand for a moment and looked up at her. 'Perhaps because our good doctor friend assures me of its values. And because it's an excuse to do all the things I want to do.' He paused and grinned at her. 'Like taking you out again.'

With great precision he ladled the jam on to the side of his plate and then added a little to the heaped cream on one of the scones. 'I should like to drive you over to Anstey's Cove in my motor car,' he said. 'We could walk on the beach and get all the fresh air of which Duncan approves so heartily.'

A motor car! Lily had never been in a motor car. Harry Coney had told her that he was about to buy one, and a van too in order to expand his business, but that seemed a hundred years ago, another life!

Her stomach did its acrobatic act again as she remembered her assignation for next Sunday afternoon. 'I'm sorry, Mr Ashe. I ...' What was she to say, what excuse to make? That she was meeting someone? He'd think she had a sweetheart. No, he mustn't believe that! But why not? It might be the best way to stop any further interest in her. Yet contrarily she wanted him to think her free. Free? That was a morbid joke! 'Not this Sunday,' she managed feebly.

'Perhaps the next one then?' he said. 'But don't make it too long, Miss Smith. I may have to go away soon.'

'To your house in Dorset?'

'First there, but afterwards I must go abroad. I could be away for quite a long time unfortunately.'

In spite of her determined resolve not to allow a friendship with him to develop she was saddened by this news as if the only bit of her life that held any pleasure, any hope, was about to be severed. She was curious too. Where was he going? What would happen to the bookshop? Was he wealthy? Who lived in the house in Dorset? A wife perhaps? The feeling of melancholy intensified.

They said little after that, merely polite goodbyes when

he had finished, and afterwards as she pondered his words she had to admit reluctantly that his going away would be the best thing that could possibly happen. She must put him right out of her stupid mind and concentrate on her meeting with William this coming Sunday.

She dressed carefully on the longed-for and yet dreaded day. She had a suit now, for the café had done well and her wages had been increased. Gladys Bailey had recommended a lady tailoress who made things fairly cheaply if you could do some of the laborious finishing yourself, and this Lily had gladly undertaken. She had gone to the market again and bought eight yards of light-weight navy blue gaberdine, and was very pleased with the result. The suit gave her much needed confidence, and she had discovered that although she disliked making garments, she had imagination and flair for the accessories.

'You'm proper handsome,' Gladys Bailey told her just as she was about to leave. 'That hat do look lovely.'

Lily had found a wide-brimmed straw hat in a second-hand shop and had trimmed it with veiling to match the suit. She carried a small pouch handbag that she had made with some of the left-over material, and with much trepidation had bought her first pair of high-heeled shoes made in shiny patent leather with bright metal buckles.

'Them shoes be a sight for sore eyes too,' Gladys Bailey persisted. 'In my day we didn't need to spend good money on fancy things like that though. They was hidden beneath our skirts. I bain't so sure that I like that new length of your'n.'

'It's only seven inches from the ground, Mrs Bailey,' Lily said. 'Much more practical.'

The old woman sniffed in slight disapproval. 'Times change, I suppose,' she muttered. 'Not always for the best, I'm thinking though.'

In spite of her nervous state Lily was amused and she had to admit that with the shorter length, shoes and stockings were more important than they had needed to be years ago.

'When'll you be back then?' Reginald Bailey had come

into the room and was looking at her with considerable anxiety.

'I don't know. This evening some time. Don't wait up if I'm late.'

''Course we will, maid. The Missis and me couldn't rest easy in our beds thinking o' you out in the dark. There be some nasty characters prowling the town at night. You get home nice and early and that'll be the best all round! And don't let your aunt persuade you to go back to Gloucester. Us needs you here, can't do without you.'

With a stab of guilt that she had told these good people yet another lie, invented an aunt whom she was to see in Exeter, Lily strode out as best as she could in her uncomfortable new shoes in the direction of the station.

To her relief the waiting room when she reached Exeter was empty and she hoped it would remain so. She had asked about trains from Bristol and judged it most likely that William would arrive in about half an hour's time. She wondered what to do, how to calm her nerves. It was only the thought of something going wrong that frightened her. Meeting her brother again after so long would be pure joy.

She walked round the bare ugly room, stared at the pictures of beaches and castles that adorned the walls, then sat down and put her hand on the bulge of her little purse to make sure that it was still there. She had taken four sovereigns from her store beneath the loose floorboard and had secreted them in the inner pocket of her jacket. She intended giving them to William to help Aunt Agnes with Ivy's expenses.

The station clock told that there were ten minutes to go before William's train arrived. She stood up, paced the floor again, and then the door opened and a woman and a small boy entered. The woman looked Lily up and down. She was fat and flustered and sank on to the bench seat and fanned herself with an abandoned newspaper. 'Hot ain't it, deary?' she said. 'For September.'

Lily had not thought it particularly warm but she nodded in agreement.

'Pretty hat you got,' the woman continued, staring at

Lily's handiwork. 'Better'n they modern things that comes down on yer face.'

Why, oh why, couldn't she go away? Lily was almost in tears. She wanted no one to witness her reunion with her brother. 'Yes,' she managed, and tried to smile at the child. He was eating a bar of chocolate, sticky fingers everywhere.

It was the last thing she registered about either of them for the door opened and a ghost stood there, a large and sturdy ghost with a sardonic smile on its face.

And it spoke in Harry Coney's dead voice. 'Well, now, here's a turn up for the books! Coming back to your loving hubby, aren't you?'

It was a command, no question. Lily stood up, backed away. This was the stuff of nightmares. The room swayed and tilted, the ground rose to meet her.

When she came to she looked up at the amused face of her husband and at the fat woman who was fanning her with the newspaper. They swam in some sort of confused and misty unreality. She closed her eyes again and thought that she must be dead, then wished that she was. Then she felt Harry's strong and roughened hand grip hers. She was pulled to her feet and she stumbled to the bench that ran around the walls of the waiting room.

The woman was holding the previously admired straw hat which must have fallen off. She held it out to Lily.

'All right now, me dear?' she asked. 'You'm proper pale. Look as though you been and met a ghost.'

Lily said nothing, but she wanted to shout out that, yes, she had seen a ghost, but a ghost that was as real and substantial as the great steam engine of which she was vaguely aware outside. She was completely unable to make any sense out of what was happening to her.

'You go and fetch her a cup a tea,' the woman ordered Harry. 'Poor maid looks proper poorly.'

'I'm not letting her out of my sight,' he said belligerently, but the woman obviously misunderstood.

'Then I'll go,' she said. 'Nice to have a good man like that what won't leave you. If you could just look after my little Eddy I'll go and get tea for all of us.'

At last Lily came to a vestige of her senses. 'No,' she said. 'I don't want tea. Please just leave me alone.' She knew she sounded impolite, but nothing mattered now except thinking straight, getting away. All she wanted to do was escape, to get away from this man. She was filled with repugnance for the face and body towering over her.

The woman smiled indulgently. 'Sorry, me dear. I never thought that you'm wanting to be on your own. 'Tis so long ago since I felt that way that I was forgetting.' She grabbed her sticky son. 'Come on, Eddy. We'm going to get some tea for you and me and leave these love-birds together.'

She winked at Harry. The child said nothing. The chocolate finished, his mouth was now filled with a lollipop, the stick protruding from his lips like some strange proboscis. They went out, the door clanging behind them.

'Well, then,' Harry said. 'Why'd you run off like that?'

Lily took a deep breath. 'I thought you were dead.'

There was a moment's silence during which she was aware of the big clock on the wall ticking sonorously like the beating of some sinister heart.

Then Harry Coney let out a great bellow of laughter. 'And you didn't think I was worth swinging for?'

Lily looked away from him and bowed her head, covering her face with her hands. Then suddenly the realization of what his very much alive appearance meant, dawned on her, engulfed her. She was no murderess. She hadn't to go in fear of her life any longer. The great burden under which she'd lived for weeks fell away, a foul infirmity suddenly sloughed off, the rope no more a stupefying threat.

But she was held now by quite different shackles, not so fearsome perhaps but terrifying, the difference between a life sentence and the gallows.

She looked up and saw that the door was between her and her husband. Without further reflection and in one sudden lithe movement she sprang to her feet and was outside. The train on the platform was just pulling out and she wrenched feverishly at the nearest carriage door, jumped and was pulled into its welcoming safety by a sturdy pair of arms. The train gathered speed and Harry Coney, running down

112

the platform, was yelling something she couldn't hear.

'That was a silly thing to do,' a voice said. 'Nearly killed yourself.'

She turned to the man who had helped her. 'Thank you.' Her whole heart was in the one word, for this stranger had saved her in more ways than he could ever know. She sank down on the comfortable seat of the first-class carriage into which she had so precipitately arrived, and wondered where on earth she was going.

Chapter Eight

Lily tried to huddle into the corner seat hoping that her agitation wouldn't be noticed, the thumping of her heart remain unheard, but the man who had rescued her kept looking up from his newspaper, glancing at her and then down again. The printed words seemed unable to hold his interest. Sometimes their eyes met and she would hurriedly look away at the countryside passing outside in rapidly changing scenes, toy cows, trees untidily dancing in uneven lines and then vanishing, telegraph wires swinging up and down in graceful continuing waves that made her feel nauseous.

If only she could ask this stranger where the train was bound, but that would certainly strike him as very strange, invite his suspicions.

Where should she go? Where was safety now that Harry Coney was alive? Her heart constricted in fear as she thought of his bed, his body heavy on hers, his lips and hands molesting her as he had done nearly every night for those past terrible months. Automatically she tightened her arms across her breast, remembering the bruises he had inflicted, the pain. She could never submit to that torment again as long as she lived. Then a fresh thought struck her, a blow almost physical in its force. Harry, alive and full of resentment and lust, was a fearful threat to Ivy. As long as she had believed him dead, Lily had been sure that her little sister was quite safe from further degradation and terror.

Had William and Aunt Agnes between them been able to give Ivy sufficient protection from him? Had they been diligent in seeing that she was never left alone? She thought of her aunt's house so close to the coal yard which Harry probably still owned, and shivered. She felt ashamed that she had been concerned more with her own safety than anything else.

'Tickets, please.'

She stared up at the man, blinked, tried to focus on her predicament, endeavoured to appear calm. The weeks of an assumed identity, a quickly invented story to cover every emergency, came to her rescue. 'I hadn't time to get a ticket,' she heard herself blurting out. 'The man waved me through, told me to pay on the train.' She groped in her pocket for her precious little bag of sovereigns and drew out one shining coin. Surely that would allay any suspicions, would be enough to get her to the next stop even though this was unfortunately a first-class compartment in which she had so abruptly landed.

'Return, Miss? Taunton or Bristol?'

She should have said Taunton, should have quickly changed trains there, boarded the very next one back to Exeter or Torquay, but before she could stop herself she had said it. 'Bristol, please. Yes, a return.'

'Fourteen shillings and sixpence.' He stamped a small piece of cardboard with his little ringing punch and handed it over to her. 'Temple Meads, next stop but one, Miss.'

She looked with both dismay and excitement at the ticket in her hand. What had she done? Why on earth had she said Bristol? She might meet Harry Coney on the station. But of course she knew very well why she had made such a quick and possibly disastrous decision. She had to assure herself that Ivy was well and safe, had to talk to William.

She tucked the ticket safely away in her bag and replaced the remaining sovereigns securely in their secret inner pocket. Then she sank back once more into the seat, glad now of the comfort and anonymity of a first-class compartment. She guessed that in third, questions might have been asked about her lack of a ticket, suspicions aroused.

Gradually she became calmer, the steady rhythm of the great engine quietening her nerves. She tried to marshal her resources, decide what she must do. She would have

115

to get herself straight over to see William first of all, hide if Harry Coney came, and get a message to the Baileys for they would be waiting up for her. For a moment her thoughts strayed to that other life, and she tried to come to terms with the two sides of herself. She knew that in Torquay she had found strengths and abilities that she had no idea she possessed, but she had also discovered a more sinister side to her nature: the capacity to deceive and to lie, to mislead good people into thinking she was someone who did not exist at all. A flush of shame spread over her face and she wondered how she would put everything right, how to retain the independent Lilian Smith and yet become Lily Penrose again, and more important still, how to rid herself of the abhorrent title Mrs Harry Coney. Divorce? Was such a thing possible for someone of her class and background? What did it cost? How did you go about it?

So deep was she in these thoughts and questions that she was almost unaware of the train stopping at Taunton, hardly registered the flat monotonous miles that followed across the Somerset levels. But when she saw the spectacular rise of the Mendip Hills her pulse quickened, and eventually she could see the Clifton Suspension Bridge spanning the Avon Gorge. She stared at its graceful lines, clear and beautiful even from this distance, and the sight took her back to the day she had walked across it with Harry. In spite of some misgivings she'd thought that marriage with him might be exciting, and that in time she would come to love him. She had even been flattered to have gained the attentions of someone older and fairly well off. She closed her eyes for a moment in self-disgust. How foolish she had been, how stupid to listen to her head all those months ago instead of to her heart.

The train pulled into the familiar station and as she stepped on to the platform Lily looked around fearfully, thinking that she would see Harry Coney leering at her from every corner. But of course he couldn't possibly be in Bristol yet. There was probably not another train in from Exeter until the evening. She judged that she had a few hours in which to accomplish everything that she had to do. As she rushed through the barrier she recalled briefly the last time she had been there, going in the opposite direction. How terrified she was then: frightened of the police, of prison, and that she would hang for that most despicable of crimes, the murder of a husband. For a second she smiled to herself. At least those fears had dropped away now. Her present predicament was far less dreadful.

'Please God, let William be in, oh let him be in,' she whispered as she stood outside the orphanage looking up at its immense forbidding walls. Then she slipped silently up the outside stairway and knocked on his door.

After a moment in which the whole world seemed to come to a standstill he opened the door and stared at her as though she had been a ghost.

'Lily!' He pulled her inside and embraced her, and then he put her away from him with a trace of impatience. 'Wherever have you been all these weeks? I've searched heaven and earth for you, and now you just arrive out of the blue.' He looked her up and down, took in her fashionable clothes. 'Thank Heavens you've come back, Lil. Are you all right?'

She sank down on the edge of his bed. 'Yes, William. I'm all right. How's Ivy?'

'Ivy?' William was completely overcome for a moment. Lily, suddenly materializing before him, looking affluent and healthy, not the pathetic waif he had imagined during his searches amongst the down-and-outs of London, had quite disconcerted him. 'She's well,' he said abstractedly. 'Flourishing, gets on happily with Aunt Agnes now.'

He continued to stand in front of her, almost afraid that she would vanish before his eyes as suddenly as she had arrived. 'It's you I want to know about,' he said. 'How did you get here? Wherever have you been?' Then he sat down beside her, took her hands in his and scrutinized every line of her face: the small upturned nose, the dimpled chin and the curly hair escaping from beneath her hat.

'You didn't get my note?'

He shook his head. 'Note? No. What about? Where did you send it?'

'To Aunt Agnes!' Lily swallowed hard as she replied. Had her aunt really betrayed her, opened her letter and passed it on to Harry Coney? 'I can't believe that she'd be such a traitor,' she said when she'd told her brother about her plan to meet him in Exeter. 'There must be some other explanation.'

'I'm sure there is. She's been a great ally, a wonderful guardian for Ivy in spite of all our fears. She won't let Harry Coney get near her, watches over her like a mother hen. Ivy's changed too. She's more gentle, more amenable.'

They talked breathlessly almost without pause, sharing news, even laughing over William's abortive journeys to London, his descriptions of the hostels he'd visited. But Lily carefully kept her side of things vague, giving nothing away.

'I must go and see Ivy,' she said eventually. 'How can I get there quickly?'

'Not very easy at this time on a Sunday unless we walk, and there's a chance we might run into that devil.'

'How could we?'

'He might go over to the yard as soon as he gets back. He goes on Sunday nights to check the horses. It's not worth taking the risk. I'd like you safely back in your bolt hole as you call it as soon as possible. I'll cycle over and tell them that I've seen you and and I can bring Ivy to meet you somewhere if you like?'

Lily brightened. 'That might be the best idea then. Could you really? I'd meet you in Exeter.'

She had carefully avoided telling her brother that she was in Torquay. 'Somewhere in the South West,' was all she had said.

'Next Saturday?'

'Sunday. I work on Saturdays.'

'And you won't tell me where you live then, or what you do?' He sounded hurt. 'I ought to know. There's no harm in telling me surely? Don't you trust me, Lily?'

She hesitated for a moment, but the thought of Harry arriving in Torquay, coming into the café, making a commotion, pulling her out, was quite terrible. 'Of course I trust you, Will,' she said. 'But however careful you are you might let something slip, perhaps to Ivy or George. Harry is pretty devious and clever at getting what he wants. It's

118

better if no one at all knows. You won't have to tell any lies if you don't know where I am. Let me keep that other part of me secret for a while.'

'If that's what you wish.' His face had a shut look, the expression she had seen years ago when their father had reprimanded him severely for some minor fault.

She put her hand over his, gripped it, and then stood up. 'I'm sorry, Will.'

'We'd better go,' he said. 'I'll come with you. We can walk to Ashley Hill Station and you can get a train into Temple Meads from there. That's the best way and we won't bump into . . . him.'

'I wish I could have seen Ivy. You'll tell her that I've been, and explain why I couldn't go over to Aunt Agnes's, won't you?'

'Of course. Stop worrying.' William took his overcoat from behind the door and put it on, grabbed his hat, looked out to make sure that no one was about, and then in silence they made their way down the staircase, out of the large gates, and along the road towards the little railway station, the place where she had often taken George and Ivy when they were little and liked to watch the huge engines puffing and grunting on their way to distant magical places.

She suddenly realized that she hadn't asked about her younger brother. She'd guessed from what Harry had said that he must have stayed in Sefton Road and had been surprised at this. But of course he had always stated firmly that he wouldn't go to the orphanage or to Aunt Agnes. 'George?' she said guiltily. 'How is he?'

'Tries to be tough just as always. He wanted to stay with Harry and there was nothing I could do about it. They get along together passably well and it appears to be working out. I see him most weekends.'

'So he's all right then?'

'I think you could say that. You've no need to worry about him anyway. He hates school and talks of nothing but going into the coal business and making a lot of money. He'll probably manage it too.'

'Will Harry take him on now that we're estranged?'

'I don't think that will make any difference. It hasn't so far.'

So I'm never to be rid of Harry Coney, Lily thought. He'll be my brother's boss, partner one day perhaps.

She and William were walking through the narrow tunnel that took the lane beneath the railway. She looked up at the curved roof which was dripping cold drops of moisture on them as it always had done and she remembered how, years ago, she had been frightened to go through when a train was coming. William would hold her hand tightly and they would run as fast as they could until they came out on the far side.

They had always been together, always supported each other in everything and it hurt her that she couldn't be completely open with him now. But she still needed his advice and help.

'Can I get a divorce, William, do you think?' she asked when they had reached the station and were standing on the small deserted platform. 'Do you know anything about it?'

'Absolutely nothing. Is that what you want?'

'Of course. Did you imagine for one moment that I'd want to be tied to Harry for ever?'

'No, obviously not. I'll have to try and find out how you go about it.'

'Would you do that for me?'

'Yes, of course I will,' he replied. 'There's a solicitor's office next-door to mine. I know the clerk. I'll make some enquiries.'

'Thank you.' She smiled at him. 'I need you, William. You won't be cross with me, will you, because I can't give you my address yet?'

He bent his head and kissed her on the end of her nose, an old childish gesture.

'The Eskimo kiss,' she murmured. 'It's a long time since you did that.'

'It's our secret bond,' he said. 'I could never be cross with you, Lil.'

She smiled and looked beyond him into the red-gold of the evening sky and for some odd reason noticed that there were no swallows. They had gone, as Augustus Ashe had told her they would, flown far away to that other secret life they lived. For a moment she closed her eyes and wished that she too could go to some distant shore where she could begin all over again. Then she thought of Augustus, his fair hair and kind intelligent blue eyes, and knew with an uncomfortable certainty that when she thought of a new future it was his figure and form she saw faintly at her side.

'The swallows have gone,' she said. 'To Africa or somewhere hot, I think.'

'Whatever are you talking about?' William sounded quite bewildered by this strange unconnected remark.

She laughed and experienced the first carefree moment in all that long terrifying day. 'The swallows,' she repeated. 'Someone told me that they leave here every autumn and come back in the summer. I knew it, of course, but hadn't thought much about it. We saw them gathering a short time ago.' She waved her hand at the almost empty sky. 'They've gone now. Sad really. It means that winter's nearly here.'

The train puffed importantly into the station, stopping further conversation. William wrenched open a door and held it for her. 'Next week,' he said. 'Three o'clock on Sunday, Exeter St David's. and I hope to have some information for you by then, something more important than swallows.'

She blew him a kiss and her heart lifted at the thought that in a few hours she would be in her lovely room with the gentle lapping sounds of the sea to send her to sleep and the twinkling lights of the boats in the harbour to give a feeling of security and peace. For the first night since her flight from Sefton Road all those weeks ago she would go to sleep without the nightmare of the gallows haunting her. Life suddenly seemed sweet again. The problems were still huge, but the worst was surely over. William would know how to deal with Harry Coney. She leaned back in the seat feeling secure in her brother's ability to care for all the complicated strands of her life in Bristol. It was her new life in Torquay that she would have to face on her own. For the first time in weeks she felt that she did indeed have a future and a fragile hope, and that knowledge was unbearably sweet.

121

After the train had gone taking Lily away to goodness-knew-where, William walked thoughtfully back to his room and wondered what to do next. Ivy and Aunt Agnes must be told the good news as soon as possible but it was important that no suspicion of next Sunday's rendezvous should leak out to Harry Coney. He hurried back to the orphanage and fetched his bike.

'I've seen Lily,' he announced when he arrived at the little terraced house.

'What?' Ivy had opened the door. 'Where is she?'

'I don't know.'

'For goodness sake!' Ivy looked at the empty pavement and the road behind him as if expecting her sister to materialize before her eyes.

William propped his bicycle against the front wall and removed his cycle clips. 'If I can come in I'll tell you all I know.'

He did not in fact tell them all he knew, merely the barest details, and said nothing about taking Ivy to Exeter the following weekend. Harry Coney's coal yard was too close. Ivy sometimes saw him on her way to school and the temptation to blurt something out might prove too great. What she didn't know she couldn't accidentally reveal. He decided that he would arrive early next Sunday morning and relate everything then.

On Monday evening he was sitting in his room, a big ledger open on the table before him. But the long list of figures jumped and jiggled about alarmingly and his ability to total the pounds shillings and pence easily in his head completely deserted him. He couldn't get the stupendous fact of Lily's return out of his mind and had just decided to walk round the block to clear his thoughts when there was a thunderous knocking on his door. He flung it open and confronted a belligerent and red faced Harry Coney.

'So, what's your part in all this?' his unwelcome visitor demanded. His eyes were hostile and his tone implied that Lily's flight from Exeter the day before had been William's fault entirely.

He looked uneasily up and down the corridor, thankful that his room was in a fairly deserted part of the orphanage.

There was an office next-door that was only used for a short time in the morning, and the remaining rooms were kept for storage. 'I don't know what you mean,' he said. 'You'd better come in.' He ushered Harry inside so that their voices should not be heard and removed a pile of books from the chair that stood in front of his desk. 'Sit down and explain yourself.' He felt more confident if his foe was seated while he himself remained on his feet.

Surprisingly Harry flopped down. 'Of course you know what I'm on about! You been meeting her, haven't you? You know where she is. Don't give me any of your damned lies.'

'I've no idea where she is. I've been to London more than once and spent hours tramping the streets and searching the hostels there to try and find her.'

'And a lot of bloody good it did! She's not there, is she, or why would she want to meet you in Exeter? I turned up instead this time, you know. Gave her the shock of her life. Bloody smart she was too, a right tart in fact, no miserable stray. Hostels! There's a laugh. She must have a fancy man to keep her in such luxury.'

William saw Harry's fists bunch in anger and felt his own face become suffused with outraged colour. 'That's not true. Lily's no whore.' He wondered how the word came so readily to his lips.

'And how would you know that?' Harry sneered, but then a defeated look crossed his face. 'But you might be right. Damned frigid bitch she was. Anyway, where is she? I'm going to get her back here and teach her a thing or two.'

'You can't do that. She wants a divorce.'

'Ha!' Harry leapt to his feet and took a threatening step in William's direction. 'So you have seen her. I knew as much. Where is she then? You'd better tell me or I'll ...'

He broke off in mid-sentence and William wondered what frightful thing was in his mind now, or was it just an idle threat? Probably it was. He forced himself to remain calm. If he lost his temper nothing would be gained. He made a split-second decision. Within limits he would be frank and perhaps that way something useful could be planned. Lily's welfare was paramount.

123

'Please sit down again, Harry,' he said as politely as he could manage. 'I'll tell you all I know.' He indicated the chair once again and seated himself on the bed.

Harry looked at him, obviously undecided, then his belligerent air faded and he sat, this time perched on the edge of the chair. 'Well, spit it out. See if we can come to some arrangement.'

His remark enraged William afresh. It was his twin sister they were talking about as though she were a commodity, a parcel. Harry seemed to think that she existed only in relation to himself.

'I honestly don't know where she is. She was very careful to give me no clue at all,' he said, his voice evenly pitched. 'Yes I did see her. She came here yesterday after she fled from you in Exeter. Then I put her on the train at Ashley Hill Station and that's all I know. She was going to Temple Meads and from there could have gone anywhere.'

'Came here?' Harry was plainly suspicious. 'And you expect me to believe that you let her go without giving you an address? If so, you're more of a bloody fool than I thought.'

William flushed at the reproach and at the obscenities that peppered Harry's speech. Before the marriage he'd never heard one swearword escape the man's lips. He'd been a cool customer for sure, making certain that he didn't show his true colours until the knot was tied. But William supposed that it was often so. He sighed, but was grateful now that Lily had been firm about not giving away her whereabouts. She was right after all. He was glad that he didn't know where she was and that he could tell the truth.

'It wasn't my decision,' he said. 'It was hers. She's determined to keep her address secret and quite adamant about not wanting to come back to you. As far as I know, the law won't allow you to force her. We're not living back in the Middle Ages. Wives aren't property any more. They have rights.'

Harry grunted in fury. 'Damned foolish law then,' he said.

William breathed deeply. 'An unwilling wife can't be much pleasure. If she's so frigid as you say ...' He paused, heartily embarrassed to be discussing such things with anyone, let alone this man who was the molester of his younger sister as well as Lily's persecutor. 'If she doesn't satisfy you,' he continued, 'well then, divorce her and find someone more to your taste.' He gulped in disbelief at his own words. Divorce was horrible, something seldom talked about, disgraceful and against God's most sacred laws. How could he possibly have voiced such unspeakable things? Yet when he thought of Lily in this man's clutches ... he blushed at the pictures that flashed into his mind ... well then, there was no other solution.

Silence reigned in the room for an embarrassing few moments and then Harry stood up, retrieved his trilby from the table where he had thrown it. 'I'll give it some thought,' he said. 'You know that a wife can't divorce her husband for adultery don't you, although a man can get rid of his wife if she's been playing false.' He laughed. 'The law might give women a few rights, but it's still firmly on the side of us men. You're wrong, my lad, women are the property of their husbands, I reckon, and always will be.'

'I'm going to find out more about it,' William protested. 'And there's another matter that needs some explaining on your part too. Before you go you can tell me how you came to have my letter and why you opened it? Lily told me that she'd sent it to my aunt.'

Harry grinned. 'Divine right, boy! She's my wife, and like I said, God and the law are on the side of husbands. Damned bloody clever of your young brother to let on though wasn't it. Recognised her writing!'

'And how did it come to be in your hands anyway?'

Harry smirked. 'Your dear loving aunt couldn't be bothered to make the journey over here. She thought you had some secret love and asked me to deliver it to you. I nearly did at first, was riveted by the thought of you, the holy William Penrose, becoming human at last and in some wench's arms.' His voice was full of sneering sarcasm. 'That was until George opened his big mouth.'

So that was it! William began to put the pieces together. He'd have something to say to George when he saw him next.

'Bloody clever lad, that young George,' Harry repeated.

'Bloody foolish lad,' William said, driven now to swear himself.

'Naughty, naughty.' Harry grinned and went to the door. He pulled it ajar. 'Till we meet again, then,' he said tauntingly, and without a backward glance he was gone, the door slamming behind him so violently that the overcoat which hung upon it jolted to the floor.

William stood staring at the garment, hardly registering it at first so maddened was he. Then he stooped to pick it up and replaced it thoughtfully on its hook. He clenched his fists for a moment, but then his face broke into a small triumphant smile as he wondered what Harry would have said if he had told him about his proposed meeting with Lily next Sunday.

On the following Saturday Augustus Ashe came into the café. It had been an amazing week for Lily, days crammed with conflicting emotions and nights when she couldn't sleep for the warming thoughts that filled her head. She had not seen Augustus for all that time and had occasionally wondered how she was going to excuse herself from the proposed outing with him on Sunday. Would another meeting with her aunt be believable? It sounded extremely suspicious to her. Was there any other story she could concoct?

These thoughts made her feel guilty as usual and she tried to concern herself with other things. How had her letter to her brother fallen into the hands of her husband? Had William found out anything about the divorce laws? Would Harry agree to a divorce?

During the whole week however, these questions, her work and everything else, had taken a subordinate place to the wonderful fact that she was no murderess! She wanted to shout it aloud, tell someone, celebrate, but there was no one to tell, no one in Torquay who knew anything at all of her circumstances.

If the Baileys wondered about the sudden change in Lily, the new buoyant spirits, they said nothing, and she had to content herself with affirming the wonderful truth over and over again alone in her room each night before she slept.

This was partly for pure joy and partly to prevent the old nightmares returning.

Frequently during the day she would cease for a few seconds from the washing up or from the endless baking, her busy hands stilled. And then her heart would lift so that she thought she herself might at any moment take off like the seagulls outside or the swallows who had gone, and glide in effortless flight into a land of magic and fairy-tale.

But these short intervals of euphoria would quickly give way to doubt and then the problems would surface, jostling for precedence. Now on this Saturday afternoon, as Augustus Ashe looked at her, ordered his scones and tea, and smiled, her heart turned right over and she knew that she wanted to be with him, wanted to forget the barriers that lay between them and all the lies she was forced to tell. She longed to confess everything to him, to be Lily Penrose, a real person again with no constraints and difficulties in the way, but equally she knew that she would never do it. Their lives could only touch for a short magical time, a few fairy-tale weeks. As soon as he knew her whole story it would be the end.

'Your scones are as delicious as ever,' he said. Then he lowered his voice for there was an elderly lady seated fairly close. 'And so are you,' he whispered.

It was the first flirtatious thing he had said to her, and she blushed furiously while alarm bells rang in her head. She told herself for the hundredth time that she must not let this get out of hand. Perhaps it was a good thing after all that she had an excuse for tomorrow.

She turned away, trying to ignore the remark, clearing the next table busily.

When she returned to him he smiled at her.

'Forgive me, Miss Smith,' he said quietly. 'That was unforgivable, a great liberty.'

She shook her head, unable to think of any suitable reply. She couldn't tell him that the words were wonderful to hear, just what she needed.

'About tomorrow,' he continued before she could bring herself to utter another word. 'I'm very sorry, but we'll have to postpone our little outing for a time. I have to go away.'

She gasped. Was the Good Lord saving her from her own

grave weakness? If so she ought to be grateful but definitely wasn't.

'That's perfectly all right, Mr Ashe,' she said primly. 'As a matter of fact, I have to go to Exeter again.'

He was silent for a moment and she wished she had said nothing. Why had she mentioned the visit to Exeter? The words had tumbled out without thought.

'How are you going to get there?' he asked.

She brushed a non-existent crumb from his table and looked at him in surprise. 'As I did last week, of course,' she said. 'There's a very good train service.'

'Then you haven't been reading the news.'

She stared at him. What was he talking about? 'No. I'm afraid I'm very ignorant about what's going on in the world. There never seems to be any time. But why should the news affect my journey to Exeter?'

'A rail strike,' he announced. 'Promised for the whole country starting at midnight tonight.'

Her spirits plummeted earthwards. A rail strike of all things! And starting tonight just when her life was complicated enough already! And William couldn't contact her of course. 'Will there be buses?' she asked.

'Some, but not many. I would have taken you but I'm going to Dorset tonight and then I shall be abroad for a time.'

Lily's heart sank even further. Abroad! Where was he going and why? For a moment the difficulties of tomorrow diminished, taking second place to this greater loss. She hoped he wasn't aware of the effect his words had upon her.

'I have an idea,' he said suddenly. 'Duncan visits a nursing home in Exeter every Sunday afternoon. He has a couple of old lady patients there who refuse to see anyone else. Rich, I think, but knowing Duncan I'm sure he doesn't go just for the money. He's a very caring chap as you've probably discovered.'

'Yes, I . . .'

'Shall I ask him to take you? I believe he gets there around three o'clock and stays for an hour or so. I went with him once.'

128

She was taken aback and tried to gather her wits together, to think clearly, to marshal all the facts and make a decision. Would William be able to get to Exeter if there were no trains? She'd have to go anyway in case he managed it. She knew her brother well. His determination could usually achieve for him anything he set his heart upon. Yet if she accepted this lift the doctor would probably discover that there was no aunt in Exeter. He'd be likely to see William and Ivy too. Her secret life would be exposed. But if she refused the offer what excuse could she make? And how would she get to Exeter? Dear God how quickly things changed, how rapidly the problems grew.

'Thank you, Mr Ashe,' she said, abruptly deciding because there was really nothing else that she could do. 'If you could arrange that for me, it would be most kind.'

Chapter Nine

George couldn't forgive himself for what he'd done. *Stupid imbecile, George Penrose*, he told himself. *George Penrose who couldn't use his brain and couldn't keep his mouth shut!*

On that terrible Sunday when Harry had gone to Exeter he had walked the streets for hours wondering what the results of his stupidity would be. He had pictured the scene many times. Lily would be waiting for Will on the station. She'd be excited because they hadn't seen each other for ages. Or perhaps she was in trouble? Maybe she needed help. Was she ill, hungry, destitute?

And thanks to her mindless lunatic brother, who would she see getting off the Bristol train but Harry Coney! A bloomin' ghost! That was what she'd see. She thought she'd killed him with that evil-looking idol. George shivered superstitiously. And there he'd be alive and kicking. Enough to give her the fright of her life. A grinning triumphant Harry Coney!

When Harry had returned neither grinning nor triumphant but drunk and alone late on Sunday evening George had not dared to ask him what had happened. And for the next two days his glowering angry face was enough to deter discussion of any sort.

By the middle of the week George had had enough. He knew what he must do. He must go to William and confess everything whatever the consequences.

His brother received him cordially enough and they talked for a few minutes of ordinary things, but George was pale and trembling, wondering how to broach the subject of Lily, how to confess what he'd done.

Then there was a lull in the conversation and William took a glass biscuit barrel from amongst the accumulation of books and pens on the table and handed it to him. 'I splashed out on some cream biscuits,' he said. 'Have one.'

George shook his head. Biscuits were the last things he wanted just now. They'd probably choke him. 'I've been stupid, Will,' he managed. He stared down at the baize table cloth and studied an elaborately darned hole without really seeing it at all. Then suddenly he realized that William had not reacted as he had expected, hadn't asked what stupid thing he'd been getting up to.

'Yes, it was rather daft,' William said.

George looked at him, first with amazement and then relief. 'You mean ... you know?'

'Oh, yes, I know. Harry came to see me, told me everything.'

'The old devil! He ain't said a dicky bird to me. What happened then when he went to Exeter? You know all about that do you, Will?'

William nodded.

'I'm sorry.' He hung his head. Sorry was so woefully inadequate. 'Can't say how ashamed I am. I'm always blurting things out. I could've cut my tongue out when I'd said that the writing was our Lil's.'

To his surprise William's tone was kind. 'Well, not a lot of harm's done, and perhaps it'll teach you to be more careful next time. It could have been disastrous. Almost was, and Lily had the shock of her life, but it turned out all right in the end, thank goodness.'

George frowned in puzzlement. 'I want to know why she didn't come back though,' he said. He had decided some time ago that there was much more to this whole matter than merely a drunken fit of rage over a book. He'd seen Ivy and Aunt Agnes now and then on a Sunday and they both had a closed up expression on their faces whenever Harry's name was mentioned. Knowing a little of Harry's lecherous appetites for women, George had begun to put two and two together. Until Lily's note had arrived he had managed to keep his horrible suspicions at the back of his mind. But since then they had haunted him and when he thought back to the night he'd found Harry unconscious on the floor he realized that he himself had jumped to the conclusion about the book. Harry had merely taken it up.

But there was still a lot he didn't understand and it was high time he discovered the truth. 'Now that she knows she didn't kill him why doesn't she come home?' he persisted. 'Where is she?'

'I've no idea where she is and there are lots of reasons why she won't come back.'

'What reasons?'

William sighed and indicated to George that he should sit down. 'The marriage wasn't happy,' he said. 'Harry was not the kind considerate husband that Lily deserved or that he might have seemed to outsiders. Perhaps you had your suspicions?'

George nodded. He'd seen Lily's bruises and to his eternal shame had chosen to ignore them. He knew his sister had often been downcast and miserable. Then there were the times he had tried to stop his ears from the noises coming through the wall from the front bedroom. They weren't the happy sounds that he remembered when his parents slept in that room.

He sat down on William's narrow bed and stared at the light bulb that swung in its inadequate glass shade from the centre of the ceiling, stared until, when he closed his eyes, he could see a round shining globe and a multitude of smaller lights dancing in his head. 'Well, I did hear noises through the bedroom wall sometimes,' he said. 'Heard her cry out. It wasn't very nice. I tried not to think about it too much.' He paused and looked back at his brother. Shame was welling up inside him again. Through his own thoughtlessness he'd betrayed his sister horribly, thrown her right back into Harry Coney's arms.

He shuddered again at the thought of his treachery. 'What do you think she'll do?' he murmured.

William ran his fingers round the inside of his stiff unyielding collar. 'She told me that she wants a divorce.'

Amazed, George sat up straight and stared at his brother.

132

'You mean, you've seen her? I thought you didn't know where she was?'

'I saw her last Sunday. She came here. She escaped from Harry in Exeter, jumped on the first train she saw and it happened to be coming to Bristol.'

'Well, of all things! Why do I never get to know nothing? I should've liked to see 'er.' George felt distinctly aggrieved.

'She had to get back quickly. She went from Ashley Hill Station.'

'Where to, for goodness' sake? Did she tell you where she's been holding out all this time?'

'No, she didn't. She doesn't want anyone to find her.'

George shook his head in disbelief. Divorce, running away, mystery whereabouts! He'd never thought it possible that all these things could happen in his family. He felt a sense of loss too for on the whole he liked Harry Coney, didn't want his image dented too much. 'How was our Lil then?' he asked. 'I mean, what did she look like? Got somewhere decent to live, have she?' He found it difficult to come to terms with the idea of his sister living on her own, managing her own life.

William smiled. 'Apart from the shock she'd had that day she seemed very well, nicely dressed too, better than I've ever seen her. She's got a job.'

'Well, I'll be blowed!' The picture that William conjured up for him was vastly different from the one George had imagined. He jumped off the bed. 'I'd best be off,' he said, anxious now to get away. But he was grateful to his brother for putting him in the picture, and his lapse over the letter hadn't had such awful consequences as it might have done. 'Keep me up to date, won't you, Will?' he added. 'I don't like not knowing things.'

William nodded and opened the door for him. 'Will you tell Harry that you've been here?'

George considered. 'Might or might not. There's no harm in anything you've told me, is there? I promised him that I wouldn't let on about Lil's note and him going to Exeter, but since he told you himself it don't matter now.'

'No, I don't suppose it does. Perhaps it's best to say nothing though. Keep mum as they say.'

'Right ho, I will. Learnt my lesson. I'll try to keep me mouth shut from now on.'

As he walked the short distance from the Orphan Homes back along Sefton Road to Harry's house, which was right in the middle of the long avenue, George thought about his brother. He'd often considered William a bit of a namby-pamby but now realized that there was more to him than he had imagined. There was strength of purpose, an iron will as well as kindness. Perhaps after all William was a brother to be proud of, someone who would always be there, a bulwark in any kind of trouble. Lily obviously thought so. He thought of William's unflagging efforts to find her in London, and it was to him that she had fled after her shock last Sunday.

Harry Coney was a different kettle of fish altogether! George reflected on his relationship with his brother-in-law. They got on well enough and enjoyed each other's company in a way, but he didn't really know him at all. He was beginning to see the flaws, to compare Harry with William, and Harry left a lot to be desired!

William arrived at his aunt's house early on the following Sunday morning and gave them the shock of their lives for he was seated at the wheel of a splendid motor car and nothing so grand had ever been seen in the road before. Ivy rushed out to look at it and stood in awed amazement. Her aunt followed and was not so tongue-tied.

'Come into money, have you, William?' she enquired, her voice slightly sour.

He jumped out and smiled at her. 'Borrowed it for the day,' he said. 'It's fifteen horse-power. That means it's as strong as fifteen horses.'

Ivy gasped and stroked the gleaming black paint as though it was indeed the flank of a horse. 'It's lovely, Will,' she said. 'but what'll happen to the horses?'

He laughed. 'We'll always need horses,' he comforted. 'But a horse wouldn't be much good for getting all the way to Exeter, would it?'

Ivy looked at him suspiciously. 'Why are you going to Exeter?'

'I'll give you three guesses.'

'You're not ... It's not to see Lily, is it?'

'Right first time. And you're coming with me!'

Ivy danced round the vehicle in delight and then stood quite still and stared at her brother as the full import of what he had said dawned upon her. 'You mean that you're really going to take me to see Lily today.'

'Yes, today. Can I come in and I'll explain?'

'Why in a motor car?' Agnes asked doubtfully. 'What's wrong with trains and where did you get it from anyway?'

'It belongs to my boss.'

'And why does he trust you with a valuable thing like that?'

'He can't drive. He arranged for me to learn, says it's something an up-and-coming accountant should be able to do. When his chauffeur is busy with something else I take him out to appointments.'

'Best stay in the front room then,' Agnes said. 'You can keep an eye on it from there. You don't want sticky fingers all over it, do you?' She glared at the little boys who had materialized from nowhere and who were staring in amazement at the vehicle. 'Off with you,' she commanded. 'Don't you dare touch.'

William followed her into the house and stood in the bay window that overlooked the road. He peered through the shiny leaves of the aspidistra and the net curtains and rapped on the glass once or twice further to deter the urchins outside.

He wondered how to broach the subject of the letter that Lily had sent care of Agnes. He'd said nothing about it on Monday night or about Harry's disastrous visit to Exeter, preferring to leave those difficult details until he could reveal all he knew. But it was Agnes who mentioned the letter first.

'You'd like a cup of tea, I suppose?' she said. 'And by the way, I've a bone to pick with you, young man.' She stopped in the doorway. 'That letter that came here for you ... I suppose you've got yourself a young lady at last? Well, that's as may be, but how d'you think I'm going to get your post over to you? Sorry and all that but it's too

135

much. It'd be better if you had your secret letters sent care of George or Mr Coney.'

'It was from Lily.'

William's words put a swift end to Agnes's air of aggrieved self-righteousness. Both she and Ivy stared at him in amazed horror. There was a moment's silence as they came to terms with what he had said.

Agnes came to her senses first. 'From Lily! And I put it right into Harry Coney's hands!' She came back into the room and flopped down on one of the hard arm chairs that stood either side of the cheerless hearth. 'What happened?'

William gave an account of all the mishaps, explained now why Lily had arrived so suddenly at his door, and then looked at Ivy. 'And most of all she wants to see you. That's why we're going today.'

'Why didn't you tell us all this before?'

'I didn't want Harry to know about today.'

'We wouldn't have said.' It was Ivy's turn now to sound aggrieved.

'I had to be quite sure. Last Sunday was bad enough for Lily. I couldn't risk it happening again.'

Agnes looked chastened. 'No, of course not. And it was all my fault.'

'What's done is done, and things haven't turned out so bad after all.' William smiled at them both. 'And now what about that cup of tea and a few sandwiches to take with us, Aunt?'

Agnes hurried out to do his bidding and to compensate a little for her foolishness.

'We could have gone on the train,' Ivy said. Motor cars were exciting but quite out of her experience.

'There's a train strike.'

Ivy gaped at him. She remembered hearing the paper boy calling out something about no trains running but she hadn't bothered to listen to any details. After all trains usually had nothing to do with her either.

Lily had a number of misgivings about the journey to Exeter. Until yesterday, when Mr Ashe had told her about the rail strike, she had been looking forward to it greatly, but now all her plans were in disarray. She had no idea whether William and Ivy would be able to make the journey. And she was nervous about going in Dr MacMullen's motor car.

'He's very easy to get on with as I expect you know,' Augustus had said to her the previous evening. 'No need to be anxious.'

He had called to see her again after the café was closed, and she had unlocked the front door and stood just inside the empty shop, embarrassed, wondering what the Baileys would think about this unexpected visit.

'You'll like Duncan even better when you get to know him. Other than as a doctor, I mean,' he had continued, and then he had smiled. 'Not too much though, I hope.' He had leaned towards her and Lily had drawn back, almost expecting him to embrace her, but he hesitated and also took a step backwards. 'I am leaving at first light tomorrow,' he said. 'May I write to you?'

Was there harm in writing letters? Lily considered for a moment and then decided that surely there was not. She had never had anyone to correspond with before but she had always enjoyed writing essays at school and the teacher had often said that she had a gift. Sometimes she had thought of trying to find a pen friend.

She nodded. 'I should like that. How long will you be away?'

She noticed a melancholy expression sweep over his face. 'I'm not sure. I have to go to my home in Dorset and then to Switzerland.'

She gasped. Switzerland! A magical place of great mountains even higher than those in Scotland, she thought, and there was a lot of snow and cows with bells. There had been a calendar once on the wall at home and every month showed another astonishing view. 'Perhaps you could send me a postcard,' she said. 'It's beautiful, I believe.'

'Yes, very beautiful, and you shall have a multitude of cards.'

There was silence between them, the only sound the lapping of the sea against the harbour wall outside and the call of an occasional gull in the darkening sky.

'I shall miss this place,' Augustus said, his eyes sweeping the bay beyond the open door. 'I've come to like Torquay very much. I sometimes think that I prefer it to my home. And I shall miss you, Lilian. May I call you Lilian now?'

'Of course,' she said, but felt dismayed for his words implied a much longer stay then she had imagined. There must be some important reason but she couldn't think what it might be.

'And I shall be Augustus to you from now on,' he declared, and held out his hand to her. 'So it's goodbye for a while.'

She put her hand in his and his grasp was firm and unbearably sweet. She wanted to throw her arms around him, keep him here for ever, tell him that he mustn't leave her, but she merely whispered, 'Goodbye, Augustus,' and her voice was prim and formal with no trace of the emotion she felt.

Then he was gone and she could feel the hot bitter tears on her cheeks and realized yet again that she loved this completely unattainable man.

The next morning was bright and sunny and Lily rose early. There was a lot to be done before church, but the sunshine today had no power to dispel the empty feeling in her heart. The shop next-door was to be looked after by Michael Dyer, the young man whom Augustus said was a friend from the army and who lived in the flat at the back.

When she walked past the bookshop with the Baileys on her way to church Lily couldn't help glancing up at the windows above, for it was there that Augustus had his own apartments. There were no lace curtains obscuring the view. He had told her that he liked to watch the sea in all its varied moods unhampered by drapes of any kind. But now Lily thought that the windows had an empty look about them. Then she glanced away across the lovely expanse of the bay and told herself not to be so stupid. The windows were just the same as before. She must forget about Augustus Ashe and get on with her life. But even as she formed the words in her mind she was planning what she would say to him when she wrote that first letter!

After the service, as she moved slowly with the other members of the congregation towards the church porch, she saw the young doctor just ahead. He paused outside and she noticed that he had a smile and a word for many of the people. Perhaps he was becoming more acceptable to his patients now, his foreignness and his lovely voice not the barriers that they had been at first. She had discovered that he came from the Highlands and had found a book and read that this meant a special part of Scotland where the mountains were wild and where the men wore kilts. She glanced at the doctor for a moment and wondered if he too ever wore such an outlandish garment.

'Morning, Doctor,' Gladys Bailey said when they reached him.

He shook her hand. 'Good morning, Mrs Bailey. You look very well today.'

'Can't grumble,' she muttered.

Lily smiled shyly at him and he took her hand in his. It was a firm grasp, warm and almost painful in its strength. For a moment it reminded her of Harry Coney's and she recalled the gentle feel of Augustus's fingers the first time they had met. She knew that it was the contrast with Harry that had attracted her to Augustus Ashe. She wanted no more of masculine power and strength.

But Duncan was smiling back at her and he held her hand a moment longer than was strictly necessary. 'Miss Smith,' he said. 'You're coming to Exeter with me this afternoon, I believe?'

She smiled. 'Thank you. I'm very grateful.'

'It'll be a pleasure. I shall pick you up at half-past two then if that is satisfactory?'

She looked round nervously, wondering who had heard and what they would think. Until recently girls had been chaperoned, and motor-car rides with strange young men were frowned upon. But she supposed that because he was a doctor it was all right! Gladys Bailey anyway had given her approval.

'Perfectly satisfactory,' she replied.

After lunch was finished and the washing up done Lily went

to her room to get ready. She put on her new suit, chose her hat carefully, added gloves and shoes to match and then went down to the café to wait.

Gladys looked her up and down as always. 'Pity 'tis only your aunt you'm going to see and not a young man. Them smart clothes wants a bit of appreciation. Still, p'raps the doctor'll like what he sees.'

In spite of her misgivings about the journey Lily wanted to laugh, for Mrs Bailey was certainly curious about the whole outing. She had been probing for more information ever since the arrangements were made.

'Doctor MacMullen is just helping me out because of the train strike. He's not likely to notice how I look.'

'That's as may be.' There was disbelief in her voice, and Lily thought that she could detect a trace of amusement on the older woman's face too. 'But be sure to get back earlier than last time, mind,' Gladys continued severely. 'Gave us a proper fright you did, coming home only just before midnight. Us thought you'd come to a bad end. Good of the doctor to take you anyway. I don't suppose you can come to no harm with the likes of him, a proper gentleman and all.'

'No, I don't suppose I can,' Lily said.

Duncan was dressed in a light tweed suit and wore a motoring cap and plus-fours. Lily thought that he looked even more handsome and rugged than when he was on his daily visits. She felt intimidated and wished that it was Augustus who was driving her today. She realized that years ago, before Harry Coney, she would have been greatly attracted to a man like Duncan MacMullen. but now his very masculinity was frightening. It threatened her.

He opened the car door for her.

'I'm glad to have such a charming and youthful companion today,' he said as he handed her in. 'The ladies I visit on Sunday afternoons are very old – pleasant and interesting, but old.' He put a blanket across her knees, slammed the door and climbed into the driving seat. 'Do you enjoy motoring, Miss Smith?'

'This is my first time.'

He turned to look at her. 'Really? Then I shall drive with great care.'

'I'm not scared,' she said trying to believe it. 'Mr Ashe asked me to go for a short ride with him last weekened, but I wasn't free.'

'His motor is much more splendid than mine.'

'Any motor car is splendid to me,' she said, and then realized that in spite of her fears, conversation was not so difficult after all. After the first ten minutes her main worries were whether William and Ivy had been able to find some alternative transport to Exeter, and if they had, whether they would be there when she arrived and so would meet Duncan MacMullen. She had gone over all the possibilities in her mind during the past sleepless night but had been unable to find any solution. Her blood ran cold again at the thought. She wanted no difficult questions asked, no possibility of exposure. She wasn't ready to renounce Lilian Smith just yet.

William and Ivy were standing beside a gleaming black motor car which was parked close to the station entrance when Duncan MacMullen's smaller Austin pulled up behind it. Lily took one look at her sister and her misgivings temporarily vanished. She had been longing for this moment for so long that nothing mattered now except their reunion. She jumped from the car and held out her arms to Ivy.

'Lil, oh, Lil!' Ivy whispered when she was released from the long embrace. 'You're all right then? We was so worried about you.' Then she pulled herself away, stepped back, and Lily could feel her sister's astonished gaze travelling over her fashionable clothes and general air of prosperity. 'You look so grand.'

Lily smiled and turned to Duncan MacMullen who had been watching in some perplexity. 'My brother William,' she said, 'and my little sister Ivy.'

Duncan showed no surprise. He merely stepped forward and shook hands with both of them. 'I'm very pleased to meet you, Ivy and Mr Smith,' he said politely. Then he turned to Lily. 'I shall have finished my visiting by four o'clock. I could meet you here just after if that would be convenient?'

'Very convenient. Thank you very much,' Lily said. She was covered with confusion over the title he had given William, frantic lest Ivy should exclaim that it was the wrong name.

'Then I'll leave you and go and make pleasant conversation with my old ladies,' he said, smiling. 'Goodbye for now.'

He had left the engine running noisily and so was able to drive quickly away.

They all watched the vehicle as it rounded the corner. Predictably Ivy was the first to speak. 'Why did he call Will "Mr Smith", and who is he anyway?' she demanded.

'He brought me over in his motor car,' Lily said. 'Because of the strike. That's all. He's a doctor.'

'We were worried about how you'd get here with no trains running,' William said. 'It was kind of him.'

Was there a trace of enquiry in her brother's voice? Lily wondered. No need of course. Now if it had been Augustus who had brought her ... she blushed and realized that in spite of her earlier wishes it was extremely providential that it was not. William was perceptive. He might just have guessed at her feelings and he would have been horrified. Rightly so.

'He looked nice,' Ivy commented. 'Fancy you being in with a doctor.'

'I'm not *in with him*,' Lily said. 'He was just helping me out of a difficulty. I don't know him very well.' She tried to banish Duncan MacMullen and the problems he posed from her mind for this precious moment. 'Gosh, Ivy, it's just wonderful to see you,' she said, staring at her sister as though she was not quite real, as though she might disappear at any moment, and then the two sisters hugged each other again. She could feel tears on her cheeks mingling with Ivy's. Duncan MacMullen and the problems he posed were momentarily forgotten.

'Aunt Agnes gave us some sandwiches and a flask of tea,' Ivy said suddenly, pulling out of the embrace and breaking the tension. 'I'm starving. Let's find somewhere to picnic and then we can tell you all our news and you can tell us yours.'

Lily brushed her tears away and laughed in delight at the sudden reappearance of the old Ivy she knew so well, and for an instant she felt completely happy and carefree for the first time in many weeks. No further mention was made of her providential lift.

They found a small woody place near the river and William brought out rugs and and the basket of food and when they were settled and had eaten there was so much to say that they looked at each other wondering where to begin, what of all the mysteries must be told first.

Lily explained about her identity, her false name, for that couldn't be a secret now. She still refused to tell them where she was living for she feared that somehow Harry Coney might discover the information. If they were ignorant nothing could be given away by accident. 'Perhaps I shall tell you one day soon, William,' she said. 'But not yet. I'm too scared of him finding me. All communication must come from me.'

'A divorce is going to be difficult,' William told her later when almost everything else had been said. 'The law is unfair to women. Husband's can't be divorced for adultery although women can. It could be for desertion but then you would be the guilty party. The whole horrid business would be dragged through the courts, your name would be mud. You couldn't defend yourself unless you went into details about everything.'

'And I would never do that.' Lily started to pack the remains of their picnic into the basket. No shame must be brought on her family. It would ruin William's career and destroy Ivy's hopes of a good marriage, and might even prejudice George's hopes of working with Harry in the coal business.

'So I'll have to stay married to him.'

William brushed bits of grass from the rug and folded it carefully. 'Not necessarily. I'm still making enquiries.'

'One course remains open to me.'

'What's that?' William placed the rug on the back seat of the car.

'Adultery!'

His face went quite scarlet. 'I didn't hear you say that,

Lily.' he declared. He busied himself loading the car and she smiled to herself. How much their paths had diverged during the past months. It was she now who was the strong one, the worldly one. William had so little experience of life. But she loved him. The bond between them was as important as ever.

Ivy had been silent throughout this latter conversation. She had looked from brother to sister understanding much more than either realized. Adultery! They thought she didn't know what it meant, but of course she did. It was in the Bible. 'Thou shalt not commit adultery!' She'd had to learn the commandments by heart years ago and had soon discovered what this particular one meant. It was obvious from various bits and pieces she'd overheard that a lot of men were guilty of it and now she'd just heard from her brother that the law said it was all right for them but not for women.

She was thoughtful as she helped carry the rugs to the motor car. William had said that it wasn't fair, but it was worse than that. It was quite monstrous. She couldn't bear to keep quiet any longer.

'That's terrible,' she said. She glared at her brother as if he was personally responsible.

Lily looked at her in surprise. 'What's terrible?'

'About the adultery,' Ivy continued. 'That your old Harry Coney can go off down to Old Market Street as many times as he likes and it ain't wrong.'

Lily was deeply shocked. What did Ivy know about Old Market Street and things that went on there?

'You think I don't know nothing.' Ivy's voice was aggrieved now. 'Well, I do. I got a friend at school who knows everything about everything and she tells us lots.' She dumped the tablecloth that she had folded behind the driver's seat.

'Then you mustn't repeat it.' Lily's voice was severe. 'Talking about that kind of filth is wrong.'

'Not as wrong as doing it,' Ivy said. 'And he does it, three or four times a week.'

'How d'you know that?'

'I hear things. Aunt Agnes talks to old Ma Baker and one or two of her other cronies. I listen to 'em.'

144

'Then you should be ashamed of yourself.'

Ivy grinned. 'But ain't you glad to know?'

'No, I'm not,' Lily said. 'Not glad at all.'

'Do you want to know something else?' Ivy climbed into the back seat and looked mischievously at her sister.

'No.' Lily said at first, then, 'Well, what?'

'He did it while you was still living with him. That's where he went sometimes.'

Lily had known about this, but had preferred to keep the unwelcome knowledge buried deep, never openly acknowledged. That her little sister had been aware of all those odious things was so appalling she felt personally degraded. Obviously she must reverse some of her ideas about Ivy. She was no longer little, no longer innocent. She knew far more than Lily herself had done at twelve years old, more than she'd known at eighteen for that matter! She got into the passenger seat and stared straight ahead.

William was busy cranking the engine. He'd removed himself during this conversation and Lily wondered how much he had heard. She wondered also how to deal with this precocious child.

'I think you know too much, Ivy,' she said, making an effort to sound kind. 'But let it be a help to you. With all that knowledge you should be able to manage your life. I was too innocent and that's just as bad. You know what happens to girls at about your age, I suppose?'

'Yes, I know. Aunt Agnes told me as a matter of fact. Proper embarrassed I was. She gave me cloths, told me what to do. I know about babies too.'

Lily sighed and for a moment wished that Ivy had been a boy. Life was so much less complicated for men. Then she thought of Arthur, of the trenches. Perhaps very occasionally women had the better part!

'Are you going to do it, Lil?'

'Do what?'

'You know. What you said. Commit adultery?'

Lily swivelled round in her seat and stared at Ivy. She was ashamed that she had so foolishly mentioned the idea. Goodness, did the child really think she had meant it? 'No,

Ivy,' she said. 'I have no intention at all of doing that, even to get away from Harry.'

'That's good,' Ivy said self-righteously. 'It's a sin. It's in the Bible. I knew you wouldn't really, Lil.'

At that moment the engine chugged into life and William clambered into the driving seat and smiled at both of them as if he'd heard nothing. Lily sincerely hoped that he hadn't.

'Ready then?' he said, and they drove back onto the lane that led to the main road, back to Exeter and their separate lives and to Lily's continuing problems, for nothing had been decided, no course of action determined. For how long was she to remain Lilian Smith, a non-person? Should she become Mrs Lily Coney once more, a runaway wife, waiting for a divorce because she had deserted her husband?

There was just one thing of which she was quite certain however. Even if legally she bore his name, she would never return to Harry Coney.

At the station William jumped out and held the door for her. 'There must be a way,' he said. 'I'll try to come up with something. When shall I see you again?'

'Can I write to you at the orphanage?'

'Yes. It's the safest way. I'm hoping to get a room or lodgings somewhere as a matter of fact, but I won't move until we've met next time and I can let you know. Are you quite sure you won't tell me where you're living. I should feel happier if I knew.'

'Absolutely certain, William. It's my only security. I know I can trust you but I should feel vulnerable.'

'It's me you don't trust, ain't it?' Ivy said, aggrieved. She got out of the car and stood looking at Lily. 'You think I'll let on? Well, I never will, honest. I hate that old black-face Coney. You oughta trust me, Lil.'

'Perhaps next time,' she said, and put her arms around her sister and hugged her yet again. 'Be good, and remember that I love you. Everything will come right in the end.'

Ivy sniffed. 'I wish you'd never married him. I'm not going to get married. Men's all the same if you ask me.'

'No they're not.' The smiling intelligent face of Augustus Ashe swam before Lily's eyes, increasing her sadness. 'Just be careful and pick the right one, that's all.'

146

'But you can't tell till you'm, married. It's then that the rot sets in.'

Lily was amused at her sister's perception but it made her feel depressed too. She forced a smile. 'That's not always true either. Think of your brother.'

'William or George?' Ivy glanced at William mischievously.

'Both of them,' Lily replied. 'They're both good.'

'They're not married yet though, are they!'

William laughed, lightening the mood of all three. Pessimism gave way briefly to hope, and at that moment Duncan MacMullen pulled up a little way behind them and waved.

Lily kissed her brother and sister, watched them drive away and then turned to Duncan. He had remained in his motor car until they had left. Now he climbed out and stood waiting for her.

'You need not have rushed,' he said. 'I'm sorry you couldn't have had longer.' He walked round to the other side of the vehicle and opened the door for her. 'Ready then?'

He drove slowly out of the town and they said very little at first. Lily had no idea how to explain the existence of William and Ivy. 'Did Mr Ashe tell you why I wished to go to Exeter?' she began tentatively.

'He merely said that you wanted to see your aunt.'

Doubt hung uncomfortably in the air between them.

'He doesn't know I have a brother and sister.'

There was still a difficult silence and then Duncan glanced quickly at her and back at the empty road. 'Do you want to tell me?'

Lily longed to tell, longed to confess everything to another human being. 'You're a doctor,' she said. 'You must hear a lot of things. And doctors never tell, do they? I mean, whatever they hear is private and safe, isn't it?'

'Perfectly safe. I listen, try to help when I can, but yes, you're right of course. Doctors have to be as silent as priests about the things they are told.'

'But I'm not your patient.'

'It makes no difference.'

'Would you listen to me, Dr MacMullen?'

His driving didn't falter and if he was surprised he gave

147

no sign. 'Do you want me to stop, to pull in somewhere?'

Lily shook her head. 'No, thank you. I should like to tell you about what has happened to me while we are driving if that's all right?'

'Certainly.'

She was silent for a while and then, with hands tightly clenched in her lap, and in a trembling voice, she started to tell her story. She began with Arthur, his needless death in the trenches, her mother's illness and death and, swiftly following that, her own disastrous marriage. She even told something of her suffering at Harry's hands and then his attempted rape of her sister, her fears that she had killed him, her terror of the gallows, the relief when she knew that he was alive, only to be followed by the fear of returning to him. She told of her false identity here in Devon, her friendship with Augustus Ashe, their shared love of books, and how the contrast between his gentleness and Harry's coarse and violent nature made Mr Ashe so attractive to her. She ended with her pleasure in the success she had made of her job.

When she had finished she was silent again and exhausted but strangely at peace, for the telling had released a great tide of emotion, leaving tranquillity in her heart like the calm that comes sometimes after a fierce storm at sea.

There were few motor cars on the quiet Sunday afternoon road and Duncan drove slowly. 'Thank you for trusting me,' he said at last. 'Rest assured that everything you've said is quite safe with me. It's an amazing story, and very sad. I'll do everything in my power to help you, Miss ...' he paused. 'What do you wish me to call you?'

'Not Miss Smith and not Lily either, not yet anyway. Will Lilian do?'

'Lilian it shall be,' he said. 'For now.' He turned and smiled at her and she felt for the first time for weeks that she was actually glad to take advantage of a little masculine strength.

'What should I do?' she whispered.

'Are you asking me for my opinion, my advice?'

'Yes, I suppose I am.'

'Do you want me to speak to you professionally or as a friend?'

'Both, I think. Is there a difference?'

'Perhaps. Many people disapprove strongly of divorce, of course, but I think that in some cases it shouldn't be ruled out. For the moment perhaps it would be best if you do nothing. Your husband could divorce you for desertion eventually. That's probably what he'll want to do and your name wouldn't be dragged in the mud too much.'

'What about my lies, my assumed name?'

'That's more difficult. Maybe you should tell Mr and Mrs Bailey.'

'And lose my job?'

'That wouldn't necessarily happen.'

'I'll think about it.'

'There's one other thing.'

Lily looked at him in surprise. 'Yes?'

It was a while before he replied and she saw his hands tighten on the steering wheel, felt his anxiety, his reluctance to continue. 'What else is there? Please don't leave me wondering, Dr MacMullen.'

Again there was a silence between them and she was suddenly afraid again. What further calamity, what other possible trouble was in his mind?

Eventually he spoke again. 'It's Mr Ashe. Be careful. You're not free, but that's not the only thing. He too has some secrets.'

'What do you mean?' She immediately thought of his house in Dorset and the stay in Switzerland. 'Do you know why he has gone away?'

Her companion nodded slowly. 'Yes, I know, but like your own secrets I can't divulge any of his reasons.'

'Has he ... has he a wife somewhere?'

To her surprise Duncan laughed. 'Well, I can set your mind at rest on that score. No. He has no wife.'

'Then why ...?'

'I can't say anything more than that. Please don't ask me, Lilian. I like and respect Augustus very much indeed and we are good friends. I don't want either of you hurt.'

149

Chapter Ten

To her surprise Lily found that her life changed very little over the following weeks in spite of everything that had happened. As far as she knew Harry was making no efforts to find her and little progress had been made in the matter of the divorce. She was sometimes uneasy about this state of affairs and had once or twice considered going back to Bristol, confronting Harry and telling him firmly that she was impatient and wanted to be free as soon as possible. So far however she had taken William's advice to wait a little longer. She was moderately content but felt that she was living in some sort of limbo and occasionally she tired of being Lilian Smith.

On the last day of the year the café had been busy and they were to open for an hour just before midnight. 'After all,' Reginald Bailey had surprisingly said, ''tis special, the end of more'n just a year.'

When she heard the church bells ringing out over the quiet town Lily felt a tingle of excitement. Perhaps they would signal a fresh start for her. Maybe 1920 would be her wonderful year at last.

'The twenties,' Gladys Bailey said. 'I wonder what they'll bring for all of us?'

Several neighbours and friends, seeing the lights flickering cheerfully from the window, came to join in the singing of 'Auld Lang Syne' and to wish each other good health and happiness. The Baileys disapproved of too much alcohol but the rules were relaxed a little for tonight and they had suggested that Lily should lay in some beer. There were ample supplies of lemonade and even tea, coffee, and a tray of cakes and scones.

Lily thought of past years as she greeted and served their customers. Her parents had never made much of this festival. Sometimes there had been a watch night service, but during the war her mother had mostly just gone to bed. She remembered sometimes being awake and hearing a few revellers in the street below, but few people in Bristol marked the passing of the old year and the coming of the new. Not many had expected to have much to rejoice over during those four awful years of war. Christmas, just a few days before, was always more important. Things were more hopeful now of course, but few families had enough money to celebrate twice.

She wondered what her brothers and sister were doing. Ivy was probably hanging out of her window, listening to the chimes of midnight and hoping for some signs of life while Aunt Agnes snored peacefully in the next room. George was no doubt enjoying himself noisily with some friends now that the restrictions laid upon him by his parents and brother were ended. And William? She smiled fondly as she thought of William. He was certainly at a service in the chapel, dedicating himself afresh to his God for the coming year. She wished that she could feel so sure of the Almighty as her twin. When finally her thoughts turned to Harry she shivered. She had few doubts about his whereabouts at this moment!

She was thinking of all this when the door opened and Duncan MacMullen burst in. He was resplendent in a kilt and tweed jacket. Everyone looked at him in amazement and he laughed and walked over to Lily, bowed and presented her with a large nub of coal and a piece of shortbread, the latter wrapped in greaseproof paper.

'Hogmanay,' he told her. 'In Scotland New Year is important. Any tall dark young man should go around with this.' He indicated the gifts he had brought and which she was now holding gingerly in her hands. 'We call it first-footing.'

Lily laughed. 'Whatever for? They seem odd presents.' She made no mention of his unusual attire.

151

'To bring good luck, prosperity and good fortune in the coming year,' he said. 'And as this is the start of a new epoch, I think it's work celebrating.'

'Sit yourself down, Sir,' Reginald Bailey said. 'Lily, fetch the doctor a glass of home made wine. 'Tis better than that beer you've bought, more like whisky.'

She laughed and doubted if he had ever tasted whisky. She fetched a bottle of the precious and seldom used elderberry wine. It had not been on display but she guessed that the Baileys felt so highly honoured by this visit that the wine might now flow freely. She brought glasses, special ones that were seldom used, dusted them and poured a little in each.

'Alcohol once a year, that's my rule,' Reginald said, but Lily noticed that he was grinning at Duncan.

She filled Duncan's glass almost to the brim and he smiled and held it up to the light. 'It looks grand,' he said. 'A very happy New Year to all of you, and peace. No more wars!'

'Peace.' The word echoed round the room and Lily knew that everyone present had lost someone in the war.

Duncan drained the glass swiftly. 'The first footer has privileges,' he said. He strode over to Gladys Bailey, bowed, and kissed her wrinkled cheek. Lily was startled and then amused as she saw the quick flush that sprang to the old woman's face and the obvious pleasure. Gloomy thoughts gave way to laughter.

He then proceeded to kiss the other ladies present, finishing with Lily. For her there was a quick kiss on the forehead and an enthusiastic hug, an embrace which reminded her, thankfully, not of Harry Coney's strength but somehow of Arthur and of long ago. For a second she was overcome with nostalgia and a longing for all that might have been.

'No sadness tonight,' Duncan said, looking at her percep-tively. 'This is the beginning of the twenties, of hope and a new future for all of us.'

She remembered that she had told him a lot about herself. He was the only one here who knew the painful story of her past. In fact he knew more than anyone, even her brother. The thought unsettled her for a moment but she looked into his eyes and was certain that she could trust him with her secrets. There was a robustness about him that gave her confidence. But there was something else too. Was it a special concern just for her that she saw? No, of course not. He was a doctor. He cared for the wellbeing of all his patients. She wasn't exactly a patient for she had never been ill but if she was ...

After they had all gone home and Gladys and Reginald had gone wearily to bed, Lily looked at the accumulated chaos of her normally immaculate little café. She would make an exception tonight and leave it all for now. They were opening later than usual in the morning. She would clear up then. She stood quite still for a few moments, listening to the sea worrying at the harbour wall for the wind was rising and she thought of Augustus Ashe. He was far away, quite unattainable, and yet he was the one person she wanted at her side during the coming year – a hopeless impossible dream!

She put her hand on the place where Duncan MacMullen had kissed her and wondered about the curious thing that he had said of Augustus. *Mr Ashe has secrets too.* She had tried to shrug it off or at least believe that it was something unimportant, but it worried her nevertheless. She bolted the door and went upstairs to her room, her mind filled with unanswered questions. The coming of the new year had brought everything into fresh focus. Before she got into bed she stared out of the window at the moon which was shining now for a moment between the angry clouds. There were lights on the distant headland and she thought of all the families there, all wondering what the twenties, as Gladys had called the next ten years, would bring.

As she thought of Augustus she longed for him, for his calm wisdom and his gentleness. She wished that he had been the recipient of all her secrets rather than the vigorous and disturbing Duncan MacMullen.

By the end of February nothing in her life was any clearer, no decisions made. Augustus had sent her postcards, ten so far. Each one was so beautiful that she couldn't imagine any place so magical as this Switzerland to which he had mysteriously gone. She dreamed about it often, both awake and asleep. It was a fantasy world which had no part in her day-to-day life. Augustus always figured in the dreams, and she felt guilty when she thought about it seriously, for both the place and the man could never be anything more to her than just an illusion of impossible bliss.

He wrote no letters, only greetings and short messages on the back of the cards. She had been disappointed at first, wanting to hear what he was doing, how he was, whom he was with. But there was no information. It was all a mystery, and her own letters to him therefore had to be short and stilted for she remembered her mother's instructions, that no girl should seem too keen, should never allow her true feelings to show.

The news which intrigued her most came from Bristol. She had seen William once in January and he still cautioned her to wait. He was sure that the first move in divorce proceedings would come from Harry for he had a new attachment, an older woman called Dot, buxom and homely, the woman who came in to clean and cook for him and George. The information had come to William from George who, although he knew it wasn't quite right, approved on the whole. He'd told his brother that he quite liked her in fact and if it made things better for Lil he supposed that it was all for the best.

Lily had been glad to hear about the agreeable Dot. She was surprised that such a person should attract Harry, and even more amazed that any woman could be persuaded to share his bed, yet she acknowledged thankfully that if her husband settled down with someone who suited him he wouldn't be a threat any more, either to herself or to Ivy. All she wanted was to be rid of him for ever.

Agnes Penrose too was relieved to hear about Harry Coney's new lady friend. In spite of her strong disapproval of the immorality of it she had to admit that everything might now be easier all round. It meant of course that Lily was probably never going to come home to live again, and so she'd be stuck with Ivy for a long time, probably until the girl grew up and got married in the distant future.

The more she thought about this however the more she came to think that it was perhaps a good thing on the whole. She had become used to the child and from time to time she even wondered how she'd managed to live all those years alone.

There was another thing too. Ivy liked animals and so did Agnes. It made a bond between them. Her old dog had died two years ago, and before Ivy came those months had been especially lonely. Perhaps one day there would be another dog.

It was in the middle of March therefore that Ivy had the surprise of her life. When she arrived home from school one day Agnes indicated a box beside the fire.

'What do you think of that then?' she said.

Ivy took one look at the puppy curled on a blanket fast asleep and glanced at her aunt with complete incomprehension.

'It's a puppy.'

'Of course it's a puppy.'

'Who does it belong to?' Ivy couldn't believe that her fussy house-proud aunt would want another dog, especially a young one.

'You, if you want her.'

Ivy took another look, drew in her breath. 'Do you really mean it?'

'I don't say things I don't mean.'

'I can keep her?'

'Don't go on so, child. Yes, you can keep her if you'll look after her properly.'

Ivy hurled herself at her aunt, threw her arms around her and hugged her tightly. 'I've wanted a dog all my life.'

Agnes returned the hug with obvious embarrassment. Then she pulled herself away. 'She's just waking up. You must take her out on to the grass. The first thing she must learn is to be clean.'

Ivy lifted the little animal from the cardboard box and cradled her in her arms. 'She's the most wonderful present I've ever had.'

'What are you going to call her?'

'I don't know yet. It ought to be something special.' She

studied the puppy gravely. 'She has a black spot on her head, but Spot is much too common.'

'Well, you'll have to decide quickly because she must learn to come when she's called. No disobedient creatures here if you please.'

Ivy was still considering the choice of a name two days later when one of Harry Coney's horses died.

'Which one?' she asked in a horrified voice when she came home from school and heard the news.

'Jane,' Agnes told her. 'Just collapsed in the shafts. Sudden it was and she didn't suffer, so no need for tears.'

'What'll poor Flo do now?' Ivy asked disconsolately. 'They've been together for years and years.'

'He'll get rid of her I shouldn't wonder. I've heard that he wants to get motor lorries. They're more up to date.'

Ivy dumped her satchel down on the table, played with her excited puppy for a few moments, and then stood up, the dog in her arms. 'But that's terrible, Aunt Agnes. Flo will be so miserable. She doesn't know nothing else but the coal yard. And they might be cruel to her, and she's old.'

Agnes sniffed. No need to mince matters she thought. The child had to learn that life was no bed of roses for man or beast.

'The knacker's yard, that's where she'll go, I've no doubt,' she said, trying to make her voice sound harder than she felt. 'She's too old to have another place now.'

'Oh, no! They can't do that to poor old Flo.' Ivy took the puppy outside and placed her on the grass, then came in again and took off her coat and threw it on top of her satchel. 'That's too cruel.'

'Put your things away, miss,' Agnes admonished. 'The end of a horse is no reason to forget all the good behaviour I've taught you.' She gathered up the offending possessions and held them out to Ivy. 'All things considered, the knacker's yard's the best place for an old horse. Quick and easy death, and she's had a good life. Say what you like about that Harry Coney, in spite of all his faults he isn't cruel to his beasts. He always sees they've got a warm stable and plenty of good hay

156

and as far as I know he never overworked poor old Jane. Many's the time I've heard him talking to one or the other quite kindly and I've seen him give them sugar lumps now and then. That's the one good thing about the man.'

Ivy shivered, but she had to acknowledge that her aunt was probably right about the horses. She'd never seen him do anything unkind and she'd often noticed that he frequently had an affectionate word for whichever horse he had between the shafts.

'Then he won't send Flo to the murderer?' This was her name for the unfortunate knacker.

Agnes laughed grimly at her, and when the coat was on its rightful hook on the hall-stand and the satchel likewise she brought a tray of little cakes out of the oven. 'He may be kind to animals,' she said, 'but he's a businessman. He'll not spend anything on unnecessary extravagances.'

'What d'you mean?'

'Keeping an animal that's outgrown its usefulness, that's an extravagance.' Agnes glanced down at the puppy who had just gambolled in from the garden. 'I hope she's done what she was put out for,' she said. 'We don't want any puddles.'

'Yes, she has,' Ivy said. 'She's learning fast.'

'Decided on a name yet?' Agnes said as she poured two cups of tea. 'If you haven't thought of one by tonight it'll just have to be Spot.'

Suddenly Ivy had an idea. 'Jane,' she said when she returned. 'I shall call her Jane after Harry's old horse.'

Nothing more was said about the possible end of the other great shire horse but all that evening Ivy was quiet and thoughtful, and when she went to bed she spent a long time lying awake trying to think of a plan. Flo must definitely not end up as meat for pet dogs, or even worse, go to France where the natives actually ate horse flesh! She was determined that she'd do something to prevent it even if it meant bearding that awful man in his den all on her own.

No opportunity presented itself however and at the end of the week she noticed that Flo was out every morning plodding along with her cart just as if nothing had happened to her lifelong companion. It set her mind at rest a little.

William told Lily about the new puppy when they next met in April. She was relieved to have some pleasant news at last and to know that her sister was relatively happy.

'Fancy Aunt Agnes allowing her to have a dog!' she said. 'She always wanted one, but Father said that they were dirty and a waste of money.'

'Well, I suppose some people think they are.' William shrugged. 'But for Ivy this puppy has been a god-send. It's given her an interest, made her think of something other than you and Harry Coney and all the horrors of life.'

Lily laughed. 'Aren't you over-dramatizing a bit?'

'Yes, I suppose I am?'

They were walking through the Exeter streets near the station. Having no excuse as before William had not been able to borrow the motor car again. The train had to do.

'So,' Lily said, 'you've told me all about Ivy and Aunt Agnes. What about Harry? Is he any nearer divorcing me?'

'You haven't been separated long enough.'

Lily sighed. 'I'm so impatient to be free of him, William. Are you sure there's no other way?'

'Not if you want to come out of it relatively unscathed. But you seem to be happy. Does the length of time matter so much?'

She was silent, wondering how to answer. Her false identity sometimes weighed very heavily upon her and she longed to cast off the past like an old skin. She had thought about it so much, and knew that whatever happened there would be difficulties ahead. A divorced woman was nearly always despised by everyone whatever the circumstances of the divorce. Would the Baileys keep her on? Perhaps she would be thrown out of house and job. And Augustus? She expected that he would react quite unfavourably, for no man wanted soiled goods. That was how she thought of herself, soiled for ever by Harry.

'You haven't answered,' William prompted. 'Are you in so much of a hurry?'

'Of course I am. He might change his mind, come looking for me, force me to go back. It's a nightmare. I want to be free of him, to forget him for ever.'

'I don't think you need worry too much about that,'

William said. 'I get all the inside information from George and he assures me that Harry and this Dot are living together now just as if they're man and wife.'

'What kind of woman is she?'

'Buxom, homely, about fortyish, a good cook and an excellent housekeeper. That's what George says.'

'I can't understand it. Does Harry still go off to Old Market Street?' Lily blushed as she asked her brother this embarrassing question but William laughed.

'As to that I'm not entirely sure. George says that he goes out some nights, but comes home early and that Dot is always waiting up for him with his slippers warming and a pot of tea brewing.'

'She seems the perfect wife, the kind of person he should have married. Perhaps everything was my fault.'

'Never think that, Lil. You were young and brought out the worst in him. Dot keeps him in order, I suppose.'

'Will it last?'

'I sincerely hope so, and if she nags him into marrying her he'll have to divorce you first, won't he?'

'So good luck to Dot.' Lily felt marginally more hopeful, but as she sat in the train on the short journey from Exeter back to Torquay doubts began to assail her. Why was this woman making a success of her relationship with Harry Coney while she herself had felt every minute with him was a disaster? William had said that it was not her fault. She must believe him firmly if she was to hold on to her fragile peace of mind.

April slipped into May and then June followed, and in Bristol it was hot and sultry. Ivy was completely engrossed with her puppy who was now growing into a mischievous and attractive little dog. Every day after school they went to the park and played with a ball until both were exhausted, and on the way home they frequently met Harry Coney returning with his empty cart, Flo contentedly in the shafts. Ivy tried to ignore him but he always grinned mockingly at her and often made some remark that invariably made her cross. She usually looked the other way or frowned at him angrily. She never replied.

She longed to know about Flo's probable fate though, for during the past week she had seen a new vehicle outside the coal yard.

'He've bought another of they motor things,' she said to Agnes one day when she returned from her walk.

'Those things,' Agnes corrected. 'He's increasing the removal and hire business I'm told but that doesn't mean he's going to get rid of Flo. He couldn't carry sacks of coal in one of those vans.'

'I'm going to ask him.'

Agnes was immediately alarmed. 'You're not to go round there, do you hear me? I promised your brother that I'd keep you well out of Harry Coney's way.'

'No harm can come to me in the daylight. His man is there too and I'll have Jane.'

The little dog looked up when she heard her name and Ivy bent to stroke her. 'You'll look after me, won't you, Janey?'

'A lot of good she'll be. I should have got you one of those great fierce Alsatians if you want protection from the likes of Harry Coney.'

Ivy laughed. 'He's not that bad, not wicked like you make out and like I always thought.' She was beginning to see another side to her brother-in-law and now, when she thought about it, she knew that she had provoked him all those weeks ago back in Sefton Road. Her guilt still hung upon her like one of the heavy sacks of coal in the back of his cart.

'That's as may be, but you're not to go round there.'

'All right,' Ivy said, but she knew quite well that she absolutely had to find out about Flo. If the lovely old horse was destined for the knacker's yard she had an idea of what she might try to do to save her. She shivered at the horrible thought, at the daring of her plan, and then went out into the scullery to wash her hands before tea.

She didn't meet the coal cart the following day or the one after that, but after the weekend, on Monday, she heard the sound of clumping hooves on the cobbles and Flo soon drew level with her. This time when Harry hailed her she forced herself to reply and she walked a little more quickly so that

160

the horse should keep abreast of her.

'How's your holy brother?' was Harry's first question.

'If you mean William, he's well.' She tried to make her voice sound grown up and offended.

'Ah, so you're speaking to me at last?'

'What if I am?'

'Just surprised, that's all.'

'I want to know about Flo.'

'What about Flo?'

'Are you going to kill her?' She glanced at Harry hoping that he was aware of her disgust.

'Kill her? Now what on earth could you mean by that, young lady? I've always cared well for my horses.'

'But you kill them when they're old!'

'If you mean that they go to the knacker's yard, well, yes. It's the best end for a faithful beast.'

'I think it's disgusting.'

'So what do you propose that I should do?'

Ivy was ready for this. 'I have a plan,' she said. 'But are you going to get rid of Flo soon?'

'That's my business.' The amusement in his voice was fading, irritation taking its place. 'Go on home like a good girl and look after your dog and your aunt and stop filling that silly little head of yours with things you don't understand.'

'I'm coming in to talk to you,' she said.

They had reached the entrance to his yard and the horse turned in at the gates which stood wide open. Harry jumped from the cart and flung down the reins and then started to unbuckle the harness.

'If I give you some money and ...' She paused, unable for a moment to go on with the idea that had come to her a few nights ago. She knew that her mother had left forty sovereigns to be shared between herself and Lily. There were four of them in the jug on the mantelpiece. She could easily get those. Aunt Agnes loved animals almost as much as she did and surely wouldn't be too cross when she knew how they had been spent. Getting some more from Lil would be the hardest part. But Ivy refused to think about that right now. Surely an old horse wouldn't cost too much to keep in hay and oats for the rest of her life?

Harry looked at her. 'Money? Now where would you get money from?'

'I got some of my own. My mother gave Lily some and she gave it to my aunt.'

'Oh, she did, did she? I never knew about that!'

'I got four sovereigns and Lil have got sixteen more for me. I could get it all if you'll promise to find a good home for Flo, somewhere she can go to be happy and do no work. A farm or something.'

Harry laughed heartily. 'Happy and do no work! That's a fate plenty of folks would like.' He shook his head. 'No such places exist, you stupid girl.'

Ivy took a deep breath and looked around to make sure that no one could see her. 'Please, Mr Coney. I'll do anything for Flo.' There were tears in her eyes now. She looked at the great horse who was cropping happily from the bag of hay that Harry had fixed round her neck. Flo was worth anything. How could anyone want to kill Flo?

Suddenly he grinned, leering at her. 'Anything? You really mean anything?'

Then Ivy was scared, really scared. She'd done just what her aunt had forbidden, had come here right into the lion's den! She could see the violent colour that rushed to Harry Coney's face. Lust was what it was called, horrible wild lust. She'd seen it before when she'd tried to get her own way with him, when she'd flashed her eyes at him back in Sefton Road, tried to coax him to do things for her. And see how it had ended up! She should have had more sense. Perhaps she was truly the wanton hussy that Aunt Agnes had once suggested, and everything, absolutely everything that had happened to Lil, was all her fault. She'd thought so for a long time and what she'd done today confirmed it.

Harry took a step towards her and she backed away. 'No, no not anything, just ...'

He seemed to change abruptly, and the amusement was replaced with swift anger. 'You silly little bitch,' he said. 'You come here and offer me what's cost me my wife and plenty of misery all round. You stand there and make stupid impossible bargains!'

162

She was horrified. What bargains? What was he talking about? Did he really think that she had been willing to ... she suddenly realized how brainless she had been. She turned, Flo's fate momentarily set aside, and made to run from the yard. But she had forgotten his strength, the power of him. He lunged at her, putting a great filthy hand on her arm and she screamed and felt her feet slipping beneath her. As she fell to the ground her little dog rushed to defend her, yelping and growling, snapping at Harry's legs and grabbing part of his trousers in her small mouth. He bent and clouted her angrily with his fist and she started her frenzied barking again, this time directing her wrath at the peaceful horse. She pulled wildly at the long hair on one of the huge legs, a tiny white whirlwind of fury.

Suddenly the great animal shook her head free of the meal bag and kicked out to shake the dog off. Harry, seeing Ivy sprawled on the cobbles and about to be crushed to death beneath those mighty iron-shod hooves, dived for the child in an effort to pull her to safety, but Flo's feet knocked straight into him, felling him and then as he crashed to the ground, one of the mighty hooves descended directly on to his coal-grimed head.

Ivy struggled to her feet, took one look at the bloody mess that had been Harry and ran out of the yard and along the street, seeing nothing, not knowing where she went. 'I've killed him!' she screamed. 'I've killed him again!'

Chapter Eleven

White-faced and with heart pounding, Ivy ran home. The front door was never locked and she pushed it violently, almost falling through it in her anxiety to be inside, to find some kind of refuge from what she had done. In the passage she encountered Agnes coming to see what the commotion was about. Ivy hurtled into her arms, buried her head in the stiffly boned bosom and sobbed wildly.

Agnes held her for a moment or two wondering what awful thing could have occurred. She looked around for Janey but the little dog was nowhere to be seen. An accident? Had Janey been injured by one of those evil motor cars perhaps, or just run away? She led the sobbing child into the kitchen and guided her towards one of the two armchairs that stood on either side of the hearth. She pushed a handkerchief into her hand. 'Now tell me what it's all about, love,' she said quietly.

'Harry Coney! He's dead, his face all ...' Ivy rubbed the handkerchief over her eyes and looked up at her aunt. 'It was my fault. If I'd never gone to ... he wouldn't have ...' The sobbing erupted again.

Unbelieving, Agnes flopped down on the other chair. 'Impossible,' she said. 'He can't be.' It was unthinkable that the cause of all their problems, the full-of-life Harry Coney, could so suddenly be ... be dead. Her heart started to beat furiously, irregularly. She put her hand on her chest and breathed deeply. 'Are you sure? Where? How?'

'In his yard. Yes, I'm quite sure. He's all bloody.'

Agnes rallied her resources. 'Then we must go and see if

there's anything we can do. Is anyone with him? Does the doctor know?'

Ivy shook her head. 'No. There's no one.'

Agnes got up stiffly from the chair. 'Then there's no time to lose.'

'He's dead, I tell you, really dead this time. The doctor can't do nothing, and they'll blame me. It's me what'll be hanged now.' Ivy started her frenzied sobbing again.

Agnes stared at her and wondered whatever could have happened. Why did Ivy say that it was her fault, and how did she come to be in the coalyard, a place that she knew was forbidden? But this was no time for speculation or reproof. Agnes put her arms awkwardly round the frightened child and tried to give some comfort. 'It can't possibly be your fault, and of course no one will hang you. He might not be dead. In fact, knowing Harry Coney I bet he's not. He's probably suffering from nothing more than a nose-bleed, and he'll be in a furious temper. Are you coming with me?'

Ivy sprang up, pushing her aunt away. 'I'll never go back there, never as long as I live!'

Agnes walked purposefully out of the room and put on her coat and hat. 'Then perhaps you'd better go and get the doctor. Where's Janey by the way?'

Ivy looked round distractedly for her little dog. She called her name but there was no response. 'I don't know.' Her voice was full of further dismay. She loved Janey best in all the world. 'I got to find her,' she called as Agnes strode out of the front door. 'I got to find Janey.'

The gates of the coal yard were wide open. There was a strange stillness, only the occasional movement of hooves on the cobbles.

'Mr Coney?' she called. 'Are you there?'

No reply. She took a few steps, looked round the corner, and then wanted to vomit or faint. Harry Coney lay face-down where he had fallen, the back of his head smashed to a pulp. The horse was obviously uneasy. Agnes could see the blood splashed on one great hoof.

She closed her eyes for a moment, almost wanted to cross herself against whatever had caused this horror, then reminded herself strictly that she didn't hold with such pagan ways. She forced herself to look once more at the man lying there, his hands and his clothes still black from the coal, and she was glad that she could not see his face. She told herself sternly that she would neither faint nor be sick and for a moment she felt a pang of distress for this man. He had some good points in spite of everything, and to go like that was a tragedy.

She turned away and retraced her steps but there was no one about in the street. Where was Dick Parker? Harry had employed him since the war. He'd been in the trenches, wouldn't turn a hair surely at the sight of blood. He'd know what to do. For the first time in her life she longed for a man and went back unwillingly to see if there was any sign of Dick. The van was there in the yard up on some blocks so he couldn't be out delivering. Perhaps he'd gone for the doctor already. She hoped so, but she'd have to do something herself anyway just in case.

What first? Police? A doctor? She walked gingerly out of the yard again, carefully avoiding the slippery trickle of blood that was seeping between the cobbles, and rapped impatiently on the front door of the nearest house to summon help.

Janey found her way home eventually and Ivy picked her up in a fierce embrace, smothered her with kisses and then sat cradling her in her arms unable to do anything else, even make a cup of tea. There was blood on the dog's coat and now it was on Ivy's dress, Harry Coney's blood. She looked at it, rubbed at it with her aunt's handkerchief, then closed her eyes on the horrible sight.

Nothing mattered any more. She would be taken off to prison and hanged as soon as the police came. Lily was free now, quite free, and she, Ivy Penrose, had rightfully paid the price for all the wicked things she had done, the things that had ruined Lily's life. She thought of the times she had goaded Harry into either being cross with her or ... or worse. And this last time had been the most dreadful. The Good Lord was punishing her for her terrible sins, would certainly punish her further. But her good kind sister was free as she deserved to be. As Ivy sat there hugging her

166

little dog she began, very slowly, to feel a glimmer of self-righteousness and hope. With this last frightful deed she had made everything right for Lily. Perhaps God would show her a little mercy. Maybe He would not send her to hell when she was hanged after all.

William had bought himself a second-hand motorbike and when a policeman gave him the news of the accident later that day he kicked the machine into life and roared round for George. He bade his brother to get on the back and, summoning as much speed as he could, rode furiously over to their aunt's house.

There he found Agnes slightly restored and in control of things but Ivy quite distraught. They sat stiffly in the front room on the seldom-used settee and the musty chairs. He concluded that such a momentous event as had just happened warranted using this dismal room.

'The police took a statement,' Agnes said. 'They blame the dog.'

Ivy turned tragic puffy eyes to William. 'They say that she got to be put down. They said it was her fault for biting the horse and she be a danger to other horses. It wasn't her fault truly, William. It was mine. She was only trying to help me.' Ivy, released now from the imminent fear of death for herself, was totally petrified at the prospect of the innocent Janey being sacrificed instead.

William sighed. He looked at the little dog in Ivy's arms and realized that this threat was more important to her than all the other problems that Harry's death had precipitated.

'They'll probably give her a second chance as long as she's tied up all the time,' he said, trying to sound confident.

A momentary flicker of hope leapt to Ivy's face and her arms round the dog tightened, but she said nothing.

'Never mind about the dog,' Agnes said brusquely. 'There are more important things to think about. Lily must be told at once of course. You must know where she is, William.'

He shook his head. 'She wouldn't tell me. I have no idea where to start looking.'

'Her photograph will be in the paper tomorrow though,' Agnes said. 'So she'll hear soon enough.'

'Photograph?' At first William was horrified. He thought

of his sister's firm wish to remain anonymous, but perhaps it didn't matter now.

'A man came round from the newspaper,' Ivy sniffed. 'He took a photo of me and Janey, and we gave him the wedding one of Lil and ... and Harry.' She indicated the empty place on the mantelpiece where the silver-framed photograph had been. 'We was glad to get rid of it. I never want to look at it again.'

'Then it wasn't very sensible to give it to the newspaper,' William said sharply. 'It'll be everywhere tomorrow.'

'I never thought of that,' Ivy said, remorse filling her once more. Could she get nothing right, ever?

'Probably the best thing all round,' George said, speaking for the first time. 'We got to get Lil home.' Then added half to himself, 'Wonder how Dot's going to take it?'

Whether he was referring to Harry's death or the return of Harry's wife, no one was quite sure.

'Dot?' Agnes sounded disconcerted. 'I never gave her a thought. Does she know?'

George shifted uneasily on the hard sofa. 'She liked 'im. She wasn't home when Will came round with the news, so I don't suppose she knows yet. She'll be busy getting 'is supper.'

'Poor soul.' For a moment Agnes pondered on the fact that this Dot, whom she had thankfully never met, was probably the only one who would mourn Harry Coney.

'I'll tell her tonight, as soon as we get back,' William said, 'Although I expect she'll have heard from the neighbours by then.' He looked at his sister who was still immersed in her grief for her dog. 'Cheer up, Sis,' he said. 'I'll go to the police station tomorrow and see what I can do about Janey. You must tell me everything that happened though.'

Ivy turned her woeful face to him. 'I don't want to do that, William. It's too bad. Just say that ... that Janey got in the horse's way and ... oh, anything that'll save her! If they kill Janey they might as well kill me too.'

The following morning Lily was in the kitchen early as usual preparing for a busy day. Now in June visitors were beginning to come to Torquay in greater numbers

168

and some of them found their way into the little café. She like the mornings especially when the sun was shining in a luminous unclouded sky as it was today. She worked cheerfully, thinking of her family as she clattered about in the kitchen. She hadn't seen William since that day in April when he'd told her more about the woman Dot, who was a paragon of the virtues and living with Harry. She longed to see her brother again and to hear the latest news. They had fixed a Sunday at the end of June, but even the two weeks that were still to go seemed a long time.

At nine o'clock, with some tables laid for breakfast and the kettle boiling, she unbolted the door and stood breathing in the fresh sea air which always delighted her. Then suddenly the door at the back of the shop opened with a crash and Reginald Bailey stood there in his dressing gown.

'Good morning, Mr Bailey,' Lily said in surprise. 'Did the sunshine get you up early?' He usually remained in bed until quite late nowadays, reading the papers which Gladys fetched for him as soon as she heard the delivery boy at six o'clock.

'It's no good morning for you, Miss, or for us.' He stood glowering at her with a newspaper in his hand. 'What's the meaning of this?' He hobbled to the nearest table and threw the paper down upon it.

'What do you mean?' Lily's heart started to thump as it had done frequently when she had lived in fear of her life. But that dread had passed, so what . . .

She bent over the newspaper, looked at her own face and Harry's staring up at her, both in their wedding finery. She gasped, unbelieving. 'I don't understand?'

'Neither do the Missis and me.' He thumped the offending photograph with his fist. 'You got some explaining to do.'

Lily tried to hold on to a shred of sanity. She picked up the newspaper and for a moment the print blurred in front of her eyes. There was a smaller picture below the large one, of Ivy and a dog. Slowly she read the story, but at first she made no sense of it. She held it more firmly, read it again. Harry was dead, killed by one of his own horses. She flopped down on the nearest chair and stared unseeing into Reginald Bailey's angry bloodshot eyes.

169

'Well then?'

'Where's Mrs Bailey?' Lily felt the need of the older woman's understanding. They had become friends and she desperately needed friendship just now.

'This,' he indicated the newspaper, 'gave the wife quite a turn. She's in bed, in the dark with the blanket over her head. You better do some explaining pretty quick.'

For a few seconds there was a terrible quietness in the room and then Lily began to speak as if in a trance. 'Yes, Mr Bailey. I am not who I seem. My name is Mrs Lily Coney and the man there is . . . was . . . my husband. I ran away from him for many reasons. The aunt I went to see wasn't my aunt at all. I went to meet my brother, my twin brother. No one knows where I am. I couldn't risk my husband coming for me, forcing me to go back to him.' Lily was amazed that she was able to say all these things so calmly when her mind was in such turmoil.

'You'll have to leave.' His voice was angry, full of outrage. 'You deceived us, told us a heap of lies. We took you on in good faith. The wife be proper upset. It could kill her. And everyone'll know soon as they reads the paper. We'll be a laughing stock, lose trade. You best clear out just as quick as you can get packed.'

Lily ran up to her bedroom, looked round at her treasures, at the picture of Cockington that Augustus had given to her. She went to the window and stared at the little boats swaying with the incoming tide, and she was filled with such an array of emotions that she saw nothing of the beauty outside.

What did it all mean? What had happened? Harry dead? For the second time since her wedding day she faced the fact of her husband's death, but now it was genuine apparently and its cause had nothing to do with her. Then the truth of her situation suddenly swept over in a great releasing torrent of pure joy. She was totally free at last.

But swiftly following came an unexpected glimmer of sadness for the man who had shadowed her life for the past year. He had been so very much alive when she ran from him on Exeter station, and he had just found happiness with Dot-somebody-or-other. But her fleeting sorrow was quickly banished. She clenched her hands tightly on the window sill and was filled once more with a sudden and glorious exaltation.

With much effort she turned her mind to practical matters. She had one small bag, not at all large enough for all the clothes she had accumulated over the past weeks, or the books she had bought, and there was no time to pack very much anyway. She would have to face the Baileys again and ask if she could come back and collect her things later.

When she went downstairs again she found the front door of the café closed and bolted and a piece of cardboard hanging on it. She turned it round and read CLOSED UNTIL FURTHER NOTICE written there in large untidy writing. Mrs Bailey came through from the back, obviously not so badly affected by the fateful events of the morning as her husband had made out.

'Well,' she said. 'Here's a to-do then. What you got to say for yourself?'

'Forgive me,' Lily whispered. 'There was nothing else I could do. I had to tell you all those lies to escape from him. There was no other way.'

Gladys Bailey sat down and indicated that Lily should sit too. She took a large handherchief from the recesses of her black skirt and wiped her eyes. 'I'm not judging,' she said. 'I know there be some awful men about and women got to put up with a lot a suffering. In spite of what my old man says, I think you been sensible and brave, and I don't want to lose you, maid.'

Lily sniffed. This was making things even more difficult. She had become very fond of Gladys Bailey. 'I'll have to go of course,' she said. 'But could I come back and fetch my things later? I can't take them all now. I need to get home as quick as I can.'

''Course, lovey, and I'll see no harm comes to nothing in your room. No one shall set foot up there.'

'Thank you.' Lily kissed her and then rushed back upstairs, glad to get away before she was quite overcome with emotion.

She took the painting that would always remind her of Augustus, two books, some underclothes and one of her darkest dresses, and stuffed it all into the bag that she had

171

brought with her when she first arrived. Then she prised up the floorboard beneath which her hoard of sovereigns lay hidden, and most of these she placed carefully in a special pocket in her petticoat. Finally she changed into her dark blue suit, added the straw hat and gloves and a pair of comfortable shoes, looked around her much-loved room once more and then firmly closed the door and went slowly down the stairs.

William was not in when Lily rapped anxiously on his door later that day. The journey had taken longer than she had expected for she had just missed the train. During all those endless hours she had tried to come to terms with what had happened. The newspaper account had been sketchy on details, the main thrust of the story being the missing wife. Herself of course! She had imagined that everyone who noticed her was staring, judging, labelling her an adulteress, an evil woman, for wives who ran away from their husbands were usually labelled so.

She stood outside William's door and knew that she must now go straight to the house, the place that had been her home as long as she could remember and which Harry had bought and had told her was his wedding present to her. It had turned out to be no present at all, the deeds being firmly in his name.

What would she find there? Would he be laid out in his coffin in the front room? Her stomach clenched in fear at the thought and her mind reverted suddenly to the day she had run away. She saw his unconscious body lying on the bedroom floor and thought of all the terrible weeks when she had believed that he was dead and that she was a murderer. And now the newspaper said something about a dog. A dog? How could a dog or even a horse possibly have killed Harry Coney?

George opened the door to her, a white-faced George, an older and more mature youth, almost a stranger for she had not seen him for nearly a year.

'Lil! Gosh, is it really you?' He stepped back as if she were a ghost.

172

''Course it's me. Where's William?'

'In town fixing things up. There's lots to do.'

'Can I come in then?'

George moved aside and she walked past him, through the passage into the kitchen. A woman rose to greet her, a buxom figure wearing a checked overall and with a red puffy face – red from weeping, Lily thought.

'You must be . . . Dot?' Lily said. It was presumptuous to address her by her Christian name but she knew of no other. She had always thought of her merely as Dot.

The woman hesitated, obviously unsure and embarrassed, but George, quickly following Lily into the room, said, 'This is my sister.'

The words hung in the air between them and then each woman simultaneously held out her hand. Lily grasped the work-worn fingers and looked into the homely face, the tear-filled eyes. This woman had loved Harry Coney. Lily couldn't imagine how that could possibly have been.

'Pleased to meet you.'

Quite unable to speak Lily nodded and it was George who once more broke the difficult silence with words that perhaps increased the awkwardness. 'He's in the front room. Do you want to see him?'

So it was as she had feared. Lily wanted to cry out that, no, of course she didn't want to see him. His dead body was the last thing in the world she wanted to look at and to remember even though, God help her, she had to be glad that he was dead.

'I'll come with you.' Dot's voice was kind. 'George, take your sister's bag. Put it on the landing for now.' She turned to Lily. 'Best get it over with straight away.'

Still speechless Lily nodded and followed her along the passage and they both stood before the closed door of the front room. Then quietly Dot opened it and there beneath the closely drawn curtains was the coffin, its lid raised. The room was dark, just a little evening sunshine creeping around the edges of the heavy damask and two lighted candles on the mantelpiece shedding an eerie glow.

Dot looked at them apologetically. 'I like to keep the candles burning,' she whispered. 'It seems reverent somehow.

173

I've always been fond of candles.'

Reluctantly Lily stepped over to the coffin and looked down. Harry lay more peacefully than she had ever seen him in life or in the imagined death of that other terrible time. Only the oval of his face was visible, for the crushing blow had been to the back of his head and was hidden by an elaborate screening of white satin.

She was unable to move, held there by a powerlessness to accept all the momentous things that had happened. She could feel the grief of the woman standing beside her, and then her own pent up emotions erupted and she started to cry. Why she was weeping she knew not, but she felt Dot's hand on her arm, a gentle loving touch.

'Come on out, deary, and I'll make us a cup of tea.'

The words were so ordinary, so matter-of-fact, that the tears flowed more abundantly.

When they were seated either side of the solid oak table that she knew so well, Lily managed to speak at last. 'You ... you were fond of him, weren't you?' she said.

Dot's tears were under control now and she smiled faintly. 'He was good to me. I came here as housekeeper first. The place was in a proper mess and they needed a woman about. Then he was lonely in the nights, and so was I. Yes, I liked him well enough. I know I done wrong but I hopes the Good Lord'll forgive me. And I wants you to forgive me too, Mrs Coney. I thought of you often when I was ... well ... in Harry's bed.'

Lily blushed. 'There's absolutely nothing to forgive, I assure you. I ran off and left him, didn't I!'

Dot shook her head. 'I got nothing to say about that. Women put up with too much if you ask me, and I know he had some bad ways. I was older, more of his age, and he treated me better'n he treated you most likely.' She paused and cut another slice of the spicy bread pudding that she had put on the table. 'Yes, I can say that I was fond of him in lots of ways. I'm used to them rough sort of men. I had a good husband and brought up three sons.' She smiled. 'So there's not a lot I don't know about the ways of menfolk.'

Lily nibbled at the bread pudding on her plate and remembered that it was a favourite with Harry and George. She

174

supposed that Dot's cooking had endeared her to them both too. She wondered what to say. She felt suddenly inadequate, as though much of what had happened was her fault, a result of her inability to manage her husband properly.

But she had no need to say anything. Dot clasped her hands round the hot cup of sweet tea and continued, 'I can see that he weren't the right one for a nice young lady like you, if you'll pardon me saying so.' She stared doubtfully at Lily, took another gulp of tea, and added, a trifle sheepishly, 'I turned a blind eye when he went off to his other women in Old Market. I never said nothing. It just made things a bit less demanding for yours truly so I didn't care that much anyway, and he weren't my husband when all was said and done so I had no right to question 'im, did I?'

'No, I suppose not,' Lily said dubiously, but Dot's words had lifted her spirits a little. There was much common-sense in what she had said. 'I can see that you were wiser than I was. He frightened me. I had no idea how to deal with him and his ...'

Dot put her cup down, reached out and patted Lily's hand. 'Of course you didn't. That kind of thing comes with the years, deary. You was too young for the likes of Harry Coney.'

Lily looked at her with sudden affection. 'Can we be friends, Mrs ... What can I call you?'

'Just Dot like your brothers do. That's all I answer to here.'

Lily smiled and the two women clasped hands across the table in a sort of mutual alliance. Lily saw the blonde greying hair of her companion drawn back into an untidy bun at the nape of her neck, at the beginnings of a double chin and at the stain down the front of the apron that she was still wearing, and wondered what exactly it was that men wanted from their women. Probably a man like Harry Coney had demanded many things and no one woman could satisfy him. Perhaps that was where she had gone wrong. For a second she thought of Augustus Ashe, but he was from another world, a different life. She drew her wandering thoughts together and considered the problems of the moment. Where was she

175

to stay tonight? Was this house her home now? Could she bear to sleep under the same roof as the dead body of her husband, the man whose living body she had so feared?

'Where should I stay?' she said, feeling suddenly glad of this woman's unexpected friendship.

'I been giving that some thought,' Dot replied. 'There be three bedrooms as you know.' She blushed. 'I had the back one when I first come, but ... well ... I moved into the front a few weeks ago. George has the middle one.'

Lily too felt her face colour. 'I don't want you to make any fuss,' she said decisively. She was quite sure that she couldn't sleep in the double marriage bed ever again. 'I'll go in the little room. It's kind of you to have me here at all.'

'This is your rightful home, Mrs Coney,' Dot said firmly. 'I shall move out just as soon as the funeral's over − before that if you want. I've a bit of money put by, so there's no need to worry about me. I got a sister too down Somerset, Bridgwater way. She'm always on about me going to live with her.'

'Please don't go,' Lily said quickly. 'Not yet anyway.' She was very glad that Dot was here, for company and to take charge of all the domestic arrangements for the time being. She suddenly longed for her beautiful attic bedroom in Torquay, yearned for the sound of the sea, for the calling of the gulls on the roof. 'We don't need to talk about the future just yet,' she said firmly. 'There are so many other things to do.'

'I'll get the back room ready for you then,' Dot said. 'There are some nice fresh sheets in the chest, all folded down with lavender. It be a pleasant room with a view over to the Orphan Homes, big too as third bedrooms go. This be a good sizable house. Harry knew a bargain when he saw one. 'Tis yours now, I reckon.'

Yes, Lily thought. *I suppose it is. After all these months of worry and uncertainty, perhaps I am not only free, I might be relatively well off as well.*

She helped Dot carry the cups and plates they had used into the little scullery which lay down two steps just beyond the kitchen. She remembered all the hours she had laboured in that horrible little place, laboured to please Harry with her

176

cooking when she would much rather have been working in the bookshop in Park Street. No, she had definitely not been the right wife for him.

Bookshop ... Torquay ... Augustus.

Full of contrition at her ungovernable thoughts, she said, 'Thank you, Dot, for being so kind.'

'It's you what's kind and understanding, Mrs Coney,' she said. 'And I'm glad to have met you at last. You've set my mind at rest, I can tell you.'

'And you mine,' Lily said earnestly. She went over to Dot and planted a kiss on her cheek. 'Let's go and see to making up that bed then. We'll do it together.'

It was Dick Parker, Harry's assistant, who saved Janey's life.

'No, 'twasn't the dog's fault,' he assured the police. 'I was under the van in the other yard fixing some'at when I heard that silly little kid come in and start talking to Harry. She didn't know I was there. 'Twas something about the horse. I couldn't make much of it, being a bit deaf with the shell shock and that. Then I heard a rumpus and tried to get a look to see what was happening. I saw Harry push her off, angry like, and the dog rightly took exception to that, but by the time I'd crawled right out it was mostly all over. There was the poor bugger lying in 'is own blood. The 'orse wasn't to blame neither. 'Twas a pure accident, but caused by the kid. A right young madam she be, by all accounts. She was up to something I'll be bound. Wants a good hiding for coming into the yard like that, ogling poor Harry. I went off to get help straight away. The kid and the dog had scarpered.'

Dick Parker repeated his story to anyone who would listen, and when it reached Agnes she stared angrily at Ivy. 'You should have had your ears boxed for going there and no mistake!' she said. 'There's a few home-truths coming out now. You'd best tell me all about it, you little minx.'

Ivy looked at her aunt, called Janey to her for comfort and cradled her tightly in her arms. 'I did it for Flo,' she said. 'I told him that I'd ... I'd give him some money if only he wouldn't have Flo killed.'

177

'Oh, you did, did you, and where were you proposing to get this money from?'

Ivy looked at the jug on the mantelpiece and Agnes followed her glance.

'So you were going to steal it, I suppose?'

'It's not really stealing, Aunt. I heard Lily say that it was mine.'

'That's as may be, but what else did you do? What did Dick Parker mean when he said that you were ogling Harry Coney and that he pushed you off? You were using those big eyes of yours to try and persuade him to do what you wanted, I suppose?'

Ivy said nothing, just looked down at the tears which were falling in salty drops upon Janey's white coat.

'How old are you?' Agnes went on. 'Twelve? I thought you'd have had more sense than to behave like that to a man like Harry Coney, and with your experience too. Perhaps you're stupid as well as wanton!'

'It wasn't like Dick Parker said.' Ivy felt the quick colour rush to her face. 'Harry grabbed at me ...'

'And whose fault was that?' Agnes questioned relentlessly.

Ivy knew now quite well whose fault it was. 'What are you going to do with me?' she murmured.

'Do? How should I know? That'll be up to William. Leave me to think in peace and quiet for a bit. Take that animal for a walk.'

Ivy threw on her coat, grabbed the dog's lead and fled from the house. Wanton! Would everyone know of her wantonness now? It was a word that she had heard before, and she knew what it meant. But she hadn't intended to be wanton, either back in Sefton Road months ago or now. Would Lily think she was wanton?

She reached the park gates and unclipped Janey's lead. She watched the dog gambol off happily and the sight cheered her a little. At least Janey was absolved, and Harry Coney was dead. She should be happy about those two things. She walked round and round the park four or five times and tried to get everything clear in her mind, tried to tell herself that nothing was really her fault, that she had only been thinking of Flo, and that couldn't be bad. Then she thought about Sefton Road. With Harry dead perhaps she would be able to go back there and live? Lily would come home and they'd be a nice happy family again just like in the old days. But what would William think about it all? He was good and sensible and wise, all the things that she was not. Would he forgive her? Could he possibly understand? And then there was George. He'd laugh probably once he'd got over Harry's death, but he might think that she had been really stupid and that wasn't very nice. He'd say it was because she was a girl.

'Please, God,' she prayed as she walked, 'let the police and everyone forget what I done, and let William forgive me, and let Aunt Agnes try to understand too.'

Her prayer was partially answered, for when she arrived home, Agnes, having thought the matter over, had become secretly a trifle amused at Ivy's outrageous deed.

'Seeing you did it for Flo, I might bring myself to pardon you after all,' she said severely. 'Animals are better than people in my opinion, and anyone who loves an old horse that much can't be too sinful.'

Ivy gulped in relief. 'Do you think William and God will forgive me too?'

Agnes hid a smile. 'William might be persuaded to do so, but I can't answer for God!'

Chapter Twelve

The funeral was an uneasy affair. Lily couldn't help recalling her mother's death, and remembered too the memorial service for Arthur. For him there had been no funeral, for his body lay somewhere in the mud of the trenches, lost, blown away, as though he had never been. She wept for both of them as she followed Harry's coffin down the aisle of the parish church.

William had suggested that the service should be held here rather than in the chapel, for Harry had often laughed at the little building and its zealous group of believers. The church was more impersonal, a place where one could call on the Almighty in death without having given much thought to Him in life.

Lily was shrouded in black. Some of her mother's clothes still remained in a trunk in the attic room at Sefton Road and she had rummaged amongst the moth-balled garments and found things both for herself and for Dot. Some shortening of hems and a considerable amount of stitching the day before had produced two reasonable outfits. There had been hats with veils too and she was glad to hide behind one of these. If she looked hopelessly old-fashioned she cared not one jot.

Ivy, in her school uniform and with the addition of a black hat, walked behind her, polished black boots clumping along noisily on the stone floor. She was crying copiously and Lily, hearing her sniffs, wondered what the tears were for. Surely she hadn't cared for this man? She knew that Dot, sitting unassumingly at the back of the church, would be weeping.

By rights she should be the one walking up here behind the coffin, Lily thought, for she was the one who mourned him most. Yet outwardly she was merely the housekeeper. Her other role in Harry's life had been kept carefully hidden.

There was a blur of faces, mostly Harry's customers Lily discovered afterwards. It seemed that he was a popular tradesman. Lily guessed that they were all staring at her, probably with hostile eyes for she was the erring wife, the woman who had so shamelessly gone away and left him.

Harry apparently had no relatives. There had been none at the wedding either. Lily was relieved about this for she would not be further judged. Had there been a mother or a sister there would have been all kinds of recriminations.

'I am the resurrection and the life. He that believeth in me, though he were dead, yet shall he live ...'

Lily shuddered. Was Harry watching her? She peered at the coffin through the black veil which covered her face.

'And though worms destroy this body ...'

For a paralyzing moment the words caused her to think of Arthur again, and all the others, Harry's own son in fact, who had been lost in that terrible useless war. *Though worms destroy this body ...* It was horrible.

Harry had wanted another son and she had failed him. Was she guilty? Had she done wrong?

' ... yet in my flesh shall I see God. We brought nothing into this world and it is certain we can carry nothing out.'

Harry had nothing now. Self-doubt assailed her as she seated herself beside her brother in the front pew. The coffin had been placed now on heavy oak trestles just a few paces away from her. She stared at the shiny brass handles, the elaborate wreath that she had ordered, and the ribboned card that hung from it. She had agonized over the wording of the message on that card. Eventually she had simply written, *'To Harry, with loving regrets, Lily'*. Yes, there were regrets. She would have liked a happy marriage, so the words didn't add to all the lies with which her life

181

had been crammed these last months.

She knelt for the prayers, and stood for the psalms, hearing little. An occasional sentence stood out now and then and sent her thoughts racing in directions that the compilers of the Prayer Book had never intended.

'I will take heed to my ways: that I offend not in my tongue.
I will keep my mouth as it were with a bridle ...'

Was this for her? Was she being rebuked for all those lies she had told in Torquay?

'My heart was hot within me and while I was thus musing the fire kindled ...'

Whatever was he talking about now? The words went on and on, spoken in the parson's melodious voice, a deep and beautiful voice with a trace of some accent that was not of the West Country, something unusual and distinctive that reminded her of someone. Of course, Duncan MacMullen. This man must be a Scotsman too. *'My heart was hot within me ...'* Could this really be part of the funeral service? A vision of Augustus flashed before her unwilling eyes. 'Dear God,' she prayed furiously, 'how can I think of Augustus when my husband is lying dead just a little distance from me?'

She had chosen the hymn herself, a familiar one sung often in the chapel, one that reminded her of childhood, of her father who had sometimes been in the pulpit, for they had no clergy, of her mother beside her, warm and loving. The words spelt security and happiness. She was briefly comforted, and as she sang each line she hoped that she truly meant what she was singing.

The hymn had not been in the Prayer Book, but she had insisted upon it, and the undertaker had grumblingly arranged for another set of books to be borrowed.

'Dear Lord and Father of mankind,
Forgive our foolish ways;
Reclothe us in our rightful mind;
In purer lives Thy service find ...'

182

That was what she wanted now, Lily thought, a simple life with no deceit, no guilty secrets.

'Drop Thy still dews of quietness,
Till all our strivings cease;
Take from our souls the strain and stress
And let our ordered lives ...'

Yes, an ordered life sounded perfect. But she was not quite sure about the last verse.

'Breathe through the heats of our desire,
Thy coolness and Thy balm;
Let sense be dumb, let flesh retire ...'

She closed her book for she knew this hymn by heart and tried to think about Harry Coney and not about Augustus Ashe.

After the interment in the little cemetery behind the church she threw the customary earth on to the coffin, took one last look down into the gloomy depths and then walked slowly away, her thoughts a mass of discordant emotions that even that last hymn hadn't been able to obliterate.

The curtains in the parlour had been drawn back now, and the June sunshine was streaming through the netting drapes. No neighbours had been invited back to the house, but there was afternoon tea for the family. Dot and Agnes had prepared sandwiches and cakes in uncomfortable co-operation during the morning.

Agnes had reluctantly accepted that Dot was to be present and was to be treated as one of the family. She tried not to think of the shameless behaviour of this woman, and the two of them had eventually managed, with some reluctance, to accept each other.

Surprisingly there was a solicitor's clerk present and when they had finished eating he cleared his throat noisily and said that he must read Mr Coney's will. Lily had not even been aware that there was one. She sat awkwardly on the edge of her chair, watching the young man as he opened his briefcase and took out a parchment tied with blue ribbon. The scene swam before her eyes and she tried to concentrate.

What was he saying? The will had been made the week after the wedding. She forced herself to sit up straight and concentrate.

Almost everything was left to the boy whom he was sure he and Lily would quickly produce. She gasped. He had been so convinced that their marriage would have issue, as the official language said, so determined to replace his lost son.

She put her whole mind to understanding this document. The solicitor's voice droned on importantly. If there should be more than one male child, everything would be shared equally. There were safeguards for herself. She was to have use of the house for her lifetime, and an income from the coal yard. If there were daughters they were to have a hundred pounds each on their marriage and a small income for life.

The young man paused and looked at her, addressing her directly. 'As you have no children, Mrs Coney, none of this applies,' he said. 'Only the last clause is relevant.'

He continued to read, and Lily could feel her whole body freeze in apprehension for the sentences were complicated, full of legal idioms, but when he stopped and just the ticking of the clock could be heard in the quiet room, William, who was sitting close to her on the sofa, turned to her and smiled, took her hands and kissed her on her cold cheek.

'Congratulations, my dear,' he said. 'Harry has left you everything.'

Two weeks passed before she could bring herself to think about going back to Torquay for her things. During that time there had been a few changes in the little terraced house in Sefton Road. Lily walked around it constantly as if in a dream, affirming to herself that it was really hers now. She was the owner, and of the coal yard too. At last she had security and independence, two of the most valuable things in the world.

Dot had told them that she wanted to leave, to go to her sister in Bridgwater, but she was easily persuaded to stay for the present and to continue as housekeeper. Lily wasn't sure yet what she planned to do with her life, and the idea of returning to domesticity, of running this house as she done when Harry was alive, didn't attract her at all. Although she had spent long hours cooking and cleaning in the café, she had been organizing the business side as well. There had been interesting challenges, and the scope to use her brain and her ingenuity.

Perhaps the coal yard would bring similar opportunities, interesting new demands, but did she honestly want to take over its day-to-day running? She wasn't sure. Dick Parker was looking after everything at the moment. George had excitedly argued that he should leave school at once and work there full-time as he had always longed to do, but William refused permission. 'Finish your education,' he had directed. 'Not much longer to go and then we'll see.'

Lily had been surprised at the changes in George. He was still the old amusing and clowning character he had always been, but he had grown up considerably in the past year. The coal yard might be the perfect opportunity for him in another year or two. He would never forgive her if she sold it now. She discussed it with William and they decided that it must be kept for the present.

'What are you going to do about Flo?' he asked her. There was a guarded look about him as though the mention of the animal held some special significance.

'What do you mean exactly?'

'Well, she seems to have been the cause of all the trouble.'

It was Sunday afternoon and they were walking in St Andrew's Park, the small green space near Sefton Road with its neat flowerbeds and closely cropped grass. Lily looked at a young courting couple sitting on one of the iron seats beside the path. They were engrossed in each other, seeing nothing else, and for a moment she wished that she had a happy untroubled marriage and no problems to solve. 'I suppose her fate is in my hands now,' she said. 'What do you think I should do with her?'

'Ivy will never forgive you if you send her to the knacker's yard. After all, she braved Harry to save that horse.'

Perplexed, Lily shook her head. 'The whole thing seems odd. I'll never find out what really happened, will I? Did he really make a grab for her? Did she flaunt herself? I can't believe that, William, not after what he tried to do to her all those months ago.'

'Don't think about it. It doesn't matter now. She was just desperate to save Flo. She's dotty about animals.'

'I'll have to go over and talk to Dick Parker, I suppose.'

'I've been,' William said. 'I wanted to take a look at the beast. She's a nice old horse, quite calm and gentle.'

Lily thought for a moment or two. Anyone's death was a tragedy, but Harry's death, for her, had been a wonderful release. She had been struggling not to be happy about it ever since the first shock had abated, but during the last day or two she had given up the effort. A widow with a string of children and no money was to be pitied, but a young widow like herself, still with some good looks, unencumbered, and with money, was very much to be envied.

'I suppose I ought to thank the horse for my release,' she said, slightly ashamed.

William smiled at her. 'Shocking of you to say so, but yes, I suppose you should.'

'Then I shall not send Flo to the knacker's yard.'

'Ivy will be delighted.'

'That's important. I want to please Ivy.'

Ivy was still living with Aunt Agnes. She had assured her sister that it was because she didn't want to change schools in the middle of a term, and Lily hoped that this was the truth and that they could resume some sort of satisfactory relationship later on. For the moment however it suited her. Nothing at Sefton Road would ever be quite the same now. She knew that they couldn't go back to how things were a year ago.

William had left the orphanage and had taken a couple of rooms in one of the houses in the avenue at the end of Sefton Road, near enough to keep in constant touch, but far enough away to be independent and separate. 'I won't be moving back,' he had told her.

Dot was still in possession of the front bedroom for no one else wanted it. George had declined when it was offered to him, preferring his own room, the middle one which, like Lily's room, overlooked the orphanage. He was able to see over the high walls at the end of the small garden and constantly congratulated himself that he hadn't ended up there after all and never would now. However when he realized that he would be the only male in a household comprised of himself and Lily and Dot, he was at first slightly indignant.

'I liked being with Harry,' he had said belligerently. 'We got on well.'

But after the first few days he had found that it suited him for the present. He was well looked after, all his needs supplied, and no laws laid down except by William now and then.

Dot had been thrilled when Lily had offered her a hundred pounds.

'Not a payment,' Lily had said, blushing. 'But because I know that Harry would have wanted it.' Privately she was relieved that he had not made another will when she first ran away from him. He could easily have bequeathed the whole lot to Dot for she had obviously pleased and satisfied him in many ways, made his last months happy. Lily was determined that she would keep in touch with her, see that she never wanted for anything. But for now the hundred pounds satisfied Dot hugely. She had obviously expected nothing.

It was July when Lily eventually returned to Torquay. As she walked along the road beside the sea she thought of that other day just a year ago when she had arrived here terrified and alone, thinking herself a pathetic victim wanted for murder, about to be hunted and then hanged. She smiled to herself and was determined that she would not be in any way subservient to the Baileys. She felt no guilt now. She had come to terms with what she had done, the lies she had told, and if they refused to condone her actions that was their decision. She would not be upset about it.

As far as she knew no one had told Augustus about the change in her life, in her status and fortunes. The Baileys had known that he was writing to her, for his postcards had come regularly and she guessed that they had read each one.

Since she had been away there would certainly have been more. But she had felt unable to write to him while she was in Bristol and she had spent many hours wondering how best to confess to him all that had happened. What would his reaction be? Would he want to continue their friendship? Would he even speak to her again when he knew every sordid detail?

In spite of all these worries however she felt excitement rising as she walked along the seashore. The tide was out, leaving an expanse of sand, and bathing machines had been wheeled down to the edge of the sea. She longed to change her clothes and to experience the cold shock of the water on her skin. She had never been in the sea, had no bathing dress, but determined that she would get one if she stayed here long enough.

On the promenade there were girls in light summery dresses, fairly short now, shorter than she could remember last season. Lily felt decidedly dowdy in last year's frock and black stockings. White was the colour now, gay white stockings. She would buy some of those too. She had money. She was a carefree rich young widow! Well, perhaps not exactly rich, not exactly carefree, but certainly independent and comfortably off.

The sunshine and the bracing sea air made her feel light-headed and full of confidence. She looked at the young men in their white flannels, blazers and bright boaters, and some on the beach wearing long droopy bathing costumes, towels draped nonchalantly around their shoulders. She wondered for a moment about them. Had they been in the war? Had they seen terrible unmentionable deeds, and did they feel the guilt that she had heard about, guilt that they had survived when millions had not? She hoped that they were suffering none of those awful things and that they were just enjoying the sunshine as she was.

She thought about the men she knew. William had been too young to be conscripted, Harry too old. Augustus? He had been in France, in the trenches, but had said little about it, refusing to be drawn. And Duncan? His wartime experiences had not been mentioned either.

Eventually she came to the harbour and quickened her

pace. She felt more optimistic now, more confident, very anxious to know what had happened to the shop, and, even more important, whether Augustus was back. She longed to see him, yet also hoped that he was ignorant of all that had happened to her. She wanted to tell him everything herself before he heard any unsympathetic account.

She wasn't sure what she expected to see. Would the café be running successfully without her, some other woman taken on hastily? Or would it be, as she half expected, closed until further notice? This seemed the most likely. She had thought of it often during her time in Bristol and had known that there was little likelihood of her returning to work there, but when she finally turned the corner and stood outside the place which had been her hideaway and precious refuge during the most difficult months of her life, she wasn't prepared for its look of utter desolation. Its windows were boarded up, obliterated by sheets of plywood nailed roughly on to the frames. The door was locked. She stared at it, transfixed, unbelieving. What had they done to her cherished little shop? Where were the Baileys?

A FOR SALE notice was fastened to the middle of one of the boards. She rapped on the door, but the sound echoed through the empty rooms and seemed to return to her, eerie and frightening. She turned away and walked slowly to the bookshop. She had determinedly ignored it until this moment, but now she pushed open its old-fashioned door and the little tinkling bell announced her arrival.

Michael Dyer, the young man whom Augustus had left in charge, rose from his stool behind the counter, obviously recognising her instantly. She noticed that his hands shook and remembered that he suffered from shell-shock. He was tall and pale with dark hair and a small moustache, and wore thick steel-rimmed spectacles. He looked as though he seldom took the advice that Augustus was so fond of giving, to take plenty of fresh air. Indeed, he looked as though he never left the shop at all.

'Mrs Coney,' he said politely, and she realized with a shock that he must know something of what had happened. He had probably read about it in the papers for Harry's death

189

had been widely reported. His voice was cultured, of the officer class.

'Good afternoon, Mr Dyer,' she said formally. 'I wonder if you know what has happened to Mr and Mrs Bailey?'

'They left. They've gone to stay with a daughter, I believe. The landlord decided to sell the shop. It hasn't been open since you went away.'

'That's a pity,' she said with vast understatement. She hesitated. Dare she ask if Augustus was back in England?

'It affects our trade unfortunately,' the young man said. 'Your café drew people to this part of town.'

'I'm sorry.' Was she being reproached for leaving so suddenly? 'Mr Ashe?' she said quickly. 'What does he say about it?'

The young man shook his head. 'I've told him nothing. He's still in Switzerland and I didn't want to bother him. He leaves everything to me. He has other financial resources though. He won't be worried. It is I who feel the loss.'

Lily stared at him, seeing him for the first time as someone in his own right. Until now he had merely been an employee of Augustus's, a useful person to have around. She thought about what he had said. Yes, of course she knew that Augustus had other resources, was rich in fact. But why was he away for so long?

'Is he coming home soon?' she ventured.

'You don't know why he is away?'

'No.' She blushed and shook her head.

'He was gassed in the war. Not as badly as some, but he has tuberculosis. He's having treatment, the very best available in Switzerland.'

Lily felt her legs weaken beneath her. Tuberculosis, TB, the dreaded scourge. She looked round for a chair. There was one at the counter and thankfully she collapsed upon it. 'That's terrible,' she said. 'I didn't know.'

The young man peered at her through his glasses. 'He didn't know himself for a long time. Then he wanted it kept secret.'

'So how is he?' The words trembled on her lips.

'Much better. He wrote to say that he hopes to come home soon. He's not sure exactly when.'

190

'And you say that he doesn't know I've left or anything about my changed circumstances?'

'No.'

Lily thought that she could detect a trace of hostility in his voice. Why had he said nothing when he wrote to Augustus? Surely they corresponded regularly? Did he know or guess that she felt more than just neighbourly concern for his employer? Did he disapprove? Maybe he considered that what she did or did not do was of no importance, not worth writing about. And he would not have expected her to return to Torquay.

A customer came into the shop and Lily jumped at the ringing of the bell. 'I'd better go then,' she said.

'I have a key to next-door.' The young man pulled open a drawer beneath the counter and handed her the large key that she knew so well, that she had used to lock up every night when work for the day was done. She cradled it in the palm of her hand.

'I sent a trunk on,' she said.

'Yes, it arrived yesterday. I directed the men to put it inside. The landlord guessed that you would be returning for your things and told me to give you his permission to go in.'

'Thank you. You have been very kind.' She turned to go.

'If you would like me to carry the trunk up to your room, please ask.'

She smiled at him. 'At the moment it's empty so I shall be able to manage.' Suddenly needing to be alone she hurried out, leaving him to his books and his customer.

The café was clean and neat, just as it had been when she left only four weeks before. Could it be so short a time? It seemed like a hundred years. Yet there was a musty smell, and some of the hated flies had returned and now lay on their backs here and there on the white table-cloths which were still in place. Lily stared at them belligerently.

There were some postcards neatly stacked on the table just inside the door. She picked them up, her heart thumping. They all had the bright Swiss stamps she had come to

191

know so well, and the short messages written in Augustus's handwriting telling her nothing, merely assuring her that he was still thinking of her, although not actually saying so. She turned them over one by one and looked at the views of mountains, lakes, cows with bells round their necks, laughing yokels in strange dress.

Who had stacked these cards so neatly? Who had taken them from the basket that was fixed to the door just below the letterbox? Who had read them? Obviously the young man in the bookshop, probably yesterday when he brought in the trunk which had been delivered by the GWR men. Was that why he looked at her strangely? Had she imagined the hostility or was it really there? And if so, why?

She held the four cards in her hands, one for each week, and read the words on each one over and over again. They had extra poignancy now that she knew Augustus was ill. She pictured him in one of those cold open wards she had heard about, where the snow and the icy wind blew round the beds. It was supposed to be the best cure for tuberculosis. The cards told her nothing of this.

She put them into her handbag and then walked slowly through the shop. The Baileys had cleared out completely. There was no sign of them at all. All their things had gone, the door to their rooms standing wide open revealing a depressing emptiness. She hoped that they were happy wherever they were. She must find out, must write to Mrs Bailey for she had been kind and forgiving, and at the time of her deepest need they had rescued her, given her shelter and hope.

Slowly she climbed the stairs, remembering the first time, the wonderful flow of relief when she saw the view, experienced the peace. Everything was just as she had left it. After a few moments of nostalgia she tried to reassert the spirit of optimism that she had felt when she walked past the beach with its carefree trippers, but she could not. The news about Augustus's illness had been too shocking.

She had known people with tuberculosis. Often they had died, but they were mostly poor, overworked, underfed. Augustus was none of those things. And Switzerland was renowned for its excellent medical centres, she told herself

192

fiercely. If you could afford to go there a cure was often possible. Perhaps Augustus would come home quite well again.

She returned to the shop, laboriously pulled the big trunk up to her room, bumping it on each uncarpeted stair. Then she opened it and looked down into its cavernous depths. She had borrowed it from Aunt Agnes and a smell of moth balls and lavender remained, a weird heady mix. She put her books and all the other possessions that she had accumulated during this past amazing year in the bottom of the trunk, then flung open her wardrobe and took out all her precious clothes and put them carefully on top. When the room was just as bare and as heartbreakingly empty as when she had first seen it, she crashed the lid down, locked it firmly, went to the windowseat and flopped down upon it.

She stared at the boats, at the sea lapping gently against the harbour wall, and in spite of the trunk sitting there in the middle of the room, knew that this was where she wanted to live. The idea came to her clearly and with a certainty that surprised her. To settle in Bristol again in the house in Sefton Road suddenly seemed a most unwelcome proposition. It would be taking a step backwards, and life should aways move forwards. Looking back on the past with regret or longing was a totally unproductive pastime. She opened the window and heard the gulls calling, felt the fresh sea air on her face, and wanted to fling open her trunk again and put everything back where it had been before.

She was completely unprepared for these fanciful dreams, and tried to reassert her common-sense, tell herself that it was impossible to stay here. She had responsibilities, obligations, in Bristol. Ivy needed her. There was the business to sort out, the house to organize.

She looked with vast dislike at the trunk sitting there in the middle of the floor for it symbolized the fact that her life here was over and she didn't want that to be so. Then a further idea came to her. Abruptly she jumped to her feet, ran down the stairs and out to the front, opened the door and stood on the pavement, staring as if transfixed at the FOR SALE notice that was stuck to the boarded up window. There was a name and an address. She memorized it quickly.

193

The future suddenly blazed with hope and excitement. Lily laughed to herself in sudden delight, went back to tidy her hair and fetch her handbag, and then strode out towards the town and the estate agent's office.

Chapter Thirteen

'Buy a business in Torquay? You must be mad.' William frowned and his voice, usually so calm and sympathetic was plainly disapproving.

'But I know how to run it. I've been managing almost everything single-handed for eleven months. It's in a good position right on the sea front, the harbour actually, and it's what I want to do, William. It would be something of my very own, nothing to do with Harry or Father or my past life.'

Lily was back in Sefton Road, the trunk upstairs as yet unpacked. She faced her brother uneasily and there was none of the usual understanding and closeness between them. They were sitting each side of the fireplace, and the coals, although damped down, were giving far too much heat for a warm July evening. The fire was never allowed to go out for it was necessary for cooking and heating water. Lily flung off her jacket, draping it over the back of her chair.

'But you'll marry again some day.' William said.

'How typical of a man! I probably won't, and anyway what has that got to do with it, with now, today, July 1920?'

'Women don't run businesses, Lily. You know that.'

She shook her head in disbelief. 'You're quite wrong. And what about the coal business? That's mine. I shall have to see that it works efficiently.' She glared at her brother and wondered why women were judged to be so inferior when she knew perfectly well that she had as much common-sense and ability as her brothers, more perhaps if the truth were told.

'That's different. There's Dick Parker for a start. He's very capable and has been seeing to things satisfactorily ever since Harry's death. I shall be able to deal with the financial side, and George can't wait to leave school and work there full-time. It won't be long before he can take over almost completely, a couple of years perhaps.'

Lily was dumbfounded. 'So you think that George will be more capable of directing a business than I am? Have you taken leave of your senses, William?'

'No, but he's keen, wants to make it his career for life. No woman can promise that.'

'He's only fourteen. Are you really saying he should take over when he's sixteen?'

William shook his head doubtfully. 'Well, perhaps I'm being over-optimistic. I shall supervise everything, of course.'

'You said that he should get some more education.'

'I've changed my mind. He hates school and it won't do any good to force him to stay. I think that perhaps he should leave next week when school breaks up for the summer. Most of his friends are leaving then.'

Lily clenched her hands in her lap, her face set in determined lines. Her brother seemed to be making all the decisions, ignoring her own ideas and plans. 'Haven't you forgotten something, William?' she said quietly.

He looked up at her, obviously surprised at the seriousness of her voice. 'What have I forgotten?'

'That the coal business is mine,' said Lily. 'You are making all the arrangements without reference to me at all.'

'But I thought that was what you would want me to do, take the worry from your shoulders?'

'As a matter of fact, it isn't at all what I want you to do. Yes, I shall be very glad of your help, but we must talk everything over together, and I should like to make some of the decisions.'

She had never had a disagreement like this with her brother before. As twins they thought alike, often acted simultaneously, had been inseparable as children. It pained her that these differences should have arisen between them now.

William flushed with embarrassment. 'I'm sorry, Lil. I merely thought that ... '

'That because I am a woman, I have no voice, no right to make choices, even for my own life, let alone for those around me? Oh William, don't get like Father, like Harry, like the men at the chapel who won't even allow women to speak in meetings. Everything is changing now, or hadn't you noticed?'

There was a long silence between them and then William spoke again and this time sounded contrite. The self-assurance had disappeared. 'Perhaps I hadn't noticed,' he said. 'But of course you're correct. Everything is changing. Right then, tell me exactly what you want to do.'

She laughed briefly. Did he really understand? Could men really change? Could they ever accept the new order, the new breed of women that the war had produced? Probably not, she thought. They would always want to dominate and rule. 'I've already told you what I want to do,' she said.

'I'm sorry I dismissed it.' He grinned at her affectionately. 'Let's talk it over.'

She was further amused by his words. 'Oh, William, so formal!' She got up quickly, went over to him and kissed him fondly on the cheek. 'We're equals, William. Let's keep it like that, shall we? Of course I want to discuss everything with you, have your advice.'

'Even if you don't take it?'

'Even if I don't take it.' Her eyes sparkled with merriment.

'Well then,' he said, 'you want to sell the coal yard and buy a café in Torquay?'

She shook her head. 'Who said anything about selling the coal yard? You're jumping to the wrong conclusions.'

'How else could you finance your hair-brained scheme?'

'I shall sell this house!' She sat down again and allowed her bombshell to sink in. 'I know as well as you do how much George is looking forward to taking over Harry's business one day. And I agree with you that he'll probably prove to be efficient and will make us an excellent income. For fourteen years old he seems quite mature. I was pleasantly surprised at the change in him.'

'Sell this house!' William stared at her as though she had taken complete leave of her senses.

Lily smiled, a slow satisfied smile. 'Yes. Why not? I've worked it all out. It will bring almost sufficient money to buy the other business and the rest will come out of Harry's insurance. I think there'll be just enough. Two businesses are better than one, William. As an accountant you should know that, and this house will only be a burden and a drain on our cash resources. Without it we might even become rich one day.'

'But, Lil, you can't sell this place. It's been our family home ever since I can remember.'

'That's not a good reason for keeping it. Should I hang on to it just for Dot and George? You've got your own lodgings in Stanley Avenue, Dot wants to go to her sister in Bridgwater or somewhere, Ivy can stay with Aunt Agnes or come down to Torquay with me and help run the café, and George can either go and lodge with Aunt Agnes ... ' She giggled at this preposterous idea. 'Or he can share with you, or more sensibly, we can renovate the big room above the stable at the coal yard for him. That way he'll be on the spot for looking after things and be free of rules and regulations. It should suit him.'

William shook his head, not in disagreement, more in amazement. 'You've got it all worked out, haven't you!'

'I suppose I have. I'm just finding out about myself and the things I can do. And I like Torquay. It's beautiful and ... oh, lots of things, William! I suppose that I want a new life. I want to forget the past.'

'Won't Torquay make you remember the past?'

'Not at all. It was a sort of haven, a sanctuary that meant a lot to me when everything was falling apart, when I was so alone and terrified.'

William stood up and went to the window with its bleak view of next-door's wall. Eventually he turned to Lily and took her hands in his. 'We'll go down to Devon and you can show it to me,' he said. 'But, as you've so firmly reminded me, the decision is yours. You have the money. You're the boss, Lil.'

His tone was warm-hearted now, and tender in spite of the words. The old relationship was partially restored, yet there was a barrier between them and she supposed that it

198

must be her new status, her independence. Yet she wasn't unduly dismayed for she knew that to own property, to have resources and a little wealth of one's own, was a wonderful and liberating asset. As her mother had said, a woman should have a little hoard of sovereigns as a weapon against the world. But Elsie Penrose had never envisaged the amount that her daughter would one day control, a house and a business and an account in the building society with quite a substantial sum written there between the red covers of the little bank book.

To Augustus and his class, Lily supposed that it was not great riches, but by the standards of most of the people she had lived amongst for all her life it was certainly plenty. And God willing, she would work hard so that she would have enough to help her family and especially her sister. Ivy should never need to depend on any man. For a woman that was freedom! Like the labourer in the Bible who put his talents to work and was so greatly praised, she too would make her capital increase as quickly and as hugely as she could manage.

'I shall own two businesses, William,' she said. Then more humbly she added, 'But I shall need your help, of course. After all, as an accountant, you're the expert with facts and figures, and girls don't understand these things!' She grinned at him and they both knew that she didn't mean those last words at all.

It was the end of August before the house was sold and the deeds of the little Torquay café were firmly in Lily's name. Everything had worked out to her satisfaction and she was to move down at the beginning of September.

George, much to his delight, was established in his own room above the coal yard where he was to work under the direction of Dick Parker. William would look after the office side of the business in the evenings and at weekends.

'We'll try not to take on anyone else for the moment,' Lily had decreed. 'We'll see how things go, and we must make sure that Flo is well looked after, not overworked, and given every consideration.' She still felt indebted to the old horse for unwittingly ridding her of Harry, but was careful not to voice this shockingly wicked thought. She felt guilty even thinking it.

Ivy was thrilled about the promise that Flo should never go to the knacker's yard. 'That's wonderful, Lil,' she had said with tears of joy in her eyes when she first heard this piece of news. 'But what'll you do with Flo when she's too old to work?'

'I'll think of something,' Lily had replied. 'Probably find her a field somewhere in Devon and a nice stable for the cold nights.'

Ivy had beamed ecstatically. 'Then I'll come to Devon and live with you. When can Flo retire?'

'As soon as we can afford it,' Lily said. 'It'll cost a lot, and we'll have to get another horse, won't we?'

Ivy shook her head wisely. 'Don't expect so, George wants one of them smelly motor things. He've got one for the furniture, of course, but he wants one for the coal as well.'

'We'll see.' Lily privately hoped that Flo's strength would hold out for another year, or at least until the café was really prosperous again.

Aunt Agnes had accepted all these changes stoically and had made one surprising offer. Thinking that she might be lonely when Ivy and Janey left, she had told George that she would cook the occasional meal for him now that he was living above the coal yard. Although she didn't on the whole approve of men, and she considered boys to be even worse, she had decided that it might be a good idea to keep an eye on her nephew, perhaps lead him in the way he should go. And she needed a strong pair of hands sometimes to fetch and carry. Yes, she would cultivate George. She had another dog now for company, a shaggy stray of doubtful origins, but the animal, named Bella, spent most of her time gazing at her new mistress and saviour with adoring eyes, and this Agnes found totally satisfying.

Clearing out the house that had been their home for as long as Lily and her family could remember was a traumatic affair. Most of the furniture was to go to Torquay. The property there had been emptied of everything apart from the tables and chairs in the café.

George's new room had to be furnished but he told Lily that he wanted very little. 'Just a bed and table and chairs,' he said. 'I don't fancy doing any cleaning, and I don't want nothing what's got to be taken care of.'

Aunt Agnes was asked if she would like something to remind her of her brother and she chose a clock that she had long envied, a small mahogany table and some pictures. Lily was especially delighted and amused by her choice of one picture in particular. It was the painting which had always adorned the wall above the large double bed in the front bedroom. It bore the bizarre message 'Thou God Seest Me'. Lily could remember looking up at it when she had lain in disgust and terror beneath Harry Coney's thrusting body and had often wondered, during those times of horror, why this God who was apparently watching them did nothing to help her. She had supposed that it was because He was a male God and presumably took pleasure in the humiliation of women. If this wasn't so why had He decreed things in a way which was so monstrously unfair?

She was inclined to forgive the Almighty a little now however, for He had definitely come to her rescue, but that didn't mean that she wanted that picture in her new home, either to remind her of His all-seeing eye, or to bring back any of those sickening memories.

She grinned to herself as she took the dusty painting down. The words were entwined around a scene of mountains and rushing water. The artist must have thought that God liked those things. Well, perhaps He did. They reminded her for a moment of Duncan MacMullen. She hadn't given the Torquay doctor a thought lately, but resolved that when she returned to Devon she would seek him out and persuade him to tell her more about Augustus's state of health. He probably wouldn't enlighten her very much, but she could try anyway.

She removed an ancient cobweb and the body of a dried up spider from the back of the picture and then she turned it to the front again and polished the glass vigorously. She wondered where Aunt Agnes meant to hang it. Her bedroom?

201

Certainly it was more suitable for a spinster's domain. Her thoughts turned to Dot, and Lily couldn't help wondering, with wry amusement, what she had thought about these stern Biblical words when she had adulterously lain in this bed with Harry.

She carried the picture downstairs and wrapped it carefully in brown paper and placed it in the passage ready to be taken over to Aunt Agnes.

Dot, who was leaving for Bridgwater the following day, glanced at the parcel as she dumped an over-full suitcase beside it.

'Suppose that's the holy picture?' she said.

Lily grinned at her. 'Yes. All ready for Aunt Agnes.'

'Good luck to her then. It gave me the shivers.'

'I suppose if you live alone it might be nice to think of God always watching you.'

'Better her than me.' Dot shrugged her shoulders. 'I could never see why Mr Coney left it there.'

'Neither could I,' said Lily.

On the first Saturday of September William brought the removal van over to the house and he and George loaded everything that was to go to Torquay into it. The things that George wanted were stacked in the front room to be taken to the coal yard later.

Lily looked around at the denuded house and shivered. 'Well, this is it then.' she said. 'Goodbye to the past. Our new lives are beginning.'

It had been decided that Ivy should go to live with Lily in Torquay and she was dancing about on the pavement with excitement, her little dog barking and jumping up and down beside her. There was a space for her and Janey behind the passenger seat, and her own few belongings had been loaded earlier. Suddenly she stood still and looked solemn. 'It was sad leaving Aunt Agnes,' she said. 'And it's sad leaving this old house for ever. Even though I wasn't living here, it was still sort of home. Do you feel sorry about leaving it, Lil?'

'A little bit I suppose,' she replied. 'But you'll just love Torquay, I promise. And we can come back and visit Aunt

202

Agnes and George and William, and you can walk up and down this road if you want to and look at the outside of the house.'

'That'll be funny, thinking about new people living here.'

'It happens all the time to lots of families. We've just been lucky, staying in one house for most of our lives. Go and say a last goodbye to the place now if you want to.'

Ivy walked slowly inside, went through every room and then came out again. 'It's not like home any more now it's empty,' she said. 'I usually thought about how it was before Ma died anyway. I never liked it really after it belonged to Harry. That wasn't your fault of course, Lil,' she added hastily, 'but I don't think Mother and Father would have wanted him to buy it.'

'But if he hadn't, it wouldn't have been mine now to sell,' Lily said. 'Come on, no more sentimental feelings. Get Janey and yourself into the van.'

The last thing they saw that day of Sefton Road was George standing beside the privet hedge at the front of the house waving to them as William drove carefully away. He was to cycle over to the coal yard later.

Two weeks passed before Lily felt able to open the café for business again for there was much to do, things to buy, and Ivy to be settled into her new school.

'We want to catch the last of the tourists though,' she said to her sister. 'If they know about us they'll come back next summer.'

Ivy was enthusiastic, longing to work as a waitress in her spare time. 'I might get some tips,' she said. 'Especially if I smile nicely at the men.'

Lily was partly amused, partly horrified. 'If you behave like a trollop, I shall ban you to your room.'

'Only joking,' Ivy told her. 'I'll be good.'

There had been no time at first to seek out Duncan MacMullen, and Lily felt apprehensive about it anyway. It might seem presumptuous to ask questions about Mr Ashe. But one day, when the café had been open for just a week, he called. There was no one else in and he sat down and ordered coffee.

'I've heard about all the changes,' he said. 'I had to come and see for myself.'

Lily pushed a curl back from her forehead. 'You knew that I had bought this place?'

'Nothing much remains secret around here for long. A doctor hears almost everything.'

'And people know that Lilian Smith has turned into Mrs Coney?'

'Many do. There's been a lot of speculation. The newspaper article was much talked over of course.' He stirred two heaped teaspoonfuls of sugar into his coffee and then looked up at her and smiled. 'Most people who knew you and your marvellous teas are pleased that you've come back.'

She laughed. 'A form of cupboard love?'

'Perhaps.'

'Do you know what happened?'

'I too read the newspaper report, but knowing also what you had told me I was able to fill in the gaps.' He went on stirring his coffee, staring into its swirling froth. 'You must have had a very difficult time. I thought of you often and wondered what you would do. I was delighted when I heard that you had bought this place. I told myself that it probably meant you felt able to start a new life.'

'Yes.' Lily's mind flew back to that time on the way from Exeter when she had unburdened herself to him. He knew so much about her, but she had nothing to be ashamed of now and there were no secrets any more. Relief and happiness filled her heart, emotions to which she was becoming very accustomed lately.

'I shall always be around if you need any help,' he continued.

Lily wondered why a busy physician should be so concerned for her welfare. 'Thank you. I hope I'm not going to be ill!'

'I wasn't thinking of that.' He smiled. 'You look very healthy and very charming. I hope I can be your friend as well as your doctor.'

She blushed. 'Thank You. I should like that.'

Their conversation was cut short by more customers coming into the café and when she had served them and

204

Duncan MacMullen had gone, Lily realized that she had said nothing about Augustus Ashe.

By the end of October the café was making a moderate profit although custom was beginning to lessen as the shorter days arrived. News from William however told Lily that the coal business was really doing well as it always did at this time of year. The two businesses complemented each other, one for the summer, one for the winter. Orders for coal were increasing every day as people started to stock up with fuel for the winter months. Customers had got used to Harry not being there, William reported, and George was brilliant, cheerfully chatting up the housewives, old and young alike, and making them laugh as he carried in their sacks of coal on his sturdy back. He was very popular.

Lily thought that she would increase his wages after Christmas if William thought it a good idea. There was the small motor lorry to be bought next year as well. She knew that George had set his heart on modernizing everything, and the lorry was the first priority.

'Good,' Ivy said when Lily told her that she was planning this purchase. 'Poor old Flo can be retired and come to live here in Torquay with us.'

'We'll have to buy a field then,' Lily said. 'So we shall need to economize in other ways. I'm not made of money.'

Augustus continued to send postcards, none of them with any news of what he was doing in Switzerland or of when he was returning. Lily had quite a collection now and she bought a photograph album and fixed them carefully on to its pages with little gummed corners so that she could remove them and read the few meagre words that he had written on the back whenever she wished. They were still addressed to 'Miss Lilian Smith'.

Every time she bought a postcard of Torquay to send to him she wondered what she should say, but still signed them merely, 'Lilian'. Measuring her conduct by his she too gave no information, allowing him to continue in ignorance of the changes in her life. She wrote of small unimportant things, sometimes of a book she had read, the weather, the sea, any interesting customers who had come into the café, but of herself she said nothing. It would be impossible to tell him the whole complicated story on a postcard or even in a letter, and although the telling would be difficult however it was done she knew that she would feel more confident when she saw him face to face. The sudden jump from single impoverished girl to rich widow would need a lot of explaining.

She went into the bookshop occasionally. Although the shop mainly stocked antiquarian books, there was sometimes a volume in the window that took her fancy. Michael Dyer was usually uncommunicative. If she decided to buy he would take her money, wrap her book carefully, and nod as she left. Only once had he told her anything about Augustus, and he apparently wished never to repeat the confidences he had made. The friendship between herself and Augustus was completely disregarded as though it did not exist.

On one dull November day she could contain her curiosity no longer. 'Have you any news of Mr Ashe?' she enquired, trying to sound as disinterested as possible. 'You said back in July that you expected him home.'

'He had a slight set-back. He hopes to return to England for Christmas.'

Lily put out her hand to steady herself against the counter. She was taken aback, felt dizzy with shock. What kind of set-back? Why had Augustus not told her? She stared at Michael Dyer. Yes, there was definite hostility in his face now. 'A set-back? You mean his illness has become worse?'

'Only temporarily. If he says that he intends to come home then he must be greatly improved.' His voice was impatient. He obviously wanted to close the conversation.

'Do you think he's cured then?'

'I hope so.'

She recovered herself, took her change and her book but couldn't resist some further questions.

'Do you ever mention the café when you write to him?'

'I informed him that it had been sold.'

'But not who had bought it?'

'I allowed him to think that you are working for the new owner.' He was staring resolutely at the counter, not

206

meeting her eyes, his words formal and stilted. 'He told me that you write to him. He refers to you as Miss Smith so I concluded that you did not wish to enlighten him further. Consequently I have said nothing. I have no knowledge of your changed circumstances anyway. Mr Ashe must have no worries, nothing to intrude on his peace of mind.'

The weather was damp and dull. It was one of those hushed and subdued days when the sea fades imperceptibly into the misty sky and when even the gulls seem to possess less of their bounce and vitality. Christmas was just one week away and Lily had received no further cards or any message from Augustus. There had been no opportunity to talk to Duncan either.

She decided to close the café early for there were always fewer customers on Mondays, and seldom any after six o'clock. She had told Ivy that they would put some decorations up, make the place look cheerful for Christmas. They had been out the day before and brought in holly and branches of feathery evergreen from the woods. It was stacked in the little yard at the back, covered with some old sacking against the dampening drizzle.

She was just about to choose some of the best pieces to bring inside when she heard the tinkling of the door bell. Swiftly she wiped her hands and realized that she had not yet bolted the door or put up the CLOSED notice. She went through to the shop and then stood transfixed, staring at the tall pale young man who was smiling at her.

'Miss Smith,' he said. 'I'm so glad you decided to stay on here. Michael told me that there had been changes, that this place had been sold. You told me nothing on your postcards.'

'Augustus.' She could say little more than his name. She put her hand to her unruly hair and pushed it back from her forehead. If only she had known he was coming!

'I'm sorry to come so unexpectedly.'

They stood looking at each other and then he laughed. 'We're so formal, and after all these months.'

'Would you like some tea?'

'Yes please, and scones.'

207

Then Lily laughed too and he came over to her and took her hands in his. 'It's wonderful to be back, and wonderful to see you so little changed. I want to hear all about you, everything that has happened to you during these long months, and whether you're still happy here with your new boss.'

'My boss?'

He lowered his voice. 'The person who bought this place. Michael told me that it had been sold and the Baileys were gone.'

'Yes some weeks ago.' Lily suddenly felt her apprehension giving way to a quite inappropriate amusement. Perhaps it was just nerves but surely there was an amazingly funny side to the surprise she was about to spring upon Augustus? However she wasn't ready yet to embark upon her story. She must keep it until just the right time. She switched her attention to him.

'My news can wait,' she said. 'You've been ill, Augustus. You should have told me.'

He dropped her hands and his eyes were guarded as he continued to look at her. 'I wish Michael had said nothing about that. I didn't want you to know. But I'm healed now. The doctors are confident that the illness won't recur. My time in the trenches caused it, of course.' He smiled. 'I certainly feel quite robust and strong again, and I'm certain that Duncan will agree with that diagnosis when I see him tomorrow.'

'I do hope so,' she said. 'I was so worried about you.'

'That gives me a little selfish pleasure,' he admitted.

He had already removed his hat and put it on the stand. Now he removed his coat and sat down at his usual table. 'I want to forget that I was ever ill.'

'Of course,' she said. 'I'll get us some tea and something to eat.'

She went to the door, turned the CLOSED sign to the outside and shot the bolt.

At that moment Ivy bounced into the shop from the back. She stopped abruptly and stared at the newcomer. 'We're closed, aren't we?' she said pointedly.

Lily remembered her lies to Augustus. No brothers or sisters, she had told him.

'This is Mr Ashe,' she said quickly. 'Our neighbour. He owns the bookshop next door.'

He smiled at Ivy. 'Good evening,' he said. 'I'm sorry to come so late.'

Lily realized that he was trying to place her sister, wondering how he should greet her. Perhaps he thought she was the new owner's daughter. Well, he was nearly correct. Only the relationship was wrong!

'Miss Smith is just going to get me some tea,' Augustus continued apologetically.

Ivy gaped at him. 'Miss Smith?' she said. 'That's not her name any more.'

Chapter Fourteen

It was the moment Lily had been dreading, longing for, dreaming about, all of those things, the moment she had wanted to prepare for carefully, and now she was precipitated right into a rush of explanations. In the presence of her sister too.

Augustus was looking from one to the other, enquiry written large upon his features.

Lily was speechless for a moment then she turned to Ivy. 'Go and make us some tea,' she said brusquely, 'And bring cakes and scones.'

'Sorry, Lil,' Ivy muttered. 'The gentleman took me by surprise, calling you Miss Smith.' She looked aggrieved.

Lily winced at her sister's broad vowels and for one treacherous moment wished her back in Bristol. 'Go and get the tea, Ivy,' she directed more firmly this time. 'And hurry.'

Ivy turned rebelliously and Lily could hear her clattering about in the kitchen making much more noise than was necessary. She looked at Augustus, took in the clean elegant lines of him, the cravat tied at his neck, the smart suit, the startling fair hair and blue eyes which, for so long, she had hungered to see again.

'There's so much you don't understand,' she whispered. 'I don't know where to begin.'

'I'm very sorry for my mistake. I presume that you must have married while I have been away?' He sounded deflated, his buoyant air quite gone.

'I'm a widow,' she said without preamble. There was

no reason now for any evasion. She pulled out the chair opposite him and sat gingerly upon its edge. 'My married name was ... is ... Mrs Coney. I never was Lilian Smith. My Christian name is Lily.' She bowed her head, not wanting to see the rejection which she was sure must follow. Instead she was aware of movement, of his hand reaching out across the table towards her. She looked up and slowly responded, until their hands met on the white starched tablecloth. 'I thought you wouldn't ... that you'd be appalled by the lies I've told you, by my deception.'

'I don't know the reasons yet, but I'm sure you had good ones, and when you want to tell me, I'll be here for you ... Lily.' He paused over the name and smiled at her. 'It's far more charming than Lilian. Suits you very well.'

She felt tears of relief threating her now fragile composure. All the unfitting amusement of a few moments ago had vanished. 'Yes. I'll tell you. I've wanted to do so for a long time, ever since you took me to Cockington.'

Ivy pushed the door open, a tray in her hands. 'Tea and cakes for two,' she announced. She saw their clasped fingers, and waited until they had sheepishly withdrawn their hands before she put the tray down on the next table and started to lay places in front of them, plates, cutlery and cups and saucers.

'Ivy is my sister,' Lily announced before there should be any further misunderstanding. 'She's living with me now, partly to keep me company, and partly because my parents are dead as I told you. That at least was true.'

Augustus got to his feet and held out his hand to Ivy. 'I'm very pleased to meet you, Miss ...' He looked enquiringly at her.

'Penrose,' she said. 'But just Ivy'll do very well.'

'Ivy then,' he said.

She shook his hand very formally. 'I'd better go and leave you two love-birds then, hadn't I?' she said. 'Got everything you need?' She examined the table carefully, moving the milk jug closer to her sister, placing the cakes just so. She had been helping Lily in the café after school and was proud of her newly acquired skills as a waitress. When all was to her satisfaction she looked at the two of them and Lily desperately hoped that she was not about to wink. It would be just like Ivy to be deliberately provocative.

She merely grinned mischievously however and walked to the door. 'If you need anything else, just give me a shout.'

'She seems very efficient,' Augustus remarked.

Lily pushed nervously at the curling strands of hair that had escaped from the bun which she wore at the nape of her neck. 'I'm glad to have her,' she said, aware that sometimes the sentiment was not exactly true.

He nodded. 'Of course.' He took one of the home-made cakes that Ivy had placed before him and cut it carefully into pieces, and Lily, watching him, wondered how he could manage to eat anything at all at a moment like this.

'She's only thirteen.'

He looked up in surprise. 'At school then, I presume?'

'Yes. I also have two brothers.'

He finished the cake and wiped his mouth on the napkin that Lily had laundered to stiff perfection, before he replied. 'Older? Younger?' Was there a trace of unease in his voice?

'William is my twin, and George is almost fifteen,' Lily told him, and immediately visions of George floated disagreeably before her eyes. She knew that she would dread the day he and Augustus met. 'William is an accountant, or at least training to be, and George ...' She sipped her tea willing it to give her strength. 'He has left school in order to help with my other business. He is very good at it, very efficient and popular.' Those last words tumbled out in an effort to atone for her unworthy feelings. Was it the coal business she was ashamed of or was it George himself with his working-class voice, his grinning, joking presence?

Augustus settled himself more comfortably in the wicker chair, stirred sugar into his tea, and if he was surprised at these revelations, gave nothing away. 'So you are a twin?'

She nodded. 'William and I have always been close.'

'I envy you that,' he said. 'And you have another business then as well as this?'

Here we go, thought Lily. *Now or never.* 'Yes, a coal and removal business. George and another man do the manual work and William oversees the management side.' She shifted uneasily in the squeaking chair, drank the dregs from her cup and set it carefully down upon its saucer before she felt able to continue. 'It was my husband's business of course. I had nothing to do with it until now.'

'And he died recently?'

She closed her eyes for a second. How to go on? How was she to tell this man whom she loved the whole complicated story, the story that might send him from her for ever?

'Have you plenty of time?' she asked quietly. 'I should like to explain everything so that there are no more misunderstandings between us.'

'All the time in the world.'

She got up and closed the door which Ivy had left slightly ajar, and then started the long and involved tale. First there was her engagement to Arthur, his unnecessary and frightful death followed by her mother's illness, the family's poverty and Harry's offer of a home and financial rescue. She told of her misery when she realized what a fearful mistake she had made with her marriage. And then came the difficult part, the details that mustn't disgrace her sister. 'I thought that I should be hanged like Tess,' she said. 'I was sure I had killed him. That was why I ran away.'

'My poor, poor child,' he said, and once more his hands were outstretched for hers. 'But why ... Tess?'

'*Tess of the d'Urbervilles.* You remember, she was hanged for killing her husband?'

'That Tess ... yes of course. And you really thought ... dear God, how frightful! So all the time I've known you, you've been suffering that terrible burden?' He shook his head in disbelief.

'Until a few weeks ago, yes.'

'How was it that you took so long to discover that your husband was alive?'

'None of my family knew where I was. William searched for me. He went to London more than once. I had been too frightened to leave an address with them. I wanted to change into a completely different person.'

When her story was complete she fell silent and was aware of his blue eyes fixed upon her. Still fearing his reaction

213

she shivered, looked down at the tablecloth, examined every mark upon it. An eternity seemed to elapse before he spoke.

'Will you marry me, Mrs Lily Coney?'

Was this all a dream? Was she hearing correctly? Was it some bizarre joke? After the appalling story he had just heard he couldn't possibly be offering her an honourable marriage. And what about his own background, the secrets mentioned by Duncan MacMullen?

'I don't understand.'

'I'm asking you to marry me, Lily,' he repeated quietly. 'I know we haven't known each other for very long and I realize that you know little about me, but while I was away I thought of you constantly. I didn't know then whether the treatment for my illness would be a success or whether in fact I should ever come home. But here I am, cured and whole, and I love you. I want to carry you off and make you completely happy.'

She felt tears of amazement and relief on her cheeks as his hands clasped both of hers and she was aware of the warmth and the strength of him.

'Do you ... could you manage to love me a little?' His voice was humble.

How could she say that she had loved him ever since he had first walked into the café so long ago? She could find no words to answer.

'You came back to Torquay after your husband's funeral. Can I detect some hope in that?'

She managed to smile. 'Perhaps you can, Augustus,' she said.

'Then you will marry me? You'll say yes?'

She wanted to shout to the world that yes, of course she would marry him, right now, tomorrow, next week, as soon as she possibly could, but common-sense prevailed.

'I ... I don't know. It's too soon. I don't know anything about you, about your Dorset home.' The words seemed to come from someone else, a sensible career woman, the owner of two businesses, not a silly girl in love with a dream. She didn't know which she was, which part of her would win.

214

'I shall take you to Dorset as soon as our engagement is announced.'

She allowed him to pull her to her feet, to draw her into the tight circle of his arms, and her doubts vanished at once. She knew that the dream girl was winning over the common-sense one. She had never, in all her months of marriage, felt like this. Only long ago with Arthur had she experienced such happiness and fulfilment.

He held her for a moment more, kissed her gently on her cheek, and then to her dismay put her away from him, his hands on her shoulders. There was no fire in him answering hers, none of the eagerness that she expected. But she sensed fondness and concern, attributes she valued highly. Her months with Harry had taught her that those things were just as precious as passion and lust. In fact a marriage without genuine love was a recipe for disaster and misery.

'Say yes to me, Lily, and we shall go and buy a ring. Saturday perhaps?' Even if there was no sign of urgency in his body there was much in his voice.

Although she knew that her answer could only be yes, she knew too that she must have a little time. 'That's too soon,' she whispered. 'Give me a little while, Augustus. I must see William before I can make arrangements.'

He kissed her again and she felt the brush of his lips on her hot cheek like the soft touch of thistledown. He dropped his hands from her shoulders. 'Can we sit down again?' he said. 'There's one thing that I must tell you.'

Fear shot through her like a shaft of ice. Was this the mystery, the fearful secret of her imagination?

They seated themselves once more at the little table and she anxiously pushed the cups and plates aside.

'Something saddens and embarrasses me,' he said. 'And I must make sure that you know before you agree to marry me.' He paused for a moment and Lily held her breath wondering what awful thing he was about to reveal.

He continued slowly, 'Because of my illness and the possibility that some infection might linger I ... I won't kiss you on the lips. Can you bear that, Lily? Can you forgive me? I told you that I'm quite well now, and I

215

certainly feel hale and hearty, but I couldn't take any risks. I love you too much for that.'

She wanted to laugh and cry and shout all together with relief. She shook her head. 'I don't mind that at all, Augustus. I don't mind that at all.'

It was only later, when she lay alone in bed, that fresh doubts began to surface as they always did at night. The thought of marriage with Augustus seemed now to be beyond belief, almost preposterous. She couldn't imagine why he should want to marry her, and so quickly too. They were of different classes. How would she manage, how fit into a life-style that would be so unlike anything she had ever known?

She turned this way and that, lay on her back, stared at the ceiling which was dimly visible, and thought of all the problems and unanswered questions. Even though she loved him, was it sensible to throw away all her newly found independence, her precious freedom? What would happen to Ivy? Where would she live? Would it mean another change of school? What about the two businesses? And Augustus. Perhaps he wasn't healed at all in spite of what he said? Could one ever be certain of a cure for tuberculosis?

Angry with herself, she wondered why she was so prone to see the difficulties instead of rejoicing in her incredible good fortune. She sat up in bed, thumped her pillows in an effort to make them more comfortable, lay down again and tried to banish all these troublesome questions. She must go to Bristol of course, see William. Just talking to him would help sort things out in her mind.

Then, as sleep was about to release her, another disturbing thought brought her swiftly back to unwelcome wakefulness. The marriage bed! How could she endure it again, and yet how could she not? She stared through the open curtains at the moon which, having appeared from behind clouds, was now shining full into the room. She threw back the blankets and went to the window and looked down at the shimmering path of light reflected on the gently rippling water.

'There must be more to lovemaking than I know,' she whispered aloud. Lovemaking! That word had nothing whatsoever to do with the nightly miseries she had suffered

216

with Harry. Would it be different with Augustus? She leaned close to the glass and watched the boats swaying lightly on their ropes and eventually she smiled to herself. 'Yes, it will be different with Augustus,' she whispered aloud. 'With Augustus it will be perfect.'

In spite of the coldness of the December night she felt a sudden glow of warmth and happiness. She crossed her arms across her breast and knew that the magic of moonlight on water, the peace and beauty of the quiet night, had worked like a benediction. For now anyway her problems faded away. She crept back into the warmth of her bed and slept at last.

The following weekend she went to Bristol. On Saturday night she closed the café early, put on her warmest dress, a low-waisted wool with thickly pleated skirt and coat to match, and she and Ivy climbed into Augustus's motor car. He had insisted on driving them to the station.

'Look after her for me, Ivy,' he said on the platform as he helped them into the first-class carriage. 'And tell that brother of yours what a good chap I am!' He winked at her and produced a bag of toffees which he thrust into her hands.

'Thank you, Mr Ashe,' she called as the train moved out. 'I'll do my best for you.'

Lily was already seated and she waved sedately. Then she blew him a kiss through the dirty glass, the train gathered speed, rounded a bend, and Ivy flopped into the seat opposite.

'I like him,' she said. 'Gosh, Lil. Are we really going to be gentry?'

When they reached Bristol they took a cab straight to Aunt Agnes's where they were to stay for the one night. They sat up late drinking endless cups of tea and catching up with all the news, and early next morning William arrived noisily on his motor-bike.

'I can't believe it,' he said critically, after they had greeted each other. 'I just can't beleive that you want to marry again so soon, and someone whom you hardly know.'

217

'Don't sound so pompous, William,' Lily said. She was just clearing away the breakfast things when he arrived. 'Sometimes I can't believe it either, but I've known Mr Ashe longer than you think. He was my neighbour for much of the time when I first went to Torquay.'

'He's nice,' Ivy butted in. 'Fair and sort of delicate-looking, about as different from old black-face Harry as you could get.'

'Don't speak disrespectfully of the dead,' Lily directed, 'and I don't want your comments either. Go and wash up.'

Ivy grinned at William and flounced out. 'All right then,' she said. At the door she turned and looked mischievously at her brother. 'I think he's rich, by the way. He've got a big house in Dorset. What do you think of that?'

'I don't think anything,' William said. 'It's what he's like that matters, not how much money he has.'

''Tis important though,' Ivy added as she retreated. 'I'd like to be gentry.'

'You'll have to learn to speak properly then,' Lily said. 'You might try right away.'

When both Ivy and Aunt Agnes were out in the scullery and the door closed, Lily and William looked at each other.

'Are you really serious?' he asked. 'It's too soon, Lil. People won't like it if you marry so quickly after Harry's death.'

'We could be engaged for a longish time.'

'But you'd be committed. Why not wait for a few more months, a year perhaps? That would be more decent.'

'He doesn't want that. He suggested buying a ring this weekend. I should be engaged to him now if I had agreed.'

William shook his head doubtfully. 'I don't like all the rush. It's odd. Is there anything else you haven't told me?'

Lily hadn't said anything about Augustus's health. She hesitated. 'Well, yes. He's been in a sanatorium in Switzerland. He was gassed in the war and it brought on tuberculosis apparently. But he's better now, quite cured seemingly.'

Alarm spread over William's face. 'He may say so, but are you sure?'

'How can I be sure? He's had the best doctors, the most expensive treatment.'

'I don't think you should go ahead with this marriage, or even an engagement,' William said decisively. 'Something appears odd about it to me, Lil, and surely you've been hurt enough. I couldn't bear to see you harmed again. And TB is very infectious. You must know that.'

Lily sighed. 'Of course I do, but Augustus is very thoughtful.' She remembered his concern that he should never kiss her on the lips, and blushed. She could never say that to her brother though. 'Augustus would never harm me, William. I just know that. He's gentle and kind and honest. He wouldn't mislead me. He'd never want to cause me any kind of distress.'

'Perhaps not intentionally. I must come down and meet him. I should like to talk things over with him before you give a definite answer'.

'I want you to do that of course,' she said. 'You must meet Augustus, and I hope you'll like each other, but all my life I've had people telling me what to do, William. Over this I must make my own decision.'

'Of course, but we're twins, Lil. We've never had secrets from each other.'

'Well, not many,' she corrected. 'But while I want your approval, I don't need your consent. Sorry, William. Try to understand, please. Brothers don't control their sisters any more you know!'

He grinned at her. 'I'm aware of that, Lil. But I still feel responsible for you somehow.'

'Thank you. I appreciate it, and it's nice to feel protected, but women aren't chattels any more. I'm in charge of my own life now. Some of us have the vote. We are equal.'

He laughed. 'Not easy for us chaps to accept, however liberal we think we are. But you're right of course. When can I come down to Torquay?'

'Next weekend? You've already seen the café. You were pleased with that. Now approve of the rest of my life!'

'I hope I shall.'

She smiled at him fondly. It would take a very long time, she thought, before men lost their bossy ways.

219

Lily had redecorated the first-floor bedroom above the café making it into a large and handsome living room. The view over both the inner and outer harbours was almost as spectacular as from her bedroom higher up, and she wanted, for the first time in her life, to choose her own furniture, to have a place where she could entertain friends and relax in the few precious hours when she was not working.

She had stripped off the garish wallpaper with its huge red poppy heads and, knowing nothing of paper hanging, had found a young man willing to put the paper of her choice on the walls for a modest sum. She had chosen a creamy background with a delicate tracery of leaves, and to this she had added the painting of Cockington and two other pictures, one an old etching of Bristol to remind her of home, and the other of some wild place in Scotland, mountainous and challenging. This had appealed to her, made her think of all the possibilities of travel that might open to her one day now that she was free and had a little money of her own. It reminded her of Duncan MacMullen too. He was tough and sturdy like his native mountains, a sort of bulwark and a defence against the possibility of Augustus's health deteriorating. She knew that she would always feel a sense of security as long as Dr MacMullen was there to consult and advise.

The house was not fully furnished yet for there had been little time to search the second-hand furniture shops for just the things that appealed. She had found a comfortable chaise-longue, very old and in need of refurbishment, and over this she had temporarily thrown a bright patchwork quilt. She had placed it in the bay window so that she could occasionally put her feet up and look right across to the blunt-nosed outline of Berry Head in the far distance. There were frequent boat trips across the bay to Brixham in the summer and she dreamed of going there with Augustus, of standing on the deck and imagining herself on some exotic cruise in far-off tropical seas.

Two modern arm chairs and a mahogany table with its matching dining chairs completed the furnishings of this room so far. The carpet was still the old one that she had found there for it was good, threadbare in places but very beautiful, and she guessed that it had been in place for many years, perhaps dating back to the time when the house belonged to some wealthy merchant who had used this room as his main bedroom, and had not needed the indignity of changing his front room downstairs into a café.

There was little time for dreaming however and this weekend William was coming so she must see that everything was spick and span. He had seen the house before she made any improvements but now she wanted to impress him, to assure him that she was successful and capable of running her own life.

Augustus had been invited to come for dinner and he arrived promptly at seven o'clock on Saturday evening. Lily had seen him only briefly during the week for he had been to Dorset again. She was tense and nervous as she opened the door to him. He bent to kiss her on the cheek, and she blushed as she took his overcoat, his hat and cane, and remembered that he had said this was the only kiss he would ever permit even after they were married.

'Are you well?' she whispered, anxiously searching his face for signs of health that would help to allay William's fears.

'Yes. I'm glad to report that I am bursting with health. Duncan tells me that I can lead a perfectly normal life again.'

Lily was reassured and wished that she had invited the doctor to dinner too. He might have stressed this good news and so reassured her brother a little more. His company would have been pleasant too. For a moment she was disappointed and inclined to be cross with herself. 'We should have invited Dr MacMullen,' she said.

Augustus nodded. 'It would have been nice but he's probably busy. His partner likes the weekends off. A family man. Duncan however has no commitments. He seems a confirmed bachelor.'

'Perhaps he has an attachment in Scotland?'

'He's never said so.'

Lily thought that the young doctor must have plenty of admirers for he was certainly handsome. Then she banished him from her mind and preceded Augustus up the still uncarpeted stairs to the living room above the café. She had not invited him in here before and he looked around appreciatively as he followed her through the door.

'Lovely,' he said. 'I approve your taste. Where did you find these beautiful things? I'm sure that you'll be able to make something really spectacular out of my crumbling old house in Dorset'.

Her heart leapt with pleasure. He intended to include her in that part of his life then. Perhaps her fears about that house were quite unfounded, no mysterious secret lurking there.

'I'll do my best,' she said, then more nervously, 'would you like a glass of sherry?' It was the first time she had presided over a dinner party, certainly the first time she had cooked for anything so grand.

'Thank you.' He watched her pour, took the glass from her and stood with his back to the fire. She detected a slight nervousness in him. 'Is your brother not here yet?' he said.

'He's still in the bathroom. He managed to fix the ancient gas geyser for me and so he's having a long hot bath. He came by motor-bike, rather cold and dirty in this weather.'

Augustus shivered 'I should say do. Jolly brave of him if you ask me. Dusty too with the roads in the state they are. I've brought some wine by the way. Left it downstairs with my coat.'

Lily glanced at the small table on which she had placed glasses, the bottle of sherry and one of brandy. She had no wine. She had little experience of such things. It was one of the details she would have to learn about.

'Thank you, Augustus,' she said. 'Ivy can fetch it.'

Chapter Fifteen

When the swallows were in the Devonshire skies again, when Harry Coney had been eleven months in his grave, and when Lily was just six months short of her twenty-first birthday, she married Augustus Ashe.

She had not been to Dorset, had not seen his family home in spite of his promise to take her there, but she had resolutely laid her fears to rest on the day that she agreed to marry him. That had been in February. They had immediately gone into Exeter, bought a ring with the largest solitaire diamond that she had ever seen, and on the way home he had stopped the motor car in a field gate, placed the ring on her finger, and told her again that he loved her and longed to see her mistress of Ashcote.

'I want to take you there as my bride,' he said. 'Not before. As soon as we return from our honeymoon we shall go to Dorset. I've ordered some repairs and improvements – not too many of course because you must choose how you want things. Ashcote has been empty for a long time and needs some refurbishment before you see it.'

This last piece of information had surprised her. 'But you go often. How can it be empty?'

'Perhaps empty is the wrong word. I have staff there to look after everything, a housekeeper and her husband and a gardener and a few others, but the main rooms have all been closed since my mother died, the furniture sheeted down. I don't want you to see it like that.'

'But I shouldn't mind. It wouldn't worry me at all.

You said that we should go when our engagement was announced.'

'I know I did. It was foolish. I was thinking of it as it used to be. I want it to look beautiful again before we go. Would you forgive the change of mind? Could you be patient?'

He had looked at her with such devotion and such pleading that, although she had hestitated at first, she quickly set aside her misgivings.

'Of course, Augustus. If that's how you want it I'm happy to wait.'

It was only a house after all, and with Augustus at her side and his ring on her finger she had everything she wanted. She was filled with happiness. The old merriment, the high spirits that had been so much a part of her nature when she was growing up, when she was in love with Arthur, returned, and she almost forgot Duncan MacMullen's mysterious warning. It had probably just been to do with the consumption, she decided, and that was over now. Augustus was healed. Ashcote was the only mystery left and that, she concluded, was an exciting one. She was to be mistress of a house with servants. Occasionally she was apprehensive, but mostly the idea gave her little shivers of pleasure. Ivy was certainly delighted.

'I'll be able to come and live there in the holidays, won't I? You won't send me back to Aunt Agnes?'

'No, of course not.'

'Me and her got on well in the end, but I'd rather be in a big house in the country, seeing as I'm going to be gentry.'

An expensive boarding establishment for young ladies had been suggested for Ivy's last years at school, and to everyone's surprise she had agreed, but on one condition. 'I'm not going to a posh school where they'll laugh at the way I talk,' she had said firmly, and then added with a mischievous grin, 'If you can get me some elocution lessons though, so that I'll speak refined, maybe I'll get to like it.'

The lessons had been arranged, Ivy's speech speedily improved, and she had started after Easter. Her uniform had given her great pleasure and she announced to George, who had laughed at both this and her posh voice, 'If you don't change too, Georgie love, I don't think you'll be allowed at the wedding or at this Ashcote place.'

'And how'll I get on with all me customers if I speak la-de-dah?' he had said.

'You must have two voices,' Ivy told him severely. 'One for the family, one for the streets. You can do it perfectly well. You're the clever one. Get some practice. You won't let me beat you surely?'

Thus challenged, George too had managed to perfect two idioms and by the time Lily's wedding day was imminent he considered himself to be two different people. He thought the idea a great lark and had thrown himself into perfecting both roles with mirth and enthusiasm. His wardrobe now contained an expensive suit and a pair of white flannels, smart shirts, ties and cravats. 'I intend to marry a toff one day too.' he told his brother. 'I hope Lily manages to find a beautiful heiress for me. Then I'll give up the coal.'

William, looking at the handsome figure of his previously ragamuffin brother, was amazed at the metamorphosis. 'And what'll this heiress say to marrying a former coalman?' he had asked a trifle cruelly.

'She'll like me muscles,' said George.

Lily had made arrangements to let the café to a new tenant for a limited period, although not the rest of the house. 'I intend to keep it,' she announced. 'It means a lot to me. I have no intention of selling it. One day we could make the café into a parlour again, and could come here for holidays.'

She had named the property Rose House. 'Not very original,' she had told an amused Augustus, 'but it seems right somehow.' The thought that she actually now owned those sturdy walls with the three bay windows one above the other all looking out across the sea to Brixham, gave her immense pleasure, a sense of security and a degree of power over her own life.

'The penniless little girl that I had thought to marry has changed,' Augustus had remarked, mirroring her thoughts. 'I am about to wed a rich widow.'

'Not really rich,' Lily had replied, although she knew, with a little inner flicker of pride, that the coal yard was doing well, giving her a steady income. She had bought the lorry that George craved and this was used for coal deliveries, thus easing Flo's load considerably. The van was kept for removals. Both George and Dick Parker had fairly handsome wages now and William too was benefiting for she paid him well for overseeing the accounts and supervising generally.

The rent from the café would also bring a small but regular income. She remembered her mother's advice. A woman needs her own money. Lily resolved that however much she loved Augustus, however secure and happy her marriage, she would see to it that she was always in control of her own capital, and that she had some steady profits as well.

Her wedding dress was made in a creamy taffeta, quite straight, and she wore a cape over it with a delicate feathery neckline that flattered her lovely features. During the last happy and exciting weeks she felt that youth had returned to her, and when she looked in the mirror she saw that the worry lines had disappeared and her eyes sparkled as they had not done for months.

The dress was short, its hemline not far below the knee. 'We're in the twenties,' she reminded a disappointed Ivy, who had imagined a great romantic crinoline with a train yards long which she would carry proudly down the aisle. 'It's my second wedding, remember, and I'm not some kind of princess.'

To emphasize her advanced and emancipated status she had her hair bobbed so that the heavy bun gave way to carefully arranged marcel waves that were far more trouble to fix in place. At the hairdressers she had asked that her long hair, instead of being swept up and put in the bin, should be bound firmly into a switch. This had been done and she had put it away in a box, tied it with ribbon and placed it in the big trunk which was to stay at Rose House. 'It's a symbol of my bondage,' she told Ivy. 'I shall keep it for ever to remind me that I must never again be in servitude

226

to anyone as I was to Harry. When you are older you can have your hair cut off too.'

They were to be married in Torquay in the beautiful Trinity Church. Augustus chose Duncan MacMullen for his best man, and Lily was glad of this. Duncan would be a pillar of strength, a sort of bulwark. Not that Augustus needed support, but nevertheless, she was happy that he would be present, and was decidedly relieved that Michael Dyer had not been chosen. The young bookshop assistant continued to give her unaccountable shivers and she was sorry that he had been invited to attend the reception, but Augustus had insisted upon it. 'We have very few friends,' he had said. 'And I couldn't possibly leave Michael out.'

'Have you no relations?' Lily had asked in surprise when she was writing out the guest list.

'None that matter or that I want at my wedding.'

She had felt some uneasiness at this revelation but tried, with moderate success, to put it from her mind. His parents were dead, there were no brothers and sisters, and probably most of his male acquaintances had been killed in the war. There was no possible reason to infer any sinister cause for his refusal to have the ceremony in Dorset or for the absence of family and friends.

However, on her wedding day, when she saw through her veil the almost empty pews on his side of the church, she experienced a flicker of anxiety. But as she stood beside him at the altar and saw the warmth of his smile, and when he turned towards her and she heard his ringing vows to love and cherish her as long as they both lived, then the moment of disquiet was banished. She was giving herself willingly and happily to this man whom she loved so much. The last weeks had been quite miraculous and she was sure that the magic would never desert her now.

And Duncan was there too, standing beside Augustus, strong and capable, a further cause for calm and tranquillity. As best man he was perfect, Lily thought. She was grateful for his loyalty. He had been a good friend to both of them for a long time now. His strange warning to her some time ago must have been laid aside, or perhaps whatever it was that he had referred to no longer troubled him.

Outside the church he smiled at her, and she returned his smile and felt a warm glow of security. With Duncan in charge everything had so far gone smoothly, all the little details of the wedding perfectly co-ordinated. And in the more serious matters of life too she knew that he would always be there for them, his concern always staunch and without self-interest. Occasionally she had asked herself why he was so devoted in the friendship he offered and had found no answer. He was just ... just Duncan, a thoroughly good man.

Although there were so few guests Augustus had insisted, to Ivy's delight, on a small but luxurious reception in the Imperial Hotel. However this didn't entirely make up for the lack of exciting new male relatives. 'You'd have thought he could have produced a few cousins or friends, wouldn't you?' she whispered to Aunt Agnes as they entered the dining room that had been reserved for them. 'Dr MacMullen's all right, but too old. And in a skirt too!'

She giggled behind her hand for Duncan was wearing full highland dress and this attire had caused much comment as well as admiring glances.

'Shush,' Agnes whispered back. 'Dr MacMullen is certainly not old. No more than thirty if you ask me, and a more charming escort you couldn't wish for.' She frowned severely at her niece. 'Not all folks are as lucky as you, Miss, with a nice family and two handsome brothers as well. Be grateful.'

Agnes was not usually in the habit of praising anyone, let alone her younger nephew, but George had just come into her line of vision and as she looked at him she considered that it must have been her influence that had wrought such a miraculous change. He was resplendent in one of his new outfits and as far as she could see was on his best behaviour, his street voice strictly curbed.

However she failed to hear him whisper to Lily a little later when Augustus was absent for a few moments, 'You done well for yourself, our Lil. Am I going to get an invitaion to the posh house then?'

228

Lily grinned at him. 'Yes, I expect so. If you promise to behave. I haven't been there myself yet.'

William, overhearing, frowned. It seemed strange that she had not visited the family home. It was the one thing that worried him. He hoped that there was nothing ominous about this singular fact.

The honeymoon was to be spent in London and Italy. They had a first-class compartment to themselves and sat in corner seats staring at each other, scarcely believing that it was all true, that they were man and wife at last. Augustus leaned forward and clasped Lily's gloved hands. 'Mrs Ashe,' he whispered. 'I've thought about it, dreamed about it, for so long.'

'But you haven't known me for that long.'

'It feels that there has never been a time without you.'

She smiled at him. 'Now you're being fanciful,' she said. She thought about her new name, Mrs Ashe. Another name to become accustomed to. Lily Penrose, Lily Coney, Lilian Smith, Lily Ashe. This last didn't quite possess the right ring to it. Lilian Ashe would have sounded better. Perhaps that was how Augustus had thought of her in his mind? He had first known her with that false name and identity, Lilian Smith. She smiled to herself. Was poor Lilian Smith quite dead and buried now, rising again as Mrs Lily Ashe? 'Lily Ashe sounds strange,' she said aloud. 'Mrs Lily Ashe.'

'But you're Mrs Augustus Ashe, my wife,' he said. 'That sounds wonderful.' He squeezed her hands tightly in his and then released her and sat back in his seat watching the sea, for at this point on the journey between Torquay and London the railway line ran right beside the beach.

Lily too looked at the waves, grey now reflecting the darkening sky, and for a brief second her mood of happiness was quenched slightly. Had she really once again submerged her identity completely into that of another human being? Why did it have to be so? Why must a woman lose her name, her father's name and even her Christian name, on marriage? She repeated the words quietly to herself 'Mrs Augustus Ashe.' Then more loudly she said, 'Mr and Mrs Augustus Ashe perhaps, but I am Mrs Lily Ashe. I don't want to lose my name again, Augustus.'

He picked up the newspaper which was lying on the seat beside him and scanned the headlines before he replied. 'It's customary for a wife to be called by her husband's first name, I believe, but of course, my dear, if you want to be Mrs Lily Ashe, I wouldn't dream of insisting that you have it any other way.'

The hotel was one of the best and the room he had booked for two nights before they were to leave for the continent was luxurious, the furnishings gilt-painted and opulent. There was even an adjoining bathroom. Lily had never seen anything so grand. Dinner too was a splendid affair but she found herself picking at each course, eating little.

Augustus on the other hand appeared to have an excellent appetite. 'Are you well?' he asked, looking anxiously at the large piece of steak which the waiter was about to bear away.

'I'm fine,' she said. 'Just not hungry.' When the waiter had gone she leaned across the table. 'The meat was raw,' she whispered. 'There was blood all through it.'

Augustus laughed. 'Rare, my dear. That's how steak should be served.'

Lily sat back in her seat considerably shaken. What a lot she had to learn. She vowed never to order steak again.

Augustus was immediately concerned at her downcast face. He glanced around to make sure that he could not be overheard. 'We're both tired,' he murmured. 'Don't think that I shall ... shall worry you tonight, dearest. If that is why you're not eating, please relax. We have all the rest of our lives.'

It was a strange speech and Lily blushed. She wasn't at all apprehensive about this first marriage night. She had thought about it, compared the possibilities to that other terrible time when she had been innocent and ignorant, and under Harry's hands and urgent body had suffered so much. She was sure that nothing like that could happen with Augustus, and she loved him, wanted him, was totally ready to give herself to him. So why was he telling her that he wouldn't ... worry her tonight?

She too glanced around, embarrassed in case anyone had heard him or knew that they were on their honeymoon. All the other occupants of the dining room were intent on their own concerns however, and, reassured, she relaxed a little. Of course she reminded herself, he had been ill, very ill, possibly nearly died of the consumption. She must look after him, see that he never did too much, never overstrained himself.

She put her hand over his on the starched table cloth in a motherly gesture, and in that moment she did indeed feel motherly towards him. 'I'll enjoy my dessert,' she said a little mischievously. 'I always liked puddings more than firsts.'

The bed was huge and it had a great canopy above it supported on four elaborately carved posts.

'I specified a four-poster,' Augustus said. 'Like the one we have at home.'

He was wearing a long nightshirt when he came from the bathroom and he climbed into the bed beside her but kept a respectable distance between them. Lily wanted to reach out for him, pull him into her eager arms, but instead lay still, outwardly composed. He was obviously tired. He had said so, and she must not show her own youthful energy, must never allow him to think that she was either more healthy or more eager for lovemaking than he was. It was one of the rules of life that all women knew. Never start anything, leave the man to lead, lie back, be submissive in everything. Well, not everything, she thought, but in this part of marriage, definitely yes.

He moved towards her, kissed her gently on the cheek. 'We should sleep well,' he said. 'It's wonderful to have you beside me, Lily. I love you very much.' He turned away from her, put out the light, and she remained quite still, hardly daring to move for fear of disturbing him. She couldn't believe that her longed for wedding day was ending like this. For a long time she lay in the semi-darkness and thought that perhaps everything would be right in the morning. His strength would be renewed and their marriage would be consummated then. Unaccountably she thought of Duncan MacMullen and for a treacherous moment wondered what it would be like to be married to him. Then she laughed at herself. No, he would be urgent, lustful perhaps, just a trace like Harry Coney.

231

She felt guilty for thinking so, for of course Duncan was a gentleman, an honourable man, but she was quite sure that it was the very reverse of those masculine things which had attracted her at first to Augustus. If her new husband was a little less than passionate, well, that was all for the best. She wanted security and love, and above everything else, kindness.

There was an abundance of pillows on the bed, two each on top of the long bolster, and gingerly she eased herself up a little and pulled one out from beneath her shoulders, slid it down and put her arms around it, hugging it for comfort.

When Lily awoke the next morning Augustus was standing at the window, a warm dressing gown over the nightshirt. For a moment she wondered where she was for she had been dreaming. She sat up in bed and looked at him. The pillow she had been holding so tightly was on the floor.

'I've ordered tea,' he said as he turned to smile at her. 'It should be here any moment.'

She forced an answering smile. Perhaps they both needed tea, the great restorer. 'That's nice,' she said. 'I've seldom had tea in bed.'

'You shall have it every morning when we get to Ashcote.'

She wanted to tell him that she would rather have him in her arms than all the tea in the world. She wanted to jump from the luxurious silk sheets, run to him, pull him back into bed beside her, strip off those foolish constricting clothes. Instead she pulled the sheets up to her chin like a shrinking Victorian bride. 'I shall like that,' she said. Privately she wondered who would bring it to her. Would he? Was that how he saw himself? In her experience if anyone brought tea in bed it was usually the wife.

A knock at the door interrupted her thoughts. She watched while the waiter, carefully not looking in her direction, placed the tray on the table and then withdrew, closing the door quietly behind him. Augustus, as if answering her question, poured milk and tea into the delicate china cups and handed one to her. 'Your servant, madam,' he said with a bow and a mock grin.

She wondered if he would get back into bed to drink his.

But he carried it to the window and stood there until he had finished and then placed the cup and saucer carefully on the tray again and looked at her. 'Do you want to bathe first?' he asked.

She could feel tears threating now and leapt from the bed. 'Yes, please.' She pulled her robe around her shoulders and went into the adjoining bathroom, wrestled with the geyser and eventually lowered herself into the scalding water, caressed her skin with the sponge and scented soap that was provided and lay there wondering what could possibly be wrong. Her careful composure of the previous night was fast disappearing. Was there something in her appearance that he found distasteful? Dear dear God, she couldn't possibly have made another frightful mistake could she?

She towelled herself vigorously, carefully covered her eager yearning body with the robe and went nervously into the bedroom.

'Ah, you've finished,' he said. 'I shall try not to be long. I want to show you the National Gallery after breakfast, one of my favourite places.' He smiled at her again and went into the bathroom. She noticed that he was carrying his clean undergarments over his arm.

Some of Lily's distress receded when they stepped out of the hotel. The sun was shining and a day of excitement lay before her, a day full of luxury, new sights and sounds, her first day of marriage to the man she loved. She resolved to enjoy every minute, to put her misgivings behind her. She was in the capital for the first time in her life, an attentive new husband at her side, no distressing secrets in her life to be hidden, no worries about money, pretty clothes to wear, and no Harry Coney to lie beside in misery tonight. She should be the happiest woman in the world!

Augustus was a wonderful companion, attentive to her every need. We are good friends, she thought, and that is important.

She stared in amazement at Nelson's Column, fed the pigeons, and then looked in awe and wonder at the impressive frontage of the National Gallery. Once inside its great doors she realized how little she knew about art, or about anything that Augustus would think important, and wondered for another dismaying moment how she could ever make a suitable wife for this man who was staring with such passion at the painting of a sea battle. How could such a picture inspire that kind of devotion she wondered when he hardly dared to look at her last night.

'Do you like water-colours?' he said, and without waiting for her answer continued, 'These are Turners. He's one of my favourite artists. He was something of a visionary, a dreamer, a bit like myself.' He turned to her and smiled. 'Forgive me, my dear, perhaps you don't know me well enough yet.' He touched her hand briefly. 'Look at this one,' he said. "The fighting Téméraire". I would give everything I have to own that.'

They stood for a long time before the painting and Lily was dismayed. How could anyone say such a thing? It was incomprehensible to her. Yes, she thought, it was a fine picture. She could see that the colours were good, the frame very beautiful, but she didn't think she would want it over any fireplace of hers, let alone give everything she had worked so hard for to own it.

She was wise enough however to say nothing. She knew that anything she uttered was likely to betray her ignorance. She walked beside Augustus pretending to appreciate the paintings to which he was so deeply devoted and occasionally she stopped beside one or another that he was inclined to pass by.

'I like the ones with people in,' she said, hoping the words didn't sound too stupid. 'I like to see their faces, especially the women. I wonder about them, what kind of lives they had all those years ago.'

He looked at her indulgently. 'Then we shall go to the Portrait Gallery,' he told her. 'You would like that.'

Her heart sank. Some of the London shops would have been more to her taste. But she said nothing, trailed round with him until her feet were hurting unbearably in the fashionable patent leather shoes she had chosen so proudly for this honeymoon. Eventually she felt that if she saw many more pictures hanging so stupidly row upon row in their over-heated galleries, she would scream. She wanted lunch, wanted fresh air, wanted to walk in old shoes over green

234

fields, wanted her husband's arms around her, wanted his kiss on her lips.

The afternoon was more to her liking. They found an expensive shoe shop and laughed together over the choosing of a pair of comfortable shoes and then walked in Green Park, took a cab to Buckingham Palace hoping to see the King, and finally went to Westminster Abbey.

Dinner was excellent, the wine of the very best, and Lily, choosing from the menu carefully, this time enjoyed each course. Afterwards, replete and exhausted with her day of sight-seeing, she wanted, perversely, nothing more than a comfortable bed and long hours of uninterrupted sleep tonight. However it was not to be. Augustus pulled her into his arms, kissed her on her cheeks, each side again and again, never her lips, kissed her neck and then, gently pulling her nightdress open, her breasts.

In spite of her tiredness she responded, excitement replacing last night's despondency. She had been foolish to worry. Everything was going to be all right after all. She had frequently felt inadequate during the day, had shown her ignorance of many things, but now it was she who was the experienced one. She guessed that few men were unpractised, but Augustus, with his time at the Front, and then the long months in a sanatorium, probably hadn't had many women.

It soon became obvious to her that there may not have been any at all for his fumblings were quite inexpert, so different from the frightful demands of Harry Coney, and when at last he was successful she felt a little frisson of pleasure but it was quickly extinguished. Suddenly he seemed disinterested as though he had withdrawn from her mentally as well as physically. He lay still for a moment and then slid from the bed, pulled his nightshirt over his head and padded to the bathroom.

When he returned he lay on his back beside her again, but once more with a space between them, only his arm stretching out to touch her. 'Not very good, my darling,' he whispered. 'My fault entirely. When we get to Venice everything will be better. We shall not be so tired.'

Venice, she thought, Venice. A place she had seen in

pictures, a town where water ran instead of roads, another place full of paintings and works of art that she knew nothing about. Would its magic work for him? Would he love her properly there? She gripped his hand. 'I love you, Augustus,' she said.

As in London, Augustus had chosen one of the best hotels and Lily was awed by its position and its luxury. She stood on the balcony of their bedroom on the first morning and thought the scene before her too magical to hold any reality. She gripped the old stone balustrade, warm even now in the morning sun, and stared in wonder at the expanse of water below, the buildings rising right out of it, looking almost as if they floated.

Augustus came and stood beside her. 'Like it?' he said.

'Like it? That's not the word at all. I've never seen anything so astonishing in my whole life.'

Augustus laughed. 'Astonishing! Yes I suppose it is when you first see it. The wonder of Vencie never leaves one really.' He pointed to a great dome in the distance. 'That's the Church of Santa Maria Della Salute,' he said. 'One of my favourites. We shall go there.'

'Santa Maria Della Salute,' Lily repeated, trying to copy the ring of the Italian words. 'It sounds far more exciting than plain old St George's at home, doesn't it?'

'Italian is a beautiful language.'

'Did you learn at school?'

'A little, but I've been here a few times. I came with my parents when I was a child before the war. My mother was particularly fond of Venice.'

Lily sighed. The gulf between them seemed to widen with every new experience. 'I should like to learn.'

He smiled. 'Not strictly necessary,' he said. 'You'll always be with me.'

She wasn't altogether pleased with this remark. It irked her new sense of independence. 'I believe the most splendid church is St Marks, isn't it?' she said, trying to sound knowledgeable. She had managed to find a little guide book to Venice before she left England and had read it dilligently. Although it had not prepared her for the

236

splendour, it had given her a few facts which she had stored in her memory.

'We shall go there this morning,' Augustus said. He looked at her with pleasure and she was glad that she had been able to show a little intelligence. 'But breakfast first.'

Lily gaped at the silver and gilt trolley that was wheeled into the room a little later, and at its lavish array of food. If only Ivy could see all this, she thought suddenly, and George and William too. Whatever would they make of such luxury? She laughed a little at the idea and then gave herself up to the enjoyment of it.

That whole day passed in a magical panorama of new sights and sounds. The soft light of the warm Italian sky and the water's reflected radiance added a beauty to the mellowed old stones for which nothing in Lily's entire life had prepared her. She had expected a degree of boredom, but not for one moment was she bored, and when she sank into a scented bath before dinner she knew that this had been one of the most wonderful days of her life.

When she told Augustus this and saw his eyes upon her she wondered if it would end with a different kind of magic.

Much later, after they had dined, danced beneath the hundred glittering lights of the great chandeliers, and then drank the champagne which was waiting for them in their room, Augustus attempted to make love to her again.

Lily shivered in suspense and expectation as he climbed into bed beside her. He lay for many minutes quite still, and then he turned to her, took her into his arms, and kissed her, not passionately, not on the lips, but yet with a determination and resolve that she found odd. She held him tightly, rejoicing in his success, but wondered afterwards whether it was at this moment that she knew there would never be deep sensual love between them, that there was something not quite right about the sort of love Augustus was offering her.

There was little physical satisfaction for her at all in his lovemaking. Any enjoyment came only from their togetherness, from her sense of security, and yes, from her slight feeling of superiority. She would never reveal this of course, but she thought about it frequently afterwards.

In everything else Augustus was the one to do the giving. He was her superior in knowledge, in wealth, in experience, but she soon realized that in bed he felt inadequate. By the end of the honeymoon she knew that he was vastly grateful to her, thankful that she didn't laugh at his incompetence.

After Venice they toured in Italy. Lily enjoyed almost every moment of it and by the time they returned to England she had decided how her marriage would work, how she would cope with her husband's lack of a normal man's desires. She decided that she would always be there for him when he wanted her, however seldom this was, but that she would never try to seduce him. The one and only time she had attempted to pull him into her arms he had turned from her, causing her to recoil in dismay. That would never happen again.

But if one part of their union was unsatisfactory their friendship should be supreme. She was determined that she could manage quite well without frequent lovemaking. In her months of marriage to Harry Coney she had had enough to last a lifetime, she told herself firmly. Being wedded to Augustus was a completely different way of life. She was confident of his love. That was the most important thing.

As if to compensate he was constantly buying her presents. In Venice there had been elaborately wrapped little gifts every day, jewels, perfume, flowers, chocolates, vases decorated with a tracery of silver and gold.

'You are making me into a very spoilt wife,' she had told him.

'You deserve all of it.'

There had been a strange edge to his voice, a sadness, and she knew that he was striving to make up, in the only way he knew, for what he perceived to be his failings. It made her want to weep for him, it made her love him even more.

On the last night of their honeymoon after he had tried unsuccessfully to make love to her she had cradled him in her arms and had wept in spite of her desire not to betray her feelings.

He had been aware of her tears, had brushed them gently away. 'I'm sorry,' he had said. 'Can you put up with me, Lily? Is this enough for you?'

She knew that she would never forget his grief and his humility. 'Of course it's enough for me Augustus.' she whispered. 'I love you.'

She was quite determined that whatever the future held, it would always be so.

Chapter Sixteen

Ashcote Manor was surrounded by trees and by its own fertile acres and lush woodlands. Augustus and Lily arrived in early-June to the constant hum of bees over the clover fields and the last stammering calls of a cuckoo from the orchard.

Lily had been nervous and ill at ease during the drive from London. She had pulled her cloche hat down low on her forehead and held the collar of her coat tightly around her neck for Augustus had decreed that they must drive with the hood down as it was such a beautiful day. She sensed a nervousness in him too.

He turned the motor car into the drive through tall wrought iron gates that stood open and Lily saw the house for the first time. She clapped her hand over her mouth in awe. Its golden beauty was quite breathtaking in the glow of the afternoon sun, but she was dismayed as she stared at its ancient walls, at the great size of it, and at the door which swung open at the sound of tyres on gravel.

The middle-aged man who had opened it stood for a moment looking at the motor car, then he walked down the steps towards them. Augustus jumped out, came round to the other side of the vehicle and held the door for Lily. He nodded curtly at the man. 'Everything all right, Dunne?' he said. 'You had my instructions carried out.'

'Yes, perfectly, sir.'

'My wife,' Augustus said to him as he took Lily's hand and helped her out.

'Welcome to Ashcote, Madam.' The man bowed slightly.

'I hope you'll be comfortable here.'

Lily noticed that his eyes didn't meet those of Augustus, that he kept his glance firmly lowered, and wondered if she was imagining the feeling of antagonism between the two men.

'I'm sure I shall,' she said, wondering if she could ever be comfortable in such a vast place. Augustus led her to the entrance. 'Dunne and his wife keep the house running very efficiently,' he told her. Then almost as an after-thought he turned back to the man. 'Is Mary well?'

'Quite well, thank you, Sir. She'll be in the hall waiting to greet Mrs Ashe.'

'Good. Have you engaged any more staff to look after us?'

Ted Dunne nodded. 'A maid for Mrs Ashe and another girl to help in the kitchen.' He held the great front door for them to enter.

A maid? Lily couldn't believe that she had heard correctly, but didn't comment. She had learned that if she kept her mouth firmly closed she couldn't utter anything foolish.

'Bring the luggage up will you?' Augustus ordered. 'And we should like tea in the parlour. My wife is very tired.'

Lily's tiredness had quite left her, but she knew that he liked her to show some weakness now and then, some need of his help, so she nodded. 'That would be nice,' she said meekly.

Mary Dunne was a stout comfortable-looking woman and Lily glanced at her with relief. Here was a possible friend, if one was allowed to make friends with one of the staff. She felt that she needed a friend just now and smiled at her.

Unlike her husband there was no condescension or hostility in Mary's attitude, just open kindliness and warmth. 'Welcome home,' she said. 'Glad you've got here safe and sound. I'm a bit afeared of motor cars.' She then addressed Lily directly. 'Do you want to go up first or shall I get the tea straight away?'

'I'll go up and have a quick wash,' Lily said, 'if that's all right?'

'Whatever you wish, Mrs Ashe,' Mary said, and Lily realized that her usual vigilance had deserted her. Those last words had been a mistake. Whatever her friendly smile might convey, this woman was still a servant and she, Lily Ashe, the mistress whose pleasure and convenience must come first. It was a new concept and Lily knew that she must get used to it quickly if she was not to betray her humble origins. She wanted to shout out that she was just a woman, just Lily, that she had never had things done for her before, that this new status was totally alien and confusing. But she merely smiled politely as she had done in the hotels to which Augustus had taken her during the past weeks.

'The master bedroom is ready,' Mary said to him. 'And the plumber has completely re-done the bathroom, as you directed.'

They were still standing in the entrance hall. It was stone-floored and cheerless and Lily shivered in spite of the warm sunshine outside. She glanced through the open front door. 'I should like my suitcase.'

'Ted'll be taking them up. He'll go round the back way.' Mary swung open another door behind her. 'This way, Madam.'

Lily gasped as she glanced at the room beyond. This wasn't a house at all. It was a museum. She had had enough of museums during the past weeks. She had not thought to live in one.

She walked slowly through as if in a dream. There were sad heads of animals staring reproachfully down at her from the walls beside the guns that she thought must have ended their lives. But there were more ancient armaments too — swords, shields, fearsome-looking pistols all fixed to the cold stone. And right down the middle of the room was a long table. Lily stared at the vast size of it, at its well-worn and gleaming wood, and immediately wondered at the endless hours of labour that must have been bestowed upon it in order to achieve that luminous shine.

Augustus sensed her amazement, perhaps was even aware of her dismay. 'This is the Great Hall,' he said. 'My father insisted that it should remain as it has always been, but the house has more comfortable parts.' He took her arm gently and steered her towards the stone staircase that was visible beyond a great archway. 'It is Tudor of course.'

Lily only had vague ideas of what Tudor meant. Something to do with the first Queen Elizabeth, she remembered. She wondered what response to make to such an incredible announcement. How did one live, actually live, in a house of such great age? A large painting of some long-haired and elaborately dressed gentleman looked down at them from halfway up the stairway.

'Sir William Ashe,' Augustus said. 'The house was presented to him for services he rendered to the state in 1620. It's been in our family ever since.'

'And you are the last one of the line?'

Augustus looked at her sharply. 'At the moment, yes,' he said.

The man in the picture appeared to be leering at her. She turned away, and then suddenly understood everything, why she was here, why Augustus had married her, what was expected of her. She held the future of this great house in her hands, or rather her body. Of course, Augustus had to have an heir. She was just a means to an end. It was an archaic idea, but it fitted this house, this strange marriage, this trap into which she had so enthusiastically fallen.

She said nothing until they reached the bedroom. Completely unaware of her thoughts, Augustus flung open the door with a flourish and Lily had another shock. This room was lovely, but it was fit for a princess, not for the ordinary girl she still considered herself to be.

A huge four-poster bed stood in the middle, but the drapes and the bed coverings were obviously quite new, crisp and beautiful. Impulsively she sat upon it and found to her surprise and delight that it was soft and comfortable – inviting! Her spirits began to revive. If Augustus needed an heir, then he would have to make love to her often however difficult he found it. And that suited her splendidly. She would like a baby very much, lots of babies perhaps.

She hadn't thought much about babies until now, although she had frequently wondered why she never found herself in the family way when she was married to the over-sexed Harry Coney. Dear God, perhaps she was barren? A shiver of horror passed through her and she wanted to laugh hysterically.

But no. It couldn't be. She would banish the fearful idea as speedily as it had come. She would have at least ten babies! There would be no poverty to consider, life would be easy and pleasant. She guessed that if she produced the required heirs she would be waited upon hand and foot, her every whim pandered to. There would be a nanny and more servants. This great house needed children.

Perhaps she could get used to this amazing life that providence had hurled at her! She wanted to hold Augustus in her arms in this splendid bed, to pull the curtains around it and to make babies right here in the place where she guessed members of his family had been conceived and born for generations.

Augustus stood at the window overlooking the garden. He turned to her. 'Does it meet with your approval?'

She held out her arms to him. 'Yes, oh, yes! I want to see the rest of the house as soon as I can. If there are a few more rooms like this I know I shall love it.' She thought he would come and sit beside her for a moment, kiss her on the cheek, his customary kiss, but he remained where he was.

'I have to go to Torquay soon. There are some things I have to see to in the shop. Will you mind if I leave you just for one night?'

She stared at him unbelieving. 'What do you mean? Are you saying that you are going alone?'

'I can deal with everything more quickly on my own, dearest, and be back here before you know it. You won't be frightened or lonely will you? Dunne and his wife live in the house, and you have your maid, and there are other servants.'

She was appalled and shocked. 'Can't I come with you, Augustus?'

'As I said, I want to make a flying visit to the bookshop. There are things I have to do.'

She knew that it must be an excuse. Michael Dyer had managed the bookshop alone all those months when Augustus had been in Switzerland. Why should he want to keep the place anyway? she wondered. How was it that the owner of a great house and estate like this should bother about a paltry little shop? It was another mystery.

'You really mean you are going to Torquay and I have to stay here?' She was quite distraught.

He hesitated. 'I want you to stay, Lily, to get used to it.'

'But I have years and years to get used to Ashcote. I should like to go to Torquay, to have a look at Rose House. I have interests there too, you know.'

'I shall see that Rose House is all right.'

'But we could call at Ivy's school on the way. I promised that I would visit during the term.' She was angry, an unaccustomed sensation lately.

'I could do that for you too.'

'But she's my sister. I want to see her. What is the matter with you, Augustus?' It was the first argument they had had and Lily was quite horrified. Was she really being ordered about like some meek little Victorian wife?

Then Augustus did come over to her, sat beside her, even put his arms around her. 'Please, Lily, do this for me,' he said. 'I have things that I need to ... to arrange. I shall leave on Sunday and return early the next morning, I promise. It's only a few hours really.'

She looked at the familiar flush on his handsome face and knew that she mustn't cross him. She had secretly read books on the dreaded consumption and was terrified that he would become ill again if he was upset. And what did such a short time matter out of a whole life after all? 'Very well, Augustus,' she managed. 'I shall stay and explore your lovely house.'

'Our house,' he said gently. 'This is your home now Lily. Ashcote Manor is yours and you are its mistress.' He squeezed her hands in both of his. 'Forgive me for leaving you so soon. I promise that mostly we shall go to Torquay together. I shall set things up so that I don't have to go so often.'

She still didn't understand what he was talking about.

'If you want to visit your family in Bristol sometimes without me, I shall not mind,' he continued, confusing her further. 'I think it's a sign of a good healthy marriage that each partner has some time to themselves.'

There was a knock at the door and Augustus sprang up and opened it. 'Thank you, Dunne,' he said curtly as the man carried the first of the suitcases into the room.

Ivy, at thirteen, felt herself almost too old for school, but as she settled into the expensive boarding establishment that Augustus had chosen for her she realized that many girls stayed until they were at least sixteen and then often went on to something they called a finishing school. She thought this a perfectly terrible idea, but if it was necessary in order to join the ranks of the upper classes, she was willing to submit to it.

The first days had been difficult, and at the wedding she had confided to George that she wasn't sure how she was going to survive. To her older brother however she had been more positive. 'I'm determined that I shall become a lady,' she had told him. 'After all, there can't be many girls like me who get such a wonderful chance to better themselves!'

William had smiled at the words and at the new voice in which she uttered them. The elocution lessons and the few weeks at the new school had already worked a vast change in his little sister.

The school was in Somerset. 'Only about thirty miles from Ascote,' Augustus had said. 'Near enough to visit easily.'

It was housed in a substatial country house, not so old as Ashcote, but by Ivy's standards positively ancient. At first she had been uneasy about living in the midst of fields and wide acres of open land. 'I prefer the town,' she had said airily on her first day, and then had added, 'but my sister is marrying into the Ashe family from Ashcote Manor in Dorset, you know, so I suppose I must get used to the country.'

There were stables behind the school. In spite of her love of animals, Ivy refused to visit them. She was very ashamed of her inability to ride and scared of saying something about Flo. A cart horse, however noble, was hardly likely to enhance one's image in a snobby place like this.

'Do you hunt?' It was the question she had been dreading and it had come at the end of her first week.

'Actually, no.' She had enunciated the words with care for she had rehearsed this scenario many times in her mind. 'One of my relations was killed in a riding accident and my parents wouldn't allow it. I shall have to learn one day, I suppose.'

The lie was only a small one. Harry had been a relative, and although it wasn't quite a riding accident she could think of no other excuse for her inability to ride, an activity which every other girl in the school apparently adored.

As she spoke the horror returned. She could see Flo, could see those great hooves, and Harry Coney lying there on the cobbles, his blood seeping slowly between the blackened stones.

The girl who had questioned her had looked at her strangely, but then the subject had been lost in the whirl of settling in, and the problem of the dreaded riding lessons was shelved.

Having to share a dormitory with six other girls was another tribulation. She was embarrased to undress in front of them in spite of her brand new under garments, and was always aware that they were watching her, trying to sum her up, for undoubtedly she didn't quite fit the pattern. By constant vigilance however Ivy was able to live her new life without giving away anything of her roots.

The occupant of the next bed was a delicate-looking girl with long curly hair tied into bunches on either side of her face. It gave her a vulnerable look, made her appear young and defenceless, and it was to her that Ivy, with her street knowledge and hard won assurance, warmed. They were soon firm friends and in a letter to her sister, Ivy wrote. *'I have a friend already, a girl called Alice Hamilton-James. I think her name is absolutely splendid, don't you, Lil? Very posh! We sit together in the classroom. I'm not going to tell*

247

her or anybody about the coal yard though. That would be the very end.'

One day at the beginning of June when Lily was still in Italy, Ivy was sitting on a wooden bench outside in the sun trying to learn the poem that had been set that morning. She found it difficult to concentrate for thoughts of her sister kept intruding. She was longing to see her, to hear all about the fabulous honeymoon. There had been postcards sent to the school, amazing views of Venice and the Italian Lakes, but the news was only about the weather and the hotels and the presents that Augustus was constantly buying her. Ivy longed to talk. She wanted to find out whether Lily was truly happy at last.

She forced herself to look down at her book and decided that when she married she would go to Greece for her honeymoon.

> *'The Isles of Greece! The isles of Greece,*
> *Where burning Sappho loved and sung,*
> *Where grew the arts of war and peace,*
> *Where Delos rose and Phoebus sprung!'*

She sighed and wondered what it all meant. Who was Sappho? Obviously she had not been listening properly this morning to the lesson about Byron or she would know. The poetry sounded good though even if she didn't understand it. She hoped that her friend had been attending. Alice would enlighten her later on.

Just at that moment one of the older girls, Miranda Cosgove, a prefect, walked along the path from the tennis courts. She stopped in front of Ivy.

'I've just heard that your sister is married to Augustus Ashe,' she said.

Ivy looked up at her, squinting into the sun. 'That's right. How did you know?'

'My mother told me. I've had a letter from her this morning.' She swung her racquet in an arc around her head. 'What did you think of Ashcote Manor?'

Ivy was mortified. How to say that she had never been there? 'I'm going for the summer holidays,' she said. 'Mr

248

Ashe is having it done up. He didn't want the family to see it before it was ready.' She placed her bookmark in the page she had been studying and closed the book.

'You mean you've never visited?' There was a sarcastic note to Miranda's voice.

Ivy sat up as straight as she could and shaded her eyes. She couldn't see her questioner very clearly for her face was etched against the blinding sun-filled sky. 'No, I haven't, and that makes the summer holiday even more exciting.'

'What about your parents?'

'They're dead.'

'So where's your home?'

Ivy was both uneasy and angry now. She stood up. 'Why are you asking me all this? None of it has anything to do with you or with school.' She knew that it was greatly daring to speak to one of the high and mighty prefects like this but she just couldn't help it.

'I don't suppose your family knows about Augustus Ashe then?'

'What don't we know?'

'That he's a nancy-boy.'

Ivy felt the colour rush to her face and her heart thumped wildly. This was a term of abuse that she had heard occasionally in Bristol and never thought to encounter in a respectable place like Barnfield School for Young Ladies. It meant something frightful, something only talked about in hushed whispers. She wasn't quite sure what.

Miranda continued, 'I live quite near Ashcote. My parents used to know Mr and Mrs Ashe, and my sister went to dances there when she first came out.'

Ivy forced herself to be calm. 'What are you talking about?' she said.

'Don't you know? Aren't you an ignoramus then! It means, my dear child, that he's different, doesn't like girls. He prefers men.'

'It's a wicked lie!' Ivy was horrified. It couldn't be true especially as he had married Lily. 'Mr Ashe is quite honourable,' she said in her best and recently acquired enunciation. 'I'm sure it can't be true of such a perfect gentleman as my brother-in-law. You have no business to

249

say such a wicked thing.' She gritted her teeth in fury and clasped her book tightly in her hands. Then she started to walk in the direction of the house.

'Not so fast, Ivy Penrose,' the girl said. 'Come back and sit down and I'll tell you all I know.'

In spite of herself Ivy hesitated. She couldn't leave it like this. Even if there was no truth in it, and of course there wasn't, she must hear everything that there was to hear and try to stop such a terrible rumour. She retraced her steps.

'Sit,' Miranda repeated, just as though she was talking to a dog. She indicated the wooden garden seat which Ivy had just vacated. She put her tennis racquet on the grass and seated herself confidently upon the bench.

Reluctantly Ivy perched herself right on the very edge, as far away from her as possible. 'Tell me then,' she said angrily.

'My sister liked him. They were friends, but he never touched her. You know, how men do. Never kissed her. She got fed up eventually and found someone else a bit more manly.'

'Perhaps it was her fault?' Ivy was even more furious now. How could a man be condemned on such flimsy evidence?

Miranda smiled disagreeably. 'No such luck. He was the same with all the girls. He was popular, you see, good-looking too. A lot of them fell in love with him.'

'I'm not going to believe you. Anyway, people change.'

'Do you really understand what I mean by a nancy-boy?'

Ivy was not going to reveal her ignorance. 'Of course I do.'

'Well then, you must know that he won't change. Your sister is in for a packet!'

'How dare you!' Ivy wanted to hit the smug self-satisfied face of the girl beside her as hard as she could, and a stream of strong Bristol abuse rose to her lips, but she controlled both impulses. Her beautiful new life seemed to be falling in tatters about her.

'What'll you do to keep me silent?'

'Kill you,' Ivy said quietly and with venom. 'Kill you,

that's what I'd like to do for saying such an evil thing!'

It was Miranda's turn to look taken aback. 'Don't be so dramatic. You'd hang.'

Hang! All the old terror that Ivy had suffered, first for Lily and then for herself, came back and the trees and beautiful lawns in front of her seemed to sway and heave.

'So what will you give me for my silence?'

The words brought Ivy back to reality, if it was reality. 'There's nothing I can give you. I haven't anything, and you wouldn't dare.' Was she being blackmailed? Ivy had read about such things and longed suddenly for William, for Aunt Agnes, for the comfortable streets of Bristol. Her new changed life had completely lost its charm.

'Just see if I wouldn't! But I'll leave it for now,' Miranda said. 'But give it a lot of thought, won't you, you silly little jumped up nobody!'

Ivy could think of little else for the rest of the day and as she dredged her memory for everything she knew about the awful accusation that Miranda had made, she remembered that she had read things in the Bible, of all places, about this sinful state.

That night she took her Bible, put the cover of another book around it and carried it to the lavatory. There in the only place where she could be private she searched for the relevant passages. She found the verses fairly easily for she was familiar with the Good Book as Aunt Agnes always called it. She knew her way around its many sections and authors. She remembered that it was St Paul who had so fiercely denounced the kind of things that Miranda had talked about.

She had often puzzled over these verses, wondering exactly what they meant. Nice girls were not supposed to think about such wicked goings on even if they were in the Bible. Certainly they must never be talked about, so she had not been able to ask anyone for an explanation. It hadn't mattered too much before, but now it was of the utmost importance.

She sat on the lavatory seat, and in the dim light that

251

filtered in through the high window she read the mystifying words again:

> ' ... *the men, leaving the natural use of the woman, burned in their lust one toward another; men with men working that which is unseemly and receiving in themselves that recompense of their error which was meet.*'

She closed the flimsy pages, pulled the flush and surreptitiously crept out, hoping no one would see her leaving the lavatory with a book clutched in her hands. And if they discovered somehow that it was a Bible they would laugh at her, thinking her especially holy. She felt herself to be the exact reverse.

It was difficult to concentrate on school work for the rest of that day, and in bed she found herself imagining all sorts of frightful things. As well as the horrible thought of Augustus being ... like that, there was the fear of what Miranda Cosgrove might do. Was she really a blackmailer?

Then another thought struck Ivy. If what she said was true, Augustus could be put in prison, couldn't he? She tried to remember what she'd heard in Bristol. There was something about two men who ... Ivy tossed and turned in her narrow bed and the words came back to her. Her aunt had been talking in hushed whispers to a neighbour and Ivy had listened guiltily. Both men had been taken off to prison apparently for doing something shocking. Suddenly she could hear her aunt's voice loud and clear, full of self-righteousness. The whispers had changed to a monstrous anger. 'Wicked fornicators,' Agnes had said. 'The Lord will punish them, I'm sure of that, just like the Good Book says.'

Ivy had not questioned the judgement then, but now that it, whatever 'it' was, threatened her own family, her sister's happiness, she was filled with horror. If both God and the law were so fiercely ranged against such unimaginable deeds, and if Miranda Cosgrove was right, there wasn't much hope for Augustus.

Did Lily know? What had the honeymoon really been like? What did men actually do together? How could they ... it wasn't possible, was it? Could Lily ever have a baby?

Eventually Ivy managed to sleep but the unanswered questions were with her just as strongly when she awoke red-eyed and desperate in the morning. She knew that she would have to talk to someone, find some answers, and she must see Lily as soon as possible.

Augustus left for Torquay after lunch on Sunday. They had attended morning service in the ancient parish church and Lily had sensed the eyes of everyone in the small congregation fixed firmly upon her. Afterwards she had been introduced to two or three families. She had nodded and smiled her way out, and then, a little later, in the warm drizzle of a damp summer afternoon she had stood at the great front door of Ashcote and waved her husband off.

'Tomorrow,' he said as he kissed her, 'I shall be back in time for lunch.'

With that she had to be content, and on her own in the great house, she wandered disconsolately from room to room. Her maid, Mildred, a local girl, had weekends off.

Ashcote was an amazing place. The portraits that adorned almost every wall fascinated her. There were many of children, most of them fair-haired like Augustus, all wearing elaborate clothes of long ago, and she stood before each one studying the childlike features. Some looked bold and fearless like Lady Charlotte Ashe whose likeness was drawn in pastels. In Venice Lily had learned from Augustus how to differentiate between the various art forms. She had told him that she liked portraits and he had taken her to many galleries. Now she had an abundance of portraits in her own house.

She spent a long time staring at Lady Charlotte. The child was about eight years old, Lily thought, and there was a lofty arrogance in every line of her aristocratic features. Lily wondered what it was like to be female in those days, about two hundred years ago she judged by the clothes. She hoped the little girl had a happy life. She moved on to others, a much younger child in Elizabethan dress clutching a doll. She must be the child of the first Sir William.

These were mostly the ancestors of the man she had

married, the man who had just dumped her in his beautiful home like some acquired possession and then had gone abruptly away after only two short days here. She felt quite desolate. He had given her no further explanation for his unexpected departure. As Lily wandered from room to room she decided once more that she had been right in her previous thoughts about her position here. She was just continuing the pattern of Ashe wives, married, kept in luxury, given no importance and nothing to do except produce heirs, preferably male heirs of course. She was both amused and a little angry at the idea, yet she reminded herself that it had been her choice. She had wanted Augustus, had dreamed of him when there had been no possibility whatever that her dreams could ever become reality. And she had heeded no advice or warning, either from her brother or from Duncan MacMullen. She resolved that she would make a success of this marriage however difficult and strange it might sometimes be. Her children would look like those on the wall. She would have their portraits painted. Once again Ashcote would come to life.

Suddenly she thought of the house in which she had grown up, and she laughed to herself at the difference between Sefton Road and Ashcote Manor. She could never have imagined that one day she would be mistress of such a wonderful place as this. It would have to compensate for whatever else might be lacking.

In Sefton Road there had not been one family portrait! A few photographs used to stand on the mantelpiece and on the sideboard in the front room. There was Granny Penrose and her mother's parents facing each other from their small silver frames, and a larger one of herself and the rest of the family taken at the beginning of the war just before her father went off to France.

Was Augustus really aware of the background from which he had hauled her, the difference between them? Why had he chosen her? Surely there must have been other girls of his own class who would have been happy to provide him with an heir? Men were scarce now since so many had been killed in the war, and Augustus was handsome, rich, eminently desirable. The question still nagged. Was it truly because he had fallen in love? If so it was like a story book romance, almost like Cinderella. She smiled to herself. Although her father had been a teacher, and her brother was an accountant they were still only just above the working classes. There was a great gulf fixed between the aristocracy and everyone from the lower orders. Lily stared rebelliously at a huge portrait of one of the autocratic male ancestors and she knew that if she were Ivy she would rudely put her tongue out at him!

She thought of George and the coal yard and the funny side of the situation struck her again. She peered at the gold-etched name plate beneath the painting. 'Sir Richard Ashe' it said. She couldn't imagine what this resplendent character looking down at her now would say if he was faced with George as a new member of his exalted family!

'When would you like tea, Madam?'

Lily turned and smiled at Mary Dunne who was standing in the doorway, round and comforting and not at all disapproving. Lily glanced at the little gold watch Augustus had bought for her in Venice. 'When you are ready, Mrs Dunne.'

'I shall serve it in the drawing room in ten minutes then. Unless you would prefer to have it in the parlour?'

'The drawing room will be fine. It's very beautiful. I shall enjoy eating there.' *But not so much as I should if my husband was beside me,* Lily said to herself sadly.

She walked along the endless corridors, through the Great Hall with its intimidating weapons and the dead eyes watching her and into one of the lovely rooms that Augustus had ordered to be decorated. There was a great fireplace dominating one wall and new curtains at the windows. Lily looked with approval at the long brocade drapes which were a warm rose colour and at the paintings, mostly scenes of woodland and river rather than portraits to look down and criticize!

The table in the centre of the room was not fashioned in heavy oak like the huge one in the hall. It was elegant, oval in shape, and the surface glowed with much polishing. Lily knew nothing of old furniture, but she ran her fingers gently over the grain. This was much more to her liking.

But the room was chilly and now in June there was no

fire, merely a mass of logs hidden by an embroidered screen. Lily looked at it and decided that after tea, as it had stopped raining, she would go out into the gardens and pick a huge armful of branches and flowers and make an arrangement to stand there. She would pick red and yellow blossoms to match the curtains and give an illusion of warmth. She longed to be outside for she could see that the sun was shining brightly now.

Mary Dunne nodded agreeably when Lily suggested her plan. 'A lovely idea, Madam,' she said as she set the tray on a small table near the window. 'I haven't time to do such things, and no gift either.'

'It'll keep me out of mischief,' Lily said, and then immediately regretted the words. It was a stupid thing to say. Depression overtook her. For the first time in her life she had absolutely nothing important to do.

Then suddenly like a knife wound a new and unexpected thought seized her. Could Augustus have another woman, in Torquay perhaps, whom he loved and could not marry? Might that explain why he was not very ardent when he made love to her? Was he going to visit her tonight? Could that be what Duncan MacMullen had tried to warn her about?

She closed her eyes for a second and saw Duncan's honest handsome face, his caring smile. Oh, Duncan, Duncan, she thought, why couldn't I have fallen in love with someone uncomplicated like you?

Then, infinitely shocked by her disloyalty and by the shameful idea that had just come to her, she tried to smile at Mary Dunne and hoped that her feelings weren't obvious.

'I'll get some vases,' the housekeeper was saying. 'You'll want big ones. I'll get them washed and put ready for you in the conservatory.'

'Thank you,' Lily managed. She drank her tea and went out into the lovely summer garden and started to pick flowers. There was nothing else to do.

Chapter Seventeen

Lily tossed restlessly for most of the night, imagining her husband in another woman's arms. With Harry Coney she hadn't cared, with Augustus she felt that her whole world would collapse if there was any truth in her suspicions. How could she survive if she must live with this jealousy eating away at her happiness?

In the morning Mary brought breakfast to her room and she looked dismally at the thin slices of white bread lightly buttered, the egg in its delicate china cup, and wondered how she was to greet Augustus when he returned. She ate little and was downstairs in time to open the door to him, forestalling Dunne who was hovering in the background.

He had kept his promise, had returned early as he had said he would. He greeted her affectionately and she noticed at once the fresh spring to his step and the healthy colour in his face, a great contrast to how she felt. 'Torquay air has done you good,' she said, hoping he wouldn't notice the trace of bitterness that she was unable to keep from her voice. What else had given him that glow of cheerfulness and unaccustomed vigour?

After he had kissed her he turned back to the vehicle and took a wicker basket from the passenger seat.

'I've brought you a present,' he said. He carried the basket carefully over the gravel and put it into her arms. 'Open it.'

What was this? A peace offering? She looked in gingerly for there was an animal of some sort inside. She placed it on the ground and opened the door at the front. A small face appeared, a tiny dog with enormous eyes that regarded her anxiously. The little creature came slowly out of the basket, revealing long shaky legs and a small perfect body. It shook itself uncertainly, and then as Lily stooped, the puppy jumped up at her, the tiny paws reaching just above her ankles, clawing at her stockings. She scooped it up and held its little squirming body firmly to her breast, allowing it to lick her face and neck with its baby enthusiam.

This totally unexpected gift took her completely by surprise, caused her defences, her suspicions, to come crashing down like a heap of cards. She looked over the puppy's head at Augustus. 'Was this why you wouldn't let me come with you?'

He didn't answer her question. 'I hope you like whippets?' he said. 'There's a breeder in Exeter. I went there yesterday and chose the prettiest pup in the litter for you. I picked her up this morning. Do you like her?'

The puppy was licking her fingers now and Lily laughed in delight. She had always wanted a dog but there had never been time or money. This little animal who was chewing her hands with needle-sharp baby teeth was the perfect present and when she looked at Augustus she thought that she could see tenderness in his eyes. Had she been wrong? Was her jealousy completely mistaken? 'Like her? Oh, yes, Augustus,' she murmured. 'You couldn't have given me anything more wonderful.' He had no idea how wonderful, for his present had reassured her, given her back her trust.

'Do you mind its being a whippet?'

'No. She's perfect.'

'There have been whippets at Ashcote for more than two hundred years,' he said. He stroked the little dog who licked him enthusiastically in return. 'Have you seen them in some of the portraits?'

'Yes, I have. I was looking at the little girl, Lady Charlotte, she has one. I remember thinking that ...'

'I must have read your thoughts.'

Lily felt quite unworthy. While she was suspecting him of being unfaithful he was planning this lovely surprise for her. She wanted to gather him to her along with the puppy,

258

tell him that she loved him very much, but the dog filled her arms and Dunne was watching in the background. Instead she said, 'We'd better let her run about a bit before we go inside.'

'Have you been all right on your own?' he asked her later when they were sitting on the terrace together waiting for Mary to bring coffee. 'I've been thinking of you here, picturing you in our home. I was looking forward to coming back this morning.'

She wanted to ask him why he was so anxious to go away then, but quickly banished the disloyal thought. 'I found things to do,' she said, 'but I'd much prefer it if we could go to Torquay together next time.'

He ignored this remark. 'Tell me what you've been up to?'

She shrugged her shoulders. 'Flower arranging, that sort of thing.'

'I noticed,' he said. 'Very beautiful. There have never been flowers since my mother died.'

'You don't mind?' She wondered if she had made a mistake.

He smiled brightly. 'Of course not. The place needs a woman's hand. Mary is all right, but has no imagination of course. One doesn't expect it in the servant classes.'

Lily turned horrified eyes upon him. How could he say such a thing when she herself came from those very ranks? 'I don't think that's a very kind remark.'

He looked amused. 'Perhaps not. She's a very admirable woman.'

Lily changed the subject. 'Tell me about my house in Torquay, Augustus. I've been thinking that perhaps I should close the café when the lease runs out at the end of the year and make it into a second home for us. That front room could become a splendid drawing room, and the one above would be our little private parlour.'

He took out his pipe and tobacco and fiddled for a long time, filling the barrel and finding a match before he replied. 'I don't think that would be a very good idea. The café seems to be running very efficently. The new couple open

259

on Sunday afternoons now so I went there for tea. Of course there were no scones without you to make them.'

It was a long time since Lily had made scones, or anything else for that matter. In this great house she was definitely not welcome in the kitchen. 'If we renovated Rose House for ourselves, I could make you some. I should have a kitchen again and we wouldn't have any servants to watch and pry. We could be on our own sometimes. If you intend keeping the bookshop you'll want to go there occasionally. Your little flat wouldn't be very comfortable for the two of us, would it?'

He glanced at her sharply. 'Definitely not, but I presumed you would prefer to remain here at Ashcote with all its luxuries during my short business trips to Torquay?'

She felt a tremor of disquiet again, the suspicions briefly returning. Why did he want to be away from her? Why couldn't the bookshop be left to the unfriendly but efficient Michael Dyer?

'But I like Torquay, Augustus. I love the sea. I want to go back there often. Surely you can understand that?' She stared at him resentfully.

He took a few tentative puffs at his pipe and when he spoke his voice was soft, conciliatory. 'Of course, my darling. But there's no need to make any great changes to Rose House for the moment. We can stay in a hotel when we visit. The Imperial is very comfortable and has wonderful sea views. We'll go quite soon if you wish. And they'll probably allow us to take the dog too. What are you going to call her by the way?'

'Tessa. I thought of it immediately.'

'Any special reason?'

'Tess. You know. Tess of the d'Urbervilles, the girl whose story used to haunt me.'

He laughed. 'Ah, yes, of course. The one who was hanged. I don't think I like the choice.'

Lily stroked the little dog who had settled sleepily in her lap. 'She'll replace that other unhappy Tess in my mind.'

She watched him blow smoke into the air, watched it circle and curl upwards, and then he started to cough.

'Augustus,' she said hesitantly, 'should you be smoking?

260

I mean, will it not do some harm to your lungs? Might it not make you ill again?'

'I had hoped that I was cured,' he gasped.

Alarmed Lily jumped to her feet, set the puppy on the ground and took the pipe from his outstretched hand. 'Are you all right?'

He turned away from her and pressed a handkerchief to his face. 'I'll be fine in a minute or two,' he managed. 'Don't worry.'

But Lily did worry. She watched him anxiously as he coughed, but as the rasping sounds grew less she sat down again, and eventually he turned towards her, put his handkerchief away, and took her hand in his.

'Sorry, darling,' he said. 'I shall give all my pipes to Dunne, should have done it ages ago. Now let's think of something else. Have you any plans for the garden?'

She took a deep breath and tried to comply. 'I should like some large stone pots here on the terrace,' she said. 'I think it would look less bare. I could plant them myself.'

'Just say the word and I'll see that you get whatever you want.' Augustus quickly regained his composure and they sat for a long time in the peace of the summer garden, saying little, watching the puppy who was now digging arduously at some of the weeds that were growing between the old stones. Lily wondered if this was the time to broach the subject that had been on her mind for some time. Yes, perhaps it was. Augustus obviously didn't want to talk about his illness and the coughing that had surprised and frightened both of them. He needed something to divert him.

'There is something else I want,' she said, and then quickly before her courage could desert her, added, 'could I have a certain old horse, a cart horse, here for her retirement, Augustus?'

He looked at her in astonishment. 'A cart horse? I'd hoped that you would learn to ride. I should like to buy you a mare. In fact, I've already made some enquiries, and I thought of suggesting to Ivy that she might like one too, to be stabled here so that she can ride during the school holidays.'

'Thank you,' Lily said primly. 'I'm sure Ivy would be thrilled about that and I should like to learn to ride, but

I really must find somewhere for Flo.'

'Flo?'

'The last of the coal horses. She's been a faithful servant for years and I can't send her to the knackers yard.'

Augustus laughed and Lily turned to look at him. He seemed better. She had been right. The silliness of her request had amused and diverted him.

'Then Flo shall definitely come here,' he said. 'The two riding horses can be her companions. I'm glad to be able to do something to please you, Lily.'

'Thank you. Thank you so much, Augustus.' She breathed the scent of the lilac, heard the birds in the delicate branches of the birch tree at the edge of the terrace, and all the uneasiness of the night receded once more. She should be the happiest woman on earth. She glanced at Augustus beside her, so loving, so affectionate, so willing to agree to most of the things she wanted. Then she turned away from him and looked at the old walls of the great house, and finally she picked up her puppy and kissed her on the nose. How could she ever ask for anything more?

That night Augustus made love to her in the big bed with its beautiful hangings, its delicately scented sheets, and he was more passionate than she had ever known him, his loving more intense. He gave her pleasure, satisfied her in a way that surprised and delighted her. Perhaps this was going to set the pattern for the future? Maybe all those hesitant gropings during their honeymoon were now a thing of the past.

He was more confident, more eager, and it was the same the next night and the next. Lily hoped that her suspicions had been completely ill-founded and wouldn't return. If that was so she would be completely happy.

Ivy heard about the plans for Flo when she received Lily's next letter, and she was delighted. The old horse would be at Ashcote probably by the time school finished for the summer holidays. Flo would be exchanging her years of labour in the Bristol streets for long carefree days in a meadow. Ivy knew that even if the animal's presence reminded her of Harry Coney's death she wouldn't mind because that had been a *good thing*. It was to Janey's frightened yapping and Flo's well-aimed response that she and Lily owed so much. Ivy sometimes felt a flicker of guilt about this, but usually managed to banish it without too much trouble.

There would also be horses to ride. Ivy read this with some misgiving although she knew that this skill was essential to her new role in life. There was a new puppy at Ashcote apparently and Janey was to be taken there too. Ivy had missed her little dog and this last piece of news delighted her. The summer holidays began to appear extraordinarily exciting.

If only Miranda Cosgrove's horrible accusations and threats could be removed then Ivy decided that she would be almost in heaven.

She read the letter again. Augustus intended to drive to Bristol himself and make arrangements for Janey and Flo to be transported down to Dorset, Lily wrote. Surely someone who cared for animals like that, she thought, couldn't be guilty of the frightful things that Miranda said and wasn't going to be condemned to some awful punishment like the Bible predicted.

Ivy's friend, the curly-haired Alice, had just finished reading her own letter. The two girls were in the school entrance hall, the place where post was distributed every morning, having already been opened and censored by one of the staff.

'Anything nice?' Alice asked. 'You look pleased.'

'Augustus is buying me a pony,' Ivy said.

'That's absolutely topping.' Alice beamed at her. 'Any other good news?'

Ivy hesitated. How did you tell a friend, even a nice easy-going friend like Alice, that you cared deeply about a cart horse?

'He's bringing my dog to Ashcote too,' she said, quickly deciding that it would be very unwise to mention Flo and the coal yard just yet. 'My aunt has been looking after her in Bristol.'

'Lovely. Will you invite me?'

This was quite a new idea. Ivy thought about it for a moment or two. Having a friend to stay was another part of her new life that needed adjustment. But it sounded fun on the whole. 'Of course,' she said, 'if Lily and Augustus are willing.'

'This is the first time I've seen you cheerful recently,' Alice said. 'I've been a bit worried in fact. It's that rotten Miranda Cosgrove, isn't it?'

Lily looked at her in alarm. Had Miranda already been gossiping? 'What do you know about it?'

'About what?'

'About Miranda threatening me the other day?'

'Threatening? I saw her telling you off about something. I could see you both from the window. What have you done?'

'I haven't done anything.'

'Then whatever ... ?'

Ivy folded her letter and put it back into its envelope. 'I should like to tell you, Alice. You're my best friend. After lunch, in the orchard. No one will overhear us there.'

There was just half an hour of free time at midday and the two girls flung themselves on to the grass under one of the old apple trees.

'Now tell me,' Alice directed. 'I'm all ears.'

Ivy decided to launch straight into the painful subject however much it shocked her well-bred companion. 'Do you know what a nancy-boy is?'

Alice, who had been lying flat on her back staring up at the thick canopy of leafy branches above their heads, now sat up straight and stared down at Ivy. 'As a matter of fact I do.'

'How? I didn't think nice girls knew about such things.'

'I had two older brothers. Both were in the Army. When they came home on leave they used that expression occasionally. They wouldn't tell me what it meant, just laughed at me. I was quite little then, but I overheard it again last year when two of our workmen were talking. I asked Frank again and in the end he told me.'

'I'm glad you know and I don't have to explain. I didn't know you had brothers?'

'Just one now. Billy was killed in '16 and Frank was

264

wounded in the third battle for Ypres the year after. A blighty wound. It saved his life. He lost a leg and they couldn't send him back, thank goodness.'

Ivy sat up and stared at the peaceful scene before her, the shrubs in full flower, the rose bed fragrant and beautiful. The horrors of war, as well as her own problems, seemed for a brief moment, remote, unreal, as though nothing cruel and disagreeable should have any power to hurt and maim.

'My father was killed in France,' she said slowly, 'as well as my sister's first fiancé.'

'I'm sorry,' Alice said, then shrugged her shoulders. 'There were so many killed that my parents are grateful they still have one son.' She paused and, like Ivy, stared straight ahead and she too was still and silent for a time. Then she turned to Ivy again. 'But why did you ask me about nancy-boys and what on earth has it to do with Miranda Cosgrove, for goodness sake?'

Ivy put a piece of grass in her mouth and chewed the end. It calmed her nerves. 'Promise you won't say a word to anyone?'

'Of course I promise. We're friends.'

'Miranda says that my new brother-in-law is one. You know, prefers men to women. I can't believe it, Ally.'

Alice didn't speak for a few moments and when she did she was flushed and angry. 'That's frightful! Frightful of Miranda, I mean. It must be a lie. Men like that don't get married. Perhaps she's trying to get at you for some reason?'

Ivy shook her head. 'I haven't done anything wrong. She's never picked on me before. Perhaps it's true!'

'You musn't believe that.'

'I try not to, but she's put the doubt in my mind now. I've got to find out the truth. She asked me what I'd give her to keep quiet.'

'What?' Alice jumped to her feet. 'That's blackmail. She can't. That's just too stupid. She'd be expelled.'

'But to expose her I'd have to tell about Augustus, wouldn't I? And even if it isn't true it would still be awful for him and my sister.'

'What do you mean, *even if it isn't true!* Of course it's

265

not true, you ninny. I tell you, he wouldn't have married your sister would he if . . . ' she paused. 'If he preferred men to women.'

Ivy looked at her in gratitude. 'Thanks, Ally,' she said. 'I hope you're right. You've made me feel heaps better anyway. I'll try not to worry any more.'

'Of course I'm right,' said Alice firmly. 'No one like that ever gets married. It's not possible.'

The two girls walked slowly back to school and during the afternoon Ivy tried to concentrate on her work, but that night she took the three sovereigns from their hiding place in her wardrobe. The gleaming gold gave her a sense of security. She knew that it was against the rules to keep money or valuables in the dormitory. Everything must be listed and handed in for safe-keeping, but she had been quite determined, when she first came to Barnfield, that she would have the means of escape ready and under her control.

Lily had given her five sovereigns for the school bank. It had seemed a vast amount of money and she had handed over two of them. The other three she had hidden and now she held them in her hands, turned them over and over and clenched them tightly in her fist before putting them away again. She shivered a little, for the feel of them made her remember those others that had been given to Aunt Agnes from her mother's little hoard, the ones she had stolen and had used to try and bribe Harry Coney. It seemed a century ago now, a different life.

She had done that for Flo, but now the honour of her family was at stake. Here was the possible means to keep Miranda quiet. In spite of Alice's comforting words there was still a niggle of disquiet in her mind about her brother-in-law. The doubts had been sown and would not easily be dislodged.

It was towards the end of term that Miranda cornered her again.

'Thought about what I told you?' Her voice was sarcastic.

'Of course I have,' Ivy said. 'And I'm quite sure it's not true.' Her voice was firm. She had no intention of handing over her precious sovereigns unless there was no other action to take.

Miranda laughed. 'Wait until you've been to Ashcote. When you've discovered that I'm right, we'll talk again.'

On a golden day in the middle of July, Ivy, with a mixture of both excitement and trepidation, was waiting for her sister. Lily had written to say that she would arrive during the morning and that Dunne would be driving. Ivy hoped that he would be wearing a proper chauffeur's uniform. She needed something to boost her self-confidence, especially if Miranda Cosgrove should be watching.

The big Humber drew up with a scrunching of gravel at the front door of the building where a number of trunks were waiting to be collected and a bevy of excited girls flitted about with last minute luggage. Ivy spotted her sister immediately, for she had been hovering around the entrance porch for the last hour.

Yes, he was in uniform. She watched with some awe as Dunne got out of the car and opened the door for Lily, holding it while she stepped sedately down. *Just as though she's always been a real lady,* thought Ivy with amusement.

She ran down the front steps and threw her arms around her. 'Gosh, Lil. It's wonderful to see you!' In the excitement of the moment she forgot, for one instant, her posh new voice.

Lily returned her embrace with enthusiasm and then stood back and looked at her. 'My, you've grown, even in four short weeks,' she said.

Ivy laughed. 'I hope not. You're imagining it. It's my new dress.' She swirled around and the delicate crêpe-de-chine spun out from her tiny waist. It was a pretty style but Ivy had at first been unenthusiastic about it, thinking that she would have preferred a straight and more modern look. But there had been admiring remarks from many of her friends and she had decided that perhaps it was becoming after all. There was plenty of time to look grown up and modern in the future.

'I'm glad you're pleased with it,' Lily said. 'Now where are your boxes?'

267

'Just one and a small bag.' She pointed to a large black trunk with the word 'Penrose' painted across it in large white letters.

Dunne, who was standing nearby, immediately nodded, and with the help of a school porter, manhandled it on to the back of the vehicle and strapped it carefully in place. Ivy stood watching him, still slightly bemused.

'Augustus sends his apologies for not driving here himself,' Lily said.

That's all right.' Privately Ivy was relieved that her brother-in-law hadn't come. Miranda might have made some frightful comment in too loud a voice. It was too awful to think about.

Just as she was about to climb into the motor car, Alice ran down the steps. 'Bye,' she whispered. 'Have a lovely time, and don't forget what I said. It was just a load of old tosh.'

Ivy grinned at her. 'Thanks, Ally. You enjoy yourself too. I'll try to arrange for you to come over during the hols.'

'Topping,' Alice said. It was her favourite word.

Dunne was standing now, holding the door for her and Ivy, feeling like a princess, stepped into the back of the vehicle and settled herself beside Lily.

'What's a load of old tosh?' Lily wanted to know.

'Oh, nothing,' said Ivy airily.

The journey was unexceptional but to Ivy it was pure magic. Even the graceful sprays of foxgloves which lined the country lanes in abundance seemed in full accord with her fanciful feelings, for as the big Humber swept past they appeared to bow their heads in homage. There were poppies too, great masses of them in the hedgerows lending their regal crimson to the scene. But even though the journey was so perfect, Ivy's first glimpse of Ashcote deprived her of all power of speech for at least a minute.

Before she would go into the house however she demanded to see Flo, and followed Lily out to the big field next to the garden. There, wonder of wonders, was the old horse contentedly grazing. The great animal looked up as Ivy called, whinnied and plodded over to the gate.

268

Ivy stroked her nose gently. 'We owe everything to Flo, don't we, Lil?'

'I suppose that's a wicked thing to say really, but yes, of course you're right.'

The two sisters smiled at each other conspiratorially and wandered arm in arm into the house.

The afternoon was quite perfect. First there was a reunion with an excited Janey, an introduction to Tessa, the new puppy, and then a tour of the house. It was not until Augustus returned that evening that all Ivy's fears and forebodings returned. At dinner he announced in a very confident and matter-of-fact voice that he planned to go to Torquay for three days next week and that as Ivy was here he presumed that Lily would prefer to remain at Ashcote?

It was Lily's tortured expression as he said this that alerted Ivy and sent shivers of apprehension through her. What was wrong? What did her sister suspect?

That night in her luxurious bed in the most beautiful bedroom she had ever known, sleep deserted her. Miranda Cosgrove's haughty and self-satisfied voice haunted her throughout the sleepless hours, and she found that Alice's confident assertions had lost their power to comfort. It was Miranda's words that dominated now.

Augustus was at his most charming the next morning at breakfast.

'Have you any plans for your first day at Ashcote?' he asked Ivy as he helped himself to bacon and eggs from the silver dish that Mary had placed on the sideboard.

Ivy was quite bemused by the luxury. 'I think that Lily is going to take me for a walk this morning,' she said hesitantly, suddenly shy. She finished her porridge, and unsure what to do or say next she looked at her sister waiting for a lead.

Lily nodded. 'Yes. It's a lovely day, and I promised the dogs.'

Augustus laughed. 'I've some things to see to on the farm so I'll leave you two girls to enjoy the sunshine. Don't get lost.'

Lily smiled at him affectionately and for a moment Ivy

269

wondered if she had been imagining the distressed expression on her sister's face last night.

'We couldn't get lost in our own grounds, could we? Lily said. Then she turned to Ivy. 'Are you having something cooked? There are scrambled eggs and sausages as well as bacon.'

'I couldn't possibly.' Ivy looked at Augustus's heaped plate and felt quite nauseous. To think that her sister now had someone to prepare all this food, to wash up, even to make the beds. It was quite unbelievable.

Lily was pleased to have Ivy at Ashcote, proud to show her round the beautiful house and excited at the prospect of six whole weeks of companionship for she was often lonely. Augustus spent a lot of his time on the farm, both in the farm office and actually working on the land with his men. Lily was pleased about this for it showed that his health was improving, but it meant that there were long lonely hours for her to fill. Now with Ivy here there would be things to do, shopping expeditions to Dorchester perhaps.

Augustus had bought her a motor car of her own, a brand new Ford saloon. It had cost him nearly five hundred pounds and sometimes when she looked at its sleek and gleaming black body she could scarcely believe that it was truly hers. During the past weeks she had been learning to drive. With care and with just a few more lessons she considered that she might be proficient enough to venture out without Dunne as chauffeur. That would be a wonderful freedom.

After breakfast they toured the gardens and then called to the dogs and walked through the gate in the high stone wall and eventually were in the meadows that lay beyond.

'It's so beautiful. Is this really all yours?' Ivy said. 'Whatever would Mother and Father have thought about it?'

'I don't know about its being mine,' Lily replied. 'But it's certainly part of the estate. I had no idea that it was so vast. I thought Augustus just owned a small country house. I knew there was a farm but not all these rolling acres.'

They walked in silence for a while and from time to time Lily took sidelong glances at her sister. Ivy was fourteen now and there was a remarkable change in her since the old Bristol days. She was more friendly and amenable, anxious to please, polite and considerate. The new school had certainly wrought a miracle. Now that their age difference was less noticeable Lily hoped that they might become really close friends. She had always felt the need of a friend. Perhaps a close relationship with a sister was even better.

'Remember the little garden at Sefton Road about the size of a postage stamp, and the orphanage beyond the wall?' Ivy said suddenly. 'To think that I was afraid that I might be sent there when Mother died!'

'I gather that Barnfield is slightly better then?' Lily said with a smile.

'Better! I should say so. It's generous of Augustus to pay for me. Is he very rich, Lil?'

'I'm not sure. I know that the long time he spent in the sanatorium in Switzerland cost a lot of money. But there doesn't seem to be any shortage. I told you about my new motor car?'

'Yes. I want to see it.'

'I'll take you for a ride.'

'That'll be wonderful. Gosh, won't George be jealous.'

'I suppose he might.' Lily thought of her brother and the memories of Bristol came rushing back as they often did, for the contrast with her present life was so great that she sometimes felt that she was living a dream. 'Remember the outside lavatory and the coal to be shovelled into the stove each day?'

'And washday,' Ivy added.

Lily looked down at her hands for a moment, soft and pale now, and thought of the rough feel of them after she had helped her mother years ago with the weekly wash, and then later in the café how red and sore they had been after she had finished the mounds of dishes each evening. Now she mustn't even attempt to carry things from the table. Augustus had engaged even more staff since they had returned from Italy.

They were walking beside a hedge fragrant with honeysuckle and Lily sniffed and closed her eyes for a second in pure delight. Then with some difficulty she plucked a stem heavy with blossom and handed it to Ivy. 'Georgeous, isn't it?' she said. 'I can't remember having any of this in Bristol, or Torquay for that matter.'

Ivy took the proffered twig absently and waved it about without considering it at all. 'Are you really happy here, Lil?' she asked.

It was a strange question and there was a seriousness about it that Lily had not expected from her young sister. She looked at her searchingly. 'Why do you suddenly ask that?'

Ivy shook her head. 'I just wondered.'

Chapter Eighteen

During the weekend Augustus was both the perfect husband and the faultless host. He put his big Hillman at their disposal, driving them wherever they wanted to go, and after church on Sunday he produced a surprise hamper that he had asked Mary Dunne to prepare and announced that they were going to the seaside for a picnic. There was a special beach he knew where he used to play as a child. The dogs were to come too and it would be possible to bathe as the little cove was usually quite deserted.

Ivy was completely entranced by her brother-in-law, totally won over by his charm and his concern for her every comfort. Miranda Cosgrove could say whatever she liked, this delightful man couldn't possibly be guilty of those horrible crimes. The disconsolate expression that she saw on her sister's face now and then must be due to other things, a slight indisposition perhaps. All this rich food probably didn't agree with her. That must be the reason for the occasional worried frown. With these explanations firmly in place, Ivy set herself to enjoy her long holiday.

The Sunday picnic was a complete success, something Ivy felt she would remember with delight for ever. Then on Monday morning Augustus left them to their own devices and went to oversee some work on the estate.

'We'll go to Dorchester to shop,' Lily said. 'I think I can pluck up enough courage to drive that far.'

Ivy looked at her sister with approval. A woman who drove her own motor car was well along the road to freedom and she heartily applauded such things. She had been studying the work of the suffragettes at school and sometimes wished that she had been born just a few years earlier so that she too could have chained herself to the railings of parliament or thrown stones through shop windows shouting the famous slogan: Votes for Women.

'I'm glad we've got the vote,' she said.

Lily laughed. 'Whatever brought that on? What has getting the vote to do with shopping?'

'Just you driving a car, being independent. I hope I shall be like that one day too.'

'Work hard. Get a good education. That's the most sure way. I was just lucky.'

Ivy switched her thoughts rapidly again. She didn't want to think about school just now. Life was too exciting. 'What are we going to buy?'

'I want some material for a dress and hat to match, some ready-made undergarments if possible, and a pair of comfortable shoes. And I thought we might get you something a bit more grown up than those gathered frocks of yours. There's a good ready-to-wear shop in town.'

Ivy jumped up from the breakfast table and swirled round in delight. 'A crêpe-de-chine gown with a low vee neck and in a dark colour, black perhaps?'

'Most certainly not. You need something for everyday. Crêpe-de-chine would be no good for walking the dogs, would it now? I thought a nice plain serge.'

Ivy pouted and then laughed. 'Perhaps I could have one of each,' she said. 'Come on then. Let's go. I'm looking forward to my first real shopping expedition.'

By lunch time their purchases were almost complete. Yards of material, two frocks for Ivy, and various other parcels were safely stowed in the car and Lily suggested lunch in the lavish Three Nuns Restaraunt.

'Funny name,' Ivy said as they settled themselves at a corner table. 'Was it started by three real nuns?' She giggled at the idea.

'I should hardly think so.' Lily removed her jacket and a waitress swooped from nowhere to take it from her. 'I didn't offer such service in my café,' she said. 'Customers usually had to deal with their own coats.'

'Do be quiet,' Ivy whispered. 'Gentry don't run businesses.'

They ordered melon to start and Ivy looked with suspicion at the unfamiliar fruit. 'Why are we having this to begin?' she asked. 'I've never seen one of these.'

Now it was Lily who looked around to see if anyone had heard the give-away words. She put her finger briefly to her lips and they both grinned. 'It's delicious. We had lots in Italy.'

Just as Ivy was finishing the last luscious mouthful she saw a tall elegant woman enter the restaurant. She stared at the lovely clothes, the air of assurance and poise, and then she almost jumped up out of her chair for trailing behind her was Alice.

'Lil,' Ivy said, 'that's my friend. You know, the one I told you about, the one we've asked over to Ashcote. Can I go and speak to her?'

'Yes, if you've finished, but don't rush,' Lily directed quietly. 'And watch yourself.' She too had registered the arrogant look of the woman who was now imperiously handing her coat to a frightened waitress. Obviously a born aristocrat, the type of person that she, humble Lily Penrose, could never attempt to emulate.

Excitedly Ivy crossed the room, forgetting to address the mother first, forgetting her manners completely in her happiness at seeing her friend. 'Alice,' she said when she reached their table, 'it's lovely to see you. Did you get my letter inviting you to Ashcote?'

'Yes. It came on Saturday.' There was no acknowledging smile, no warmth. Alice was strangely silent and withdrawn.

Rebuffed, Ivy hesitated, and then the woman looked at her coldly. 'You are Miss Penrose, I presume?' she said. 'I'm afraid that I shall not be able to allow Alice to come to see you at Ashcote.'

'But ... but we were both very much looking forward to it, Mrs Hamilton-Jones,' Ivy said quickly. 'I have so much to show Alice. I am sure she would enjoy ...' Her voice trailed off beneath the disapproving gaze.

'Quite impossible, I am afraid. You can see each other at school next term.'

275

'Mama, I ...' Alice turned pleading eyes to her mother.

'My mind is absolutely made up as I told you when you first mentioned this plan so please do not argue, Alice, especially here.'

Ivy looked at her friend and sensed that she was upset and ill at ease. 'It's all right,' she murmured, and turned and went back to her sister, sure that everyone in the restaurant was staring at her.

Lily had heard nothing of the exchange, but she had noted the cold reception, the strained looks. 'What was that all about?' she asked.

Ivy shook her head. 'I've no idea. Her mother looked at me as though I were a lump of coal or something worse. She won't let Alice come to Ashcote.' Tears came to her eyes and she angrily brushed them away.

Lily sighed. 'Only to be expected with people like that. We have to get used to it. It's one of the problems of moving out of our class. I suppose she's found out about our background?'

Ivy sat down and replaced her napkin on her lap, smoothing out the spotless starched linen. This new life was more complicated than she had thought. Perhaps Bristol was altogether a more comfortable place to be after all!

The next course was brought to the table. They had ordered plaice and both watched as it was exquisitely served.

'I don't know that I'm very hungry now,' Ivy said.

'Of course you are,' Lily replied. 'It's I who should be feeling squeamish.'

Ivy looked at her sister in alarm and saw, instead of the pallor she expected, a rush of colour spreading across her face.

'I think that I shall be able to do my duty for Ashcote after all,' Lily whispered.

'You mean ... ?'

'Yes. Hush. We don't want the whole restaurant to know, do we!'

Ivy was delighted, the hurts of the last five minutes giving way to pleasure. 'That's wonderful, Lil. Just wonderful. Why are you telling me now, here of all places, though?'

'For assurance and comfort, I suppose,' Lily said. 'To

assure myself that whatever the world thinks, my child will be the heir to Ashcote.'

Augustus was to leave for Torquay on Wednesday morning and promised that he would return on Friday. Lily was despondent about it and said nothing to him of her hopes.

'I've to see the doctor first,' she told Ivy. 'I must be sure.' She didn't add that she felt so distressed about this longer visit to Torquay that she was quite unable to give him any hint of the good news. She determined that she would make another attempt to show him how much his absences upset her.

The night before he left she broached the subject again. She was sitting at her dressing table in the privacy of their bedroom. 'Couldn't you sell the bookshop?' she demanded, looking at his reflection in the mirror. 'After all it's a strange sort of hobby for someone like you, Augustus. You told me that it was given to your mother as a present, a sort of plaything to keep her occupied. You don't need it for any financial reason, do you? In fact, I'm quite sure that it doesn't even pay for itself.'

He was just about to get into bed. He turned and stared at her back. 'No, it probably doesn't, and no, of course I don't need it for the income. Michael needs it though. It's his home, all he's got.'

She flinched and gripped the silver handle of her hairbrush so that it cut into the palm of her hand. 'So you keep it for his sake?'

'Precisely.'

'Why then do you have to go so often? Can he not run his life himself?' She knew that she was being the interfering wife but she couldn't help that. Her suspicions still niggled, still caused her frequent unrest. Was she being stupid, jealous of nothing? Or was there another woman whom he met there in the privacy of that little flat above the shop? It made sense. It made sense of everything: the quick marriage proposal, the desire not to wed one of the local aristocracy, and his willingness therefore to marry out of his class in order to get an heir. It even made sense of his need to keep on the right side of Michael Dyer for he must be helping in the deception. And of course it would explain the animosity that she and Ivy had experienced in Dorchester. Perhaps people knew. The wife was usually the last one to find out.

'I don't understand why you are so bothered about my visits to Torquay.' He climbed into bed. 'You must accept them, Lily. I don't ask much of you, but this I do ask. I shall never get rid of the bookshop, so please don't mention it again.' There was a hardness in his voice that she had never known before.

She brushed her hair with short vicious strokes. Now that it had been cut she hadn't the satisfaction of the long flourishes that she had always enjoyed. Eventually she rose, took off her robe and reluctantly got into bed beside him, but she kept very much to her side, leaving as much space as possible between them. 'Very well,' she said. 'I don't understand but I shall try not to mention it again.'

The post arrived soon after Augustus had left and Lily took the letters that Dunne had placed on the table in the Great Hall and sorted them. There were two long brown envelopes that must go into the study to await her husband's return, one from William which she picked up with great pleasure and a pink envelope addressed to Ivy. She carried these two out into the morning sunshine and sat on the terrace to read hers. Ivy was out somewhere with the dogs, probably in Flo's field she guessed.

William wrote that all was well in Bristol, the coal yard going from strength to strength and George was thrilled with the new lorry. Much better than poor old Flo and her rackety cart he decreed. Lily laughed at this and envisaged 'poor old Flo' thoroughly enjoying her retirement with her every need catered for. There were two sleek young mares in the next field and an old donkey sharing her own paddock. There was a handsome stable too ready for when the weather should turn.

On the second page William announced that he was sitting some important accountancy exams next year and if he passed he might be taken on as a junior partner in his firm. Lily thought of her parents as she read this, and her promise to her mother that nothing should come between their precious elder son and his ambitions. Well, she had done her part. William had come first in everything. There was no more she could do. It was up to him. She had other commitments now, other duties.

Just at that moment Ivy came bouncing round the corner of the house, the dogs in hot pursuit. She ran across the lawn and up the terrace steps. 'Lovely morning,' she shouted, and then collapsed on one of the seats that Lily had installed there.

'Letter for you,' Lily said. 'A pretty pink one.'

Ivy jumped up again and took the envelope. 'From Alice.' She ripped it open anxiously and scanned the one page inside. Then she sank down on to the seat again, pushed the excited dogs impatiently away and stared at the words as if in a trance.

'What is it?' Lily saw the angry frown on her sister's face.

Ivy hastily folded the page, replaced it in the envelope and jammed it into her pocket. 'It's nothing,' she said.

But she stared straight ahead of her with haunted frightened eyes and Lily knew that it must be far from nothing. She remembered the disdainful look from Alice's mother when they had met in town. 'Whatever it is, Ivy, you must tell me,' she said. 'I won't have that woman upsetting you. Tell me.'

'No!' Ivy gave her one dismayed look and rushed across the terrace into the house.

Lily jumped up and followed her, but more slowly. She was unaware now of the staring eyes of Augustus's ancestors as she climbed the great stairway. What possible calamity could have brought that frightened look to her sister's face? What on earth could have been written in that letter to cause such sudden distress?

There was no lock on Ivy's bedroom door but it was firmly closed and Lily paused outside, unsure whether to enter. She could hear sounds of sobbing. She put her hand on the doorknob. 'Ivy can I come in?' she called.

No reply, more sobs. Reluctantly Lily turned the knob and opened the door a crack. Ivy was sprawled on her bed, the letter screwed up on the floor. She didn't move and Lily went into the room and closed the door quietly.

She sat on the bed and stroked her sister's hair which was a mass of unruly curls, having escaped from the confining ribbons. These too were on the floor where Ivy must have thrown them.

Then suddenly she sprang into life. She thrust Lily aside and jumped off the bed, gathered up the crumpled letter. 'You mustn't read this. It's a pack of wicked lies,' she shouted.

Lily tried to remain calm. 'Then if it's lies it can't hurt us, can it?'

'Oh yes it can. It can hurt all of us.'

Lily stood up and held out her hand. 'You must give it to me, Ivy. Whatever your friend says is my concern as well as yours.'

Ivy went to the window, the letter still in her hand. She stood for a long time and stared out at the sweeping lawns, the fertile acres. Then finally, after what seemed to Lily an eternity, she turned and threw herself into her sister's arms and sobbed wildly. Lily held her until the weeping stopped and then gently she took the crumpled page from her fingers, smoothed it out and read:

Dear Ivy,

I am so very sorry about my mother's outburst in Dorchester on Monday, and even more sorry about what I have to tell you.

Apparently Miranda Cosgrove wasn't lying. As soon as I told my mother about you and that you had invited me to Ashcote she nearly had a fit! Your brother-in-law was well known in the county as being what Miranda said and no local families will allow their daughters to visit, or their sons for that matter!

I shall stand by you whatever happens at school next term and we will think up a plan to outwit Miranda. Try not to worry too much. I feel sure that Mr Ashe must have changed or he would not have married, would he? I have also wondered whether the rumours were first put about by someone who had a grudge. But once someone gets a bad name it seems to stick.

Cheer up, old thing, nothing is as bad as it seems, and I'm your friend.

Love from Alice

Lily read the letter over twice and still it made no sense, yet it filled her with dread, with a frightening sense of some hidden and mysterious doom that lay in wait for them all. Ivy was sitting on the bed now quite motionless. Lily wanted to shake her. 'You must tell me everything,' she demanded. 'For goodness sake, Ivy, what are these accusations and why does no one visit here? Whatever has Augustus done that merits this?' She waved the letter about furiously.

Ivy couldn't get the words out, couldn't say those awful things. She gripped the bedspread twisting its beautiful frills into creases.

'Does he ... has he got some girl into trouble?' Lily said in a strangled voice. 'Is that what she's trying to say?'

'No. Oh, no, Lil. If that was it I could bear it.'

Lily felt cold all over. If it wasn't another woman, perhaps even an illegitimate child, then whatever was it? What could possibly be worse?

'He ... they say that he doesn't like women ... that he's like those men in the Bible who prefer ...'

Then all at once Lily understood. In a flash she grasped the reasons for all the mysterious things that had hitherto mystified her. Duncan's words were clear as crystal now. Augustus's fumbling efforts to make love to her made sense.

She was almost bereft of reason for a moment and then she turned to Ivy and laughed hysterically. 'I'd thought he was being unfaithful to me,' she said. 'That he had a woman in Torquay. But he's not, is he? He couldn't be. He loves me, Ivy, and he married me. Don't you see? All those things that were said about him were in the past. If there was any truth in them long ago he must have forced himself to change. I'm going to have a child!' She gripped the letter in her hand as though it had become a talisman, almost as if it had brought her relief instead of suffering.

281

'It's all right, Ivy. You don't have to be upset at all now.' She patted her completely flat stomach. 'This baby will clear Augustus's name. It will confound all the trouble-makers. If he was ... one of those ... I wouldn't be expecting his heir would I?'

Ivy's face wore a forlorn expression. 'I don't know. Perhaps they can be both?'

'Definitely not.' Lily wasn't too sure about this but she preferred to believe that it wasn't possible. Surely a man had to be one or the other?

'That's not all,' Ivy said. 'There's worse.'

'What do you mean? There can be nothing worse than such a foul rumour.'

'Miranda Cosgrove, one of our prefects, started it all.'

Lily examined the letter again. 'You mean that you've been discussing Augustus at school with this ... this Miranda somebody? That's dreadful. You had no business to.'

Ivy groped for a handkerchief and blew her nose noisily. 'I couldn't help it. She cornered me one afternoon. She says that she's going to tell everyone if I don't give her something to keep quiet. She's a prefect.'

Lily was furious now. 'That's blackmail! Prefect or no, she could be arrested for it.'

'And what good would that do? Everyone would be talking about Augustus.'

Lily gritted her teeth, smoothed out the letter as best she could and put it back into its crumpled pink envelope. 'We'll see about that,' she said with stony determination. 'I shall go to see your headmistress and confront her with all the facts before term begins. Blackmail has no power if there's no secret.'

'Don't do that, Lil,' Ivy wailed. 'All my friends would think that my sister was married to a na ...' She stopped in mid-word and clapped her hand over her mouth.

Without thinking, Lily reached out and slapped her right across the face, a stinging blow. 'If you say that, then you're as bad as they are. Nancy-boy you were going to say, weren't you? It's my Augustus you're talking about.' She was so angry that she felt no remorse for what she had done. She flung the letter onto the floor and strode to the window, staring out, seeing nothing.

Then she turned and walked steadily to the door, not looking back. She slammed it behind her, ran along the landing and down the great curving staircase. She went out into the garden, crossed the terrace and instinctively slowing her pace in case she should be seen, walked over the lawns and out of the gate that led to the wood. Her world had suddenly gone to pieces, had split apart as surely as it had done in her life so often before. Before, when she thought she had killed Harry Coney, and longer ago than that when she had stood beside her mother's death-bed, and again on that terrible day right at the end of the war when she held the telegram in her hands and looked down at the words announcing Arthur's futile death. Those moments had all been terrible, and this day stood with them, and she knew that she must struggle once more to overcome, to survive yet again.

It was a long time since she had thought of Arthur, but now she could see his face as clearly as she had seen it when he had bent to kiss her goodbye on the station in that distant summer of 1918. 'Arthur, Arthur,' she sobbed aloud to the silent trees. 'Why did you have to die? None of these awful things would have happened if you had come back to me. We might have been poor but we would have been happy.'

She came to the spot beside the river where some previous occupant of Ashcote had thoughtfully placed an iron seat, and slumped upon it and watched the rippling water, low now because there had been little rain during the past weeks. She sat there for a long time, her mind roving over all the events of her life, and finally coming again to this latest hour and its startling revelations.

What she had said to Ivy in that first flush of relief that there was no other woman, was true. At least she hadn't to worry about that any more. And Augustus had changed surely? He had made a great effort to assume normality, to marry, to produce an heir for Ashcote. She wiped her eyes on the sleeve of her dress. It was up to her to help him overcome his . . . his unnaturalness, to make him happy as best she could.

She got up and prepared to go back to the house wondering how best to plan what was to be done. She was sorry that she had slapped Ivy for she needed her help and co-operation. Augustus must know nothing of what had passed between them.

She retraced her steps slowly along the river bank. There were still things that didn't quite tie up, like the Torquay visits which continued to puzzle her. If there was no other woman, what ... ? She frowned, stared into the rippling water, and then unaccountably into her mind sprang a picture of Michael Dyer's unfriendly face. Instantly she knew the truth! She stood quite still. The birds still sang, the river continued to flow, and in the tree above her head a squirrel stopped in his headlong flight and stared down at her. But she was hardly aware of any of those things. She clasped her hands together and realized that the truth had been there all the time waiting to destroy her, but veiled. Now the veil had been jerked viciously from her eyes. Or perhaps it was like a jigsaw with the pieces coming grimly into place revealing the odious whole.

It was for his ... his lover that Augustus kept the bookshop. He had said as much in fact, and still, in her stupid innocence, she had not guessed. She recalled how her flesh crept so strangely whenever she had talked to Michael Dyer, and understood now the coldness of his manner towards her. She had felt repugnance when Augustus had mentioned that Michael had been to Ashcote once to sort some of the books in the library, and had blamed herself, wondering why she was so unsympathetic, so uncaring about his sufferings, his shellshock.

She stumbled, half blindly, along the grassy path and her anger increased with every step. Michael Dyer, Michael Dyer, Michael Dyer! The name went round and round in her head as she walked. So it *was* possible for a man to be both, to have a man as his lover, and to take a wife, to make love to her as well, even to father a child.

Why had she been such a fool, why had she not seen it before? Oh dear God, Augustus was being unfaithful to her in the worst possible way, with ... with *a man!* She wanted to be sick, wanted to have a bath, scrub herself all over, even wanted to rid herself of this child she was carrying, Augustus's child, the child of filth and degradation. She would drive to Torquay, would find out the truth and would accuse him and Michael Dyer to their ashamed faces. For the second time in her life she wished her husband dead!

Chapter Nineteen

Ivy was nowhere to be seen when Lily returned to the house. *And no wonder,* she thought, *after the way I treated her. There was no excuse for that slap.* After looking in the obvious places she made her way through the endless passages to the kitchen and pushed open its great door. Mary Dunne and a maid were inside and she was aware of their surprised expressions. It was not often that she ventured into this hot and unpleasant place.

Mary wiped her hands on her apron and smiled. 'Lunch won't be long, Madam,' she said. 'Were you wanting it outside? 'Tis quite warm enough and I could serve it there if you wish?'

'No, thank you, Mary. The dining room will do quite well.' She didn't add that she wanted nothing, indeed felt as though she would never be able to face food again. She forced a measure of calm into her voice. 'I just wondered if you've seen my sister recently?'

'I saw her running for dear life just now.' Mary nodded towards the window which looked out on the gardens at the rear of the house. 'Both dogs were with her. Most likely she was making for that cart-horse's field. My husband says she spends a lot of time over there. You'd think a young lady would prefer to be riding her pony wouldn't you, rather than messing about with a great beast like that what isn't no use?'

Normally Lily would have smiled at this and made some remark about Flo's charms, but she murmured a further thank you, shut the door behind her and went up to her

286

room. She didn't think, after all, that she could face Ivy just yet.

At lunchtime she sat at the table hoping her sister would return and that the slap would be forgiven. This was no time to quarrel.

Ivy came in hesitantly a few minutes later and sat down without looking at Lily.

Mary Dunne followed her and put a plate of cold meat on the table, a bowl of lettuce and tomatoes, some potatoes carefully sliced and anointed with her own home-made salad dressing, and a dish of beetroot also sliced. 'From the garden,' she said of the latter. 'In fact all of it have come from the garden. Nice and fresh. There's nothing like home-grown.'

'Thank you, Mary.' Lily shook out her napkin and spread it on her lap. 'It all looks splendid.' She hoped that the dogs would be around to eat her share of food.

'There's a fruit pie for dessert and some cream. Ring when you're ready, Madam.'

Mary was a mixture of homely servant who kept her place and would-be friend. Lily found this confusing, but knew that on no account must Mary catch any whisper of the things that had been said between herself and Ivy this morning. She waited until the door was closed and Mary's footsteps had echoed through the hall and were lost in the distance. Then she reached out across the wide table, stretched her hand towards her sister. 'I'm sorry I hit you, Ivy.'

Ivy sat motionless, her mouth set in despondent and downcast lines. Then she put her hand to her face, held it over the place where Lily had slapped her. 'You've never struck me before,' she said. 'Ma did now and then when I was really naughty, but not like that.'

'Please forgive me, Ivy. I've said I'm sorry. What more can I say? I was so shocked and upset by what . . .'

Then Ivy looked up and also reached out across the table. She grasped her sister's hand, stopping her in mid-sentence. 'Don't say no more, Lil, any more I mean. What I said or nearly said was awful, enough to make you very angry. I'll never say or think those horrible words again.'

Lily felt tears of gratitude in her eyes. 'Thank you, love.

Calling him that horrible street name cheapens everything somehow ... even if it's true.'

Ivy stared at her. 'So you think it is?'

'I believe it might be.'

'Oh, Lil, that's terrible. I thought with the baby and that ... that it proved it wasn't?'

'We'll see. I don't want to talk about it any more. Not yet anyway.'

Ivy helped herself to a generous portion of meat and salad. 'I never thought girls who went to posh schools would know about all those kind of things. Will you go to see Miss Walton about it?'

Lily had forgotten about her promise to see the headmistress of Barnfield, but now she reconsidered, tried to order her thoughts. If Augustus was really being unfaithful in this terrible way, then the girl, Miranda, was right of course. But even so, blackmail was a serious offence. She picked drearily at the one slice of meat she had forced herself to take, and knew that whatever she decided to do would be frightful. There was no easy way at all.

The troubles of the morning had not affected Ivy's appetite. She added a large spoonful of chutney to her plate and then stared at Lily thoughtfully. 'If this baby you are going to have proves that there's no truth in these rumours, then everything's all right, isn't it? I can tell Miranda Cosgrove myself and that'll shut her up. If it doesn't, perhaps you could write to Miss Walton instead of going to see her. I could threaten Miranda that you'd tell about the blackmail.'

'I want to talk to Augustus before I decide what to do,' Lily said as calmly as she could. She speared a pickled onion on the end of her fork and crunched it furiously.

'You're going to tell him?' Ivy nearly spluttered a mouthful of food into her napkin in her sudden fright.

Lily felt a great rush of love for her sister, and sorrow that she was causing her such problems. She had thought that by marrying Augustus she would bring only happiness to her family. 'I must,' she said.

'Oh, Lil, is that really necessary? Couldn't we deal with it ourselves and never let on? It'll be awful.'

'It's awful anyway,' Lily said curtly. 'I shall go to Torquay tomorrow.'

There was complete misery now on Ivy's face. 'It's all my fault,' she said. 'If you and Augustus fall out, I'll never forgive myself.'

'Of course it's not your fault, you little ninny. There's only one person to blame!'

Ivy sniffed tearfully. 'But I thought you said it was all lies?'

'I've reason to believe that ...' Lily stopped in mid-sentence. How was she to tell Ivy that Augustus had a male lover? That as well as being a ... the offensive words sprang into her own mind now ... as well as having those awful tendencies, he was actually being unfaithful in this appalling way?

'What do you believe?'

Lily shook her head. 'I'm going to Torquay.'

'How are you going to get there?'

'I'll drive.'

'It's a long way. You'd need company. You couldn't possibly go on your own. Could I come?'

'Certainly not. Sorry, love, but I must do this alone. I'll come straight back.'

Ivy shrugged her shoulders. 'All right then. If that's what you want.'

'It's not what I want, for goodness sake!' Lily almost shouted the words. 'It's what I must do.'

When Mary brought in the pudding she looked at Lily's plate suspiciously. 'Not to your liking Madam?'

'It's fine. I'm not hungry.'

Mary cleared away the things and then set the golden-crusted plum pie on the table. 'Perhaps you'll try a bit of this?' she said. 'There's real clotted cream just like you get in Devon too. My mother came from down Dartmouth way and she showed me how to make it. Now eat up, I don't want any left. There's another pie and a big bowl of cream in the larder for me and Ted and the rest of us.' She put the used plates on a tray and then quietly retreated, giving no sign whether or not she was aware of the heavy silence in the room.

Lily felt her stomach heave as she looked at the glass bowl of rich yellow cream, thick and crusted, but Ivy helped herself to a generous portion of both pie and cream.

'Come on, Sis, have some,' she said. 'It looks delicious. I remember that you always liked afters better'n firsts.'

Lily smiled a little at the old Bristol voice that she guessed Ivy had deliberately used in order to cheer her up, but shook her head and began to wonder how she was to accomplish the journey to Torquay alone. She very much feared all those miles of country roads let alone the confrontation at the end. Would she be able to find the way? What about petrol? Dunne always saw that the car was ready to drive. She had no idea where the petrol went or how to put it there. She knew that Augustus took a can of the stuff when he went on a longish journey. She had only ventured around the estate roads and into Dorchester a couple of times. Torquay was a different prospect altogether.

'I think that I shall go by train after all,' she said half to herself. 'Dunne can drive me to Dorchester.'

'Then you won't be back in a day.'

'Perhaps not, but you'll be all right here. You can have Janey and Tessa in your bedroom.'

Ivy made no more objections. 'Be careful, Lil,' she said in a motherly grown-up sort of voice. 'Augustus is nice. I like him a lot. If Miranda Cosgrove was the cause of you and him falling out, I'd kill her.'

'And how would you do that?'

'Make a doll and stick pins in it. I'm told it works.'

In spite of her despair Lily managed to laugh. 'I love your loyalty, Ivy, but we don't want any more funerals.'

'Only trying to make a joke,' she said.

Lily left the following morning. Neither Mary nor her husband made any comment about this sudden decision. Dunne was dressed smartly in his chauffeur's uniform, ready for the short journey to the station. He carried her one small suitcase down and put it in the back of the motor car.

Ivy looked at it suspiciously. 'So you do intend to stay overnight then?'

'I hope to come back this evening, but thought I'd better

290

be prepared to stay just in case ... ' Lily's words tailed off. In case what? she wondered dully. In case Augustus persuaded her that he was quite innocent of the rumours, in case they should have a lovely romantic reunion together. *Some hopes,* she thought angrily. *He would never take me with him to Torquay, so he isn't likely to be very pleased to see me there this afternoon!*

She seated herself in the passenger seat and glanced back at Ivy as Dunne started the engine. 'Hope to see you tonight, darling,' she called as confidently as she could manage, and she waved an immaculately gloved hand at her sister. Ivy looked forlorn and lonely standing there on the top steps in front of the great house and Lily wondered for the second time whether all this wealth and grandeur was bringing happiness to either of them.

The vehicle carried her smoothly down the drive and through the tall wrought-iron gates. What she discovered in Torquay would answer that question once and for all.

She shivered in apprehension and hoped that the new suit she was wearing and which had been recently made for the summer would give her the confidence that she lacked. It was a pretty jade colour and she had ordered a hat to match fashioned in the latest crushed velvet. It was trimmed with a large feather and she touched it nervously and wondered why she had not chosen a simple cloche style as she usually wore. This more fashionable design didn't allow for resting one's head back against the seat and that was what she wanted to do just now, close her eyes and go to sleep and forget the horrible purpose of this journey. Instead she sat up straight and stared unseeing as the motor car sped through the narrow lanes to Dorchester.

She didn't speak at all, and Dunne, austerely correct, made no comment. She wondered what he was thinking and what he knew.

At the station he waited as she bought her ticket and then handed her small suitcase over to a porter. She knew that she was quite capable of carrying it herself.

'Will you be all right now, Madam?' Dunne asked guardedly.

'I shall be fine, Dunne, thank you. The train will be here

291

in half an hour. Please don't wait.'

'Shall I meet the last train?' he asked.

'I shall telephone if I want you to do that, but I may get a taxi.' Lily marvelled at herself in spite of her agitation. Augustus had recently had a telephone installed at Ashcote and although she had not used it yet and the idea of it frightened her a liitle, she knew that she must appear to be completely confident about such things.

He nodded, touched his cap and turned to leave and she watched him with a fearful heart for she was on her own now and was about to face one of the most difficult things she had ever had to deal with in her life. There had been plenty of other formidable situations to confront during the past few years but surely none so fraught at this.

Torquay was bright and sunny, the station reassuringly familiar to her and she politely declined all offers of help and of taxis. She deposited her suitcase in the left luggage office and set out to walk with as determined a stride as she could manage. The three-quarters of a mile along the sea front to the Old Harbour was just what she needed to calm her nerves, to concentrate her thoughts.

Tor Abbey Sands looked beautiful, a happy place to be on this August morning, and she looked with envy at the families enjoying the sunshine and the sand. She didn't slacken her pace but she saw children playing, running in and out of the sea, laughing together, fathers sitting in deck chairs, some of them with handkerchiefs knotted over their heads against the sun. Families, families, families! She wanted to cry. It wasn't possible that she and Augustus would ever be a family now, not with this awful thing that Ivy had discovered, this frightful disgrace that she was soon to expose.

She made a slight detour, took one of the paths in the Royal Terrace Gardens so that she could delay by a few minutes the moment of confrontation, but then she gritted her teeth, and strode resolutely round the familiar harbour with its boats moving just a little in the gentle swell, and soon she saw the dear familiar lines of her house, her very own Rose House, its three bay windows one above the other and the door standing open welcoming visitors to the café on the ground floor. She wanted to run into it, run up the two flights of stairs to that lovely haven of hers at the top of the house, the place where she had found comfort and peace, but she knew that she would not. Even though only the café was let, there was someone else in occupation and if she appeared at all it must be as the composed and confident landlady. Her refuge was lost to her at present.

She stopped and glanced through the window but she hardly registered the few families having lunch there for all her thoughts now were on the bookshop next door. She hadn't dared look at it yet.

Her heart was thumping fearfully but her feet led inexorably the few steps along the pavement towards the old bay window with its enticing display of books that once she had contemplated with such excitement. For one moment she recalled the first time she had met Augustus here, the immediate accord, the easy friendship in spite of their greatly contrasting backgrounds. She had thought herself so much in love with him then. It could have been centuries ago, yet in fact was only a few months.

She opened the door, heard the bell ring and looked straight into the pale enquiring face of Michael Dyer.

'Mrs Ashe?'

Apart from those two startled words he seemed to have been struck dumb yet for that matter so did she. Neither spoke but just stood looking at each other and the air was heavy with their shared hostility.

'Lily!'

It was Augustus's voice that brought her to her senses, made her look around vaguely for a chair as the walls on all sides appeared to spin.

'What on earth are you doing here?'

She gripped the counter unnerved by the frostiness of his voice. 'I had to talk to you.'

He seemed quickly to take control of himself. His tone changed. He came around to where she was standing, took her arm, led her gently through the door at the back of the shop to the little office behind. 'Sit down, dearest.' he said. 'I'll make you some coffee. Is there something wrong? Has anything happened? You could have telephoned.'

She sank on to the proffered chair and closed her eyes for a second. Now in his presence she realized how much she still loved him, how precious he was to her, and was filled with loathing for the young man in the shop who, she was dimly aware, was now talking to a customer. Perhaps none of it was true, perhaps that terrible Miranda somebody was just making mischief. Oh dear God, how could she know what to do? She gripped her handbag so tightly in her lap that she could feel her comb inside bulging through the soft leather, hurting her. At last she spoke.

'Can we go out?'

'Yes, we'll have some lunch. You look as if you need it. I know a nice place. Then you can tell me what's wrong.'

She watched as he took his coat from the peg on the wall. It had been placed carefully on a hanger and he took equal care in putting it on, buttoning it with maddening slowness in spite of the warm weather outside. He took his silver-topped cane and his hat and then turned to her.

'Ready then, or do you want the bathroom?'

She blushed. 'No. I'm ready.'

He stood back and she walked before him through the shop. She kept her eyes fixed on the ground and was careful not to look at Michael Dyer.

Once outside Augustus opened the passenger door of his motor car which was parked at the kerb side. 'We'll drive there,' he said. 'It's a hotel overlooking the sea just a mile or so along the coast.'

She made no comment but climbed in and sat quietly while he started the engine. He took the sea road which led past Mead Foot Sands and then turned slightly inland, and still they said nothing to each other.

The hotel was high on the cliff with sweeping views over the steep and beautiful coastline of Torbay. Lily had seldom been up here, for while she had lived in Torquay she was usually too busy. Just once she had walked along the footpath on to Hope's Nose, but that had been in the early days. She had been alone, and the magnificence of the rugged cliffs below had caused her to gasp in amazement. Now she stared down at the sea and hardly saw its shimmering beauty.

Augustus parked the car and helped her out. She could feel the tenseness in him and wondered what he was feeling, why he had not questioned her.

'Before we go in,' she said, 'I think we should talk. I don't want anyone to overhear what I have to say.' There were gardens sloping down a little way towards the cliff edge. She indicated them. 'There's a seat.' She walked away from him across the lawn. She could feel him following unwillingly. She sat down on the bench that had obviously been placed to make the most of the spectacular views.

Augustus stood uneasily and then sat down beside her. 'Now, what is it?' he said eventually. 'Don't keep me in suspense any longer, Lily. It must be something important to bring you here like this. Tell me.'

She took a deep breath. No good would come of prolonging the agony. She closed her eyes shutting out everything beautiful and forced the horrible words from her lips. 'There have been rumours at Ivy's school, frightful things said about you, Augustus. That you ... that you are not as other men. That you don't like women.' She could hear the sea far below worrying at the rocks and then she opened her eyes and looked down, saw the luminous blue of it blending almost imperceptibly in the distance with the cloudless sky.

For a time he said nothing. There was no sudden anger, no flare-up of rage. She would have preferred that. She longed for a quick and confident denial, but there was none, just a quiet acceptance of what she had said. This was the most appalling response that she could imagine.

'So it's true?'

He shifted uneasily on the hard seat. 'Yes, its true, or partly true. I should never have married you, Lily.' He spoke slowly, the words seeming to be dragged from him unwillingly.

Her whole world fell apart. 'Why did you then?'

'I love you. Strange as it may seem to you, I love you.' He turned to look at her and tried to take her hand, but she pulled away from him.

'How can you possibly say that when you have admitted that you don't like women?' She felt a terrible anger rising in her now.

He put his head in his hands. 'I can't feel the things that most men feel when they see an attractive woman. I've known it for a long time, have tried to fight it, but it's never been any good. It's part of me. The world says that it's a bad defiling part and I find that difficult to accept. But the love I have for you is different, something that has nothing to do with that other kind of love.'

'So that's why our honeymoon was so disastrous!'

He looked up at her and as their eyes met she realized the power of those last cruel words and the pain they must cause him. He had been so kind during that holiday, had done everything for her happiness. But at that moment she didn't care. Let him suffer now as she was suffering.

'Is that really what you thought?' He stared at her like a dog cruelly beaten by a loved master.

In spite of her anger there was a sudden stab of sorrow for him. She tried to find something to say that might mitigate the hurt a little. 'I thought it was my fault that things weren't right, Augustus,' she said quietly. 'That I was unattractive to you, that I was doing something wrong.'

He shook his head. 'Never, Lily. You were wonderful. You did nothing wrong'.

But as he spoke she knew that there was a monstrous truth in what she had said. She was indeed unattractive to him! Which thought brought her immediately back to Michael Dyer. She shuddered. 'There's more, Augustus, that I must know.'

He was staring straight out to sea now, his eyes inscrutable, his whole body tense and taut like a spring strained to its full capacity.

'I believe that you have someone else. You are unfaithful to me. You have ... you have Michael Dyer.'

She wanted him to jump to his feet. Again she wanted his furious denial. She wouldn't have minded if he had hit her just as she had struck Ivy. She would have welcomed it. But he sat there as though turned to stone, cold solid stone and he said not one word.

She jumped up and stood in front of him. 'So it *is* true. You come down here to Torquay to be unfaithful to me in the most terrible, the most frightful way of all. Even another woman would have been more bearable than this!'

She turned and ran from the garden, not knowing where she was going, but found herself on the footpath that led directly to the Bishop's Walk, a difficult and undulating pathway that wound around the steep cliff side. She stumbled almost blindly along it, tears streaming from her eyes and her fashionable shoes causing her to trip constantly on the rough stones. What she intended to do she neither knew nor cared. In fact she longed to fling herself from one of the many high viewpoints along the way and end all the agony and frustration of her life once and for all.

Chapter Twenty

Augustus remained where he was for a long time, the sun failing to warm him and the chill in his heart making him shiver repeatedly. How could he save his marriage? How continue to have the love of the two people who meant most to him in life? He felt *himself* to be two people in fact, two parts of a whole, two parts that were in complete conflict with each other. The one was respectable, honourable, but the other, the hidden side, was base and totally contemptible, sinful and to be utterly abhorred. That was what he had been brought up to believe. He knew that almost everyone accepted those views, and if they did not, then they kept quiet about their opinions.

When his parents had discovered him one day years ago in one of the stables with a boy from the village they had been outraged and horrified. Vast sums had been paid to the lad's family to keep quiet, and from that day Augustus had been rejected by his father and despised by his mother. He remembered his bewilderment and misery during the following months and years, his efforts to be normal, to dance with the girls his mother was constantly forcing upon him. Then came the war and blessed relief, and afterwards fulfilment at last. As he pondered the dilemma he was now in, every shred of his boyhood suffering returned to haunt him.

And now, if his love for Michael was known as Lily implied, it would be labelled despicable and dirty. It was of course neither of those things. It was pure and beautiful and he couldn't bear the thought of that relationship being dragged into the dust, paraded for all to condemn. Arrest was perfectly possible, was in fact very likely. 'Damn them all,' he said aloud. 'Damn the ignorance and bigotry that creates such laws, that forces us to conform.'

Slowly he got up and retraced his steps to his motor car. There was no point now in trying to follow Lily along the path. He knew where it joined the road. He would drive there and wait for her. He had no idea what to say, yet he knew that he would have to make the agonizing decision between his wife and his lover. Lily or Michael? He was racked with self-loathing for he also knew that he should never have married Lily. But all the regrets in the world wouldn't make the problem any easier to bear or the choice less difficult. And that choice must be made soon, today, within the next half an hour!

Should his future life be a pretence with Lily? If he chose this way he would be able to vindicate his accusers, and enjoy all the comforts of life as a country squire for years to come. Hopefully there might even be a son in time to fully exonerate him and to secure the future of his family name, for to his relief he had managed to aquit himself successfully as a husband quite a few times. It had not been too unpleasant either and Lily had been gentle and patient with him, never allowing him to feel inadequate or incompetent.

The other choice entailed a rejection of his marriage, a messy divorce, the loss of Lily whom he loved deeply in a brotherly way, the exposure of his affair with Michael, certain arrest and eventual imprisonment. He would lose everything, Ashcote too. Put coldly like that there was really only one way he could go. Yet could he bear to lose Michael? The thought was almost as frightful to him as losing life itself. But either way he would lose Michael.

He parked at the end of the short cul-de-sac where the footpath ended and sat for a time in the private and safe cocoon of his car pondering his total misery. Then he climbed from the vehicle. He felt sure that Lily would not have reached this spot yet. He walked in the direction from which she would come, his mind veering from one solution to the other in anguish and despair.

299

Eventually he saw her as she stumbled around a bend and his heart went out to her in a mixture of compassion and sorrow. She looked bedraggled and lost, as though she too had come to the end of her endurance, and through no fault of her own, he reminded himself with shame.

He held out his arms to her and to his joy and amazement she ran into them. He clasped her tightly. 'I love you, Lily,' he murmured. This at least he could honestly say, for he did love her, perhaps not with his body, but with his mind he certainly loved her, and needed her forgiveness whatever they decided to do.

He buried his head in her windblown hair, for the fashionable hat was missing now. 'Can you possibly forgive me?' he whispered, and the words sounded quite preposterous to him.

In spite of everything Lily knew that she didn't want to lose him. Whatever happened, whatever he did or did not do, this man was the one she loved, the one she had promised to cherish and care for in sickness or in health, till death parted them. Well, his malady was a sickness, wasn't it? If only he would give her his co-operation surely she could help him overcome it, get well again? And she carried his child. That should bring him back to her. It was her trump card. If he would promise not to see Michael Dyer again she might be able to forgive him, but she remained silent, giving no immediate answer.

He led her to the motor car, helped her in, tucked a rug around her and then got in beside her.

'Where would you like to go?'

She shook her head. 'I don't know. I suppose I want to go home.' But where was home? Was it Ashcote? That depended completely on Augustus now.

'I shall drive you to Ashcote as soon as we've found somewhere else to have lunch,' he said.

'But we haven't settled anything. You haven't told me anything. I still don't know what you intend to do.' She was near to tears again.

'What do you want me to do?'

She couldn't believe that he was asking her this. 'It must

300

be obvious. Surely you don't need me to tell you what is right?'

'Perhaps I do. Perhaps I need to hear it from your lips, Lily.'

'And would you do as I ask?'

There was no reply. He gripped the steering wheel as if it were his only means of support.

'I want you to promise me that you will never see Michael Dyer again.'

There was a terrible silence between them. She was frightened. What was this strange incomprehensible thing between two men that had such power? Was she underestimating its intensity and depth? So grounded was she in the Bible that her mind immediately went to the ancient friendship that until now she had never questioned, David and Jonathan, the two whose love for each other was held up as something honourable, an example to be followed. She remembered the words that she had read so many times in Sunday School, the childish drawings she had done of the two young men clasped in each other's arms. David had said in his lament to Jonathan after his death in battle that their love for one another 'was wonderful passing the love of women'.

But had there been anything sinister and wrong in that ancient alliance that no one noticed or perhaps allowed themselves to think about? 'Passing the love of women.' She said the words aloud almost without realizing that she had done so.

'What was that?' Augustus looked at her strangely.

'Just some words from the Bible.'

Silence again, and then at last Augustus spoke, slowly, thoughtfully, every word sounding as though it was wrung from him in agony. 'It would kill Michael if I told him that our relationship was at an end.'

At this Lily felt rage and resentment rise in her yet again like a mighty flood, displacing all her efforts to remain cool and understanding. Any thoughts of self-sacrifice, of helping him to change, disappeared.

'So you intend to continue your filthy, disgusting behaviour, do you?' she shouted. 'Then you'll end up in prison, Augustus Ashe, for make no mistake, there are people in Dorset who are quite aware of what you are like. I despise you from the bottom of my heart. All right, you have inclinations that I cannot begin to understand and I was prepared to forgive, for strange as it may seem, I loved you too. But to expect me to wave happily goodbye to you every time you leave me for your ... your whore ... is completely unthinkable.' She flung open the car door and stormed out. 'And I don't need any more support from you, or from your great uncomfortable house. I shall see that my baby is born far away from your perverted influence.'

She stumbled away from him back the way she had come with no thought of where she was going. She ran as fast as her unsuitable shoes would allow, but just as she had almost reached the place where the path curved away out of his sight she tripped and fell heavily, her ankle twisting beneath her so that she could only cry out in pain and lie there helpless and outraged on the dusty ground.

Augustus gasped. What had she said? Baby? Had he heard correctly? Had those fumblings in their great double bed really resulted in this already? He was out of the car in a flash, tearing towards her, bending over her, whispering loving comforting things, telling her that he would indeed never see Michael Dyer again, that he loved her, that he would sell the bookshop, give it to Michael, anything, if only she would forgive him, love him again, come back to Ashcote, give him a son, stand by him. She could have the whole world if she wanted it.

He scarcely knew what he was saying. The only thing that mattered in that one blinding moment of revelation was that he should take her back to Ashcote, cherish her, love her, give up everything for her and their child. He would try to be normal, the clandestine nights in Torquay would be over, the fear of discovery would be at an end. This child would put everything right for ever.

Lily was helpless, the piercing pain in her ankle overcoming all her objections, all her fierce resolutions. He carried her to the car and she cried out in pain.

'I shall take you straight round to Duncan MacMullen. If he's out then it'll have to be the hospital.'

Duncan took one look at them and ushered them into the surgery. He carefully examined Lily's ankle, diagnosed a severe sprain but nothing worse, bound it firmly and commanded rest for at least a month.

'You must put no weight on it at all,' he said. 'Let everyone wait on you.'

'Everyone does already,' she managed.

He looked searchingly at her ashen face. He was obviously aware of the tension between herself and Augusutus and it was equally obvious that he was making every effort to appear as if he saw nothing wrong.

'How do you like that great house Augustus has told me of?' he said, trying to make inconsequential conversation.

'It's bigger than I thought. Very beautiful of course.' Her voice was flat, disinterested.

He nodded and washed his hands in a china bowl that was set on a sturdy marble washstand. 'Well, it's good to see you in Torquay again, Mrs Ashe, but it was foolish to walk on that rough footpath in such fashionable and unsuitable shoes.' He grinned at her. 'I trust Augustus will buy you a flat ugly pair for your next visit? By the way,' he continued, 'your tenant can't make such delectable scones as you used to do. I miss them.'

'I think I've forgotten how to make them myself,' Lily said, trying her best to sound normal while her heart was breaking. Had she been alone she would have told Duncan everything as she had done on that long ago day when he had taken her to Exeter. She knew that his advice would be sound and that he would comfort her in a way no one else could.

Conversation was difficult. Augustus said little and Lily noticed Duncan looking at him curiously from time to time. Nothing was said of the baby. The landlady was persuaded to bring sandwiches and a pot of tea but it was only Duncan who ate heartily.

'Sorry I can't spend more time with you,' he said when they had finished. 'I've a great list of calls to make this afternoon. Now take care, both of you. Drive her carefully, Augustus.'

He stood at the door and waved to them as they left and

Lily turned and watched him until they rounded the corner and his sturdy comforting figure was lost to her. She wished that he lived closer, that she could see him more often.

They drove to the station to collect the suitcase which she had left there and then straight back to Ashcote. 'Michael can send my things on,' Augustus said.

They hardly spoke during the first part of the journey, each concerned with their own private agonies. All the questions between them waited to be resolved. The bitter words that Lily had spoken just before she fell still hung in the air, threatening, not yet repealed. She had not answered him when he had bent over her and given all those fine promises. Was it just because of the baby? Was the assurance of an heir for Ashcote so important that Michael Dyer must make way, take second place, even be rejected altogether? Could she dare hope for that?

When they were just a few miles away from Ashcote Lily decided that she must know the answers to these things. She couldn't face Ivy and the servants with so much uncertainty and pain in her heart.

'Did you mean what you said?' she murmured. 'Will you truly ...'

She got no further. Augustus interrupted her. 'I shall visit my solicitor tomorrow and ask him to make the bookshop over to Michael. I shall not see him again.'

Lily gasped and turned to look at him but his eyes were firmly fixed on the road ahead. Her first reaction was one of relief and triumph. She had won. Yet doubts and misgivings quickly followed for she was aware of her husband's misery. What had she done? Could they live together in harmony after this?

'Is it just because of the baby?' A frightful question but she had to know.

Another breathless silence between them, tense and fraught, full of unspoken monstrous thoughts.

'Not just because of that.'

'What then? You said you loved me. Is that really true, Augustus?'

'I love you, Lily. Not perhaps as fully as a man should love a woman, but I do love you. I shall be faithful for the rest of my life, I shall care for you and our child if you'll let me, and in time, and with your understanding, I hope that I shall be as satisfactory a husband as you could want. Will you give me that chance?'

Lily breathed deeply. So what she had hoped for could become fact. She might be able to help him change, become normal. And what was the alternative? She went over all the possibilities in her mind. She could leave him, find somewhere to live in Bristol, for Torquay was quite out of the question now with Michael Dyer living there, hating her.

But the future heir to Ashcote couldn't be brought up in an ordinary house, in an ordinary street, go to an ordinary school, could he? The child might even be taken from her by law. Her baby would be given into the care of a nanny and she would never cuddle him, tuck him into bed. He would become a stranger to her. She felt cold all over as she thought of this possibility and clenched her hands over her stomach in fear. Then there was Ivy of course. Whatever would happen to Ivy, her new life, her new school, her ambitious dreams? And there would be the horror of seeing Augustus, the father of her unborn child, mocked and ridiculed, arrested and imprisoned for the crime of loving Michael Dyer. Their child would be tainted as he grew up. The shame of his father's life would follow him wherever he might live, for he would bear the name Ashe and that would be enough to condemn him for ever.

Lily sat in the car tense and deeply troubled but the more she considered, the more she knew that there was only one course of action open to her now. Augustus must be protected so that their child should be protected. She must stand by his side and face the suspicions and condemnations of the world, assert that all was well, that the rumours were merely that, unfounded stories with no truth at all. With his help and co-operation she could do it. She had lived a lie, many lies, before in her life, and she would do it again with perfect skill.

Yet the thought of resuming her marriage as though nothing had happened was completely abhorrent, couldn't be done. She was quite sure that it would be impossible to blot from her mind the image of Augustus and Michael

Dyer together. She shuddered and knew that it would be a long time before she would be able to accept her husband into her bed again. Perhaps she never could.

She looked across at him. He had asked if she would give him a chance. 'Yes, Augustus,' she said quietly. 'I will give you another chance. But I must have a bedroom to myself.'

He accepted her condition calmly. 'Of course,' he said. 'You will keep the big room and I shall have a bed made up in my dressing room. Will that do?' He took one hand from the steering wheel, reached over and grasped hers, pressed it firmly in his, but said nothing more and she guessed that he was unable to speak for she saw tears on his face. Whether they were tears for her or tears for Michael Dyer she couldn't begin to imagine.

Michael Dyer! The name suddenly pierced her yet again twisting in her gut like a murderer's knife. Would he remain silent? In the face of his rejection would he be loyal and say nothing? Or would be become bitter and betray Augustus?

Perhaps reading her thoughts Augustus said, 'We shall have nothing to fear from Michael. I know he'll be trustworthy. If he gave me away then he would be giving himself away after all.'

Lily flinched. Perversely she wanted to hear nothing good of Michael Dyer, yet at the same time she was relieved. 'I'm glad. I just hope you're right. Will you really give him the bookshop? Won't that look suspicious?'

'I shall sell it to him for a small sum. That way there will be no possibility of gossip. Don't worry about those things, Lily. I shall see that he has money to pay for it, but you have my promise that I shall never see him again. I shall abide by that. Just trust me.'

She could hear the anguish in his voice and she knew that she must probe no further.

Eventually Ashcote came into view for it stood on a small rise. Its beautiful golden stone glowed in the early-evening sunshine and her heart leapt in unexpected pleasure. She knew that however hard the next months, years even, were going to be, she had made the right decision. This was her child's inheritance and she could never take it from him. The generations of Ashe wives would look down at her from their portraits on the walls of the house and she was certain they would approve.

Mary Dunne fussed around her, prepared a special meal, and made no comment about the extra bed to be prepared for Augustus.

Lily was grateful for this unquestioning loyalty but she knew that Ivy wouldn't be so easily satisfied. She shrank from giving explanations tonight but she supposed that it must be done.

Later Augustus announced that he had things to do in the library, and she and Ivy settled themselves in the small parlour. This room had a homely air and Lily had tried to make it her own in many ways. Her foot was carefully propped up on a stool and some colour had returned to her cheeks.

'So you came back?' Ivy said, somewhat unnecessarily.

'Yes, and everything is going to be all right.'

'You mean that there's no truth in what Miranda said?'

Lily took a deep breath. She wanted to tell another lie, say that there was indeed no truth in those frightful assertions, but she looked deeply into her sister's eyes and knew that she couldn't deceive her. 'There might have been in the past, but that's all over. Augustus is my husband. We have a proper married life as must be obvious because I am going to have his baby. That's all we need to say to stop the rumours. You must tell Miranda this on the first day of term, and if she persists in her persecution, then I shall come to see your headmistress at once. Blackmail is a very serious crime. She would be severely punished.'

'I hope you won't need to come,' Ivy said. 'I want to forget all about it.'

During the next few days Lily's ankle mended slowly but her heart would not be comforted. She looked at Augustus every day, loved him, wanted him and yet was repelled by him. He was away frequently, but for short periods only, and always just to Dorchester to see his accountant or solicitor. As far as Lily knew there was no direct communication between him and Michael Dyer.

The pregnancy was confirmed, an eminent gynaecologist engaged, and everyone informed. William and George came down to Ashcote for a weekend towards the end of August to give their congratulations and to see the house, and both returned to Bristol impressed and slightly intimidated by its grandeur and great size. Neither had any inkling of the tension that was gradually damaging Augustus's fragile health, and causing Lily such unhappiness.

Along with Ivy, both Lily and Augustus had managed to put up a united front. 'No rumours of anything wrong are to reach Bristol,' Lily had instructed before the visit. 'William has enought to worry about. He has to study for his next exams.'

Ivy had laughed in spite of the seriousness of the remark. 'You'll never change, will you, Lily Penrose?' she had said. 'Still putting William first, aren't you!'

'Suppose I am? It's how I was brought up.'

Ivy returned to school in the middle of September and Lily missed her cheerful boisterous presence, but had little time to mope for two days later a body was found washed up on Mead Foot Beach. It was an item of news that she would never forget.

The man had been climbing the steep cliffs near Daddy Hole Plain and must have fallen, the newspaper said. It was a foolish thing to do, especially for someone still suffering from shell-shock. But, the article continued, the war left its mark in many ways, often made men unstable. This young officer had been a hero. He had won the Military Cross on the Western Front. Michael Dyer was a man to be honoured, and would be given a fitting funeral.

An envelope arrived for Augustus from Torquay on that very morning. Inside was one sheet of paper, one sentence written upon it in Michael Dyer's distinctive handwritting. 'Remember the good times.' There was nothing else, just those stark words, a message from the dead.

Augustus stood for a long time, white-faced, staring at the thick piece of deckle-edged paper. It shook in his hand.

He handed it to Lily. She too stared, transfixed, the words stringing together, making no sense at first. Then she knew. Everything was suddenly clear. This one sentence, in its very brevity, said all there was to say. Michael Dyer had won after all. Lily felt that she was condemned. She was the guilty one, for she had stolen Augustus from him, had brought to an end their mystifying and powerful union. Michael Dyer's death was her fault and hers alone.

However unwholesome his devotion to Augustus seemed, however repellent to decency, to the law and to Lily's strongest instincts, yet there was a power in it that she completely failed to understand. She had no idea how to react, what to do, or what her future would now be.

She watched helplessly as Augustus became enveloped in a great blanket of despair. They lived silent separate lives, neither wishing to communicate. But then, after two days of misery he made a surprising request. He asked Lily if she would go with him to the funeral. Her heart sank at the suggestion. It was the last thing in the world she wished to do and yet she was moved that he wanted her, needed her perhaps in this moment of his deepest anguish. But how could she possibly go through with such a bizarre and terrible ceremony knowing the frightful truth and yet saying nothing, appearing composed and fairly unmoved? To the outside world, this man was just her husband's former employee, the victim of a simple accident.

They were sitting opposite each other at breakfast and she looked into Augustus's ravaged face, saw the pallor and agony in it, and her own desolation gave way to pity for him. In spite of everything she realized that in a way she still loved him and if there was to be any sort of life for them both and for their coming child it was she who must be strong, must set her own needs aside just as, years ago, she had promised her mother she would do for William. She sighed and wondered if it must ever be so for women.

'It will be hard, Augustus,' she said eventually. 'But yes, if you want me to come, I will.'

Chapter Twenty-one

To Lily's surprise the church was almost full when they arrived. They were shown to a pew at the rear, a place that was not in any position of importance and she was grateful for this for she had dreaded being conspicuous.

She studied the backs of the assembled congregation. She had never thought of Michael Dyer as a member of a family. He had been, to her, a lone character, someone who had existence only in the bookshop, his fascination with old books giving him a sort of matching antiquarian aura. She realized now how wrong that judgement was. There were a great number of relatives, mostly women. Were they cousins? Sisters? Did they know anything of the truth?

Duncan was sitting a few rows in front. She could only see the back of his head, but longed to go to him, to be comforted, to feel his strength. What did he know? Had he genuinely thought that Augustus would renounce his affair when he married? Perhaps Augustus had convinced him that this would be so.

She watched wretchedly as the coffin was carried down the aisle. There was the body of the man who had wrecked her marriage just as surely as she had wrecked his happiness, destroyed his very life. Yet in his dying he had not been malicious, had not sought revenge. A verdict of accidental death had been returned and accepted by the authorities and the Press. There was no suspicion of suicide. He had set up the whole poignant deed with skill and competence so that it should appear a simple accident. Only to Augustus . . .

to his lover … in those few tragic words, had he revealed the truth.

Lily thought of all these things throughout the hymns and the prayers and she realized that she should be grateful to Michael Dyer. Filled with jealousy and despair, as he must have been, he could have ruined Augustus and cast a blight on their unborn child that might have lasted for ever. Just one whiff of the truth to the newspapers would have brought complete havoc to everything Lily valued most.

At last the service was over and she closed her eyes as the procession of mourners walked slowly behind the coffin towards the church door. She preferred not to see again the shining wood, the name plate, the wreaths. Was one of those from Augustus? He had said nothing of flowers.

She pulled on her black gloves and quietly followed him as he too walked solemnly out.

The interment was another penance for Lily. She stood beside Augustus in a non-feeling trance and tried to blank the proceedings from her mind. There had been too many funerals in her life. She was grateful that they were not to have the further agony of the reception that was to be held afterwards in a small hotel on the sea front. Augustus had politely declined, giving his wife's state of health and the long journey back to Ashcote as reasons for their early departure.

At last it was over and they turned away, walked through the churchyard to the enclosing privacy of their car. Lily wondered what she could possibly find to say during the coming long painful miles to Dorset.

Augustus drove carefully, his hands gripping the steering wheel and his eyes fixed on the road ahead. They had reached the other side of Exeter before Lily, greatly daring, asked the question that had nagged at her for the past terrible days. 'Augustus,' she whispered, 'do you blame me for Michael's death?'

The car swerved violently and Augustus wrenched the wheel round to correct the swing. He pulled over to the verge and stopped, leaving the engine running.

'Of course I don't blame you,' he said. 'You are going

311

to give me a child, an heir. That was what Michael couldn't face. If there was any fault it was mine.' At last he turned to her. 'Can we make another fresh start, Lily?'

'Perhaps,' she whispered, but the sound of the engine and the wind in the trees snatched the word away so that she had no idea whether he heard.

Back at school at the start of the new term Ivy greeted her friends with confidence. The news that her sister was expecting a baby would certainly disarm any unpleasant threats and taunts from Miranda Cosgrove.

Alice was the first person to hear. 'Guess what?' Ivy announced with barely suppressed triumph, 'I'm to be an aunt!' The girls had managed to get beds side by side in the dormitory and they were both unpacking their things.

'Gosh, that's topping,' Alice said. She let the frock she had just pulled from her large trunk drop onto the floor. 'Really, truly? Do you mean that your sister and Mr Ashe have ... ?' She giggled. 'Just wait until my mother hears! She'll have to apologize to you, and as for old Miranda Cosgrove ... well, she won't have a leg to stand on. All those tales must have been malicious rumour.'

'I jolly well hope so! Ashcote is going to have an heir anyway. Lily and Augustus are over the moon about it.'

Alice picked up the dress and put it on a hanger. 'Funny how spiteful people can be. Perhaps it all started because some girl was rejected by Mr Ashe, Miranda's sister probably. He's very handsome, I'm told. I'll bet it was only jealousy.'

This was just what Ivy needed to hear. Alice's straightforward assessment was exactly what she wanted to believe. All her worries of last term had been unnecessary, and those frightful verses in the Bible didn't apply to Augustus after all.

The next day she confronted Miranda. 'My sister is going to have a baby,' she said without preamble.

'I don't believe you. Unless she's been off with someone else?'

Ivy was immediately rigid with anger and shock. Was there no end to this girl's wickedness? 'That's a terrible thing to say. You could get into serious trouble for saying that. It's . . .' She tried to think of the right word.

'Slander?' Miranda supplied for her. 'Not if it's true. So there's going to be an Ashe heir after all! Well now, what a triumph.'

Ivy was on her way to a French class, her books clasped across her chest. She gripped them so tightly that she was almost devoid of breath. 'What do you mean by that?' she said, aware of the sarcasm in the other girl's voice.

'Just that no one believed there would be. If there isn't a son the house goes to some distant relative.'

Ivy stared at her. 'And how would you know a thing like that?'

Miranda's hair hung in one thick plait over her shoulder and she tossed it back arrogantly. 'My mother knows everything.' Her tone implied that this was the end of the matter.

'Well then, you'd better write and tell her about the baby. She won't know *that* yet.'

'She probably does.'

The conversation wasn't going at all as Ivy had planned. 'I told my sister about your . . . your threats.' she said frostily. 'If you spread lies about my family Lily is going to come and see the headmistress and then you'll be in trouble.'

The older girl laughed. 'Very well then, you little nobody! I'll keep my secrets to myself for the time being. Perhaps when the precious baby arrives he may look like somebody quite different from sissy Augustus Ashe.'

Ivy was beside herself with fury, but Miranda flounced off in the direction of the sixth-form common room and there was absolutely nothing more that she could do about it.

She recounted all of it in whispers to Alice later that day.

'I shouldn't worry too much,' her friend said. 'Don't take any notice of that horrible creature. You know that your sister's baby is an Ashe. When he's born all the rumours will disappear. You just wait and see!'

'I hope you're right,' Ivy said with feeling. 'Lily needs something nice to happen to her. She's been unlucky rather a lot.'

'Oh?'

Ivy shrugged her shoulders. 'Her fiancé was killed in the war and our mother died.' She wasn't about to relate all her family's recent turbulent history even to Alice and hoped those two facts would do. 'Her baby might be a girl,' she said, hoping to change the subject. 'Why does everyone presume that it'll be a boy?'

'It's simple. Just wishful thinking. Ashcote needs an heir so it must be a boy. Jolly unfair, I reckon. I suppose it's the name that counts.'

'So if it's a girl, poor old Lily must just go on having more and more babies until she produces a son! Miranda was right about one thing then, that the house must go to a boy?'

'Afraid so, old thing. That's life. But your sister will go on having babies anyway, I expect. Once you're married that's your lot. Another bit of unfairness, but I blame God for that.'

Ivy was shocked. 'That's blasphemy. You can't blame God.' But as soon as she had said it she knew that you could, for He had ordained things so. She thought of some of the Bristol streets, particularly down St Paul's, and the pathetic women who lived there. Some of the husbands were often drunk and violent especially on a Friday night. She'd heard Aunt Agnes talking about it. There were strings of dirty bawling children too. 'I don't think I want to get married,' said Ivy.

'Rubbish. Of course you do. And if you're rich, having children isn't so bad really. Your sister will have a nanny and servants. No hard work.'

This was a slightly more cheerful idea. The Penrose family had never been part of the squalor of those Bristol streets of course, but poverty had always been a distant threat, a trap into which you could fall if you came upon hard times. Lily had risen far above all that now. Alice was right. Money made everything easier. Lily would have her babies in comfort and luxury, and Augustus would be vindicated. Perhaps the future looked rosy after all.

'Well, if I ever get married, it'll have to be to someone rich,' she stated firmly.

314

'And I'll be your bridesmaid,' Alice said with a laugh.

The two girls linked arms and walked along the path that led to the tennis courts. Thanks to Alice's cheery and light-hearted attitude Ivy's troubles seemed to have diminished and she was filled with a sense of well-being. It was just great to be young and rich now in England in 1921 with all of life stretching before you – the best time and place in all the world in fact. And she had a friend too. She and Alice had vowed permanent friendship. What did Miranda Cosgrove matter after all?

When she heard the news of Michael Dyer's accident Ivy gave it little thought. Strange that he should have been climbing though. She hadn't seen much of him while she was living in Torquay, but he hadn't struck her as the kind of person who would be interested in sporty things. Still you never knew, and he'd been in the trenches and got a medal or something, so he must have been brave. Ivy remembered those cliffs. They weren't far from Rose House and she'd walked there a couple of times. They were impressive, but jolly dangerous. There was no doubt about that. Perhaps Michael Dyer had merely slipped from the footpath? She shivered and resolved that if she went there again she'd be very careful, and if she had the dogs with her she'd be sure to have them on leads.

Thankfully no one at school knew about the Torquay bookshop or Augustus's connection with it so she was able to put the whole affair of the unfortunate young man right out of her mind. Hopefully life was going to be fun from now on and she wasn't going to let anything else worry her. She was determined to work hard at her books, improve her riding during the holidays, even agree to go to the finishing school Lily had mentioned. By the time she was grown up she would be completely refined, a real lady! *Nineteen-twenties, here I come,* she wrote in her journal, *Ivy Penrose, one of the gentry!*

Back at Ashcote both Augustus and Lily made great efforts to resume an outwardly normal life. It was important that Ted and Mary Dunne and the other servants should have no suspicions about the state of their marriage. Lily still couldn't contemplate sharing her bed with Augustus and he appeared to be quite content with the arrangement.

When she next visited her doctor she came back with the message that she had to take great care for there was a chance that she would miscarry. Everyone knew that this precious heir to Ashcote was more important than almost any other consideration at the moment so her small lie was easily believed and the separate sleeping arrangements were not commented upon.

Augustus still worked on the land, but his hours outside became shorter with the decreasing light and as September gave way to October Lily began to worry about his health. The pallor was back in his face, and it was combined sometimes with the unhealthy flush, the cough, and always with a constant tiredness.

'Are you sure that you are well enough to go out today?' Lily asked him one morning as he looked in dismay at the steadily falling rain.

'I shall stay inside,' he replied. 'There are a lot of papers that need my attention.'

His easy compliance frightened her for he had ignored all the signs of his returning illness until now. He had even started to smoke his pipe again occasionally in spite of her objections.

'The solicitor is coming this afternoon,' he continued. 'I think I told you. There are some forms to sign before the shop is finally handed over to the new buyer.'

To her relief he had put the bookshop up for sale the week after Michael Dyer's death. She knew that he had meant Michael to have it, and now all he wanted was to be rid of it as speedily as possible. The contents would be sold too he told her apart from some medical books which were to go to Duncan.

Lily, thinking about this, wondered frequently what she should do with her own Rose House when the lease ran out at the end of the year. The tenant had written to tell her that he would be leaving then. It would be empty again. Could she ever bear to go back there and constantly see that other shop next-door? Would she think of Michael Dyer every time she passed its bow-fronted windows?

And what would she want Rose House for anyway? Ashcote was her home now, the place where her child must be born and where her life would henceforth be lived. The great Elizabethan house encircled her, sometimes trapped her like a monstrous web. It was beautiful no doubt, and parts of it had been made comfortable and homely, but just lately it was becoming more like a prison than a home. This thought had been gaining ground in her mind more and more lately and it frightened her. In spite of all the luxuries she sometimes longed for simpler times, days when the need to work, to earn a living, dominated every hour.

That afternoon, while Augustus was closeted with his solicitor in the library, Lily called to the dogs and went to look at Flo and her donkey companion and the other two horses. Ivy's pony, Beauty, was happily grazing but the great cart horse, closely followed by her own Jess, ambled over to the field gate at her call. Flo was looking sleek and contented. Lily held out her hand with one of the sugar lumps which she had brought and her mind returned to the coal yard. Flo always reminded her of Harry Coney.

She shivered a little, reviewing her life. Was there some evil eye that had bewitched her when she was small? Both parent's dead, Arthur's untimely death, then marriage to Harry Coney and now ... now a second ill-starred marriage. Could anyone be as unlucky, and would adversity follow her throughout her life? She put her free hand on her stomach and hoped that the child growing so surely there would put an end to the jinx that had beset her during the past few years.

She left the horses and walked through the fields and woods of the estate. The rain had stopped and the sun had come out weakly for a time. She picked her way carefully for the path was muddy in places but the scent that arose from the newly dampened earth was intoxicating and the trees were splashed with the pale gold of autumn. The hedgerow elms stretched into the sky above her and she was enchanted by their beauty. The big sycamore looked as if it had put on a brilliant scarlet cloak and finches were darting in and out of the hawthorn bushes. A thrush flew closely across her path.

317

She looked up at the little scudding clouds and thought about the swallows, wondering where they were now. It was some time since she had seen them around Ashcote. She hoped that Africa, or wherever it was they went in winter, would be hospitable to them. They would always be special to her for it was Augustus who had first drawn her attention to the arrival of these elegant little birds that heralded spring. By the time they returned next year her baby would be born.

Eventually she retraced her steps and was met by Augusuts. He was walking towards her along the river bank and she was immediately struck by his stoop, the slow ambling footsteps, and the way he relied on the stout walking stick in his hand. He was like an old man, she thought, and her heart went out to him in sympathy and love. She was finding now that forgiveness was becoming easier and she knew that she would look after him, cherish him as she had promised in the wedding service. Although her bed was still out of bounds for him they had become friends again. Yet it was because of this very friendship that she was more and more aware of the strength and intensity of his private grief for Michael Dyer. For Lily as well as for Augustus it was a constant anguish.

The dogs ran to him and greeted him exuberantly, their muddy feet making marks on his immaculate trousers. He spoke to them, threw a stick for each, and cared nothing for the mud.

Lily watching him was full of regret. If only there had been no Michael Dyer, no rumours, no unfaithfulness, how happy they could have been.

'Has the solicitor gone?' she asked.

'Yes. Everything is settled, all my affairs sorted out.'

She felt a stab of fear. 'What do you mean, your affairs sorted out? I thought he was coming to see about the bookshop.'

'I decided that it would be prudent to see to other things while he was here.'

'Can you tell me about them?'

He smiled at her, took her arm and tucked it into his as they walked along the path towards the house. 'Of course, my dear. Firstly there is the matter of our child. I had to get everything right for him.'

'What do you mean?'

'He will inherit Ashcote and I have to make provision for you should I die.'

Again the thrust of fear in her heart. 'You are not going to die, Augustus.'

'We all must die some time,' he said. 'Only foolish men refuse to acknowledge that fact.'

They walked a little way in silence after that and then Lily said tentatively. 'You always assume that we shall have a son. We are just as likely to have a daughter. What happens then?'

Another silence. Then he stopped walking, stood quite still and there was only the sound of the wind whispering in the trees. 'If there are no sons, then Ashcote goes to a cousin.'

'You mean that we lose everything?' She was stunned. 'That's monstrously unfair.'

'If I had only daughters they would lose the house and land on my death,' he said. 'The estate is entailed that way. It has been so for hundreds of years. There would be money of course, ample provision to set up another home, and a generous income for life for all of my dependants. You would also always have the right to visit here, but that's all.'

'Then we shall go on having babies until we have sons,' she said, shivering a little at the idea.

He looked down at her, kissed her gently on the cheek. 'But the child you carry will be a son,' he said. 'I know it. I have a feeling, a certainty that this is so.'

Alone in the big bed that night Lily thought again about the responsibility that had been thrust upon her. She put her hands over her stomach protectively and her mind travelled back to the history lessons she had enjoyed when she was a little girl. History was one of her favourite subjects. There was that monstrous King, Henry the Eighth. He had needed a son and had disposed of his first two wives because they couldn't oblige him. She smiled to herself at the irony of it. His despised daughter, Elizabeth, had become one of the greatest monarchs to sit on the throne of England. Ashcote was built during her reign and the house was shaped like an 'E'. E for Elizabeth. At school Lily had always liked hearing about the great Queen. She could never, in her wildest dreams, have imagined that she would one day become mistress of a real Elizabethan manor house. As she thought about it she decided that if it was a little daughter she carried her name should be Elizabeth, and she would see that no reproach ever fell upon her because she was just a girl. Still cradling her stomach in her hands and continuing to smile she fell asleep.

'We shall have a ball,' Augustus announced, 'for your twenty-first birthday. It's years since we had anything like that at Ashcote.'

After the first flush of pleasure Lily began to see the problems, obstacles that rushed through her mind one after the other in an endless procession. The first took the shape of Miranda Cosgrove and all her ilk. The neighbours! There were half a dozen or so big houses within a twenty mile radius and Lily had visited none of them.

'But who shall we invite?'

'Your family, Duncan MacMullen, some of Ivy's friends and their parents.'

'I don't think it's a good idea, Augustus.'

He looked at her in surprise. 'I thought you would be delighted.'

She sighed. 'It's very sweet of you, but I should prefer a little house party for the weekend with just my family and Duncan perhaps, no one else. We could invite them for Saturday, and maybe you could take me into Dorchester on the Friday. That's the actual day of my birthday and I've heard that there's going to be a Valentino film that week.'

Augustus laughed. 'I suppose I could bear it for your sake although I can't see what all you women see in the man. I thought that you were thrilled to be liberated, as you call it. I can't imagine anything more contrary to women's emancipation than a film about an Arab Sheikh.'

'It's only fantasy,' Lily said. 'Do you mind not having a ball, my dear?'

'Whatever you want.' Augustus's voice suddenly lost its enthusiasm. There were very few hours in the day now when he showed much interest in anything other than his health. She knew that he had forced himself to suggest the ball. He was probably thoroughly relieved that she had declined.

Lily's birthday was on Armistice Day so there was sadness as well as celebration. At eleven o'clock in the morning she was sitting at the beautiful desk that had been her present from Augustus. She had arranged her papers and pens, coloured scented envelopes, and a few photographs, and wished that she had a great number of friends to correspond with. Then the old grandfather clock chimed the eleventh hour and she jumped up, stood for the two-minute silence that she knew would be kept all over the country and Empire in remembrance of those who had fallen, everyone thinking first of their own loved ones and then of all the millions of others unknown.

For Lily there were three whom she was sure she would never forget. Arthur was first of course. His features were blurred in her memory now, but she stood very still and felt him close to her, remembered the feel and the male smell of him, his rough uniform. It was not an officer's uniform such as Augustus had worn. Arthur had been a private, an ordinary Tommy.

As the seconds passed it was her father who came next. She had loved him very much throughout all her childhood years. Then her mother seemed to smile through the mists and she found herself smiling back, longing for her living presence and wishing that she might see her coming grandchild. *Perhaps she will. Who knows whether or not the dead are aware of what we are doing, of how we are?* She shivered a little. In some ways it was a chilling idea.

Lastly, fleetingly, Michael Dyer's face came into her unwilling mind, the man whom she had hardly known, for whom she had no feelings other than antipathy. Yet now, in company with all those others, she felt that his death had been a sacrifice of war as surely as if he had perished in the trenches.

She was still thinking of him when Augustus came into the room. But the silence was over, the ghosts departed.

321

'Dunne will drive us to see "The Sheikh" tonight,' Augustus said. 'Mary is also anxious to see it so I told him that he could bring her too. That is, if you don't mind?'

Lily laughed to herself. It seemed strange to be going out to celebrate along with one's housekeeper, but, she reflected, *IT shows how much I have changed, how much I have become accustomed to the ways of my betters, that I should even think it odd at all.* 'That's fine, Augustus,' she said, hiding her amusement. 'I look forward to it very much.'

The following day William arrived with George, Ivy was fetched from school by Dunne, and Duncan MacMullen came in time for lunch.

Ivy immediately wanted to rush out to see Flo and she dragged the resplendent George with her. 'Steady on, Sis,' he grumbled. 'I'll mess up me good clothes.'

'That doesn't matter,' Ivy said. 'Flo'll be upset if you don't come and talk to her.'

'A load of codswallop,' George commented as he allowed himself to be taken outside. 'She's a lucky old sod if you ask me. Ought to have gone to the knacker's yard long ago.'

'Don't you dare say such a thing, George Penrose.' Ivy guessed that he was teasing but she made her voice sound cross anyway. 'And mind how you speak,' she directed. 'None of your Bristol street talk for Ashcote, if you please.'

The horse was in one of the old stables now that the weather was cold and damp. George stroked her nose and gave her a sugar lump, one that Ivy noticed he had surreptitiously brought with him. Flo crunched it enthusiastically and then nuzzled his hand. 'Motors haven't got anything on you after all, old girl,' he whispered to her affectionately. He went inside the stable and looked her over. 'They take good care of you too, don't they?' He ran his hand down her coat. 'Yes you're a lucky old sod.'

'George! I told you to mind your tongue.' Ivy glanced round, hoping that no one had followed them from the house.

322

'Sorry,' he said. He patted the horse again and then rejoined Ivy outside. 'But she is. She's a lucky old ...' He grinned at his sister. 'All right. Don't worry. I'll be good. I can speak as posh as you when I want to.'

They walked slowly back to the house. 'Why is that Duncan somebody or other here?' George asked suddenly. 'He was best man, wasn't he?'

'I think he was Augustus's doctor in Torquay,' Ivy said. 'He's a friend. They both like him. I do too. He's nice.'

'Married?'

'No, of course not.'

'Why of course not?'

'Well, he'd have his wife here wouldn't he if he were married.'

Later that day when she and Lily were alone in the bedroom fixing her hair she asked her sister about Duncan. 'Has he a sweetheart?' she said.

Lily paused and looked at Ivy's reflection in the mirror. 'Not that I know of.'

'A pity.'

'Why?'

'Just waste of a nice man,' said Ivy dreamily.

The little party was a success and although Augustus was tired he made a great effort to entertain his guests. However Lily saw Duncan looking at him with obvious concern now and then. She longed to talk to him privately but there was no opportunity until the following morning. He had apologized for having to leave straight after breakfast in order to be back in Torquay for afternoon surgery.

Lily walked with him to his motor car for Augustus had not risen yet. 'It's not like him to lie in bed,' she said. 'I know he would have wanted to see you off himself. He was so glad that you were able to come.'

'I suppose you know that he's very ill?' Duncan said quietly. 'We talked a little when I went up to say goodbye just now. He asked me to ... to make sure that you understand.'

A chill entered Lily's heart that had nothing to do with

the dank November morning. 'I know,' she whispered. 'We haven't talked about it.'

'I think you should.'

'I wish you were still his doctor. Will he get better again, Duncan, like he did in Switzerland? He's looking forward so much to our child being born.'

He didn't answer her question directly. 'I'll come whenever you want me,' he said. 'But your doctor here is very good, I believe. Augustus won't go abroad for treatment again. He's just made that quite clear to me.'

Lily looked at him in dismay. 'But if that's his only hope, why won't he?'

Duncan shook his head. 'I think he knows that there's little use this time. He wants to be with you for as long as possible. He told me that he feels too guilty to go away and leave you.'

'I've forgiven him. There's no need for more guilt.'

'You must make sure he knows that, Lily. Tell him.'

'I thought he did know?'

'In the state he's in, he needs telling over and over again.'

Lily brushed tears from her eyes and pushed back her unruly curls. 'Thank you, Duncan,' she said. 'Thank you for reminding me. You've always been a good friend. You tried to warn me about Michael Dyer long ago, didn't you?'

He nodded. 'I was never sure whether I was right in saying what I did, in just giving you the merest hint that there were things you should know about. Perhaps I should have said more, but I hoped that you would find out from Augustus. I've always been careful not to betray a confidence from patient or friend.'

'I wouldn't have listened then whatever you had said. I loved him so much that I refused to acknowledge any problems.'

'Loved? Past tense?'

She hesitated but only for a second. 'No, not past tense. I still love him.'

Duncan gripped her hands with both of his. 'Keep on loving him, Lily. He needs your strength and courage now more than ever before.'

324

She smiled through the tears. 'He shall have them always.'

Duncan released her, swung his motor car into life, climbed into the driving seat and was quickly gone. She stood quite still until the sound of the engine was just a faint hum in the distance. She felt desolate, as if he had taken her resolve and her strength away with him down the curving drive, through the great gates, and away into the world beyond, a world of normality and freedom and happiness. Lily went back into the house, back to Augustus, to the smell and atmosphere of illness and decline. She knelt beside the bed, and put her arms around him.

'You're going to get better,' she said resolutely. 'I absolutely command it.'

He smiled at her. 'You really want me to?'

'Of course I do.'

'Then I'll get up,' he said. He pushed the eiderdown and blankets back and swung his legs over the edge of the bed. 'What has Duncan been saying to you?'

Lily wasn't surprised at the question. She got to her feet and fetched his dressing gown and held it out for him. 'Just that he had to get back for afternoon surgery.'

'Nothing else?'

'That you are too stubborn to go to Switzerland.'

Augustus frowned. 'Stubborn, yes. I'm determined not to leave you again for so long.'

'It might not be for long. You would get better quickly there.'

He pushed his arms into the warm garment, pulled it around his thin body and knotted the belt tightly.

'I'm not leaving you, Lily.'

'Is there any reason? Duncan said that you ...'

'Ah, so he did say something more?'

Lily didn't want to say the word 'guilty' but she had promised to forgive, and forgiveness needed a trespass. *Forgive us our trespasses as we forgive ...* 'He said that you felt guilty. You have no need to feel that, Augustus.'

He went to the window and stood looking down at the misty November garden. 'No need?' His mood changed suddenly. He became tense and withdrawn. 'I don't think

325

I shall ever feel free from guilt,' he said. 'I've harmed the two people I love most.'

Lily was dismayed. Although she knew that he would never forget Michael Dyer, yet she hoped that he would put that part of his life behind him eventually. But here he was talking about him again, talking about him to her, reminding her of his adulterous love for this man! How dare he! And then she knew, chillingly, that though she could forgive him, her forgiveness alone would never be enough to banish the ghosts. He needed a full and free pardon from Michael Dyer too. Duncan was only half right when he had said that Augustus needed to be sure of her forgiveness.

She gritted her teeth. She must do something about it for there was no other way to bring him back to her and to their child. 'Michael has forgiven you,' she said, forcing the unwelcome words from her lips. 'That last message he wrote told you that.'

He turned to her and his expression was fierce, his eyes staring and angry. 'No it didn't,' he said. *'Remember only the good times!* Some hopes of that! All I can see is his dead body smashed to bits on the rocks because of my desertion, and when I look at you I can see only the misery I've caused you and, dear God, am continuing to cause you.'

She stared at him, horrified, wondering how she could go downstairs, talk to William, to George and Ivy, continue as if nothing had happened, as if she had not just heard those awful things from the man she loved. If only she had never started this conversation!

She pulled herself up very straight. It was important that her brothers should have no suspicion that anything was wrong. William would worry and probe and George would gossip in Bristol, tell Aunt Agnes probably. She shuddered at the thought. Ivy was perceptive, but she already knew more than the others and wouldn't comment.

She looked at Augustus severely and summoned the no-nonsense tones that she had learned years ago from her mother. 'I've told you that I forgive you, Augustus,' she said. 'The past is over. For the sake of our child you must put it behind you. If you want my forgiveness to continue, then please don't mention Michael Dyer's name to me again. Go and have a bath and come down for coffee.' She stared at him, willing some of her strength and purpose into him. 'William is looking forward to talking to you,' she continued. 'He wants a tour of the house. You promised him yesterday that you would show him the parts that are closed and that he didn't see last time.'

Still Augustus didn't move and Lily wondered what more she could do. Some stronger motivation was obviously needed to bring him back to normality and to her. She walked over to him, took his hands in hers and put them on the gentle swell of her stomach. She even managed to smile. 'For your son,' she repeated. 'For him you must renounce the past and get well. You must be strong.'

At last, as if returning from far away, his arms went round her and he held her close. She forced herself to relax in his embrace.

'I don't deserve you, Lily,' he whispered. 'I don't deserve you at all.'

Chapter Twenty-two

The name of Michael Dyer was not mentioned again between Augustus and Lily, and outwardly their marriage was happy. But Augustus's health deteriorated rapidly, until by Christmas he was keeping to his bed for most of the day.

Lily had suggested to her sister that, under the circumstances, it might be more pleasant to stay with Aunt Agnes for the holiday. Ashcote was bound to be gloomy and there was the risk of infection too. Ivy wrote back to say that although she would like to visit her aunt for a couple of days, she couldn't bear to stay in that *little* house in Bristol for the whole holiday. She thought of Ashcote as her home now and wanted to be with Lily anyway to support her. No, she wouldn't get too near Augustus and wasn't likely to catch anything. She was too healthy. She had to see Flo and Janey and go on with her riding lessons anyway.

When Lily read this letter she smiled to herself and admitted that she really wanted Ivy to come. She was a breath of fresh air, a link with the past. There was little to laugh about now in the big manor house and Lily often felt stifled, longed to get away just for a few hours, but it was seldom possible. Augustus hated to have her out of his sight for long.

She rather dreaded the coming of Christmas, yet with Ivy here there would be someone to talk to, a reason to decorate part of the house perhaps. No other members of the family would be visiting. William was courting seriously and wanted to spend the holiday with his sweetheart's family. George of course had a life of his own. No one knew what he did with himself, but he had many friends and Lily had long ceased to worry about him. Aunt Agnes had also declined the invitation.

Dunne fetched Ivy from school the week before Christmas and she flounced into the hall laden with packages and full of the healthy exuberance of youth. Lily hugged her and for a fleeting second envied her. It seemed a long time since she herself had felt any trace of such careless freedom.

'Are we having a tree?' Ivy demanded, looking round the Great Hall. 'This place needs a bit of livening up.'

'There's one in the small parlour,' Lily said. 'It's waiting for you to decorate as usual. We can put another in here if you like. There are plenty in the woods. We could have something much bigger.'

Augustus came down later in the day, approved the attempts at Christmas decorations, and smiled at Ivy. 'We'll have a really jolly Christmas,' he said. 'I'm glad you came, my dear. Your sister needs someone cheerful around.'

Looking at him, Ivy doubted very much whether anyone would have a very jolly time. She tried not to show her dismay at his appearance but later, when he had gone back to his room she whispered to Lily, 'Oughtn't he to be in hospital? I mean he ...' She stopped, embarrassed.

Lily sighed. 'He refuses to go and won't have the local doctor now. He seems to have fallen out with him for some reason. Duncan comes most weekends and he'll be here on Boxing Day.'

Christmas Day was as merry as they could make it. Augustus came downstairs briefly for lunch, and then to Ivy's relief went back to bed. She and Lily took the dogs for a walk in the afternoon, the fresh air making a welcome change from the stifling heat that Augustus liked in the parlour. The gardener was kept busy chopping logs and Dunne was constantly stoking the huge fireplaces.

The following day Duncan arrived and after he and Augustus had been closeted for an hour in his room, Lily was called in.

'I've persuaded Augustus to get some treatment,' Duncan said.

Lily breathed a great sigh of relief. Augustus was sitting in an armchair beside the fire, a blanket over his knees. He held out both hands to her and she went to him and knelt on the rug at his feet.

'Duncan tells me that the sanatorium in Torquay is very good.' he said. 'And the doctor in charge there is very knowledgable and pleasant, though Duncan himself would be my own personal physician. And the sea air is the best in the world. Would you mind, my dear?'

Torquay! The one place she had imagined he would never want to see again, the place that was bound to remind him of all she wanted him to forget. She looked across to Duncan for help and clarification.

He nodded. 'It's one of the best places. I don't think you could do better.'

'Not as good as Switzerland surely?'

'Almost.'

'I told you that I shall not go abroad again.' Augustus tightened his grip on Lily's hand. 'Torquay will be quite adequate.'

She could see that his mind was made up. 'Very well then,' she conceded. 'If that's where you want to go, Augustus, then I shall go with you of course.'

'I should be grateful for that, but you need not stay all the time. I should like to think of you here at Ashcote.'

'I could live in Rose House,' she said. 'The lease has almost run out. It will be empty soon.'

He looked at her strangely. 'Are you sure you would like that?'

Rose House! Suddenly the future looked a little less dismal to Lily after all. Like it? *Yes, oh yes. I can be myself, Lily Penrose, Lily Ashe, my own mistress with my own kitchen, my own possessions around me. But what about the shop next-door? The bookshop? Could I live so close to the place where ...* She told herself to be sensible. Nothing as insubstantial as memories or ghosts would stop her reclaiming her own house and with it her independence.

330

'I should love to live there again. I shall stay there as long as you're in the sanatorium.'

She felt a sudden tension in him. 'But our child must be born at Ashcote,' he said. 'Promise me, Lily. You must come back here well before he's due.' His hand was hot and clammy, agitation in every line of him.

'Of course.' she comforted. 'The future heir to Ashcote must be born at Ashcote. I'm well aware of that. Don't worry, Augustus.'

He relaxed and lay back on the cushions that had been arranged at his back. He released her hand. 'As soon as Ivy goes back to school we shall go to Torquay then,' he said. 'Duncan is going to arrange it.'

Rose House was quickly refurbished and redecorated. The café was turned into a drawing room, the kitchen at the back transformed, and a new bedroom made on the first floor. The room in the roof which had been Lily's precious haven would be Ivy's domain when she was not at school.

By the middle of January Lily was living there again and Augustus was established in a splendid room of his own in the sanatorium. It had great open doors along one side and an abundance of fresh air that blew straight in from the sea.

'If anything is going to cure me, this will,' he said, sounding more cheerful than for a long time.

'It's jolly cold,' Lily said. 'But that's the best treatment.' She shivered in spite of her fur coat.

'You mustn't stay too long,' he directed. 'I don't want you risking your health and that of our baby. An hour a day is quite enough, and you must promise that if that's too much, you'll make it even less.'

She smiled at him and thought sadly that his concern was probably more for their child than for her. 'I'll look after myself,' she said. 'And tomorrow I shall wear even more clothes. Just concentrate on getting better, Augustus. You have to be quite well for the Christening, you know. Have you thought of a name yet?'

'I've been considering,' he replied. 'Oliver perhaps?'

'Oliver Ashe? I don't think it sounds right.' Lily frowned

331

as she put the two words together. 'How about Clifford? That goes better with Ashe doesn't it?'

He nodded. 'Maybe it does. Yes, Clifford is a capital name.'

'And Elizabeth if its a girl?' she said.

'Why that particularly?'

'Because of Ashcote and the queen whose initial it was shaped for.' Lily wanted to add, *The girl who, by being a girl, disappointed her father but became a great queen,* but she refrained and smiled at him instead.

'It will be a boy,' Augustus said firmly, then closed his eyes and fell asleep as he did very frequently now.

The remaining days of January passed swiftly and by February Lily's visits to Augustus were seldom for more than half an hour for he tired very quickly. For the rest of each day she busied herself in her house, walked both dogs on the cliffs, and always remembered Ivy's instructions to keep them on leads whenever they were close to the many sheer drops to the sea far below.

Every day she cooked for herself and occasionally for Duncan who came to see her now and then. She was glad of his support and friendship. One day she asked him if he could bring himself to tell her more of the relationship between her husband and Michael Dyer. Although she tried to put it behind her, yet it remained a constant source of unease, something that, in spite of her aversion, she wanted to know more about.

'Why *did* he marry me, Duncan?' she asked. 'I torture myself with that question still.'

For a long time he was silent. He was sitting in front of the fire, a plate with one of her scones on it balanced on his knees. 'He loved you, Lily,' he said. 'He still loves you very much. He often tells me that. It seems that every time he says it, the very words take away some of the guilt he continues to feel.' He paused for a moment and stared into the comforting flames. 'Because both the Church and the law condemn homosexuals so severely, they are often very sad people. Of course they must be secretive about what they do, and people despise them − wrongly in my opinion. They miss out on one very important thing too.'

Lily was surprised that he should defend men who suffered from a deviation which was so strongly condemned.

'What do they miss?'

'As well as never being able to live openly with the person they love, they can never have children with that person.'

She was dismayed by this, for although it was obvious, of course, it confirmed what she had long suspected of Augustus. 'So you're saying that he married me just to get an heir for Ashcote?'

'I've told you that he loves you, but yes, there was that as well. I can't mislead you. He needs a son more than most men.' Duncan ate his scone slowly before he continued. 'Men usually want sons of course,' he said. 'But for Augustus it was vital. If you want to understand, then ask him, Lily. Talk to him. He's very ill, but not too ill to tell you his deepest feelings. I think it would help him, would clear his mind. In fact he told me yesterday that there is more he wishes to say to you but he dreads the telling. You must encourage him to unburden himself before ...'

'Before he dies?' Lily forced the words from her lips. 'I'll do my best,' she said.

The following day the weather was lovely, a golden winter day with sunshine and blue skies. Lily looked from the window and thought how sad it was to be lying on a sick-bed on such a day. She brushed the tears from her eyes and wondered what to wear for her visit to the sanatorium. In spite of her plentiful wardrobe, selecting an outfit was becoming increasingly difficult now that she was in her seventh month. But her fur coat was large and comfortable and when she was with Augustus she always kept it closely wrapped around her body for warmth. She chose a hat with care however, one of her prettiest, and arranged her hair so that it curled seductively beneath the brim.

Augustus looked up at her and smiled when she entered the sunny flower-filled room but she was shocked at his appearance. Every day he seemed weaker.

'You look very beautiful,' he said.

She sat down beside the bed and he took her hand and

pressed it tightly in his. She was always surprised at the strength of his grip. Perhaps it was the only way now that he could assure her of his love. But was Duncan right? Did he love her? Had he loved her when they married? What kind of love had he been able to offer when his heart was given to another? What was it that he wanted to tell her? What more could there be? She shrank from what she might be about to hear.

'Augustus,' she whispered, 'tell me you love me. If you do, please say it.'

'But I have told you,' he said, and his eyes were full of pain. 'I've told you that I love you over and over again. Why can't you believe me?'

She felt wretched, sorry that she had asked. But Duncan had said they should talk before it was too late. 'I suppose ... because of ... of Michael.' Now she had said it, dared to say that name in his presence when she had vowed to herself that she never would again, and still he held her hand as tightly as before, still he looked at her with all his heart in his eyes. 'I must know whether you needed me, or needed to be married because of your name, Augustus? Because of the Ashe name and your house.'

He turned away from her, still holding her hand. 'I couldn't bear to lose you now.' The words were murmured into his pillow and she had to lean close to hear them.

'You'll never lose me,' she whispered. 'Never, Augustus. I promise.'

When he looked at her again she could see tears in his eyes, but a faint hope too.

'Can you bear the truth and still come here each day, still hold me until ...' A violent fit of coughing stopped his words and a nurse rushed in to look after him. When it was over and his bed linen changed Lily saw that there was still a trace of blood on his lips. She felt shamed that she might have been the cause of this fearful attack, but he reached out for her again.

'I want to tell you,' he said. 'I've wanted you to understand ever since we first met, but I was afraid of losing you.'

She smiled at him and pressed his hand on her breast. 'I've promised,' she said. 'If it won't distress you too

334

much, say whatever you must. Nothing will make me leave you now.'

His voice was faint and shaky but she leaned close to listen. It was a long tale of woe, of misunderstandings and cruelty from parents who were horrified at their only son's behaviour. 'My father added a codicil to the will,' he said. 'If I did not marry and have a child by my thirty-fifth birthday I should lose Ashcote. Without that codicil, I would have kept it until my death, but he was so disgusted with me that he made that further condition.'

She didn't move, did not reject his hand which still clasped hers. But now she understood. Now she knew why he had married her in such a hurry, and knew too why he couldn't marry anyone of his own class for they must all have been aware of what he was, perhaps even knew about his father's frightful will. Miranda Cosgrove had been right about everything.

And so he had chosen her, Lily Coney, a girl who had foolishly fallen in love with him, cast herself very conveniently into his arms!

She could feel tears in her eyes and couldn't move to brush them away. They found a pathway down her cheeks and dropped on to the fur collar of her coat.

'Will you still come?' The question was wrung out of him. 'The thought that you were bound to discover all this after my death has haunted me, but it was always fear of losing you that kept me silent.'

'I shall still come,' she whispered. She bent to kiss him on the forehead and her lips tasted the salt sweat of him.

He started to cough again and the nurse came quickly. 'I think that's enough for today, Mrs Ashe,' she said, and Lily looked at her sharply, wondering if she had overheard any part of their conversation. Surely not. Their voices had been low, inaudible, she hoped, to anyone outside the room.

She was loth to go and kissed him again in spite of the unbearable coughing that racked his body, the bloody froth on his lips. The nurse pushed her away, a frown of disapproval on her face.

Lily sobbed as though her heart would break that night in Rose House, and her two dogs crept upstairs when they

335

heard the crying and were soon on her bed and eventually in it. She cuddled both in her arms, especially Tess, the little whippet that Augustus had given her.

He died peacefully a few days later, a day when the wind blew cold from the north and the sea was grey and comfortless. Gulls screamed in the wild skies on that day, echoing the feeling of desolation that filled Lily's heart. She began, without thought or plan, to pack her things ready to go back to his house, to Ashcote, her prison.

'But he died in peace,' Duncan told her. 'In confessing those things to you about his past, he seemed to cast off all his worries and burdens. Don't reproach yourself for anything. You were the perfect wife to him right to the end, Lily.'

Ted Dunne fetched her the following day and they drove in near silence all the way to Dorset. The funeral was to be in the village church where members of the Ashe family had always been buried. Lily went through the formalities scarcely conscious of anything she did and during the following days Mary Dunne and the two dogs were her only comfort.

But gradually she became aware of other things. The gardens at Ashcote were white with snowdrops and in sheltered nooks Lily found primroses blooming. Although the weather was bleak and dull there was the occasional golden day when the birds sang and everything conspired to lift her spirits from the depths in which she floundered. On one such day she wandered further than usual and found herself in a little hidden dip in the hills. To her surprise there was a roofless cottage hidden among the trees and amongst the bare branches of oak and hawthorn she saw one tree covered in golden blossom with a haunting pungent scent. She broke off a small piece and closed her eyes as she breathed the glory of it. She carried it carefully back to the house and sought out Mary to find what it was. A tree bearing blossom like this just now when all the other trees were bare and desolate was almost a thing of fantasy. She had seen nothing like it before.

''Tis truly a magical tree,' the usually down-to-earth Mary

336

told her. 'Witch hazel, that's what it is. An old woman skilled in herbs and the like used to live in that cottage. They say she could cure almost anything with her potions.' Mary took the sprig and held it to her face. 'Rumour tells that if you come upon such a tree by accident when you'm feeling down, then your luck will change.'

Lily laughed. She had never believed in such things but the fact that she had found this amazing tree so unexpectedly in such a hidden and mysterious place lent a certain enchantment. 'Well, I need something cheerful in my life,' she said. 'I shall go and pick a great bunch of it tomorrow and set it all over the house.'

'Don't do that, Madam, or the magic might not work. Leave it be. Just be content with what you have brought back today.' Mary's voice was firm.

Lily looked at her and realized that she was quite serious. 'We need something in the house though,' she said.

'Catkin branches and that yellow stuff ... forsythia I believe 'tis called. Some's out already in a few places. You go and cut some of that and bring in a few daffodil buds and they'll open out in the warmth and we'll all think spring have come.'

'All right then. Daffodils it shall be,' Lily conceded. 'I think spring really is coming, Mary. We'll all feel better when it warms up a bit.' Then she thought of the swallows and was immediately sad, for they reminded her of Augustus, of the first time he had taken her out in Torquay. 'When will the swallows come back do you think?' she asked knowing quite well what the answer would be.

'Not till your baby is born, I shouldn't wonder,' Mary said. 'And that reminds me, the decorator is coming to finish the nursery tomorrow so mind and be in.'

Lily smiled. Yes, she would be in. The nursery was very splendid already. Augustus had written careful instructions almost as if he knew he would not be here to see them carried out. But everything was for a boy, and Lily hoped passionately for a girl. She felt guilty for wishing so, for a son was the only thing she could give Augustus's memory now.

Only to Ivy when she came the following weekend did she

337

confess to this disloyal wish. 'You see,' Lily explained. 'If its a girl I shall be free to leave here, to take my daughter and live my own life. If I have a son he must stay, grow up to inherit Ashcote. I shall be a kind of dowager mother. It'll feel like being in prison.'

'A jolly nice prison,' Ivy said. 'There are plenty of folks who'd welcome a prison like this.'

'Perhaps. Maybe I'm being terrible, but I shall still imagine that I'm a captive if I have to live here all my life. It'll be William all over again.'

'What on earth do you mean — William? What has poor old Will got to do with it.'

'My promise to our mother. As you know she made me promise to put him first until he had qualified. I had to give up all my dreams, all the things I wanted to do, so that William should become an accountant. She asked me to look after you and George too. Only when all those duties were done could I think of myself. It's going to be the same, don't you see? If I'm mother to the Ashe heir, his interests and life will be more important than anything I might wish for myself.'

'Gosh, Lil. I suppose you're right. I hadn't thought of it like that. Mum was a bit unfair wasn't she?'

Lily shrugged her shoulders. 'It sounds like that, but she had this female thing about sons being more important than anything else, about women always having to make the sacrifices. Whether I have a boy or girl, I shall see that I don't pass on that unwholesome idea.'

'And now you've gone and done it again,' Ivy said. 'Got yourself all tied up with a life-time job.'

'Only if it's a boy,' Lily said, patting her considerable bulge. 'Do you believe in magic, Ivy?'

'Whatever are you talking about?'

'Mary Dunne said that witch hazel is magic. I've found a lovely enchanted tree. I go there as often as I can and talk to it, ask it to see I have a little girl!'

Ivy looked at her sister and frowned. 'Now you're being quite batty,' she said.

Lily laughed again. 'I know I am. It's only a bit of fun, but somehow it sets me free. Augustus would have been horrified if he had known and so would Duncan. Men are so proper, so unmagical.'

'I don't think unmagical is a word.'

'Probably not but it perfectly describes what I mean. Of course nothing can really change the sex of the baby I'm about to produce. The magic just makes me feel good.'

At the end of March Elizabeth Ashe was born in the big bed at Ashcote, fair as the summer corn, a perfect replica of her father. Lily cried a little when the baby was handed to her, cried for her child's lost inheritance, but cried with joy for the return of her own freedom, the two emotions joining so that she hardly knew which was dominant.

She sent a simple message to Ivy. *'I was right to rely on the witch hazel after all.'*

And with the returning swallows, came the cousin who was to inherit Ashcote, a handsome man with a wife and three boisterous sons. He expressed insincere regret at having to turn Lily out and failed to understand the look of near triumph on her face. He told her that she was to come and stay as often as she liked, and indeed a wing of the house would be kept ready for her and Elizabeth to use at any time. This was a condition of the will, but he was very happy about it anyway.

She thanked him sweetly and said that if he could keep Flo and the donkey in comfort until she could make other arrangements that would be all she would ask of him. She would find good homes for Jess and Beauty as soon as possible.

'You want to keep a cart horse?' he enquired, obviously intrigued.

'Yes. She used to pull a coal cart,' Lily said with delight. 'I'm very, very fond of her.'

As Augustus had promised, there was ample money settled on Elizabeth and a handsome income for life for Lily. Even Ivy was not forgotten. Her school fees were assured and she too had a small settlement that would give her a certain independence for many years to come.

By May Lily and baby Elizabeth were both installed in

Rose House with the dogs and with Mildred, Lily's maid who had been in tears at the thought of remaining at Ashcote without her mistress.

When the day trippers were beginning to arrive in hordes in Torquay and when the lanes around Cockington were a mass of wild roses and elder flower, Lily began to feel that her heart was mending. She thought of Augustus often, but knew that she had done her duty to him as surely as she had done it for her brother and for all her family. Soon she would begin to find a new outlet for her life. For now just being a mother was enough. She gloried in her baby.

It wasn't until the summer was over and Christmas was almost upon them once more that she began to feel a certain emptiness now and then.

Ivy had come for the holiday. 'I wonder what Ashcote looks like now,' she said nostalgically as she decorated a small Christmas tree. She had regretted leaving the great house. It had given her an importance at school, a certain air of distinction that Rose House could never match.

'Very nice, I expect,' Lily said. She was intent upon laying the table for the evening meal. Duncan had been invited and they were to have their main celebration now on Christmas Eve. He was on duty for the whole of the following day. 'I'm jolly glad it's not my responsibility any more. Ashcote I mean.' Lily shivered. 'All those rooms!' She stood back and surveyed her handiwork. There were candles and holly, and a decoration beside each place. 'Just the wine glasses,' she added half to herself. She knew about wine now and had bought several bottles and a set of splendid new glasses. She held one of these up to the light, admiring the shimmering crystal.

'Are you going to marry Duncan?'

The question came so unexpectedly that Lily nearly dropped the glass.

'What did you say? Did I hear you correctly?'

'Are you going to marry Duncan? Don't tell me you haven't noticed the way he looks at you?'

'I don't know what you're talking about.' Lily set the glass down with elaborate care.

'Oh, well ...' Ivy tied another bauble on to the tree and

340

shrugged her shoulders. 'There's none so blind as them what won't see.'

'Those who won't see,' Lily corrected, and then laughed. Of course Ivy was right. In spite of her quick denial she had become aware lately of a difference in Duncan's attitude to her.

'It's nearly a year since Augustus died,' Ivy persisted. 'Duncan's waited till now, but I bet you anything he'll pop the question before the year is out. Make sure you say yes. I need a rich respectable brother-in-law!'

Lily set two more glasses on the table. The wine was in the cellar, not to be brought up until the meal was ready.

'You do like him don't you?' Ivy was more serious now.

'Yes, I like him.' In fact Lily knew that her feelings for Duncan were more than mere liking. He had been a good friend, had stood by her during the bad times, had been the first recipient of her tale of woe long ago. He was reliable, honourable, kind, all of those things, but much more too. More important perhaps he set her heart on fire! When they were together she felt alive, vibrant and awakened. His presence filled the house with sparkle and fun as well as peace and security.

Perhaps she had been aware of her feelings for a long time and had deliberately refused to acknowledge them. She looked at herself in the mirror above the fireplace. Her face was flushed and glowing and she knew that it wasn't just because of the heat.

Ivy, watching her closely, suddenly clapped her hands. 'I knew it,' she said. 'You're in love with him too.' Her voice was jubilant.

'Then I'll ask you please to be quiet about it,' Lily said. She put her hands to her burning cheeks.

Ivy refused to be hushed, but she was suddenly serious. 'Don't let Duncan go, Lil. There's been too much unhappiness in the past years, too many dark secrets. Duncan is open and honest. Nothing hidden about him.'

At that moment Mildred came in carrying Elizabeth. The baby, nine months old now was ready for bed, sweet smelling and adorable. Lily took her little daughter in her arms and buried her face in her soft nightgown. Then she held the baby aloft. 'And to have no menacing secrets must be one of the best things in all the world,' she declared loudly and with feeling.

'I let Doctor MacMullen in just now before I come up,' Mildred announced opportunely. 'He come a few minutes ago. He's taking his coat off.'

Duncan, overhearing only Lily's last few words, stood in the doorway, his arms full of brightly wrapped presents. He put them down beneath the Christmas tree. 'And what is the best thing in all the world?' he asked, grinning at them all.

Lily wanted to say, *you are,* but she resisted. 'I'll tell you one day,' she managed.

Then he came over to her, encircled both her and the baby in his arms and kissed her on the lips.

'Will you marry me, Mrs Lily Ashe?' he said as he released her.

Lily gasped, and then laughed at such a public and rather unromantic proposal. 'Do you expect me to answer that here and now with everyone listening?' She disentangled Elizabeth's baby fingers which were clutching at the pearls around her neck.

Mildred was standing at the door her eyes wide with delight. Then she came to her senses. 'I'll take the baby. 'Tis her bedtime.'

Lily kissed her little daughter and handed her over. 'I'll be up in a few minutes.'

Ivy skipped round the table and ushered them out. 'And I'll fetch some champagne,' she said following them closely and shutting the door with a flourish.

Lily stood quite still in the silence and looked at Duncan.

He took a small package from his pocket. It was not wrapped like the other presents but lay on his palm, a little red velvet box. He opened it and the diamond gleamed and sparkled with a myriad colours reflected from the flickering Christmas candles.

Without a word Lily took Augustus's rings and placed them on a finger of her right hand. The fourth finger of her left hand was bare now, the flesh slightly dented and white where the other rings had been. She held out her hand to Duncan and he slid the solitaire gently into place.

She looked up at him and smiled and knew that she had found peace at last. The days of anxiety and stress were surely over, all the dark secrets of her old life banished along with the fears and ghosts which had haunted her tormented past.

Then he folded his arms around her again and she realized that he was offering her much more than mere tranquillity. Everything that she had thought marriage to be and had so far failed to find would be hers now, both to give and to receive in abundance.

You have been reading a novel published by Piatkus Books. We hope you have enjoyed it and that you would like to read more of our titles. Please ask for them in your local library or bookshop.

If you would like to be put on our mailing list to receive details of new publications, please send a large stamped addressed envelope (UK only) to:

Piatkus Books: 5 Windmill Street
London W1P 1HF

PIATKUS

The sign of a good book